PRAISE FOR

Little Gale Gumbo

"Spicy, delicious, and filled with surprises, *Little Gale Gumbo* is a wonderful stew, a debut novel that will fill you with joy. Put it on your reading menu and enjoy!"

—Adriana Trigiani, *New York Times* bestselling author of
Don't Sing at the Table and *Big Stone Gap*

"I loved this novel like crazy. With its irresistible settings—from New Orleans to an island off the coast of Maine—unforgettable characters, and heartfelt exploration of love, family, and secrets, *Little Gale Gumbo* is one of my favorite novels of the year."

—Melissa Senate, author of *The Love Goddess' Cooking School*

"Seamlessly shifting in time to reveal the layers of a mystery, this is a poignant story of an unforgettable family bound by secrets, fierce love, and a dash of voodoo. The Bergeron sisters will stay with you long after you leave Little Gale Island. Erika Marks is shining new talent, and she has written a novel full of heart and grace." —Rae Meadows, author of *Mothers & Daughters*

"Built on a roux of charm, intrigue, and family secrets, Erika Marks delivers a savory blend of romance and suspense, bringing New Orleans to Maine in a delectable debut novel."

—Sally Koslow, author of *With Friends Like These*

Written by today's freshest new talents and selected by New American Library, NAL Accent novels touch on subjects close to a woman's heart, from friendship to family to finding our place in the world. The Conversation Guides included in each book are intended to enrich the individual reading experience, as well as encourage us to explore these topics together—because books, and life, are meant for sharing.

Visit us online at www.penguin.com.

Little Gale Gumbo

ERIKA MARKS

NAL ACCENT

NAL ACCENT
Published by New American Library, a division of
Penguin Group (USA) Inc., 375 Hudson Street, New York, New York 10014, USA
Penguin Group (Canada), 90 Eglinton Avenue East, Suite 700, Toronto,
Ontario M4P 2Y3, Canada (a division of Pearson Penguin Canada Inc.)
Penguin Books Ltd., 80 Strand, London WC2R 0RL, England
Penguin Ireland, 25 St. Stephen's Green, Dublin 2, Ireland (a division of Penguin Books Ltd.)
Penguin Group (Australia), 250 Camberwell Road, Camberwell, Victoria 3124,
Australia (a division of Pearson Australia Group Pty. Ltd.)
Penguin Books India Pvt. Ltd., 11 Community Centre, Panchsheel Park,
New Delhi - 110 017, India
Penguin Group (NZ), 67 Apollo Drive, Rosedale, Auckland 0632,
New Zealand (a division of Pearson New Zealand Ltd.)
Penguin Books (South Africa) (Pty.) Ltd., 24 Sturdee Avenue,
Rosebank, Johannesburg 2196, South Africa

Penguin Books Ltd., Registered Offices:
80 Strand, London WC2R 0RL, England

First published by New American Library,
a division of Penguin Group (USA) Inc.

First Printing, October 2011
10 9 8 7 6 5 4 3

Copyright © Erika Marks, 2011
Conversation Guide copyright © Penguin Group (USA) Inc., 2011
All rights reserved

REGISTERED TRADEMARK—MARCA REGISTRADA

LIBRARY OF CONGRESS CATALOGING-IN-PUBLICATION DATA:

Marks, Ericka.
    Little Gale Gumbo/Erika Marks.
        p. cm.
    ISBN 978-0-451-23465-0
    1. Mothers and daughters—Fiction.   2. Restaurateurs—Fiction.   3. Fathers—Crimes against—
Fiction.   4. Family secrets—Fiction.   5. Maine—Fiction.   6. Domestic fiction.   I. Title
    PS3613.A754525L58 2011
    813'.6—dc22   2011024541

Set in Cochin LT STD
Designed by Catherine Leonardo

Printed in the United States of America

For Ian, who takes my breath away.

Little Gale Gumbo

There was never anything magical in the gumbo. At least, nothing you could see. From the peanut butter–brown roux to the slender rounds of her sliced okra, Camille Bergeron made her gumbo the very same way her Creole mother had made it in her own kitchen for nearly forty years. But then, Camille should have known that a single woman from New Orleans with caramel skin couldn't arrive on the cold and quiet shores of an island in Maine in 1977 and expect to blend in, especially not with two teenage daughters in tow and a carpetbag that smelled of boiled crawfish, no matter how many times she'd hung it out.

So it was no surprise to Camille when she opened the doors to her Little Gale Gumbo Café that the islanders eyed her suspiciously over their soup spoons, even as they clamored for second and third bowls of her trademark Creole stew. It had killed them, she suspected, to admit how good her gumbo was, nearly broken them to find themselves addicted over-night to such a simple confection as a praline, charging through snow and rain to buy a brown bag of those shiny bronze disks that melted on your tongue like good bourbon.

You might have asked native islander Ben Haskell what Camille put in her gumbo to make it so special, but he would never tell. From the moment Camille and her daughters had appeared on his weathered porch to inquire about an apartment for rent, Ben's routine and guarded world was never the same.

His teenage son, Matthew, would have been of even less help, having been equally enchanted by Camille's girls, soft-spoken Josephine and headstrong Dahlia: passions that would follow him for years, no matter how hard he tried to let them go.

Because just as anyone enjoying a good gumbo could never bear to relinquish it until the bowl had been tilted and the last silky spoonful had been scooped from the bottom, so it was for all the men who fell in love with the Bergeron women, those too good and those much too bad. Letting go was never easy.

Part One

First
you make
the roux.

One

Little Gale Island, Maine
Friday, June 14, 2002
6:30 a.m.

𝓕og crawled along the island's rugged shoreline like old smoke, hugging shingled gables and steeped in the rich, salty taste of the tide.

From the bedroom window of her mustard cape, Dahlia Bergeron watched morning spread across her backyard, brushing daylight over her cold frame greenhouses in streaks of blue and gray. She couldn't remember the last time she'd risen before the sun, at least not to roll over and make love again. But the mattress beside her was empty and had been for a while now. What she wouldn't have done for a lover's company today, the smell of a man's skin on her fingertips, his hairs on her pillow.

When the phone sounded on the other side of the room, she reached it before the second ring. Most mornings she would have let it chime on and on until the machine swallowed it up, but not today. She'd known even as she hurried across her cluttered wood floor that there was only one reason anyone called this early.

"Dahl?"

Dahlia could hear her younger sister's ragged breathing on the other end. Josie had been crying. Sobbing.

"Joze, honey, what is it?"

"It's Daddy. He was here last night. He was here and he attacked Ben."

Dahlia fell hard against the dresser, her collection of perfume bottles toppling. "Oh, God, is he . . . ?"

"Daddy's dead. He's dead and Ben's in a coma."

Dahlia closed her eyes, swallowed. "Where is he?"

"Portland. He's in ICU. But the doctors won't let us see him. They said only family, and they won't make any exceptions."

"Where are you?"

"The house."

"I'm coming."

"Just stay there," Josie said. "Wayne's already on his way."

Dahlia rushed downstairs to the front door and opened it just as the station wagon came barreling up the driveway, bringing with it a damp sea breeze that tumbled through the long tangles of her black hair and raised goose bumps along her bare legs.

Wayne emerged from the driver's side, his brown hair and beard wet with perspiration, his round face flushed.

Her brother-in-law looked grimly at her over the roof of the car.

"Get dressed," he said. "Hurry."

Josie waited for them on the front porch, pulling nervously at the ends of her short red bob.

This was all her fault. She'd grown so lazy with her Voodoo. She couldn't remember the last time she'd dressed a candle or covered the steps with brick dust. Her mother, Camille, would never have let so much time go by without a protection spell, never have left herself and her family so vulnerable.

And now the man who had been like a father to Josie and Dahlia for nearly twenty-five years, the man who'd loved their mother so much you would have sworn his skin had smelled from it, their beloved Ben, lay unconscious in a hospital bed.

It was unimaginable to her.

When the station wagon appeared, Josie rushed to the railing and watched Dahlia crawl out of the passenger seat, holding the door to steady herself.

Wayne closed the driver's side and walked ahead, wiping his forehead with his arm. "Any calls?"

"I don't know," said Josie. "I couldn't stay in there alone. I was going to jump right out of my skin."

Dahlia labored up the four crooked treads to the porch, her plastic garden clogs smacking the old wood with each step. "Your husband is a heartless son of a bitch."

"Because I wouldn't stop at Clem's for booze," Wayne explained wearily, passing Josie to enter their shingled cape. "I told her we had plenty of alcohol here."

"Cooking sherry doesn't count!" Dahlia yelled after him, finally on the porch and face-to-face with Josie. "Hi, sweetie."

The sisters embraced, clinging to each other with a desperation they hadn't felt in years.

"We're supposed to just sit here on our hands while he lies there all alone, Dahl. I can't bear it."

"I know."

They parted, still holding hands.

Josie nodded to the street. "Let's go in before the vultures land."

"He wasn't supposed to get out, damn it." Dahlia pulled an ivory mug down from the kitchen cabinet and poured the last of the coffee. "He was supposed to rot and die in there."

"Well, he didn't," said Wayne, pulling a soda from the fridge.

Dahlia carried her cold coffee to the window seat and dropped into it.

"I should have known something awful was coming," Josie said, knocking the old coffee filter into the trash. "All this early heat, and that stupid fly that wouldn't leave me alone in the café yesterday. You remember, Wayne?"

Dahlia groaned. "Oh, Jesus, here it comes. . . ."

"Don't you dare make fun of me, Dahlia Rose." Josie spun around. "If Momma were still alive she would have scrubbed the steps a dozen times by now."

"Right—because that worked *so* well keeping him out all the other times!"

"Hey!" Wayne stared pointedly between them. "Just cool it. Both of you."

The sisters fell silent, looking away.

Josie's hands shook as she peeled the lid off the coffee tin. "I hate that Ben's all alone in that hospital room and they won't let us see him. I just hate it."

Dahlia stared numbly into the backyard, where Wayne's mower stood stalled in a patch of high grass. "So, who found them?"

"Who do you think?" Wayne snapped open his soda and took a long swig. Jack, of course. Dahlia rolled her head against the glass, trying to imagine what her ex-boyfriend must have thought, seeing her father again after so many years, and now with Jack being the island's police chief to boot.

Josie rinsed out the coffeepot, fresh tears spilling down her cheeks. "Poor Jack," she whispered.

"He went over as soon as dispatch got Ben's call," Wayne said. "Apparently the front door was open and Ben and Charles were just lying there at the bottom of the stairs. Jack thinks Ben went upstairs to try to get away from Charles and Charles chased him to the top and they lost their balance."

"Jesus." Dahlia closed her eyes.

Wayne walked to the sink, shaking his head. "This shouldn't have happened. We should have just filled out those request forms from the prison when they came. Then we would have known he was out."

"Well, don't look at me," Dahlia said. "Your wife's the one who thought it was a better idea to soak them in gasoline and stuff 'em in a goddamned tree."

"It was vinegar," Josie said indignantly, "and I didn't *stuff* them in a tree; I buried them around the roots. There's a difference."

"Oh, well, excuse me, Your High Priestess."

"You and Daddy never understood what Momma and I believed. You never even tried."

"What's to understand about digging a hole under a tree? And you know I hate when you call him that."

"Fine, Dahl. What am I supposed to call our father?"

"Gee, I don't know. How about wife-beating asshole? Drug-dealing shithead? Either of those would work."

"What difference does it make now?" Wayne said, taking the empty carafe from Josie's stalled hands and filling it himself. "He's dead."

Dead. The sisters looked across the room at each other, waiting for the word to sink in. All the years they had suffered their father's violence. Leaving New Orleans to escape him, only to have him follow them north to the island, as relentless as a greenhead fly. They'd been so sure he'd chase them forever.

Them, and anyone who'd ever loved them. Ben, Jack, Wayne, and—

"Matty." Josie gasped.

Dahlia rose in an instant. They raced for the phone at the same time, shoulder to shoulder across the kitchen floor.

Wayne called after them, "I'm sure Jack's already talked to him."

But neither sister was listening. It was unthinkable that their oldest and dearest friend should hear this unbearable news from anyone else. Josie reached the phone first and snatched it up. "We should try his cell."

"No," said Dahlia, over her sister's shoulder. "What if he's at work? Or driving? He'll run off the road!"

Josie agreed, already punching in the numbers. "We'll try his house first," she said.

And just like that, after so many years of their agreed truce on the subject of Matthew Haskell, the Bergeron sisters unwittingly began their unspoken contest for his affections all over again.

Two

Miami, Florida

Friday, June 14, 2002

8:15 a.m.

Fifteen-year-old Joey Ortiz was slouched in a yellow plastic chair across from Matthew Haskell's desk, scowling at his sneakers.

"Want to tell me what happened in the boys' bathroom after school yesterday, Joey?"

"What for?" the boy said. "You already know or I wouldn't be here."

"Maybe I want to hear your side of the story."

"I was smoking a cigarette. Big deal."

Matthew gave the young man a flat stare. In his fifteen years as a guidance counselor at the Wharton School, he'd learned to read his students. He called it his Crapmeter, when lies ranged from faint unpleasant odors to all-out, steaming piles of bullshit. Right now Joey Ortiz was walking through a cow pasture.

"Just a cigarette, huh?"

The young man snorted. "See? I knew you wouldn't believe me."

"One of the teachers said it smelled more like marijuana."

"It was Mr. Kline, wasn't it? I saw him in the mirror. That dude's got it in for me. You know that, right?"

"It doesn't matter who it was."

"Yeah, right. Like an old geek like him would even know what marijuana smells like."

"Hey," Matthew said gently. "That's not necessary. This isn't about Mr. Kline. This is about you. Don't change the subject."

Joey quieted, his self-impressed grin drooping until he looked genuinely remorseful.

Matthew leaned back, linked his hands behind his head. "I heard Ashley was in there with you, too."

"So what? Now it's against the rules to kiss your girlfriend? Come on, Mr. H. I've seen you and your wife kissing in the parking lot and no one calls *you* in for it."

His wife. Matthew couldn't help a sad chuckle at that, even though Holly wouldn't have found much amusement in the boy's mistake. Her continued lack of a wedding band had been the final toppling block on a precarious stack of gripes piled over ten years together.

Who knew why he'd never asked Holly to marry him. He'd never wanted to lose her, never wanted anyone else more since he'd met her, and yet he'd never been able to make that ultimate commitment to her.

She'd blamed the sisters, the island, and he'd said nothing.

"So you two were just making out then?" Matthew asked pointedly.

Joey shifted nervously in his seat. "Mostly. You know how it is, Mr. H."

"No, I don't. I'm an old geek too."

Joey reddened, gnawing at his thumbnail. "I didn't mean you."

Matthew grinned, flashing back to his own conflicted teenage years, his fumbling attempts at romance when he was fifteen, chaste in comparison, though not by any choice of his own. He would have gladly been one of Dahlia's early conquests if she'd only let him.

He took a sip of cold coffee, reminded of the last time he'd given safe-sex advice to a student. It was how he'd met Holly in the first place, when he'd been encouraged to seek counsel after the boy's parents had threatened to sue. Holly had looked so beautiful, so confident, strolling into the wine bar in her white suit. He had fallen for her at once, so relieved to know he could finally feel something for someone other than Dahlia Bergeron.

"Excuse me—Matt?"

Matthew turned to see Claire Wentz's ruddy face in the doorway. The school secretary wore a strained smile as she asked, "Can I speak with you a moment?"

Matthew moved to the door. Bad news about a student, he thought. It had to be.

Claire leaned in, looking around nervously. "I didn't want to say it over the intercom," she whispered. "It's the police for you on line one. They said they're from Little Goose Island. . . ."

"Little Gale," Matthew corrected gently.

Claire blushed. "Oh. Sorry."

"It's okay. Thanks."

But even as he moved to the phone and picked it up, Matthew felt his skin growing cold with dread. When Matthew heard Jack Thurlow's voice on the other end, he knew, somehow he just knew, but he let Jack say it anyway.

After he hung up the phone, Matthew turned back to his student to excuse himself, but the riptide of anguish pulled him under too quickly. As his coffee slipped from his hand and splattered across his thighs, Matthew saw the whole of their lives together: Camille and the sisters, himself and Ben, and Charles: twenty-five years in a single, burning instant, just before he slid to the floor.

Three

Little Gale Island
Friday, June 14, 2002
10:25 a.m.

After stalling for as long as she could, Loretta Robinson got up from her reception desk in the brick entry of the Little Gale Island police station and took the short walk to the end of the corridor.

"Margery's here, Jack. She wants to report a parking violation."

Little Gale Island's chief of police glanced over from his computer screen and gave his receptionist a weary look. "Who's she looking to burn at the stake now?"

Loretta crossed her arms. "One guess."

Jack raked a hand through his dark hair and sighed.

"Should I tell her you're on a call?" Loretta asked.

"Too late." Jack nodded behind Loretta to where Margery Dunham had appeared, her tidy white bob swinging just above her pink earlobes, wide-eyed and breathless with outrage. "Thanks, Loretta," he said, rising. He forced a patient smile. "Come on in, Margery. Have a seat."

"I can't possibly sit," Margery huffed. "This is the third time this month. That woman has no regard for the laws, Jack. I have exactly two parking spaces allocated for my antique shop—may I remind you their café has *four*?—and still I come out to find that rusted truck of hers sitting in one of mine. It's outrageous." Margery Dunham raised a plump finger. "She's a menace, Jack. An absolute menace."

"*Menace* is a pretty strong word, Margery. . . ."

"Dahlia Bergeron has always been a loose cannon. If you hadn't been so foolish over her, you might have locked her up twenty years ago and thrown away the key. Well, I've had enough. The season isn't a week old and she's already costing me potential customers."

"You know," Jack began patiently, "I think today might not be the best day to bring this up. There's been an incident this morning and I think—"

"An incident?" Margery's small navy eyes rounded with greedy curiosity. "What sort of incident?"

"I'm afraid I can't discuss it."

"I thought I heard sirens this morning! Oh, Lord, has something happened?"

"Look, why don't you go back to the front and ask Loretta if you can fill out a complaint form, and I'll see that it gets looked at as soon as possible, all right?"

"Another one?" Margery said. "What happened to my other two complaints?"

"I'm not sure, but I think the law requires at least three before I can authorize any tarring and feathering."

"Tarring and fea . . . ?" Margery's eyes slitted. "Are you making fun of me, Jack Thurlow?"

"God, no, I wouldn't dream of it," he said, steering the shopkeeper toward the door.

"Fine," Margery said tightly, shaking off his lead. "But you are the law and I won't feel safe until I know this has been taken care of. I barely made it past them in the waiting room just now. The younger one practically put a Voodoo curse on me with her eyes. They can do that, you know."

Jack looked down the hall, seeing a flash of Josie's pumpkin hair through the doorway.

Josie tugged a fresh tissue out of her purse and wiped at her red nose. Behind her Dahlia paced in front of the waiting room's curtained window.

"I feel like a bird trapped in someone's goddamned basement," she muttered, rubbing her arms.

"So sit down then," Josie said, honking into her tissue. "No one's making you do laps, you know."

"I bet you a hundred bucks I know why that old witch was here," Dahlia said, pointing to the hall.

"Oh, Dahl, for God's sake . . ."

"Didn't you see how she glared at us?"

"Margery Dunham glares at everybody."

"Well, if she files another complaint I'm going to put slugworms in her fucking window boxes."

Josie pulled her cell phone from her purse, looked at the screen, and sighed. "I wish Matty would call back."

"He's probably in the air," Dahlia said, her gaze drifting anxiously to the doorway, knowing Jack would appear at any moment. She didn't know what she would say to her ex-boyfriend. Any more than she knew why, all the years after their breakup, seeing him still left her shaky and undone.

Josie twisted her tissue around her thumb. "Do you think he blames us?"

"Jack?"

"Matty."

Dahlia didn't answer right away. It hadn't occurred to her that Matthew might blame them for their father's violence. Maybe it should have.

"I don't think he blames us, Joze," Dahlia decided at last.

"I wonder if she'll come with him."

"I don't know. He said 'I' on his message, not 'we.'"

"How could she not? She'd have to."

"She didn't come for Momma's funeral."

"That was different," Josie said.

"How was it different?" demanded Dahlia.

"She didn't know Momma."

"So what? She knew Matty, didn't she? And why do you always defend her?"

"I'm not defending her." Josie shrugged contritely. "I just think you can be too hard on people, that's all."

"And you, baby sister, always think everyone's a saint."

"Ladies."

At the sound of Jack's voice, Dahlia turned to find him leaning in the doorway, dressed in khakis and a dark blue shirt.

"Jack." Josie rose and rushed to him, her eyes bright with

yearning. "How's Ben? We tried calling the hospital but they wouldn't tell us anything."

"It's like talking to the CIA, isn't it?" Jack met Dahlia's eyes across the room, not surprised that she hadn't greeted him with the same speed. He offered her a small smile, but she refused him one in return. He didn't know what he expected.

He looked back at Josie and gestured to the hall.

"Why don't we go to my office."

It was a small room with off-white walls, tan carpeting, and a heavy oak desk that looked like it had been rescued from a one-room schoolhouse. Dahlia flopped into one of the blue molded chairs in front of the desk and glanced around, seeing a framed senior picture of Jack's teenage daughter, Jenny, on the far edge, perched beside a pitiful-looking African violet, its leaves spotted and limp. It was a miserable room, Dahlia thought. Colorless and low ceilinged. No wonder the poor plant looked like it wanted to die.

"I spoke to the nurse a few minutes ago," Jack said, clearing off a pile of papers and sitting down. "Ben's condition hasn't changed."

"Isn't there something you can do, Jack?" Josie pleaded. "It's killing us, not being able to see him."

"I know it is," he said gently, "and I'm sorry for that."

"If you're so sorry then tell them to let us in," said Dahlia. "You're the chief of police, Jack. Tell them you'll arrest them if they don't."

"I can't tell people what to do just because I'm a cop, Dahlia. It doesn't work that way."

She met his gaze and held it. "You would know, wouldn't you?"

"Don't mind her, Jack." Josie glared at her sister. "She's been drinking cooking sherry since this morning."

Dahlia turned in her seat. "And whose fault is that, dear sister?"

"Okay, okay . . ."

Jack leaned forward, his brown eyes tender. He wasn't surprised by Dahlia's reaction. He knew from experience what she was like in times of stress. No one had ever accused Dahlia Bergeron of being calm under pressure.

"I know how hard this is, okay?" he said, looking between them. "I love him too, you know."

Josie smiled. "I know."

Dahlia knew it too, but she refused to meet his eyes. She crossed her legs instead, plucking a loose thread from the hem of her shorts.

Jack sat back and folded his arms. "I called the prison this morning," he said. "According to their records, Charles was granted parole four days ago. They also said they couldn't contact next of kin because they had no family request forms on record from either of you. Is that true?"

Josie nodded ruefully, her eyes filling at once. Jack handed her a box of tissues from behind his desk. She plucked out several, making a pile in her lap.

"What would have been the point?" she asked. "Daddy was supposed to be in there for eighteen years. That's practically a lifetime."

He looked at Dahlia. "So when was the last time either of you had contact with him?"

Dahlia's foot bounced nervously, her plastic clog hanging loose and smacking against her heel. "I don't remember," she said.

"Yes, you do, Dahl," Josie said, sniffling. "Daddy called the café a few times after Momma died."

Jack frowned. "So your father knew Camille had died?"

"Ben insisted on sending a letter to the prison," Josie said. "We told him he didn't have to, but he said it was the right thing to do." She smiled weakly. "You know Ben."

"And who talked to Charles when he called the café those times?"

Josie shook her head. "Nobody. We never accepted the charges." She shaped a tissue into a point and dabbed at the corners of her eyes. "I suppose we should have," she said. "Even just once. Maybe then he wouldn't have been so mad when he got out; you think?"

She looked up at Jack with moist, yearning eyes. He gave her an absolving smile.

"I don't think a few phone calls would have made much difference, Jo," he said gently.

She smiled, sniffling again. "You're probably right."

In the silence, Dahlia stole a look at Jack, wondering suddenly whether he'd done the same.

Josie molded a new tissue around her nose and blew.

"You just couldn't help yourself, could you?" Josie said, following Dahlia into the parking lot ten minutes later. "We're in there talking about Daddy almost killing Ben and you decide it's the perfect time to take a cheap shot at Jack."

"He's the one with the grudge, not me."

"God, you're a pill," Josie said, seeing the Buick parked at the far end of the lot. "In case you've forgotten, Jack's divorced now. So maybe you might want to stop raking the poor man over the coals and just admit that you still have feelings for him."

Dahlia released the knot of her curls, shaking them out. "We're not talking about this anymore."

"Fine."

They reached the station wagon and found Wayne waiting in the driver's seat, his eyes tired under the shadow of the car's peeling visor.

"That's done then," Wayne said when they'd climbed in, Josie in the front, Dahlia in the back. The sisters didn't answer, and Wayne pulled them out into the street, steering them through the village and past the wharf.

Stopped at the blinking light at Main and Chestnut, they waited for Helen Ingersoll to push her newborn across the street in a pale pink stroller.

Dahlia looked away, dread skidding down her legs.

"It's strange," Josie said softly. "I still wonder sometimes what it would be like if you hadn't lost the baby."

Dahlia looked up to see Wayne's eyes in the rearview mirror, hard on hers, the familiar flash of panic she'd come to know so well in the years since their pact.

She turned to the window as the prickle of tears climbed her throat, and finally the light turned green.

Four

Miami, Florida
Friday, June 14, 2002
11:20 a.m.

The black *BMW* was parked against the curb when Matthew came out of his apartment with a duffel bag and his nine-year-old golden retriever, Hooper. Holly stepped out of the car wearing a white tank and linen pants, her straight blond hair pulled back into a smooth knot. Even from far away, Matthew could tell she'd been crying.

Seeing Holly, the dog lunged, pulling free of Matthew's grip on his leash and galloping down the sidewalk. Holly knelt down to accept the dog's lapping kisses, then stood to greet Matthew. When he reached her, she slipped her arms around him before he could say a word and pressed her cheek against his chest. Matthew couldn't remember the last time she'd let him this close to her, and he ached with the brevity of it. Grazing her breast when they pulled apart felt almost improper, the idea of lowering his lips to her temple unthinkable. The strange new rules of separation. He hated them.

Almost as much as he hated getting a ride to the airport in Holly's architect boyfriend's precious car.

"Oh, great." Matthew groaned when she opened the back door for Hooper. "The fucking sheet."

"Oh, forget about it," Holly said, reaching back to tear off the crisp white cover and stuffing it under the seat. Hooper leaped gleefully into the back, brushing his rear against the smooth ivory leather. Matthew swore the dog grinned.

"He'll know you took it off," Matthew said, closing the door and moving around to the passenger side.

"He won't. I'll vacuum out the back."

Climbing in, Matthew tugged his seat belt across his chest, shifting his bag between his feet. "I suppose I should just be happy King Peter let you out of the castle for a few hours. I'll be sure and send him a bouquet of lobsters when I get to the island."

"Please don't do this," Holly pleaded, her eyes filling as she steered them onto the highway. "Not on top of everything. Not today."

"It's a day like any day," Matthew said, frowning into the distance. "You used to think my jokes were funny."

"I don't feel like laughing right now. I can't imagine you do either."

Matthew studied the horizon, mute. The truth was he didn't know what he felt like, and in his confusion, laughter seemed as reasonable as tears. His father was lying unconscious in a hospital bed, barely alive after suffering a stroke at the hands of a madman. The harrowing potential of Charles Bergeron's violence had followed them all for so many years, like the moon through the trees; sometimes you could see it, sometimes you couldn't, but you always knew it was there.

The windshield began to fog with Hooper's panting. Holly pushed at a strip of lit buttons on the dashboard. "God, I hate this car," she confessed, sniffling. "All these stupid buttons."

Matthew reached out and calmly twisted a knob, sending up a rush of warm air. The windshield began to clear.

"Thanks." She swallowed. "Any news from the doctor?"

Matthew shrugged, watching the traffic. "Nothing. His condition hasn't changed. And I wasn't able to reach Dahlia or Josie."

"They left a message at the house," Holly said tightly. "You obviously haven't told them you moved out."

"I guess I didn't see the point, in case . . ." Matthew stopped, meeting Holly's eyes briefly, hoping she'd finish the sentence for him. When she didn't, he said, "You could come with me, you know. We could drop Hooper off at Maggie's."

Matthew watched Holly consider his offer, his weak brain flooding quickly with the possibility of her acceptance. Together, so emotionally raw, they'd turn to each other again. Away from that architect, that builder of bullshit, Matthew could remind Holly of their love, of what had brought them together, instead of always talking about what had driven them apart.

But the island wasn't theirs; it never had been. Little Gale belonged only to him and the sisters, and that plain and cold fact had been made clear to Holly within minutes of her first and only visit.

As the silence lingered, Matthew knew she would decline.

Finally, Holly sighed. "You know I would if I could," she said. "But work is crazy right now. Especially with Connie out on maternity leave."

Matthew frowned reflexively. Even in the blur of his grief, he felt the same sting he always did in the wake of a harmless mention of someone's pregnancy or birth announcement, each one a reminder of what he and Holly had tried for and never succeeded with. And then the jarring surge of his own resentment, the habitual belief that every innocent mention was Holly's way of blaming him, of reminding him of what he couldn't give her. When he knew it wasn't, knew it was only him blaming himself.

They both glanced at Hooper, who had perched himself between their seats, as if the dog might say something to join them again, but he could only nuzzle their cheeks.

"Yeah," said Matthew, defeated. "It's probably not a good idea."

Stopped in traffic, he watched Holly's hands in her lap, waiting for the inevitable measuring of her wrists, her ritual in the grip of anxiety, one of so many tiny and inconsequential details that he'd only recently begun to catalog in her absence.

"I put the number of the hotel in with Hoop's stuff," he said. "In case you can't reach me on my cell."

"You're not staying at the house?" she asked.

"I can't. It's a crime scene."

"Oh." She nodded. "Of course it is. I'm sorry. I wasn't thinking."

"It's all right."

When they reached the departure lane and pulled to the curb, Holly reached for Matthew's hand, gently lacing her fingers through his. "Call me when you can."

She leaned over and kissed his cheek, lingering against his jaw just long enough that he turned toward her, as if he expected to find her lips waiting, but she had already moved back.

Matthew took up his bag and climbed out, turning to find Hooper had already filled his vacant seat, the dog panting excitedly.

Matthew rubbed Hooper's coppery head through the open window.

"Don't let Peter feed him that gourmet shit," he said. "It gives him the runs. And you tell Prince Charming if I ever hear he's dragging my dog on one of his fucking bike rides again, I'm gonna kick his ass up and down Delray Beach."

Then Matthew turned to the glass doors of the terminal and walked through them, heading back, heading home.

Five

New Orleans, Louisiana
Summer 1961

Roberta Bayonne lifted the bottle of dove's blood over the shallow white dish and poured.

"I want him back for good this time, Roberta."

Wanda Johnson's voice was steady, but in the flickering candlelight of the shuttered room, eighteen-year-old Camille Bayonne could see the woman's lips quiver as she watched the burgundy liquid fill the bottom of the saucer, spreading out like a stain.

Outside, Maurepas Street bustled with activity under a relentless July sun, its shotgun porches crowded with cackling old men, its sidewalks filled with racing children. Just beyond the rooftops, the fairgrounds roared with the day's races, the smell of the stables blowing over. But inside the narrow turquoise house silence prevailed, and with it the thick scents of incense and wax. All around the three women, shadows of eager candle flames rippled up the tall, scarlet walls, turning plaster into billowing curtains, and the ceiling into the surface of the sea.

Roberta gently eased the dish of dove's blood into the center of the table.

Wanda Johnson's eyes filled. "He wants to marry her, Roberta. I'll kill myself. I swear to God I will."

"Hush," Roberta ordered. "Focus now. Camille, bring me the powders."

Camille rose dutifully and crossed the room to the sturdy armoire, her mother's medicine cabinet, and took out three small bottles. She had helped her mother work a commanding spell only once before, but she hadn't forgotten the ingredients. Spearmint, salt, and cloves. It was a strong spell, but Wanda Johnson needed one now. Camille had watched her mother make Wanda a gris-gris bag the month before, filling a square of red flannel with an odd number of stones and a knot of her lover's dark hair, and Wanda had worn her bag dutifully against her left breast for weeks, but still her husband had refused to give up his mistress.

Camille returned with the powders and set them before her mother. Roberta sprinkled equal amounts of each into a clean, wide-mouthed bowl, then turned again to Camille.

"The parchment," she said.

Camille handed her mother a square of brown paper and a quill. Roberta pushed the parchment and the pen toward Wanda and pointed to the dish of dove's blood. "Write his name five times on this paper," Roberta said. "Then you write your name on top of his. And whatever you do, make sure all the letters touch. Every last one."

Wanda nodded numbly, but her hand shook as she took up the pen and lowered the tip into the dish, over and over, until the sound of the quill tip scratching across the rough paper grew unbearable in the hot, silent room.

Camille pressed her hands into her lap.

"There." Finished at last, Wanda set down the quill and rolled her lips together to clear off the beads of sweat.

"Now fold it," Roberta instructed. "Then press it to your heart and think hard on your desire. Close your eyes and see what it is that you want."

Wanda did, clutching the folded paper so tightly that when she finally released it to Roberta, the indents of her fingers remained. But Camille knew it was the only way a spell would work. All the oils and candles and stones in her mother's medicine chest were powerless without the will of the person making the wish. It was the first lesson of Creole Voodoo her mother had taught her.

"Whatever you do, don't stop thinking," Roberta said as she set the folded paper into the bowl and rested it gently atop the powder piles. "Don't stop thinking on your wish, you hear?"

But Wanda Johnson wasn't in any danger of that. When Roberta raised a lit match above the filled bowl and let it drop, Camille saw Wanda's dark eyes grow wide, flashing with the reflection of the flame, her lips tight, stilled with resolve and purpose.

"Think hard now, honey child," Roberta whispered. "See your desire. See him come back to you."

As Camille watched the paper and powders crackle and

burn, she wondered what it was like to love someone so much, so much you'd want to die if they stopped loving you.

Wanda swallowed, breathless. "Now what?"

"Now you take these ashes and you sprinkle 'em right where—"

The jingling bells of the front door rang out, quieting Roberta. Wanda glanced up, panicked, but Roberta just flashed Camille an instructing look and Camille rose to see to their customer.

Splitting the velvet curtain that separated the front room from the rest of the shotgun house, Camille looked beyond the counter to find a white man standing by a display of healing herbs, whistling. He was lean, with thick red hair that curved over his ears in slick waves. He wore a blue suit jacket with sleeves that hit just above his wrists, and he carried a trumpet case.

She cleared her throat. "May I help you?"

The man turned to her and smiled. "Good mornin'." His voice was cheerful, his pale blue eyes bright. "Man, it sure smells good in here. What is that?"

"Incense," Camille said, gesturing to a row of shelves running along the opposite wall.

"Incense," he said, looking around. "No kiddin'? You know, I always wondered about this place."

"It's my momma's shop," Camille said. "She's in the back."

"Well." He grinned, winked. "I'll be sure and behave myself then."

Camille smiled nervously, feeling a warm flush crawl up her neck. "I didn't mean it that way," she said, then wished she hadn't.

The man sauntered toward her, swinging the trumpet case at his side. Reaching the counter, he set the case on the floor and leaned forward, resting his elbows on the glass. His voice was conversational, as if they were old friends.

"Tell me somethin'," he whispered, nodding toward the crowded displays behind her. "You believe in all this stuff?"

Camille nodded, nervously fingering the rounded collar of her stiff white blouse.

"I believe people need to feel safe," she said quietly.

The man rolled forward on his elbows, his blue eyes fixed on her, his gaze so steady that she felt compelled to draw her hand across her upper lip, sure there were fresh pebbles of sweat there.

"So does all this make *you* feel safe?"

Camille shrugged. "Sometimes."

"You know what makes me feel safe?" he asked low.

Camille shook her head, riveted.

"Love," he said. "Love makes me feel safe."

She felt a blush prickle the skin of her throat. "Must be nice."

"It is." He smiled, extending his hand. "I'm Charles. Charles Bienvenu Bergeron. At your service, darlin'."

Camille slipped her fingers inside his, shocked when he drew them up and placed a soft kiss on her knuckles.

He lowered her hand but didn't release it. "Now it's your turn."

She looked at him, confused.

"Your name, darlin'," he directed gently.

"Oh," she said. "Sorry. Camille. Camille Bayonne."

"Camille," he repeated, then once more, "Cameeelle . . . Man, that is a beautiful, beautiful name. That's a name should be a song. I think I might just have to write a song for you.

What do you think about that, darlin'? You ever had someone write you a song?"

"No."

"Oh, come on now—you kiddin' me? A beautiful girl like you?"

She smiled, pulling at the pleats of her skirt with her freed hand.

"You like music, darlin'?"

"Sure," she said. "Doesn't everybody like music?"

"Most people, yeah. But I'm talking about *real* music." His eyes grew big. "I'm talkin' about the greats. Miles Davis. Coltrane. Monk. Bird. Louis Armstrong. You ever been to Mighty's?"

Camille shook her head, the names spinning in her head, utterly unfamiliar. The truth was, she hadn't been to most places in the city. Life on Maurepas Street had always kept her busy: the simple but consuming routines of helping at the shop full-time since she'd left school, the occasional breaks spent on neighbors' porches, or short walks in City Park, or sometimes farther up along Lakeshore Drive, watching Pontchartrain's surf wash the stepped levee walls.

"I don't get out very much," she confessed.

Charles winked. "Well, baby, I think that's gonna have to change."

"Camille!"

Roberta's voice rang out from the back. Camille spun around reflexively, then turned back to him. "That's . . . that's my momma," she said, backing away slowly, as if he were reaching out to her with open arms. "I should go see what she needs."

"Oh, sure, sure. I was just lookin'." Charles Bergeron grinned and picked up his trumpet case. "But I tell you what. Maybe I'll come back and you can show me which one of these candles I gotta burn to make you fall crazy in love with me; what do you think about that?"

Camille blushed instantly, deeply, just so grateful to be able to disappear behind the curtain before he could see.

It would be a rainy and sticky Friday afternoon, almost two weeks later, before Charles Bergeron would return to the shop.

Camille was behind the counter when she heard the tinkling of bells, finding sage sticks and sweet almond oil for Miss Willa while her mother and Miss Willa gossiped in the back room over bowls of Roberta's famous gumbo. Wilhelmina Marshall was one of Roberta's most loyal customers, a shapely brunette, forty-five, with a smoky laugh that had never seen a single cigarette, and a penchant for tiny poodles that she carried everywhere, one under each arm like loaves of French bread. Some white women came to the shop pretending to know about Voodoo, but Miss Willa was the real thing. Roberta would never have sold to her otherwise.

"Told ya I'd be back."

Camille looked up, a delighted smile blooming helplessly on her face. She glanced behind her, sure her mother would appear, but the curtain remained still, the deep rumble of Miss Willa's laugh still a safe distance beyond the doorway.

Camille gestured to his empty hands. "No trumpet today."

"You mean Donna?"

"Donna?" Camille gave him a dubious look. "You named your trumpet?"

"She came with it. Got her from a man in Florida says he

found her floatin' out a flooded house during Hurricane Donna a few years back. Said he thought it was some kinda miracle. Picked her up and she played like a dream. Said it seemed only fair to call her Donna, and I do agree. Don't you?" Camille nodded enthusiastically. Charles stopped to draw in a deep breath. "Hey, don't tell me y'all are sellin' incense that smells like gumbo now?"

Camille giggled. "Nope. That's the real thing."

"Smells good."

"It is," she said proudly. "People say Momma's gumbo is the best in the neighborhood."

"Do they now?" Charles positioned himself as he had his first visit, leaning across the counter, close enough this time that Camille could smell his minty cologne and see flecks of lavender in his eyes. And freckles! She'd never seen so many freckles on a man: great, big constellations of them, even on his fingers. "But I don't bet you bother with that, though, huh?" he added coyly. "A beautiful girl like you don't waste her time workin' over a stove."

"It's not work to me," Camille said. "I love to cook. Especially gumbo."

"For real?" Charles raised a thick red eyebrow. "What's so great about makin' gumbo?"

Camille shrugged. No one had ever asked her that before, and even though she'd never really thought much about it, an answer poured out of her. "It's kind of like the spells," she said. "Finding all the ingredients, getting the roux just right, knowing if you don't, it won't work. Then when it does . . ." She paused, looking up to find him staring at her, enthralled. She smiled and looked away, embarrassed. "I guess I just like it, is all."

"Yeah, I can see that." Charles rolled forward. "Think you might like to go out with me as much as you like makin' gumbo, Camille Bayonne?"

Camille felt the blood rush against her temples, a fierce, dizzying torrent.

"You remembered my name," she said.

"Course I did. You remember mine?"

"Charles," she said softly, meeting his eyes. "Charles Bienvenu Bergeron."

His smile grew long.

Behind them, the poodles barked madly, Miss Willa's playful scolding, then the rustle of chairs across the wood floor. Their time was running out.

Charles leaned even closer and whispered, "How soon can you meet me at the corner of Fortin and Gentilly?"

"I—I don't know." Camille swallowed, not sure which terrified her more: meeting him or not meeting him. "It's hard to say. . . ."

"An hour's easy to say. Try it."

Camille smiled, blushing. "An hour," she whispered obediently.

"There you go. That wasn't so hard, was it?"

Floorboards creaked as footsteps neared. Charles pushed off the counter, walking backward toward the door.

"An hour," he said, then grabbed at his breast pocket. "Gonna be the longest hour of my life, Camille Bayonne."

Camille barely got in a small wave before she felt the rush of hot air from the back room, smelled the citrusy scent of Miss Willa's perfume blown in and heard the shrill scamper of poodle nails tearing at the wood floor.

Roberta stepped behind the counter, glancing at the door as it shuddered closed. "Who was that?"

"Nobody," Camille said. "Just a friend."

But Roberta had only to see the helpless smile on her daughter's face before a fierce panic gripped her. For weeks now, the cards had delivered news of a dark visitor entering her daughter's fragile heart. Roberta had warned Camille over and over, but Roberta should have known better; some men were stronger than her spells.

"A friend, huh?"

Miss Willa and her poodles were already at the window, sweeping aside a panel of dyed silk just in time to see Charles sprint down the street and slip into Flap's restaurant at the corner. Willa came back, the rapping of her tiny heels like a clucking tongue.

"I know him, Bertie," she reported. "He's a white fella from the parish. He plays at Minnie's with Leroy."

Roberta frowned. "What do you mean, *plays?*"

"What do you think I mean, sugar? Music."

"Nuh-uh," said Roberta firmly. "Minnie wouldn't let a white boy play at her club."

"She lets *him*."

Roberta considered that, stumped. "Then he must be good."

"That's what I heard." Miss Willa grinned wickedly. "And not half-bad at the trumpet, either."

When Camille reached Gentilly Boulevard at four o'clock and Charles was nowhere to be seen, the disappointment was immediate, like a hard shove from behind. Rain had arrived, fat, heavy drops, and she'd ruined her best shoes on the walk over, soft ivory flats with tiny salmon bows on one side, not to mention wilting her neatly rolled hair that now hung just above her shoulders and clung to her cheeks in thick clumps. She could already hear her mother's voice, the unmistakable tone of *I told you so*, and her throat felt thick when she swallowed.

So when the maroon Impala pulled alongside her, she didn't pay any attention to it, until the driver's-side door flew open. In an instant, Charles was beside her, sweeping her under his umbrella and steering her to the car.

"Your chariot awaits, darlin'," he said, throwing open the passenger door. Camille climbed in, the warm, brassy smell of old leather filling her nostrils.

Charles dashed in the driver's side, shaking the rain from his hair. He turned to look at her and smiled.

"Man, you look like an angel," he said. "I wasn't sure you were gonna come."

"I wasn't either," she confessed.

He smiled. "But you did."

"I did."

"And you know what I gotta say to that?" He slammed both palms into the center of the wheel, forcing a shrieking burst of the horn. Camille jumped, embarrassed for a moment as everyone on the sidewalk stopped and spun around, then buoyant and carefree when the horn quieted and Charles's high-pitched laugh filled the car in its place.

She was still smiling when he pulled them out into traffic.

"Where are we going?" she asked.

Charles tugged out a tight roll of bills from his jacket pocket, turning them in his hand as if they might catch the light, and he grinned.

"Wherever we want."

He took the long way, driving them up the lush stretch of Uptown, along St. Charles and through the Garden District, past the old mansions with their deep galleries and endless gardens. The rain had let up, so Camille rolled down her window to catch the thick perfume of confederate jasmine, the air so much cooler under the canopy of live oaks that reached across the neutral ground. It was nothing like her neighborhood, where there were few trees to shade the smoldering concrete. *No wonder people uptown never sweat,* she thought as Charles steered them down Oak Street.

"Welcome to Mighty's!"

He pulled them in front of a bar with a neon saxophone above the door and helped her out of the car, then through a pair of heavy doors and down a wood-paneled hall to a long mahogany bar that gleamed under a ceiling tiled with squares of painted tin. Camille could hear the crashing and settling of objects just beyond a narrow doorway, the tinny sound of cymbals moved into place, the shuffling of feet, instruments being tuned.

"It's early," Charles said, helping her into a seat at the end of the bar. "Things don't really get movin' till later, but I figured we wouldn't push our luck, this bein' our first date and all."

While Charles leaned across the bar to order their drinks and chat with the bartender, Camille studied him in careful glances. He was very handsome; there was no denying that. If not for his broad nose, he might have even looked feminine, his features so fine, his mouth remarkably full, his pale lashes long and curling.

The bartender set down her Coke and a bourbon for Charles. The brown liquor looked like melted gold to her. She wet her lips.

"I could tell you were wondering about this," Charles said, pointing to his nose after he'd taken a swig. "Broke it a few years ago. I used to be a boxer, but I decided I liked usin' my hands for playin' the trumpet better, so I quit it."

Camille nodded and watched Charles drain his bourbon and order a second.

"You ever play here?" she asked, noting the way his left knee bobbed up and down to a silent beat.

Charles tugged out a five from his wallet and left it on the bar. "A few times. I got a gig tomorrow night at Rhino's on Royal. Maybe you wanna come hear me?"

"I don't know." Camille played with her straw. "My momma doesn't like me being in the Quarter late by myself."

"You wouldn't be by yourself. You'd be with me." He pulled out a pack of cigarettes from his suit jacket, shook one out, and slid it between his straight, white teeth. "Your momma don't trust me—that it?" he asked, snapping open his lighter and holding his cigarette over the flame until the end sizzled, red as his hair.

Camille shrugged. "It's not you. She doesn't trust most people."

"Most *men*, you mean. Or maybe just white ones like me and your daddy."

Camille's eyes lifted to his, blinking with surprise. But of course he'd guessed. Her skin was so much lighter than her momma's, her eyes more hazel than chestnut.

Charles snapped his lighter shut, tossed it on the bar beside his fresh drink. "I'm sure she thinks I'm too old for ya. But you know what I say to that?" He pointed at Camille with his cigarette. "I say age is just a number. Just look at you, for example. How old are you?"

"Eighteen."

"See? Now, that's what I'm talkin' about. I'd have said you were more like twenty. Maybe even twenty-one."

"Really?"

"Oh, yeah, really."

Camille smiled, her posture straightening reflexively.

"I bet you got a lotta boyfriends, huh?" Charles asked, scooping up his drink. "Beautiful girl like you?"

Camille shrugged. There was Franklin Dupre, but he didn't count. She'd decided just last week that someone who cared only to press himself against you in the produce department at Schwegmann's didn't count as much of anything. "No," she said. "Not really."

"Aww." Charles winked at her over his glass. "You're just sayin' that so I'll think I've got a real chance."

Camille leaned down for her straw. She wondered if he did this often; then she reminded herself it wasn't her business, and that she had to be grateful for this drink, this moment. It could be her only night with him, and she'd have wasted it worrying about something she couldn't change even if she wanted to. Men had to be men, Momma had always said, and a woman was a fool to think she was special enough to change one.

"You want a sip?" he asked, gently nudging his drink toward her.

Camille waved with both hands. "Oh, no, I couldn't."

"Sure, you could," he said. "A small sip. Ain't nobody gonna care."

He inched the glass closer. She sighed, biting her lip a moment longer; then she finally took it, wincing when the bourbon hit her nose, then her throat.

She coughed, her eyes watering.

Charles grinned. "Not like a Coca-Cola, is it?"

Camille shook her head, sipping her soda to wash away the sting.

Charles took a long drag off his cigarette, watching her intently, squinting as the smoke drifted up to his eyes. "You been without your daddy a long time, darlin'?"

"Long enough." Camille looked down. "I don't think about him much anymore. Momma and I take care of each other."

"I can see that," Charles said, "and that's real nice to see, but a girl's got to find a man to take care of her eventually. Gotta let go of the things that keep her from bein' a woman. It's the natural order of the world."

The natural order. Camille hadn't ever thought much about that. Her own world had always been filled with women whose lives seemed perfectly functional without the constant, or even infrequent, attention of men. She wondered what Charles meant, but she didn't dare ask. Already his talking was making her skin flush hot from her ears to her toes. She wondered whether a person could get drunk on just one sip of bourbon.

His hand closed over hers, his fingertips hard with calluses. "You don't need all that Voodoo when you got a man to love ya, Camille," he said low, his eyes fixing on hers. "Ain't no potions more powerful than that."

Ten minutes later, the band began to play. They walked through the narrow doorway and took seats around the crowded stage, their voices quickly lost in the swell of sounds, the air thick with the smell of perspiration and warm beer. Looking around at the other tables, the men and women wrapped around one another, fingers and feet tapping, cigarette paper crackling and smoke rising all around, ice cubes tumbling in emptying glasses, Camille felt weightless, blissful, free.

When Charles moved in to kiss her, she tasted the nutty flavor of liquor. When he slipped his tongue through her tight lips, she could smell her own breath, strange to her suddenly. When she opened her eyes she could see the band over his shoulder, the sharp points of light reflecting off the brass, exploding like sunbursts.

Driving home under a half-moon, the night air still moist with the day's humidity, Camille felt sure she was changed, as if the smoky smell on her would be permanent, washed from her clothes but never from her skin. When Charles pulled up in front of her house at nine, Camille took the stairs with shaky legs, glad for the railing. At her front door, she didn't notice the redbrick dust her mother had sprinkled over the threshold until she was already inside, but she should have expected her mother would try anything to keep Charles Bergeron from coming into her daughter's home, or heart.

There was no use in trying to wash it off; Camille knew that much.

Better she work her own spell. And fast.

It *would be three* weeks before Charles brought her to the Creole town house on Royal Street and the shuttered room with the widest brass bed Camille had ever seen. Afterward, she lay on the mattress while he dressed, listening to the pounding of the rain on the balcony and watching the gentle spin of the ceiling fan, trying not to think about how much her body stung. Charles told her not to bother putting on the same clothes she'd arrived in, but gave her a box filled with tissue paper and a flowing velvet minidress that he helped her into, his fingers smelling of tobacco and the coppery scent of his trumpet: hot, salty metal.

When Camille came home, her mother was in the kitchen,

spooning rounds of praline syrup on waxed paper, the smell of warm sugar still heavy in the air. A feeling of fleetingness overcame Camille, swift and sudden, as if she had come home to someone else's life without warning. She didn't know why but she wanted to cry.

"You never cook with me anymore," Roberta said, her voice so sad, so weak that Camille didn't recognize it at first. "I can't remember the last time we made gumbo together. I'm beginning to think you forgot how."

"I couldn't forget, Momma; you know that."

Roberta drew in a shaky breath. "He's taking you away from me, Camille. And you're letting him."

"That's not true."

"Yes, it is." Roberta stopped a moment to wipe her eyes with her sleeve. She sniffed. "All these things he buys you, he doesn't get that money from playing music, baby girl. You know that, don't you? He no more makes money playing that trumpet than I do making these pralines. He gets his money from the track. Only reason he ended up on our street in the first place was 'cause we're spittin' distance from the fairgrounds."

"I don't care how he makes his money."

"Well, you should. He's trouble, Camille. Baby girl, he is so full of trouble. Dark, dark stuff. Powerful stuff. Just like I told you I saw."

"They're just cards, Momma."

Roberta looked up, her eyes washed with hurt. "You never used to turn your back on the cards," she said tightly. "Not ever."

Camille looked away, knowing it was true. She had grown up listening to her mother's premonitions, so used to letting the cards dictate her every move, the warnings somehow always working to keep Camille close to home, to keep her quiet and full of fear.

Maybe Charles was right. Maybe it was time for her to find her own magic, her own spirits. Maybe she didn't need the spells anymore.

"Oh, Momma." Camille came up behind Roberta at her post at the stove and wrapped her arms around her mother's narrow waist, burying her cheek against her shoulder, feeling the bones there under the thin cotton of her dress.

"Seems like all of a sudden you're in such a hurry to run out on me," Roberta said, her voice failing as she began to weep. "Why him, Camille? What's so great about him?"

"He thinks I'm beautiful, Momma."

"You are beautiful, baby. You don't need a man to tell you that."

"But I do," Camille said softly.

Then she walked to her room and closed the door.

Almost two months later, Camille was walking down Gentilly when Franklin Dupre saw her from his seat in Junie's Po' Boys and darted out of the restaurant and across the street to reach her. He called to her several times but she refused to slow her pace, forcing him to run to catch up to her before she'd turned onto Lapeyrouse.

"Well, look who it is," he said, pulling alongside her. "Queen Camille."

"You don't have to be nasty, Franklin," she said calmly. "I never did anything to you."

"Just stopped seein' me, is all."

"You never said we were going steady. Not once."

"These fancy new clothes you're wearin'. I don't even recognize you anymore."

"You knew me well enough to cross the street raving like a lunatic."

"Yeah, well." Franklin frowned at the sidewalk, driving his hands into his back pockets. "I've been comin' by the shop. Didn't your momma tell you?"

"She told me."

"So it's true?"

"What?"

"You and that white dude."

"His name's Charles, Franklin. Charles Bienvenu Bergeron. And I don't really see how it's any of your business."

"Well, excuuuuse me." The young man sucked in his cheeks. "You think he's somethin' else, don't you? Well, I don't bet he told you that he been to jail almost as many times as I got fingers, huh? Or that he gets so high some nights he can't even hold up that skinny ol' trumpet of his. He tell you all that, Mr. Charles Been-whatever Bergeron?"

Camille walked on, silent, her eyes still fixed on the end of the block. Franklin studied her awhile, waiting for her answer, but he could see she wasn't going to budge.

"Yeah." He snorted, defeated. "I didn't think so."

When they reached her porch, she took the stairs carefully, elegantly, just like she'd seen the other musicians' girlfriends do when they'd all march out of the clubs.

Franklin waited a long moment on the bottom step. When Camille reached for the screen door, he threw out a hand as if he were swatting a slow fly. "I'll see you around, Queenie."

Camille didn't answer, but she didn't go in either. She waited on the threshold, where Roberta's redbrick dust still appeared every morning. She waited until Franklin was back on the other side of the street, headed back into Junie's, thinking to herself there was one thing she knew, one thing that Franklin Dupre didn't.

She was carrying Charles Bergeron's child.

Roberta honked into a Kleenex, then dragged it across her red-rimmed eyes.

"He won't marry her. That miserable bastard won't marry her."

Miss Willa leaned across the kitchen table to offer Roberta a fresh tissue. Roberta took it. "You don't know that, Bertie," Willa said gently. "He's crazy about her."

"Parker was crazy about me too before the baby."

"Yeah, he was crazy, all right," Willa said, wrinkling her lips. "Crazy like a loon."

"Men like that don't stick around, Willa. Believe me, I know. There's always a bigger payout somewhere down the line. A prettier girl. A faster car."

"Don't be so sure." Miss Willa peeled a cooled praline off its sheet of waxed paper, admiring the disk's smooth finish. "He stuck around this long, didn't he?"

Roberta shrugged, turning her gaze to the window, where she could see a group of girls jumping rope in the street, and she sighed. "I could kill him."

Willa nodded toward the middle of the table, where a small pile of black dog hair sat neatly in a ring of salt, and she grinned. "Looks like you've already tried."

Six

New Orleans, Louisiana

Spring 1962

"It's been almost a month since I've seen you," Roberta said when Camille came by the shop in her third trimester, feet and ankles bursting like boudin sausages. They sat in the kitchen while Roberta stirred a pot of red beans, the air fragrant with onions and thyme.

"I've been so busy, Momma. Getting ready for the baby and all. There's just so much to do."

"Especially when you're doing it all on your own," Roberta said. "I remember."

Camille said nothing, just blew on her coffee, not wanting

to admit that Charles had lately been spending less time at the apartment, that all of the last-minute preparations for the baby had fallen on her, and that anytime she mentioned it, Charles grew sullen, even angry.

Roberta glanced over at her daughter. "Been blessing the house with the Florida water I made you?"

Camille frowned contritely, thinking on the bottle of Voodoo holy water that sat under her sink, untouched. "A few times," she lied.

Roberta shook her head. "You can't treat the spirits like canned goods, Camille. Store 'em up in case of emergency, thinking they'll be there when you need them. They get their feelings hurt, they won't stick around." Roberta dropped a few bay leaves into the pot, folded them in.

"I know," said Camille. "I haven't forgotten."

Roberta gave her daughter a worried look, then set down her spoon and reached into her skirt pocket. "Here." She held out a filled red velvet bag tied with a black ribbon and smelling of rosemary and lavender, her mother's favored protection herbs.

"Momma," Camille said, gently but firmly, "you didn't have to do that. I have plenty of bags I can fill myself. I'm telling you I'm fine."

"And I'm telling you I know what I feel." Roberta set the gris-gris bag on top of a tin of pralines and slid them both into a brown bag.

"Just take it," she said, folding her daughter's hands over the top of the bag. "For me."

Camille carried the bag back to the peeling-plaster studio apartment Charles had found them on Rampart. Coming in, she was overcome with a bout of fatigue and fell asleep on the daybed, rousing when she heard Charles's uneven steps in their tiny corner kitchen. She stirred, rising slowly to keep from getting dizzy, as she had been finding herself lately.

"What the hell . . . ?"

Too late she remembered her mother's gift. Charles came at her with the small red sack in one hand, their dented garbage can in the other. He waited until he was right in front of her before he thrust the bag into the can, sending up a puff of rotten food, the smell so wretched Camille was sure she'd throw up.

His blue eyes narrowed. He looked suddenly old to her, the harsh light of the kitchen turning one side of his face a jaundiced yellow. "I told ya I didn't want that bullshit in my house, Camille."

"It was just a little something from Momma," she defended weakly, swallowing down her nausea. "A gift, Charles."

Charles took the can back to the kitchen and shoved it under the sink, closing the cabinet with his foot. "Baby, how many times I gotta tell you, you don't need all that anymore? I'm your husband and I'm the one that keeps you safe. Not some bag of chicken bones. And I sure as hell don't want you or your momma teachin' my kid any of that crap, either. You hear me?"

She nodded dutifully, rising to make his dinner of catfish and fried okra, then watching him across the table as he ate. She was relieved when he pulled out his trumpet later on, playing her a lullaby just before they climbed into bed, then pulling her swollen body against his erection, shuffling the moist sheets until he could slide inside her.

It was a comfortable routine, she thought, watching the blown curtains fold into ribbons as he thrust into her. The rage and the release. She'd heard about men who did far worse than raise their voice, or say hateful things. Some men hit and seized and shook.

She was sure Charles would never hit her, certainly not while she carried their child, and she was right. He waited until two months after Dahlia was born, when Camille had detected the smell of another woman's crotch on his chest hair. He dragged her from their bed and hit her so hard she fell back against the dresser, knocking down the mirror and shattering it all over the rug into tiny shards that sliced her knees as he held her afterward, sobbing with his apology.

Josie came on a damp, overcast day, almost twenty-eight hours after her first feeble push. It would not occur to Camille for many years that her daughters came into the world just as they would inhabit it. Dahlia, bold and insistent, had burst out a week early and with eyes wide-open, while Josie had lingered long in her mother's womb, finally peeking out two weeks late, refusing to open her eyes for several minutes, as if she still hoped there was a chance she might be put back in.

"She's perfect," were Charles's only words when he finally arrived home from two days away, reaching for the red-haired infant with arms outstretched, too fixated to even grant his wife and first child a proper hello on his way through the bedroom. Camille could still recall the chilling look in his eyes when he'd first seen Dahlia at the hospital, the flat sound of his voice as he'd said, "She's too dark. She shouldn't be that dark." But in Josie, there would be no confusion, no doubt.

"She looks just like my mother," Charles whispered, tenderly lifting Josie out of her crib. "Jesus H. Christ, ain't that somethin'."

For almost an hour, he walked the porch with Josie wrapped

in a blanket, leaving Camille inside to mop at her forehead, her neck, her breasts so swollen with milk she was sure they were filled with rocks.

Roberta and Miss Willa were fanning themselves on the porch when Camille visited several months later with the girls, cradling one child on each hip as she came up the steps.

"Now, you come give those precious babies to me," Willa said, drawing both girls into her arms, much to the outrage of her newest poodle, Lucifer, who found himself deposited on the porch floor. The sisters filled their tiny hands at once with Willa's beaded necklaces, beguiled. "Come on, now, sugars," she said, pressing the screen back with her hip. "Auntie Willa's got some Voodoo dolls that need dressing."

Mother and daughter poured glasses of sweet tea and sat side by side on the unraveling wicker swing, watching the neighborhood children chase one another up and down the street.

"Seems awfully hot for long sleeves," Roberta said evenly.

Camille said nothing, just sipped her tea, but it was hard to get anything past the lump in her throat.

Roberta reached for her daughter's hand and held it. "You and the babies can always come stay. I can protect you here. But out there . . ." Roberta's eyes misted. "Out there he's too strong."

Camille nodded, rubbing her mother's hand. "He's trying, Momma. I know he is."

"It's not always enough to try, baby girl. A man's got to *do*."

Lucifer trotted to the edge of the porch and flounced down in the sun. The delighted squeals of the babies came floating through the screen, Willa's laugh like a plucked harp.

Looking back, Camille would wonder how it took her so long to fall out of love with Charles, even though the longing stayed, immediate and jarring, when she'd catch a glimpse of that handsome profile, or when he'd play the trumpet for her and the girls, and that bright, rich sound would fill their apartment. In the months after Josie was born, Camille believed Charles might finally do right by them all, his admiration for Josie was so strong. But not even nine months later, Camille watched him greet a blond woman on their porch who was dressed in a pinched silver dress that looked like it was made out of aluminum foil. Their heads were close as they conferred; then Charles came back inside while the woman waited, her back to the door, puffing madly on a cigarette.

"She needs a ride home," he said matter-of-factly, and Camille had responded in kind, "Fine." But it would be the first night he simply didn't bother coming home, the first morning he would return stinking of another woman's juices and not even bother to change before he collapsed into his chair at their breakfast table and took his morning coffee and grits.

That night Camille considered her mother's offer for refuge for the first time in three years of marriage, and she even packed a small bag for the babies, but she didn't leave.

She wouldn't have another chance. A few weeks shy of Josephine's first birthday, Roberta died of a heart attack in her kitchen.

Camille didn't leave the house for almost two weeks.

The girls grew quickly, riding rickety bicycles up and down the levee and climbing the branches of the great oaks in Audubon Park, whatever they could do to steer clear of their father's unpredictable moods. Sometimes Charles's temper would land him in prison, as it did in the spring of 1970, when he was sentenced for punching an officer during a Mardi Gras parade. For nearly two years afterward, Camille and the girls rented a room from Lionel Morrow and Roman Winters in their Creole cottage. Roman was a sculptor, and Lionel taught literature at the university. The men watched Dahlia and Josie when Camille worked the overnight shift at the candy factory on Decatur, letting the girls stuff themselves on bread pudding and caramel custard, then putting them to bed in one of the guest rooms with velvet canopies and crowded bookshelves that climbed to the ceiling. In the mornings while Camille slept, the men took the girls out to the courtyard, where Lionel read Thomas Hardy to Josie, and Roman showed Dahlia how to care for the gardenias and the satsuma tree. On Friday nights, crowds of friends, professors and artists, activists and drag queens, would gather at the house, and Dahlia and Josie would sneak out in their nightgowns to sample skewered shrimp and pluck fat, shiny olives from unsupervised martinis.

When Charles was released in the summer of 1972, he came for them in a peanut butter–brown Dodge Dart, and waited in the car while Camille and the girls packed their things with aching hearts. They returned with Charles to the Quarter and a drafty apartment on Bourbon Street two stories above Adam's Serpent Strip Club, where girls in sheer tops and heart-shaped pasties beckoned men from arched doorways. When Camille found Dahlia mimicking the topless dancers' poses in front of the window a month later, Camille demanded they move. Charles found them a new home in the Irish Channel, two blocks from a bar that happened to be looking for a trumpet player for its weekend band. The lavender-and-ivory raised shotgun was bathed in sun, and there were children the girls' ages on either side of the house. Camille grew contented, enduring Charles's bleaker moods and bursts of rage, working protection spells when he was at work, and taking ritual baths in milk and mustard seed after he'd gone to sleep, and in the years that followed, while Charles drifted in and out of jail for one offense or another, Camille traded her minidresses for flowing caftans and her straightened curls for an Afro.

She grew strong. Not quite strong enough to leave, but strong enough to keep her wits about her, to raise her daughters to have regard for their history and their home, and to speak civilly but firmly to Charles's lovers when they arrived at her door flushed and strung out, hoping to spare her daughters the truth of their father's infidelities.

But even at thirteen, Dahlia knew.

"You don't have to pretend, Momma," Dahlia announced one stifling Monday afternoon when she was helping their mother take down drying sheets off the porch. "I know who those women are who come around."

Josie sat in the porch swing behind them, giving a bottle to Miss Margie's new baby boy.

Camille gave her oldest daughter a warning look. "Watch you don't drag my nice clean sheets all over the floor, Dahlia Rose, and don't worry so much about who's coming and who's going from this house, you hear?"

"Yes, ma'am," Dahlia said.

"Why do you have to upset Momma like that?" Josie asked when Camille had gone inside with the laundry.

"Me? He's the one who's upsetting her, not me. And why are you always defending him?"

"Because he's our daddy," Josie said weakly, carefully shifting the infant in her small lap.

"Yeah, well, he's crazy." Dahlia dropped into the swing beside her sister. "Do you know what he does at night? He locks the doors and he hides the key in the broiler. He doesn't know but I saw him do it once. That's how crazy he is. We're like his prisoners."

"We are not," Josie said. "And don't talk so loud. You'll scare the baby."

Dahlia shrugged. "Look for yourself tonight if you don't believe me. All I know is, I'm never getting married."

"That's silly. Everybody gets married."

"Not Mrs. Kemper's boarder, Miss Clarice," said Dahlia. "She takes lovers instead. A whole bunch of them. I heard Momma talking with Miss Willa about it the other day, and you should see the way men look at Miss Clarice when she walks down the street, like they forgot how they got there or something. I want men looking at me that way, following me around so I can tell them to bug off when I'm bored instead of the other way around."

"But if you don't get married, you can't have babies."

"Who said I wanted babies?"

"Well, I do," said Josie, smiling down at Randolph. "I want five. Three boys and two girls."

Dahlia frowned. "All I know is, I don't ever want to fall in love if it means some man thinks he can lock me in at night, or tell me where I can go or when I have to be home to fix him some meal that he's too drunk or high to even eat—"

"Shh," Josie ordered, seeing their father come down the street. "I heard Momma telling Miss Margie that Daddy might get laid off at the dock."

"Good," Dahlia said. "Then maybe Momma will leave him."

"Don't say that. I don't want Momma to be alone."

"She's not alone. She has us."

Charles came up the steps in his work clothes, the smell of grease filling the porch. "Shit, don't tell me you got yourself a baby now, Julep?"

"No, sir. It's Miss Margie's. His name's Randolph. Isn't he precious?"

Charles nodded next door. "Well, you give him back and get in there and help your momma, both y'all. I got a gig tonight."

"Yes, sir." Josie rose obediently, the infant pressed protectively to her shoulder.

They took their seats around the table while Camille served up heaping bowls of red beans and rice.

"Mmm," Charles said. "These are some good beans, Camille."

Camille handed a bowl to Dahlia. "Josephine made them."

"No kiddin'? You make these all by yourself, Julep?"

Josie nodded, blushing. "Yes, sir."

"Well, damn, girl!" Charles slapped his thigh. "You gettin' to be a real good cook. Just like your momma." He reached out and tore off a hunk of French bread, glaring at Dahlia as he dunked it in his bowl. "When are you gonna start helpin' out in there?"

"Dahlia helps out plenty, Charles," Camille said, serving herself at last.

Charles snickered. "Yeah. Helps herself to eatin' it."

Josie reached for her sweet tea, feeling the familiar prickles of an impending fight crawl up her spine.

"Sure don't take after my side," Charles added, chewing his bread roughly. "All the women in my family are tiny little things. Like Josephine. Bergeron women got stomachs like birds."

Dahlia looked across the table at Charles. "That must be why Aunt Vivian is as big as an ostrich."

"Dahlia," Camille said, her eyes pleading, but Charles was already on his feet, moving to the other side of the table, where Dahlia sat calmly shoveling in spoonfuls of red beans.

He slammed his palm next to her bowl, causing the whole table to shudder.

"What's that you just said, girl? I don't hear so good all the way down there."

"Charles, please," Camille said, rising nervously. "Leave her be."

"Answer me, goddamn it."

Josie gripped her napkin in her lap, her stomach lurching.

Dahlia lowered her spoon, refusing to look up at him. "I said, your sister Vivian is as big as an ostrich."

Without another word, Charles snatched the spoon from Dahlia's hand and struck the side of her face with it, leaving a fat teardrop of red beans just below her left eye.

"Charles!" Camille rushed from her seat, shoving her husband out of the way and moving to Dahlia, but Dahlia had already wiped herself clean.

"Jesus, it wasn't nothin' but a little tap, Camille. Girl's gotta know better than to disrespect family like that."

Josie stared down at her bowl, too afraid to look up as her father walked behind her chair. Seated again, Charles reached out and touched her cheek. Josie flinched, startled, but he didn't seem to notice.

"Not you, though, Julep." He smiled. "I ain't never gotta worry about you."

That night, Josie crept from her room and into the kitchen, wincing as she opened the broiler door, so afraid to hear its usual creak. She reached in with trembling fingers and gasped, feeling the jagged shaft of a key.

Seven

New Orleans, Louisiana
Fall 1977

November arrived, breezy and mild. Camille had taken a job cutting hair at a beauty parlor while Charles had been serving a six-month sentence for drug possession. He called to announce his release the day before Thanksgiving, though he wouldn't arrive until the next morning, just in time to make sure Camille had fixed his favorite holiday dish: roast turkey with oyster dressing.

"I'm home!" he called out, blowing through the front door shortly before noon. "Where y'all at?"

Camille summoned a pleasant smile when Charles swept by her, heading first to Josie to deliver a loud kiss to her forehead and a squeeze so hard that Josie swore he left the imprint of his shirt button in her cheek.

"Smells good, Camille." Camille nodded, wondering how he could smell anything over the stench of liquor on his own breath. His celebratory round at the Oyster Shell on the way home, no doubt. "Looks good too," he murmured, stroking her bottom.

Camille stepped aside to stir the gravy. "Glad you think so, Charles."

"Let's speed this up," he ordered, dragging a finger through the dish of sweet potatoes and sucking it clean. "I got a gig this afternoon at Lucky's."

"On Thanksgiving?" Camille asked.

"Work's work, baby." Charles looked around. "Where's your sister at, Julep?"

"Outside," Josie said. "In the back."

"What the hell she doin' out there? Didn't she hear me come in?"

"I'm sure she didn't," Camille said, lifting the turkey out of the oven, knowing just how to distract him.

Charles's eyes grew big. "Damn, that is a good-lookin' bird. Y'all get Dahlia in here while I go take a piss. Then we eat. I'm starved."

Camille nodded to Josie, who then walked to the back of the house, pushing open the screen door to find Dahlia laying down mulch on a rose bed.

"Daddy's home," Josie said. "Didn't you hear?"

"Sorry. I don't have the news on out here."

Josie frowned at her sister's filthy hands and thighs. "He's gonna hit the roof if he finds you out here looking like that."

"I'm sure. Only thing worse than being a convict is getting dirty on Thanksgiving. Maybe I should be the one going to jail."

"Dahl, please don't start," Josie whispered. "Momma's made a really nice meal, and Daddy seems happy. Don't ruin it. Let's try and be like a real family today, huh?"

"We *are* a real family," Dahlia said, annoyed. She rose to her feet, wiping her hands on her seat. "It's when he's here that we're not."

"Jesus Christ, girl." Charles appeared behind Josie, zipping up his fly. "What the hell you doin' out here? Diggin' a goddamned well?"

"Dahlia grew roses, Daddy," Josie said. "You should have seen them when they were blooming. They were so beautiful."

Charles looked at Dahlia. "Get on inside and wash yourself up. Your momma needs help settin' the table."

Ten minutes later, the table was set and the sisters and Camille were seated. The turkey sat in the center of the table, its crinkled skin gleaming.

Camille looked around, shifting from side to side. "Where's your father?"

Josie shrugged, answering brightly as she reached for her milk, "Maybe he's bringing some food to the lady in the car."

Camille looked up.

"What lady in the car?" demanded Dahlia.

"The . . . lady," Josie said weakly, panic filling her as she looked between them.

Dahlia jumped up, and before Camille or Josie could stop her, she lunged across the table and scooped up the turkey in her arms like a drowsing cat.

"Dahlia Rose!" Camille cried, struggling to free herself from her chair to chase after her. Josie followed, steering around the slick trail of juice that Dahlia was leaving in her wake, and both mother and daughter arrived on the porch just in time to see Dahlia reach back and hurl the shiny bird at the black DeVille's windshield, where it exploded like a squeezed boil.

"You forgot your precious turkey, asshole!"

A scream came from the passenger seat, where a blond woman recoiled, her red-nailed hands covering her eyes.

Charles tore out of the driver's side, wild-eyed. "Jesus H. Christ!"

"Charles, leave her alone!" Camille pleaded, trying to barricade the doorway after Dahlia had run back inside, but Charles just shoved her roughly aside, shouting, "You come back here, goddamn it!"

Josie helped Camille to her feet and they raced inside. Charles slipped on the path of turkey grease, catching himself on the back of a chair before continuing his chase. "You get your ass out there and you apologize to that woman, girl! What she ever done to you, and you go and try and kill her with my goddamned turkey?"

Dahlia stopped at the table, spinning around to face him from the other side. "If I wanted to kill her, I would have aimed for the open window!"

Charles considered the answer a moment, his eyes narrowing; then he lunged across the table. Camille and Josie arrived, screaming for him to stop, but his rage was blinding. He swung the chairs out of his way, scrambling around the table as Dahlia dove beneath it.

"Charles, stop it!" Camille cried, dropping to her knees to pull Dahlia to safety, but Charles's hand wrapped around Dahlia's ankle and tugged her back. "Charles, no!"

Dahlia twisted onto her back and kneed his stomach, forcing him to free her, but he recovered quickly, catching her arm as she got to her feet. He managed a strike across her cheek, then another, harder. He had brought his hand back for a third when he sucked in a sharp breath and released her. "Son of a bitch!" he exclaimed, his back curved as he studied the streak of blood on his shirt; then they all saw the carving knife in Dahlia's hand. "You little bitch," he gasped, wide-eyed. "You cut me!"

Dahlia thrust the knife at him again, her eyes as wild as his had been, looking even wilder behind the tangled mane of her dark hair.

"Dahl, don't!" Josie wailed, sobbing now.

Camille stepped forward. "Baby girl, give me the knife," she ordered gently. "Give it to me."

"Holy *shit* . . ." Charles just kept walking backward, staring dully at his wound. It wasn't deep—they all could see that—but it was deep enough to prove that Dahlia dared to do worse if he came at her again. He looked up, stricken, as he pointed at them all, still moving away. "I want her outta here," he said, gripping his chest. "I want her gone when I get back!"

When Charles reached the doorway, he turned and stormed out, banging the screen door against the house. Dahlia dropped the knife and collapsed to the floor. Camille rushed to her, pulling her daughter against her and smoothing her hair. Josie followed, dropping down between them.

The three of them sat huddled on the floor, wrapped together in a sea of broken dishes and splattered food, waiting for the squeal of the DeVille's tires to disappear down the street.

Josie sat on Camille's bed, weeping. "What if they take Dahlia away?"

"They won't do any such thing," Camille said calmly, even

as her heart raced so loudly she could barely hear herself talk. She pulled her carpetbag from the armoire and yanked it open. "Now take out some clothes, and go tell your sister to do the same."

"But, Momma . . ."

"Do it," Camille said sharply.

Josie sucked in a sob and nodded, moving into the other room. Camille packed quickly—some clothes, a box of her oils and powders and candles, and a dozen records from Charles's prized collection in the parlor—then she set the whole pile inside the bag. She moved last to the kitchen, dropping in spices and herbs, then uncovering the jar of money she had been hiding behind the sink, rolling the bills into a neat tube. Seeing that Dahlia was too dazed to move, Josie packed her sister's bag for her, and when it came time to go, Josie even slipped Dahlia's sneakers onto her bare feet.

They took the streetcar to Canal and crossed over Esplanade to the Creole cottage, where Lionel and Roman put fresh sheets on the canopy bed and a pot of peppermint tea on the stove.

"Where will you go?" Roman asked, setting down Camille's tea.

She sighed, looking out at the courtyard where Dahlia and Josie wandered in the men's bathrobes through the forest of bamboo. "I don't know," she said. "I've never lived anywhere but here. My family was all here, but there's no one left. No one I know of, anyway."

Lionel took a seat beside her on the chaise, rubbing her back. "We'll figure something out," he said. "You can stay here as long as you need to."

Camille covered each of their hands, tears filling her eyes

as she smiled, her heart breaking. Her precious city was too small to hide them now. It was time to go.

It was Dahlia's idea to use the spinning globe in Lionel's study the next morning. The suggestion of closing one's eyes and dropping a finger blindly on a map seemed ludicrous at first, but the more Camille considered the idea, the less absurd it became. After a languid breakfast of grillades and grits, the three huddled, hands clasped and eyes wide. Dahlia offered to spin it and let her mother stop it, but Camille felt it only fair that her oldest daughter get the right to mark their destination, since it was Dahlia's idea in the first place. So it was Josie who spun the sphere of their destiny, afraid at first, then filled with a strange and thrilling abandon, sending the globe whirling so fast it nearly toppled over.

They agreed that no matter the spot, unless it was water, they'd find a way to get there, that there could be no do-overs, no second chances.

When the globe finally began to slow its crazy twist, and Dahlia decided she had kept them all in suspense long enough, she planted her finger on it, forcing it still.

They circled close to see what lay beneath.

Josie squinted. "Is that . . . Canada?"

"It says Quebec," announced Dahlia proudly, as if she had meant to choose it. "It's French."

"French," marveled Camille softly.

"Will there be Creoles there?" asked Josie, tugging her thick red braid over her shoulder and twisting the knotted end. "Like you, Momma?"

Camille felt certain of her answer. "I don't see why not."

They returned to the courtyard to deliver the glorious news

to Lionel and Roman, relieved and eager, imagining a place that would be just like home.

They would be quite disappointed. At least at first.

The farther north they went, the less color they saw, in both the people and the landscape. Stark white churches and modest homes, sprawling textile mills and open fields spotted with lumbering cows. Worst of all, the air grew increasingly chilled. Soon their breath bloomed in front of them when they stopped off at rest areas, their nostrils glued shut with every inhale.

Sitting in the bus station in Portland, Maine, waiting for the next leg of their journey, Camille wondered if Canada would be different. How could they hope to find anything as welcoming as the tropical richness of their home when the farther north they traveled, the chillier it grew? Already there was snow on the ground outside the station, pocked brown clumps of it.

They had dressed poorly, Camille realized, looking around at the other waiting passengers in their bulky layers. They may have looked cumbersome and clumsy, but they were warm. Much warmer than she and the girls in their thin jackets and thinner stockings.

They would have to amend their grand contract.

Camille gathered the girls together over hamburgers at the diner across the street and made an announcement.

"I think we should stay here," she said. "If we go much farther, I don't know if we'll survive till spring. There could be this sort of weather year-round in Quebec, for all we know."

The girls looked at each other, biting at their chapped lips.

"Where's here?" asked Josie.

"Portland," said Dahlia. "Maine."

"Not Canada?"

"Not quite."

Back in the bus station, Camille found a display of brochures highlighting area attractions and picked up one for Little Gale Island. She brought it back to where the girls sat in the waiting area and presented it.

"It's not far," she said. "A ferry ride across the bay. We could just try it. See if we like it."

"Let's," said Dahlia, rising to her feet and pulling her sister up with her.

Josie just nodded, her attention diverted suddenly by a pair of whispering old women who were gesturing to Camille's ankle-length painted velvet coat and her purple beret: Josie's first real proof that their assimilation might be tricky, no matter where they ended up.

Josie and Dahlia had taken the ferry plenty of times across the river to Algiers, but this ride was different. For one thing, it was cold. Freezing. The wind off the water cut through their cotton and scraped at their skin. Their toes prickled, nearly numb in their sneakers, their bare fingers pulled up inside their cuffs. If their mother felt the cold, she wasn't showing it. Camille stood calmly beside them, chin up, facing the frigid view, her fine features fixed in an expression of serenity and quiet determination, her hazel eyes flashing.

When they stepped off the ferry onto the town landing, the trio felt as if they'd landed on the moon. All around them, islanders marched head down against the icy evening air, wrapped like packed china in scarves and hats with earflaps, thick gloves, and boots fattened with woolly linings.

Even the smells of the island were different, Josie thought, drawing in a long, cold breath: smoky, salty air, burning wood, and gasoline. No curling vines of star jasmine with tiny white blossoms so fragrant you might walk off the curb from their scent. They would no longer hear the click of the street-car, the wail of a jazz band spilling out of open bar doors into the humid night, or the electric whir of the cicadas in the oak trees. Cicadas couldn't possibly live in such a frigid, quiet place. Josie was certain of it.

But none of that mattered. This was their home now, they agreed silently as they climbed the steep trail of Ocean Avenue, arms linked to steady one another when they slid on the slick slush that dotted the street. They found an inn at the top of the hill where the wallpaper was spotted with sailboats and sea-shells, and they inquired about a room. They had some available, the proprietor admitted begrudgingly, forced to do so when a dozen room keys hung in plain view. But there was a three-night minimum, and housekeeping didn't come but twice a week, and, oh, yes, there was an extra charge for a third person. Camille smiled pleasantly and handed over enough to cover the next four days.

They unpacked their few belongings into a dresser with crooked drawers and left to explore the town, settling eventually on a restaurant with short red curtains and paintings of whaling ships on the wall. The waitress was young and cheerful and wore her hair parted down the middle. When Camille explained that they had only just arrived from New Orleans and were looking to stay, the girl remembered overhearing Ben Haskell in the restaurant just a few hours earlier, bemoaning his lack of a tenant. His vacancy had been going on two years, she said, and he was worried that the plumbing would fail if left unused too long. While the waitress wrote Ben's name and address on a napkin, she said something, almost too quietly but not quite, about how awful it was, the way that Midwestern woman had run off and left him with a young boy to raise on his own. Camille took the napkin, folded it neatly, and slipped it in her coat pocket.

Back in their room, bathed and warm and tucked in, the girls in the beds, their mother in a roll-away between them, Camille said they would pay a visit to Ben Haskell in the morning.

The island seemed like a pleasant place, Camille said, a safe place to stay through spring. As soon as they found an apartment, she'd phone the beauty parlor and tell them where to forward her last check. Besides, she had her cards and her candles and her oils. She could put an ad in the local paper, give readings and work spells like her mother used to. Make them some money, and by summer they could move on.

Of course, she would never leave.

Eight

Little Gale Island

Fall 1977

Ben Haskell leaned his head under the kitchen sink, squinted through his glasses at the hissing drainpipe, and cursed quietly. He loved the old house, but it never ceased to exhaust him. As a growing boy tracking mud through the maze of its cold, colorless rooms, he'd imagined its frame as stone, having been oblivious to the weekly battles his father had waged, and usually lost, with the cottage's decaying parts. When Ben had inherited the house sixteen years ago, he had never imagined the patchwork of repairs he'd find behind its plaster walls, but of course, he'd not been in a position to refuse it. He and Leslie had needed a home, and Matthew had been due any day.

But for years after Leslie had left them, Ben had wrestled with the useless belief that it was the house that had driven his wife away; that if only he'd given her a new house, with tidy electrical wires threaded through perfectly drilled studs, and gleaming new pipes tucked neatly under even floorboards, toilets that emptied after every flush and sinks that drained, then maybe she would have stayed, and for months afterward the house suffered the blame. Ben could still recall the time Matthew had toddled from his bed at three in the morning to find his father berating a loose stair spindle that had slipped from its joint for the umpteenth time. Thirteen years later, Ben finally understood that it wasn't the house's fault that Leslie was gone, that some wounds didn't close neatly or heal cleanly. Just like houses.

Climbing to his feet to find a wrench, Ben heard a knock on the front door. At first he wasn't entirely sure he'd heard anything other than the house's typical moans and creaks, but when it came again, sharp and clear, he wiped his hands on the sides of his work pants and walked to the foyer. A flurry of possible visitors rushed across his brain as he reached for the knob—salesmen, a neighbor, the mailman—but when he opened the door and saw the trio on his front porch, he blinked in surprise. The woman was slight in build under layers of brightly colored fabric, with a dome of tight brown coils and skin the color of coffee with milk. Of the two girls on either side of her, the older was clearly her child, with her equally buoyant curls and dark, almond-shaped eyes, but her frame was heftier, rounder. The younger girl was red haired and slender, with peachy freckled skin and ice blue eyes.

"Good morning," the woman said.

Ben glanced at the two girls. The redhead smiled shyly. The darker one looked like she was sizing him up.

"Morning." He straightened his glasses, leaving a thumbprint of grease on the edge of one lens. "Can I help you?"

"I do hope so. I'm looking for Benjamin Haskell."

"I'm Ben."

"Oh, wonderful." The woman held out her hand, a chorus of bracelets colliding at her wrist, nearly lost under a fluttering sleeve. Ben took her hand carefully, her fingers like pussywillow branches in his rough palm. "My name is Camille Bergeron and these are my daughters, Dahlia and Josephine. The waitress at the restaurant said you have an apartment for rent."

"I do," he said, his gaze moving between the three of them. "It's furnished, but it's small. Just one bedroom."

"We're quite comfortable in small places, Mr. Haskell," Camille said. "Unless you have some sort of occupancy code issue or some other reason why we can't rent it?"

Ben paused, uncertain. His last two tenants had been single people, young men. One had even owned a dog. Ben hadn't had a problem with that. Besides, an inquiry this late in the year was nothing short of a miracle. He wasn't about to turn away a prospective tenant. Especially not a single parent. Not that the woman's business was any of his concern. Ben had never made his tenants' business his own, and he wasn't about to start.

"No," he said at last, "there's no issue of code." He pointed behind them. "It's just up the stairs. I can show it to you if you'd like."

She smiled. "Please."

It would do just fine, Camille decided, running her finger-tips over the dusty top of an empty dresser. No matter that the walls were as bleak as oatmeal and the rooms smelled of sour milk; the ceilings were high and the windows were tall and sunlight poured in. She could paint. She could bring in plants, paper lanterns, colorful tablecloths. She could light incense. She could make it feel like home.

"The stove can be tricky," Ben said, twisting the knobs on the range. "The pilot goes out from time to time. The house is old and temperamental, but the water pressure is good and the heat works well enough." He watched Camille wander around the perimeter of the apartment, the girls trailing close behind. "I did warn you it was small," he said. "I'd understand if you've changed your mind, now that you've seen it."

Camille stopped at the window and turned toward Ben, where he stood in the narrow opening between the kitchen and the living area, wondering for a moment whether Benja-min Haskell was of the same breed as the innkeeper, too clever to be outright discriminatory but not pleased with the idea of housing a Creole woman with two daughters.

Camille studied his eyes, a deep, soft brown behind his round glasses. He was really a pleasant-looking man, she thought. Not the sort who was so handsome you'd reel at first sight, but the kind whose nice looks revealed themselves over time. He had a kind face. Plenty of thick, sandy brown hair. A shapely nose. She guessed him in his late thirties, not much older than she was.

No, he wasn't like the innkeeper. His sensitivity was real.

"How much is it?" she asked.

Dahlia and Josie disappeared into the bedroom, their high

voices blending with excitement at the view of the ocean from their very own turret window.

The sisters met Matthew that afternoon when he came home from school. It was Dahlia who encountered him first, having discovered his failing orchid in the living room window and deciding it had to be moved at once.

"Hey!" Matthew dropped his books into the wing chair and charged across the room, grabbing the shiny pot from Dahlia's hands. "What do you think you're doing?" he demanded, setting the orchid gently back on the sill.

"It's getting too much light," Dahlia said flatly, and without even a hint of apology in her voice. "Orchids like filtered light."

"How would you know?"

"And I can tell you aren't misting it, either." She bent down for a closer look. "The roots are soaking wet and the leaves are like cardboard. You only wet the roots when they're bone-dry. Otherwise, you should just be misting it regularly."

"Who are you?"

"I live here."

Matthew snorted, the idea preposterous. "Since when?"

"Since an hour ago. My mother just rented the apartment for me and my sister."

Matthew swallowed, having calmed down enough now to study her at last, and deciding she was awfully interesting-looking, and tall. Maybe too tall. She was actually as tall as he was, and worse, she wasn't even wearing shoes, he realized, glimpsing her long, wiggling toes.

"You should let me keep this in my room for a while," Dahlia said. "I know a ton about plants. I could bring it back for you."

"Bring it back?" Matthew crossed his arms. "What are you talking about? It's fine."

"It's not fine. It won't survive the winter, let alone the week."

"Where's my dad?"

"How the hell should I know?"

"Dahl?"

Matthew turned to see a slight, red-haired girl in the doorway, her pale skin sprinkled with freckles.

"Dahl, Momma's been looking for you," Josie said softly, her eyes darting back and forth between the two of them, her lips lifting each time her gaze landed on Matthew. "Hello."

"That's Josie," Dahlia said. "My younger sister."

Matthew frowned at them. Sisters? They didn't look a thing alike.

"It's Jose*phine*," Josie corrected proudly, blushing as she did. "And I'm barely younger. Only by fourteen months."

Matthew turned back to Dahlia. "What kind of name is Dahl?"

"It's short for Dahlia," Josie said, walking toward them.

"Dahlia." Matthew frowned, hardly satisfied. "What kind of name is that?"

Ben appeared in the doorway then, a woman at his side.

"Matthew, this is Mrs. Camille Bergeron. I was just giving her a tour of the house. She and her daughters will be living with us now."

Matthew glanced to Dahlia, her smug smile unbearable. Beside her, Josie beamed.

What are they doing here, anyway?" Matthew demanded later that night, keeping his father company on the kitchen floor while Ben finished the repair he'd been pulled away from that morning. "And where's their father? Why isn't he here too?"

"I have no idea," Ben said, crawling deeper under the sink, "but it's none of our business. Hand me the wrench."

Matthew picked the wrench out of the toolbox beside him and pressed it into his father's outstretched fingers. "The older one thinks she's smarter than everyone else."

Ben grinned as he widened the mouth of the wrench. "Maybe she is."

"I suppose they're going to want to go to school, huh?"

"Well, of course. Raise the light a little bit, will you?"

Matthew repointed the flashlight into the cabinet, frowning at his father's outstretched legs, the scuffed bottoms of his shoes.

"They're really different, aren't they, Pop?"

"Maybe so," Ben said quietly, smiling as he twisted the wrench around the stubborn joint. "Maybe so."

Camille dropped the rag into the bucket and looked out onto the gleaming floors of her new living room. She smiled, pleased. It was a good start, but if she intended to work spells in their new home, she'd need more than just the protection of a salt-and-pepper floor wash. The space would need to be cleared out and made sacred. There was no telling what sort of negative energy might still live in these walls.

She turned to the bedroom door. It was as good a time as any, she decided, as she collected the last of her tools from the kitchen and lit a pair of white candles. For years Josie had been begging to learn the spells, and for years Camille had gently deferred her daughter's fervent requests, knowing how much Charles detested Voodoo, and knowing the wrath she'd face for sharing her beliefs. But no more. From now on she would do as she pleased. From now on her daughter would learn to protect herself as Camille had learned from *her* mother.

She came into the bedroom and gently woke Josie. Her younger daughter stirred, blinking in a confused panic, her cheeks rosy from sleep.

"What's wrong, Momma?"

"Nothing's wrong, baby girl," Camille whispered, smoothing the tangled hair out of Josie's face and taking her small hand. "I just need your help, that's all. Careful walking; the floor's slick."

Josie squinted through the candlelight as she followed her mother into the living room, but as soon as she saw the sage bundle and the bottle of Florida water on the table, Josie's bleary eyes widened, suddenly alert.

Camille picked up a book of matches. "Since it's our first night in our new house, I thought it was the perfect time for a cleansing."

Josie looked back to the bedroom. "What about Dahlia?" she asked.

Camille smiled. "Don't worry about your sister. She'll have her chance."

Josie nodded, but they both knew that day wasn't likely; Dahlia had no patience for Voodoo.

"Now, first we light the sage."

Josie watched, enthralled, as her mother held up the herb bundle and lit it, the leaves crackling as they burned. After a moment, Camille blew out the flame. The tip smoked, a luxurious silver ribbon.

She carried the bundle into the kitchen doorway, making circles with the smoke.

"The first thing we do is offer the smoke to the spirits, Josephine. We ask them to empty the space of all negative energy." Josie trailed her mother across the room. Camille continued. "You must always visualize your desire, baby girl. No matter what it is you are wishing for, see it in your mind. Use the candle flames to help you find and keep your focus. Your spell is only as strong as your desire. Understand?"

Josie nodded quickly, urgently, fixing her gaze on the pair of candles that burned on the table. Camille turned the bundle to Josie, just enough so that her daughter would move through the smoke. "This is called smudging," she said. "It seals your wish. And you must always draw your circles clockwise, toward the future."

Josie nodded again, her lips moving as she repeated her mother's instructions to herself. Clockwise. Always clockwise.

When the bundle had ceased to smoke, Camille set it in a saucer, picked up the bottle of Florida water, and sprinkled it liberally throughout the room. Josie followed her mother from one corner to another, inhaling deeply, remembering when she'd first asked why they called it Florida water. Camille had explained that it was once a popular cologne before becoming the Voodoo holy water, and that the original bottles had a picture of the Fountain of Youth on their label, which was believed to be in Florida. Josie had always loved the water's sweet, citrusy smell, even before she'd known what it was. It was her mother's scent: lemon and clove, a touch of cinnamon, and a hint of rose. Josie had sworn she could recall the smell of it even before she could walk, but Dahlia had told her that was impossible.

"Almost done." Camille set the bottle of Florida water back on the table and lit incense; then she took Josie's hands in hers

and looked out at the room. The room seemed different somehow, Josie thought. Bigger. Brighter. Warmer.

Camille smiled. "Now there's only one thing left to say,
Josephine. Do you know what that is?"

Josie knew. She had heard her mother utter the words so
many times, sometimes under her breath, other times, when
their father wasn't around, shockingly clear.

Josie smiled proudly and lifted her face to the ceiling.

"Blessed be," she said, then again, louder, "Blessed be."

Nine

Little Gale Island

Fall 1977

Ben was behind the house splitting wood when Camille found him the next morning. She waited until he was at the end of his swing before she called out into the chilled air, waving with her free hand, the other hand growing numb as she clenched the collar of her coat around her throat.

"Good morning!"

Startled, Ben lowered his ax, wondering how long she had been standing there.

He nodded. "Morning."

"I was hoping you could tell me where the market is," she said.

Ben laid his ax over the flat top of his chopping log, flexing his stiff fingers inside his thick gloves. He couldn't imagine she planned to go into town dressed that way, but then, she and the girls had only just come from New Orleans. He thought at once of the swollen boxes of Matthew's old coats and sweaters collecting dust in the attic.

"It's not too far," he said, pointing her to the front of the house. "Just follow this street to Pine. Take a left and you'll hit Main. Larson's Grocery is just a few blocks down."

"Wonderful," she said, then laughed. "If I go too long without cooking, I get the most awful headaches!"

Ben had to wonder how she could be so bright and cheery when she must have been freezing, her breath swirling into thin ribbons around her face, his own pouring out like chimney smoke.

"Can I get you anything while I'm there, Mr. Haskell?" she asked.

"No. Thank you."

Ben reached down to the pile for a fresh log and stood it on the chopping block, glancing up as Camille returned to the path, her peasant skirt held high as she took her first careful steps down the slick, frost-covered gravel. He could already imagine the bewildered looks on the islanders' chapped faces when she walked into Larson's musty little store. Not to mention the gossip that would surely follow.

He drew up his ax, not even sure she was still within earshot when he said, "You can call me Ben, if you want."

Camille turned and smiled. "I think I'd rather call you Benjamin."

"What the hell do people eat here?" Dahlia asked, following Camille and Josie as they wandered down narrow rows of canned goods, paper products, and frozen foods.

"Dahlia Rose, please lower your voice," Camille instructed coolly, her bracelets jingling against the cart as she pushed. "I'm sure there are plenty of delicious things to eat here."

"You mean like *this*?" Dahlia held up a can labeled HASH and laughed. "It looks like dog food."

"That's enough, young lady. Put it back and keep your opinions to yourself."

"That'll be the day," whispered Josie. "So do you suppose lobsters taste just like crawfish?"

"I don't know," Dahlia said. "Why don't you go find one and ask it?"

"So long as I'm cooking, we'll eat what we always eat," Camille assured them, looking up to meet the narrowed gaze of a bearded man across the aisle, his eyes dropping quickly. She took a bag of rice and moved them forward.

"Well, I don't care what they eat," Josie said. "I like it here. And I like Mr. Haskell and Matthew too. I think Matthew has the most beautiful eyes."

"They're both lovely people," Camille said, drawing down three bags of dried beans and tossing them into their cart. "In fact, I was just thinking we should invite them to dinner tonight."

"Oh, can we please?" Josie pulled at her mother's sleeve, her voice breathless with excitement. "You could make jambalaya!"

"I could," Camille said.

Dahlia frowned. "Tonight? But we just got here."

"Exactly," said Camille. "It's never too early to get off on the right foot with new friends." She stopped at the end of the aisle and squinted down the length of the store. "Now, where do you suppose these poor cold people keep their hot sauce?"

———

"I *still don't see* why I have to wear this stupid shirt," Matthew grumbled, following his father up the foyer stairs to the apartment door in a crisp, brown oxford.

"Because it's the polite thing to do, son." Ben put his arm around Matthew and tugged him close. "So's brushing your hair," he added, grinning as he tried to smooth down Matthew's curling cowlick.

"I don't know why you're even bothering to bring those, Pop." Matthew gestured to the trash bag filled with winter coats that Ben carried in his other hand. "Most of the girls in my class wouldn't be caught dead in old snowmobile jackets."

"They would if they got cold enough."

Josie answered the door, flushing instantly. "Hi, Matthew."

Matthew muttered his greeting, glancing over Josie's shoulder, looking for a sign of her sister. From the kitchen, Camille called them in and pointed them to the table. Dahlia emerged from the bedroom, her dark hair pulled up on one side with a tarnished silver comb, her expression one of clear challenge as she took the seat across from Matthew.

"You really didn't have to trouble yourself," Ben said when Camille arrived.

She smiled. "It's no trouble."

"Momma's an amazing cook," Josie said, sitting up as straight as she could in the rickety ladder-back chair after all the bowls had been set out. "People in the neighborhood used to smell her gumbo cooking and they'd make up any excuse to stop in for a bowl. Even Mr. Avery. And Dahlia said he wouldn't get up off his porch if his ass was on fire."

"*Josephine*," Camille whispered as she took her own seat, blushing slightly, then to Ben: "She exaggerates. Pass the bread, will you, girls?"

Dahlia reached out, but Josie was quicker, thrusting the basket at Matthew, who took two slices.

"This is delicious," Ben said, wiping his mouth. "What did you call it?"

"Jambalaya," said Camille. "We Creoles like ours with tomato. It's not nearly as good as gumbo, but it is a great deal quicker to make."

Matthew took a small bite, wary of the curious rice dish flecked with chunks of chicken and sausage, while Josie stole glimpses of his profile, trying to decide whether his eyes were bluish green or greenish blue. Across the table, Dahlia stretched out her bare foot and poked Matthew in the ankle until he looked up, only to find her glancing around innocently.

When Camille rose to get Ben a second helping, Ben glimpsed the bookcase on the other side of the living room, empty except for a stack of records on the top shelf, no doubt left by the last tenant, he thought.

"Sorry about those," he said, pointing. "I can get rid of them for you."

"Don't you dare," Camille called from the kitchen. "I carted those records all the way from New Orleans."

"They're yours?" Ben looked at her, genuinely surprised.

"They are now," she said proudly, returning with his replenished bowl. "We had so many more but there wasn't time. Or room." She smiled. "One day I'll hear them again."

Matthew watched his father's eyes drift down to his dinner, Ben's brow knotting in thought.

Later that night, Matthew came downstairs to find his father in the foyer, buttoning up his coat.

"I'm going out for a bit," Ben said, tapping on his cap.

Matthew nodded, saying nothing. Just as he said nothing the next morning when Ben presented Camille with the record player he'd dug out of Malcolm Clements's shop at the end of Tuttle Road, or when Matthew caught his father wearing a small smile in his study later that afternoon, the lively swing of Louis Armstrong audible from across the house, the clear sounds of dancing feet landing on cold wood floors.

Just three days later, an early storm dropped five inches of wet snow over the island, leaving a layer of glistening ice on rooftops and car hoods, and in the week that followed, Camille and the girls could count on one hand the times they left the house. But the quarantine was far from unwelcome. While winter raged outside, warmth abounded within, and there was plenty to do in their new home. Rooms needed to be painted, Camille said. White walls would do for churches and hospitals, but not for their house.

When she asked Ben if she might add some color to the apartment, he thought she meant to change the window trim. He was shocked to find the next day that she'd returned from the village hardware store with gallons of paint in colors he suspected that Sam Milkie, the store's owner, had never even heard of, let alone mixed for a customer: China red, eggplant purple, mustard yellow, olive green.

Camille requested a few old sheets to use as drop cloths, but Ben provided more than linens. He recruited Matthew, and soon they were spending the weekend alongside Camille and the girls, their arms, elbows, and chins paint streaked, until the apartment was reborn.

The next week, when Ben overheard Camille longing for Old Paris china and velvet curtains, he piled them all into the Wagoneer and drove to a large indoor flea market in New Hampshire, Josie rolling toward Matthew every time the Jeep took on a bumpy patch of road.

That night as thanks, Camille made shrimp Creole and dirty rice for them all. After dinner they lingered in their seats around Ben's kitchen table, letting the heat from the wood-stove warm their necks and cheeks while Camille practiced her tarot readings on the men, feeling rusty after months away from the cards. She explained to Matthew and Ben about Creole Voodoo, about the spirits and the spells, and how the power of desire was the most important tool of all. She told them little things, too: That it was never wise to throw away hair combings, because birds could pull them from the trash and weave the combings into their nests, which would give a never-ending headache to the person the hair had belonged to. Or how you must never extinguish a candle with your fingers but blow the flame out and let the tiny spark endure, so a soul might briefly rest from torment.

"Momma's going to make lots of money with her spells," Josie promised them all proudly. But when a job opened up at the island's Laundromat the following week, Camille applied, much to Josie's disappointment.

"There's no rush," Ben said quietly. "This house is paid for, you know. If you need more time to get settled, I wouldn't want you to take something just because."

Camille smiled, grateful, but she'd never taken charity and

she wasn't about to start. She was hired on at the Laundromat the following week, but only because Fred Lucas's niece had just been put on bed rest with her fourth child.

It seemed that things might be falling into place. But news of Camille's skin color—too dark to pass for tan in December—and her suspiciously single status had already found its way around the island, spreading like ice crystals across a frosted window.

Ten

Little Gale Island
Friday, June 14, 2002
6:30 p.m.

Jack was shutting off the lights in the station's waiting room when his cell phone chimed. He glanced down at the small screen before he answered, glad it wasn't another reporter. "Hi, Arch."

"Jack." Portland's deputy chief sounded tired. It had been a long day for everyone, it seemed. "Sorry to be so late getting back to you," Archie Wentworth said. "Just wanted to let you know Collins is coming down first thing Monday morning to do the autopsy. I don't see the point myself, but you know how that sanctimonious prick is."

Jack knew, all right. His relationship with the state's medical examiner had never been a smooth one. Frank Collins took every opportunity he could to malign the efforts of smaller police forces, Little Gale's being one of his favorite examples of inefficiency.

"Thanks for the heads-up, Arch. Fortunately there's not much dirt to dig up on this one." Jack walked to the window and parted the blinds enough to see Main Street at dusk, the day tourists gone, the sidewalk spotted now with locals looking to unwind at Shell's or the Captain's Table.

Christ, what he wouldn't have done for a cold beer himself just then.

"I'll have the final report sent over in the next few days," Jack said, dropping the blinds and heading back out into the hall. "A few more witness statements just to round it out."

"Pretty much open-and-shut then, huh?"

"Seems it. There was no forced entry, just some broken dishes on the floor by the fireplace. Ben Haskell was probably just sitting there, having tea before bed, when Bergeron sneaked up on him. Startled him and he dropped his cup."

"Son of a bitch." Wentworth sighed. "They think Haskell's gonna recover?"

"No one knows for sure. The doctor says we can only wait and see."

"Wait and see," the deputy chief echoed. "Don't you just hate having to do that."

Matthew peered through the narrow glass insert on the ICU floor of Portland's Maine Medical Center and barely recognized the pale, unmoving man on the other side.

"When can I see him, Doctor?"

"Tomorrow." The doctor, fair-haired and slight, stood beside Matthew, holding Ben's patient folder in his hand. "We've sedated him to prevent any further damage to the brain, and we may need to keep him under sedation for several more days. Mr. Haskell, did your father suffer from high blood pressure?"

"What difference does that make?"

"A great deal of difference, actually. High blood pressure is one of the main risk factors for stroke."

"Doctor, my dad was in great shape. He still shoveled off his own roof every winter, for Christ's sake."

"Fitness only goes so far, I'm afraid. When people age, their blood vessels weaken and become brittle. Sometimes when there's stress, be it any kind of emotional or physical exertion, it can raise a person's blood pressure, increasing the volume of blood in already fragile vessels."

Matthew frowned impatiently. "So what the hell does all that mean?"

"Imagine a dry-rotted rubber hose," said the doctor, "and you've turned the spigot on high."

An image of Charles Bergeron standing behind his unsuspecting father flashed through Matthew's head. He swallowed, sickened.

"Is he going to be all right, Doctor?"

"We're confident he'll regain consciousness."

"That's not what I'm asking."

The doctor smiled patiently. "It's difficult to assess the level of neurological damage of someone who has suffered a stroke, Mr. Haskell. It takes time."

Time.

Matthew nodded dully, his gaze sweeping the room through the glass. Except for the view of Portland Harbor and all its twinkling lights, it could have been the set of a science-fiction movie, so many machines and tubes, monitors with flashing lights. Then the reality, a cold hand on his spine; his father was alive only by the grace of a pleated blue tube, his lungs expanding because of an electrical current coming through a hole in the wall.

Matthew pressed his palm against the glass, his fingers weightless, numb.

I'm here, Pop. I'm here.

Josie swore she felt it when Matthew stepped off the ferry.

She'd been in the kitchen, cleaning up from dinner, a sorry little meal of tuna sandwiches and canned soup, but it had sufficed. And besides, neither she nor Wayne had much of an appetite.

She frowned at the clock on the stove. Nine fifteen. She'd considered making up an excuse to take the car just so she could coast down Ocean Avenue to have a look at the landing, maybe see Matthew step off the boat, pretend to be running an errand. She still wondered why he'd chosen to stay on the island when Ben was on the mainland, but a part of her—a big part, too big, really—liked to think it was because Matthew wanted to be near them too, wanted things to be as they were in the old days.

She heard the patio door slide open, glanced over to find Wayne stepping in from the deck, looking drained. He crossed the kitchen to leave his empty mug in the sink. Josie smiled at him when he passed and he briefly touched her shoulder.

She tried to remember the last time they'd made love, but couldn't.

When he scooped his car keys off the table, she asked, "Where are you going?"

"The mower needs gas," he said.

"Now? It's almost nine thirty."

"I know. Clem's is open till ten." He offered her a weary smile, tugging down his Windbreaker from its hook and shrugging into it. "I won't be long."

Josie nodded, saying nothing as he crossed to plant a light kiss on her temple, knowing better than to press him. It had been an unimaginable day; she couldn't begrudge him his distance. Her father had been a burden in their marriage for so long, and even now in his death, the fog of Charles Bergeron's violence would remain in their hearts, hurtling them backward to a time they'd nearly put away, a time of suspicion and fear, when the islanders had demanded proof of their innocence before relinquishing their trust. Even Wayne, as native to the island as the stones along its shores, had been cast out for a time by people who had practically raised him, all because he'd loved a Bergeron girl.

Josie stood at the sink, listening for the sound of the Buick's engine, then the telltale crunch of gravel under tires as it pulled away, a familiar ache returning instantly, seamlessly.

"*Here you are, Mr. Haskell.* Room three ten."

The young woman at the front desk of the Sand Dollar handed Matthew his key, smiling blankly. Matthew had felt her eyes on him as he'd filled out his information, possibly trying to decide whether he was any relation to the Haskell who'd been found slumped over a dead man that morning.

Fifteen years ago, it would have been Lenora Parsons at that desk, knowing Matthew almost as well as she had known her own son Tim. But these days, the island was a new place, filled with new faces. Matthew had been spared any reunions on the ferry ride over, easily hiding himself in the thickening dark on the lower deck. To avoid the crowds on Ocean, he'd taken Franklin to Bartlett. To avoid the old house, he'd taken Orchard to Douglas, feeling guilty with every circuitous step.

It still seemed unimaginable to him that he wouldn't be climbing the driveway to the old house, wouldn't be laying his suitcase across the creaking twin bed that he'd tossed and turned in hundreds of nights in his youth, wouldn't be waking to the familiar squeal of his father's router in his woodshop: Ben getting an early start on the latest project, a bookshelf or a new bathroom cabinet. The countless Saturday mornings he and the sisters had met in the hallway, squinting and yawning, their mouths sour with morning breath as they'd collectively groaned at the noise outside.

The woodshop, the whole rambling house, was silent now. A chisel had been left on a piece of wood, a mortise started, rough and waiting to be finished.

Matthew took the two flights to his room, came in and collapsed on the king-size brass bed. A complimentary copy of the *Portland Press Herald* lay on the night table. He read the headline and dared to flip it over, dreading what he would find, but there was nothing about his father. There would be, of course, farther in. But at least today it wasn't front-page news.

He kicked off his shoes and lay on the flowered bedspread, watching the curtains curl in the breeze. He felt an instinct return to him that he had lost years ago. He wanted to call the sisters, but that wasn't right. They had never called one another; there had never been any need. What he wanted was to walk out of his room and cross the house to their apartment, as he had done so many times, for so many years.

Matthew sat up and reached for the phone. He didn't know which sister's voice he wanted to hear first.

No, that wasn't right either. He knew.

But it was too late to call.

When Dahlia heard the knock on her door at a quarter to ten, she knew it was Matthew. She'd been so sure he'd come to her first that she'd left the porch light on for him. Now, thumping down the stairs in her robe, wearing only a thin T-shirt and hiking socks beneath it, Dahlia could see the blurry shape of a man on the other side of the frosted glass panel, and her heart shuddered briefly.

But when she opened the door, she found Wayne filling out the doorway instead, his face drained, his shoulders slumped.

A fierce hope gripped her. "Ben."

"No, it's not that." Wayne tugged off his baseball cap. "I just needed some air." He gestured behind her. "Can I come in?"

"Sure."

Wayne stepped into the foyer, rubbing his hands as if he were cold. "He's not here yet then?"

"Matthew? No." Dahlia closed the door, watching her brother-in-law as he looked into the dimly lit rooms that flanked the entry. Wayne walked into the parlor and dropped onto the love seat, cupping the bill of his cap between his hands.

"I didn't mean to wake you; I just . . ." He paused, sighed. "Rough day, huh?"

Dahlia walked to the other end of the love seat and sat down, pulling her legs under her. "Yeah. You could say that."

But Dahlia knew he wasn't just talking about Charles or Ben. Josie's comment in the car had stuck with her too, finding its way through the fog of Charles's attack all night.

Dahlia blinked and felt the prickle of tears.

"Sometimes I think I should just tell Josie the truth," she whispered. "Just get it over with, so she can start hating me for the rest of her life."

Wayne looked back at his cap, his hands now practically rolling the bill into a tube. "Hating *us*, you mean."

"It was never your idea, Wayne."

"It might as well have been." Wayne tossed the hat onto the coffee table and dragged a hand down his forehead, along his beard. He stood up, too anxious to stay in one spot. He paced in front of the fireplace, staring at Dahlia's cluttered mantel, the framed gallery of portraits, all of their young faces looking back at him, smiles and laughter, reminders of an uncomplicated time. One of Matthew and the sisters on Christmas morning, mugging in front of the tree.

He reached out and slammed it down.

"Don't do this to yourself, Wayne." Dahlia looked at him. "It never would have worked. We both know that."

Wayne nodded, righting the picture. He stared enviously at Matthew's teenage face, lips drawn in an exaggerated smile while Josie looked up at Matthew with unveiled infatuation.

It hadn't been easy loving a woman who'd always wanted another man, but Wayne had learned to live with his secrets.

"We sent off the application to the adoption agency last week," he said. "Jo tell you that?"

Dahlia nodded. "It's going to happen for you guys this time. I know it."

"Jeezum, I hope so." Wayne dragged his sleeve roughly

across his wet eyes once, then twice. "Anyway." He grabbed his cap off the coffee table. "I have to go. I told Jo I was just getting gas. She'll worry."

"Okay."

Dahlia walked Wayne to the door. She stood on the porch, the sea air brushing her cheeks, and watched her brother-in-law as he took the stairs to the driveway, feeling a fierce surge of pity for him. It hadn't been easy for him to keep their secret all these years. They both loved Josie more than anything in the world; it was hard to say which of them felt the greater betrayer.

So many secrets, Dahlia thought to herself, coming back inside, looking around at the rooms of her small house, crowded with twenty-five years of their island life. She never imagined there would have to be so many.

Eleven

Little Gale Island

December 1977

The sisters' first day of school came on a bitterly cold Tuesday when the island's sky was the color of limestone, but Dahlia wasn't about to let temperature get in the way of making a first impression on the mainland boys of Portland High.

When she bounded downstairs to meet Matthew and Josie at a quarter to seven, the two already buried under layers of wool in the foyer, they blinked at her bare legs, her hand-me-down jacket flying open to reveal only a thin blouse and a corduroy miniskirt beneath it.

"Where are your tights?" demanded Josie, her own tiny hands useless in puffy snowmobile gloves, her red braids peeking out from under one of Matthew's old knit caps. "And your hat and mittens?"

"I don't need tights," Dahlia said, glancing into the nautical mirror to check her haircombs.

"But you'll freeze!"

"You will," Matthew said firmly. "It's like ice on the water. You'll catch pneumonia on the boat dressed like that."

Dahlia just shrugged, reaching for the door, and Josie knew there was no use in trying to change her sister's mind. Dahlia would risk pneumonia if it meant making a spectacle of herself. And sure enough, when they joined the crush of students who packed into the boat's upper deck, Dahlia stood out like a peacock feather in a pile of down. Josie was just grateful to have Matthew's escort, his firm shoulder against her, the smell of woodsmoke from his sweater filling her nostrils each time he shifted to let someone pass their seats.

But Matthew's escort could take them only so far. As soon as they reached the crowded halls of the high school, the three of them parted ways, and Josie felt a swift and heavy depression. In the weeks leading up to their first day of school, she had worried deeply that their arrival would be ill received. Though no one had spoken outright, Josie had seen the veiled looks of suspicion when they'd walked to and from town, the side glances in the grocery store and the post office. Matthew's allegiance was important, but it might not be enough. Within hours, Josie realized that acceptance would have to come too in the form of Marsha Daley, Peggy Posner, and Tracy Jenkins, a trio of juniors who ruled the corridors and the bathrooms, who traded shiny pearl lip gloss and scrawled their boyfriends' initials on the thighs of their jeans.

"Five bucks says I can make every one of those goons fall

in love with me by the end of the week," Dahlia announced, glaring across the cafeteria to where Marsha, Peggy, and Tracy dined with their thick-necked boyfriends in a haze of Avon perfume and Tinactin.

"Please don't," said Josie, genuinely afraid of the familiar flash of mischief in her sister's eyes.

Matthew looked up from his slab of meat loaf, a swift rush of jealousy turning his stomach.

"Old lady McGraw totally gypped me on the fries." A skinny boy with shaggy blond hair and braces arrived at their table and slid in beside Matthew, surveying Dahlia and Josie from behind thick glasses. "Who are you guys?"

"This is Dahlia and Josie," Matthew said. "This is Josh Moody."

Josie waved politely. Dahlia looked around.

"Where you guys from?" Josh asked.

"New Orleans," said Josie.

"Oh, sure, New Orleans," the boy said. "That's cool."

Dahlia leaned forward. "You have no idea where that is, do you?"

"Dahlia!" Josie's cheeks burned with embarrassment. "That's so rude."

"What? It's no big deal," Dahlia said, munching on a french fry. "Nobody does."

"It's far from here, Josh," Josie said. "Really far."

"I figured." Josh opened his milk. "Most things are, aren't they, Matt?"

Matthew nodded, his eyes still fixed on Dahlia, wondering why she always had to be such a snot about everything. "You're one to talk, you know," he said to her. "You didn't even know Maine existed until you showed up here."

Josie smiled awkwardly at Josh.

"Well, at least I didn't pretend like I knew where Maine was," Dahlia said, glaring at Matthew.

Josie buried her hands between her knees. "It's freezing in here."

"It's winter," said Matthew. "Winter's cold."

"We don't have winter in New Orleans," Josie said. "We have carnival."

"What's carnival?" asked Josh.

"Oh, it's so exciting," Josie practically gasped. "It lasts a really long time, and at the end there's Mardi Gras and parades, and you get to eat lots of king cake!"

"King cake?"

"You've never had a king cake?" Josie looked at both boys, incredulous. "Well, it's like a big cinnamon roll with lots of colored sugar on top. And there's a baby hidden inside. A little plastic baby. And the person who gets the slice with the baby in it gets good luck."

"*And* has to buy the next king cake," Dahlia added.

"Well, jeez," said Josh, moving on to his meat loaf, "that doesn't sound so lucky to me."

"It is," insisted Josie, adding proudly, "and I *always* get the baby. Don't I, Dahl? Every year."

"Me and Matt are on the debate team," Josh said. "It's a lot of fun. You guys should join."

"Oh, not me," said Josie. "I hate standing up in front of people and having to talk. I get nauseous just thinking about it."

Dahlia grinned. "Matty's on the debate team? *That* I have to see."

"Come to our meet next week," Josh offered brightly. "We're debating Scarborough."

"That sounds like fun," Josie said. "Doesn't that sound like fun, Dahl?"

"A blast." Dahlia stood up, feeling Matthew's glaring eyes still on her. "I'm getting more ketchup, y'all."

There were several tables between theirs and the condiment station, and Dahlia took her time moving through them, careful to listen for the whispering in her wake. At the row of squeeze bottles, she picked up one, found it empty and tried another. When that one too felt light, she groaned and slammed it back down. "Son of a bitch."

"It's in there. You just have to give it a good shake."

Dahlia stepped back to watch a dark-haired young man in jeans and a tan chamois shirt pick up the bottle, give a single thump to the bottom with the flat of his palm and hand it back to her.

"You're gonna need all that to get the meat loaf down," he said. "Trust me."

Dahlia took the bottle with a shaky hand, noticing the way his hair feathered over his ears and curled around the nape of his neck.

"Are lunches always this bad here?" she asked.

"They're usually worse, if you can believe it," he said. "At least around the holidays they drown everything in so much gravy you don't actually have to see what you're eating."

Dahlia smiled. "My momma says gravy's a bad cook's cheap perfume."

He laughed, revealing a pair of dimples so deep Dahlia swore the hairs on her neck straightened.

Their eyes met and held.

"I like that," he said. "Your mom sounds like a smart lady."

"She is."

Dahlia wished he'd say something else, *anything* else, just so she'd have an excuse to keep looking at him. But then a voice drew his attention back to the tables. He nodded to someone over her shoulder.

"I should get back," he said. "See you around."

"See you," Dahlia said, watching him disappear into the thickening crowd, try as she did to watch where he ended up.

When she returned to their table, Josh Moody had gone and Matthew was still glowering at his food.

"We thought you'd left," Josie said, poking holes in her meat loaf with her fork.

"I was just making friends." Dahlia squeezed ketchup over her remaining fries, glancing at her sister's plate. "Jesus, Joze, stop torturing the poor thing. Either eat it or let it die in peace."

"Making friends, huh?" Josie said pointedly. "That's not what it looked like."

"So who is he, Matty?" Dahlia asked, glancing over her shoulder.

"Who's who?"

"The guy at the ketchup stand."

"I didn't see him," Matthew answered glumly. "And don't call me Matty anymore. I mean it."

Dahlia smiled. "Whoever he is, he's a total fox. And there was definitely something between us."

"He's dating Janet Miller," Matthew said. "Jack's been dating her for almost a year now."

"Jack, huh?" Dahlia grinned. "I thought you didn't see him."

Matthew stopped, caught. He stood up. "I'm heading to class."

Josie scrambled to follow him. Dahlia took the long way around the cafeteria to drop off her tray, hoping to catch another glimpse of Jack, but he'd already gone.

"So how was your first day?" Camille asked when they arrived home.

Josie collapsed into a chair at the table, pulling her jacket around her, still frozen from the ferry ride back. "Fine," she said quietly.

Camille cast Dahlia a suspicious look as she peeled off her coat. "Just fine?"

Dahlia shrugged, coming beside her mother at the stove and stealing a chunk of corn bread. "It was school. The food tastes like crap, the teachers have their heads up their asses, and the kids gave us dirty looks."

"Dahlia Rose," Camille scolded wearily. "And stop eating my corn bread, young lady. Dinner'll be in an hour."

Dahlia tugged the comb from her hair and joined Josie at the table, hauling one foot up on the chair and balancing the comb on her knee.

"It's only the first day," Camille said brightly, still studying Josie's sullen profile as she stirred a pot of red beans. "It can take a long time to get to know people. For both sides. Surely Matthew has some friends there he can introduce you to."

"A few," Dahlia said. "But he didn't seem very interested in introductions. He hung around us all day like a bodyguard."

Camille smiled. "He's protective of you. I think that's nice."

Josie's pout lifted briefly, her mother's observation filling her with an unexpected joy. Maybe there was some hope in the day after all.

"Better dress warmly for bed tonight." Camille wiped her hands on the hem of her apron. "Ben says it smells like snow."

"What the hell does snow smell like?" Dahlia mumbled through a mouthful of corn bread.

But Josie was already on her feet and down the stairs, pressing through the front door and standing on the porch, her nose in the air, taking long, deep breaths, determined to own the answer to this small island secret.

As if the simple knowledge of the smell of snow would be all it took to earn her a way into the elite island world for good.

Four hours later, the bedcovers pulled to her chin, Josie was no closer to being an islander. "They hate us."

Dahlia rolled over and squinted into the darkness, barely making out the bump of her sister's reclining body on the other side of the bedroom.

"Who?" she asked.

Josie sniffled. "Everybody. All day at school and not a single person talked to us. No thanks to you."

"What is that supposed to mean?"

"You know," Josie said. "Why do you always have to push people so much? So what if they don't know where New Orleans is? Big deal."

"Oh, who cares if they like us or not?" Dahlia reached out and drew circles on the windowpane beside her bed where bursts of ice flakes rimmed the glass. "I certainly don't."

"You don't have to care," said Josie, "but I do. I want friends."

"And I don't?"

"You want *boy*friends."

Dahlia grinned at the ceiling. "You mean like Matthew?"

Josie sat upright, panicked. "You don't like him that way. I can tell you don't."

"How would you know? I barely even know myself what I think about him."

It was a lie and Josie knew it. She'd seen the way Dahlia acted around boys who intrigued her, and Dahlia wasn't intrigued by Matthew. Amused, maybe even interested, but not intrigued. Not like she'd been seeing that handsome Jack Somebody at the ketchup stand. Nothing like that.

Dahlia drew a lazy star on the cold glass. "Did you know that Matthew's mother left him when he was three years old?"

"Who told you that?"

"Matthew did."

"He did not."

"He did too. This afternoon on the boat, when you were in the bathroom." Dahlia crossed her arms under her head. "He said her name was Leslie and that she met Ben at the beach here when she was on vacation with her family, and that she got pregnant, so they had to get married. He said she never wanted to be here, so she just split. Crazy, huh?"

"Yeah. Crazy." Josie frowned into the darkness, deeply wounded that Matthew would share such personal information with Dahlia and not her. Maybe it wasn't true, she thought. Maybe Matthew had meant only to try to shock Dahlia. As if that was even possible.

"You didn't tell him about Daddy, did you?" Josie asked suddenly.

"Of course not. I can't very well pretend the asshole is dead if I talk about him, now, can I?"

"Don't say things like that," Josie pleaded. "It's bad luck."

"Only for him."

"Oh, forget it." Josie snuggled deeper under her covers. "I don't care what Matthew told you. It doesn't matter. He wouldn't like the things you like."

"How would you know?" said Dahlia. "You're too young to know anything about what boys like."

"I am not. And you saw Momma's cards last night. They said my love was already here. On this island. The cards didn't say anything about your love."

Dahlia groaned. "Those cards are such horseshit. They say what you want them to say."

"Fine. Don't believe them. But don't expect them to give you what you want, either."

"I don't need cards or spells to get me what I want." Dahlia rolled toward the window. She pressed her lips against the cold glass, drawing back to find the crooked oval her breath had left. "I'm not like you and Momma," she whispered. "I have plans."

Josie stared up at the ceiling, biting at her cheek. She wished her heart would slow down. She wondered whether a person could die from nerves. Tomorrow she'd ask Momma if she could start burning salt on the stove. That would slow the gossip. At least for a little while.

"You are right about one thing, Joze," Dahlia said after a while. "They don't like us here—and I don't need a deck of cards to tell me that either. We're not like these people and we never will be."

"But we have to be," Josie said softly, feeling hot tears flood her eyes. "Because if we don't fit in, then we have to go back." She wiped at her cheeks with the edge of her blanket. "And we can't go back, Dahl. We can't ever go back."

Camille was in the kitchen, humming to Dinah Washington and dropping the last dollops of praline syrup onto waxed paper to harden, when she heard a gentle rapping on the apartment door. She opened it to find Ben in the hallway, holding out a stack of quilts.

"Here are the extra blankets I promised you. Sorry I'm so late with them."

"You're not late at all," Camille said, taking the quilts and holding them against her. "Has it started snowing yet?"

"Not yet, but it will soon. The quilts might have a little bit of creosote on them. I've been fighting with the flue, as you can see." Ben gestured to his pants, the knees and thighs brushed with the same black streaks that covered his forehead. He reached self-consciously for his hair, trying to smooth back the thick waves. "I'm not usually this much of a mess," he said. "The barber in town has been out with pneumonia, so I'm afraid all of us island men are a bit shaggy right now."

"Well, I'd be glad to cut it for you, if you'd like," Camille said. "I worked at a salon. I used to cut our friends Lionel's and Roman's hair all the time."

Ben shook his head, blushing at the idea. "Oh, no, I couldn't possibly . . ."

"Of course you could," Camille said, stepping back and waving him in. "Think of it as a thank-you for the blankets."

"You mean . . . now?"

"Why not now?" she asked. "I just finished a batch of pralines, and I can never go to sleep before they cool."

Ben glanced behind her.

"It's okay," she said. "The girls are asleep."

"Oh." He reached compulsively for the back of his neck, where his hair had grown so long that some mornings it rubbed against the collar of his wool hunting jacket.

Their eyes met. "It *has* been driving me crazy," he admitted.

"Well, we can't have that, now, can we?" Camille pointed him to the table. "You sit right there. I'll go get a towel from the bathroom."

"All right." Ben took a seat, glancing around the apartment while he waited. The air smelled warm and sweet, of melted butter and brown sugar. A saucepan rested in the sink. A plate of cloudy brown disks sat on the counter. This woman really did love to cook, he thought to himself. So unlike Leslie. In every way.

"Here we are."

Camille returned carrying a towel and a comb and a small pair of shears. She swept the towel around Ben's neck and tucked the ends into his collar.

"Now, let's see . . ."

She drove her fingers into his hair, the sensation against his scalp so unexpected that Ben stiffened in his surprise. But as she drew layers of his hair first through the comb and then between her fingers, he began to relax, the delicate snip of her scissors building to an even rhythm. Behind them, Malcolm Clements's record player turned on the floor of the living room, the smoky wail of a trumpet, the pluck and purr of a standing bass. Camille hummed along, her voice smooth and in perfect tune.

"I can't tell you how much I've loved having my music back," she said. "I do hope I haven't been playing it too loud."

She had been, actually. On several occasions. But Ben hadn't wanted to tell her so. The truth was, he liked the music.

"Not at all," he lied. "I can barely hear it."

"Well, you be sure and tell me, won't you," Camille instructed firmly as a flurry of hairs landed on his hand. "I'm not used to all this quiet."

"The island can be a quiet place," Ben said.

"So I've noticed. No one says very much, do they?"

"Not really. Islanders don't like to let you know too much right away."

Camille laughed. "Not like New Orleanians. If you've got five minutes, they'll give you their life story. Whether you want it or not."

Ben smiled as more hairs rained down his cheek. "Sounds like a friendly place, New Orleans."

"It is."

"You must miss it."

"Some days," she said wistfully. "But I've brought my favorite parts of it with me. My daughters. My food. My music."

She walked around to his front. Ben lowered his gaze, feeling the skin at his neck flush; but even if he avoided the sight of her breasts, he couldn't avoid the smell of her, the puffs of rosewater-scented air as she moved her arms above him, or the way the scarlet silk of her robe clung to her hip, and the embroidered flower with deep sapphire petals that moved when she did.

"Tell the truth," she said. "Am I the first tenant to cut your hair?"

He grinned. "I'm fairly certain, yes." He might have also admitted that she was the first tenant he'd ever helped to paint a room, the first he'd ever dined with, the first he'd ever rushed to the attic for extra quilts for when temperatures dropped.

"It can be hard, can't it?" Camille said, neatening the clipped hairs above his ears. "Raising our babies alone."

Ben drew in a long breath, the gentle sweep of her fingertips along his lobe making it hard for him to answer, let alone think. "Sometimes," he said. "I really don't think about it much anymore. It's been . . ." He paused, studying his hands. "It's been a long time."

"Do you mind me asking how long?"

"Thirteen years."

Camille blinked, surprised. "So Matthew was just a baby when she left?"

"Three."

"Do you ever hear from her?"

"No." Ben swallowed hard. "She passed away."

Camille's hands ceased their motion. She drew the shears down to her side. "Oh, Benjamin . . ."

"It was a car accident outside of San Francisco when Matthew was eight."

"I'm so sorry."

"I might never have known if her sister hadn't sent word. We hadn't heard from Leslie for quite some time when it happened. Postcards, a few letters. Nothing of any real meaning. Just to alleviate some of her guilt, I suppose. But there was never any return address, never any phone number. She didn't want to be found. I came to accept that."

Camille couldn't imagine it. What she wouldn't have done for her children. But not all women wanted to be mothers.

She made a few more snips, circling him for one last look, then drew off the towel and stepped back. "All finished." She smiled at him. "You look very handsome."

Ben stood, running a hand over the back of his neck, along his temple. He glanced around the room for a clock, but found none.

"I should let you get to bed," he said. "I'm sure it's quite late."

"Oh, please stay for some pralines," Camille implored, gesturing to the counter. "They're so good when they're fresh."

"Well . . . maybe just one."

He watched Camille as she peeled several of the brown disks off the waxed paper and arranged them neatly on a small plate. The record ended, the needle thumping a moment against the smooth edge until the arm lifted and clicked itself back into place.

Regret rushed over him in the silence.

"I didn't mean to burden you with all that just now. We barely know each other."

"It's not a burden," Camille said gently. "I assure you I don't frighten easily. If you'd been through what I've been through . . ."

Her voice trailed off as she picked up the plate of pralines and carried it to the table. Ben watched her approach, concerned. It was the merest glimpse into her past, but it was enough.

He didn't know what to say. The desire to correct her secret misfortunes overwhelmed him.

"I'm sorry," he said.

"Don't be. It's all in the past." She offered him the pralines. Ben took a bite of one and let out a small moan.

"They're wonderful," he said. "What did you call them?"

"Pralines. They're sugar and cream, then butter, pecans, and vanilla at the very end."

Ben took another bite, amazed at the texture, crumbly and coarse at first, then creamy-smooth.

Their eyes met. "We don't have anything like these here," he said.

Camille smiled. "You do now."

The house was still quiet when Josie woke early the next morning. She crept out of bed and tiptoed through the living room, past Camille sleeping soundly on the hideaway, and the covered plate of pralines on the table. She knew just which drawer in the kitchen held her mother's box of powders and oils, and she drew it out slowly.

The front door creaked only slightly when she pushed it open, and the threshold groaned just once when she dropped to her knees on top of it. The brick dust felt cool in her fingers, like the sand of the island's beaches, gritty and heavy. She was careful not to get any on her nightgown as she sprinkled the powder over the boards, spreading it from one end of the doorway to the other, until her fingers were stained a deep red.

Sitting back on her heels, she assessed her handiwork and felt a swell of relief ripple through her.

There, she thought. *Just let Daddy try to follow us now.*

Twelve

Little Gale Island
January 1978

Camille might never have reconsidered selling her spells if Jeannie Potts hadn't come into the Laundromat on an unseasonably warm day, wiping her eyes on the dingy sleeves of her Mariners sweatshirt. The thirty-six-year-old mother of three teenage boys had never said more than two words to Camille in all the weeks she'd come to stuff load after load of T-shirts and gym socks into the Laundromat's heavy-duty machines, but today it seemed the poor woman couldn't stop talking.

"I'm a good mother. Raised my boys right. Maybe didn't go to church all the time, sure, but does anybody? I blame his father mostly. Sorry son of a bitch."

Camille nodded patiently, taking over folding the pile of gray briefs when Jeannie stopped to blow her nose.

"You come back and see me tomorrow, baby, you hear?" Camille said quietly. "Sometimes we just need a little help to put things right."

Jeannie's puffy eyes blinked quickly, her mouth growing slack.

The very next morning, she returned to the Laundromat and eagerly took the paper bag that Camille handed across the counter when Mr. Lucas wasn't watching.

"It's redbrick dust," she said. "You spread it across your front door every morning to keep bad energy from coming in. There's a peace candle in there too. I already dressed it for you, so all you have to do is burn it. When you do, think hard on your boy righting himself. Think real hard and don't let anything come between you and that wish. You understand?"

Jeannie Potts nodded, swallowed.

It would be another two weeks before Camille saw Jeannie again, coming out of the church's bean supper in the company of all three of her sons and smiling serenely.

By the end of that same week, almost a dozen people had come into the Laundromat looking to speak to her, wearing the same eager expression as Jeannie Potts had, their eyes growing just as round as soon as Camille began to speak.

Since she couldn't very well do spell work in the back of the Laundromat, Camille began taking customers into the apartment after work, offering rituals and selling potions and gris-gris bags from her dining room table. It was a far cry from her mother's old Voodoo shop, Camille often thought to herself as she gathered the powders and oils from her shallow kitchen cabinets, but it felt good to have her hand in her magic again, and the extra money didn't hurt either.

Dahlia, however, wasn't nearly as smitten with her mother's new career. Coming home from school to find neighbors slipping out of their apartment, most of whom barely made eye contact when they realized their hasty escape had been witnessed, made Dahlia want to jump out of her skin.

But the final straw came one raw, gray afternoon when she entered the foyer to meet Marsha Daley and Peggy Posner jaunting down the stairs from the apartment, snickering and giggling behind their hands and pushing past her out the front without a word.

Dahlia slammed the door behind them and charged up the stairs.

She found her mother in the kitchen, calmly putting away her jars, the smell of burning incense still thick in the air. Josie stood at the table, sweeping up loose powder and brushing it neatly onto a plate.

"What the hell were they doing here?" Dahlia demanded, swinging off her scarf.

Camille gave her daughter an even look through the kitchen doorway. "I'm sure you're not talking to *me* in that tone, Dahlia Rose."

"You don't know who they are, Momma," Dahlia said. "I do. They're little snots. You're so eager to spread all this stuff, you don't want to see that."

"They were perfectly polite girls," Camille said, her eyes narrowing as she reached for a bottle of anointing oil. "Certainly more polite than you're being right now."

Dahlia looked away, contrite but not yet surrendering. She glared at Josie, who hadn't dared to meet her sister's blazing eyes. "And you!" Dahlia said. "You're the one who cared so much about fitting in here. You think this is going to help?"

"Dahlia Rose, that's enough," Camille said firmly. "Your sister was only helping me. If this upsets you so much, then I can meet people in their own homes."

"That's not it." Dahlia shook her head, pleading, "Momma, these people don't care about us. Don't you get it? Right now those smug brats are walking down the street laughing at us. And I guarantee you they aren't the only ones. Nobody comes in here for your spells, Momma; they come in to see the freak show. They think we're a joke—and you're letting them!"

"I thought you didn't care what people thought of us," taunted Josie, feeling bold at her mother's side.

"I don't care about you and me," Dahlia said. "I care about Momma."

"Girls." Camille sighed, looking between them. "Dahlia, I can take care of myself, thank you very much. And I most certainly am not *letting* anyone think badly of me or my family, let alone giving them cause to laugh at us."

"You're one to talk, Dahlia," Josie said. "If anyone's making this family the laughingstock of the island it's *you*—sleeping your way through the junior class!"

"Josephine!" Camille turned slowly to her older daughter. "Is that true?"

Dahlia shrugged. "That's what they say."

"That's not what I'm asking."

Dahlia glared across the room at Josie. Camille saw the silent rage pass between her daughters and she folded her arms.

"Josephine," she instructed firmly, "I left a load of wash downstairs that needs folding."

Josie glanced quickly at Dahlia, knowing what her mother meant. "Yes, ma'am." She moved to the door, keeping her eyes down as she stepped out into the hall and closed the door behind her.

Camille waited until she heard Josie's footsteps on the stairs before she began again.

"The truth now, Dahlia Rose. Is this how it is with you and these boys?"

Dahlia's eyes lifted to her mother's, the challenge so clear. Camille watched her older daughter in the silence that followed, feeling the sting of retribution. It wasn't so different from that afternoon in her own mother's house, when Roberta had tried to make Camille see that a man's affection wasn't nearly as almighty as Camille had believed. Now she was on the other side of that cloudy glass. No wonder Roberta had been so frantic, so afraid. But Camille wouldn't be such an easy adversary for her child.

"I know how it is to be wanted, sugar. I know how good it can feel. But it isn't everything."

Dahlia sniffed. "I never said it was, Momma."

"And you think these boys will love you because you do things or say things the other girls won't?"

"I don't want them to love me," Dahlia said indignantly. "God, that's the last thing I want."

"That's foolishness, baby," Camille said gently. "Everybody wants to be loved."

"Not me. Not like that."

"What then?" said Camille. "Why else on earth would you want these boys thinking you don't have any respect for yourself?"

"I don't care what they think about me," Dahlia said, turning back to the window. "They don't know me. They don't know the first thing about me, and I want to keep it that way."

"But why?" Camille blinked at her daughter, confounded. "What's so wrong with someone knowing who you are? With letting someone—the *right* someone—care about you?"

"You wouldn't understand," Dahlia said.

"Then explain it to me," pleaded Camille.

But Dahlia's gaze remained fixed on the street. "It's my life, Momma."

Camille's eyes narrowed. "It's your life, but it's *our* house," she said firmly. "You may not think what you're doing is any big deal, but other people, *younger* people, in this house might not see it that way. Am I making myself clear?"

Dahlia answered without turning. "Yes, ma'am."

Camille moved into the kitchen, set down a pair of onions on the cutting board, and began chopping. Dahlia walked into the bedroom and shut the door behind her.

"I always wondered what this place looked like inside," Rowena Parker said a week later, watching Camille take candles down from the shelf. The nineteen-year-old sat at the table, her hands stuffed in her lap, working nervously at the buttons on her canvas coat. "I know we talked about how much, Mrs. Bergeron, but I don't have enough, so I hope you don't mind . . ."

The young woman reached into her coat pocket, withdrew two pairs of wool socks, and set them on the table. "My mother knits 'em for the Christmas fair. I thought maybe it could make up for the difference?"

Camille came to the table and took them up, admiring them. "They're lovely, Rowena."

"And real warm too."

"I'm sure they are." Camille took a seat. "This will do just fine."

Rowena smiled, revealing small, crooked teeth. "I know he loves me, Mrs. Bergeron," she said quietly. "It ain't that."

Camille nodded, calmly drawing the candles around them.

Morning, Irene.

Ben stepped into the Little Gale post office, glad for the burst of heat. Irene Thurlow, short and thick waisted, with black hair and sparkling blue eyes, waved to him from the other side of the counter. "Morning to you too, Ben. Got a big package for you. For your new tenant, actually. Be right back with it."

"Great." Ben pulled off his fogged glasses and stepped up to the counter. Margery Dunham stood waiting in a brown wool coat and matching hat, holding a stack of envelopes, her husband, Thomas, standing stiffly beside her.

"Hello, Ben," she said. "Haven't seen much of you in the village lately."

"I've been busy," he said, knowing well enough what Margery was digging for.

"I suppose you must be *very* busy with your tenant. So strange how she arrived here, isn't it? And without the husband."

Strange. Ben grinned down as he cleaned his lenses on the hem of his coat. "I wouldn't know, Margery," he said patiently, settling his glasses back on his nose. "That's not really any of my business."

"The hell it isn't." Thomas Dunham stepped forward, old pipe smoke sour on his breath. "She's living under your roof, Ben. And from what I hear, taking in customers for some kind of Voodoo ritual things. Were you aware of this?"

Ben shrugged. "There's no law against enterprise."

"Call it what you want," Margery said, "but just this morning I heard Lorna Richardson say Florence Carlisle got one done for that unfortunate birthmark on her neck."

"Really?" Ben looked calmly between the two of them. "Did it help?"

Thomas frowned at him. "Is that supposed to be funny?"

"Birthmarks are one thing, Ben," Margery said gravely, pressing a gloved hand against her cheek. "But then there's this business of Arnold Parker's daughter getting pregnant not four days after letting that woman put some kind of hex on her. Now you can understand why people are concerned."

"And then there's the older one," Thomas added. "Darla."

"Dahlia," Ben corrected firmly.

"Well, there's already lots of talk about her and some of the boys at school. Boys with girlfriends. Nice boys who may not know what they're getting into. If you get my meaning."

Ben sighed, his patience running thin. "No, Tom, I don't think I do."

"Ben . . ." Margery stepped between them, her voice softening. "We all remember how hard things were for you and Matthew when Leslie left, how much help you needed getting on with things, and we were more than happy to help you, because that's what neighbors do for one another." Margery paused, glancing nervously at her husband. "We'd hate to see you go through it all over again, that's all."

"Here you are, Ben." Irene Thurlow returned, hoisting a long, flat box onto the counter. "Got Fragile stamps all over it. I gave Donnie grief when he brought it off the truck, tossing the poor thing around like a bluefish. Lord."

Ben took the box and turned it over before Margery could peek at the return address. "Thanks, Irene."

But walking back out into the crisp morning air, Camille's box under his arm, he felt a brief but twisting shame creep out from under his indignation.

The Dunhams were right. The island had been incredibly kind to him and Matthew when Leslie had gone. For most of those early weeks of abandonment, Ben didn't know what he would have done without his neighbors.

"What is it?" asked Josie, eyes wide and hands clasped under her chin as Matthew and Ben stood at the table and pried open the thickly taped corners of the cumbersome package.

"Whatever it is, it's wrapped up like a mummy," said Matthew.

"Easy, now," Ben said. "We're getting close."

They peeled and peeled until the layers of cardboard and felt thinned enough that it took only one gentle tear to reveal a telltale splash of turquoise.

Camille drew in a delighted gasp. "Oh, they didn't," she whispered.

Ben helped her pull away the last of the covering and soon the canvas emerged, a vivid landscape of brightly colored cottages under an orange sky.

"It's that painting of the Quarter, Momma," Josie said. "The one at Lionel and Roman's that you loved so much."

Camille smiled, her eyes filling with tears. "They always promised it to me, but of course I never in a million years imagined they really would."

Matthew frowned at the brightly colored painting. "Who are Lionel and Roman?"

"Friends of ours," said Josie. "The most wonderful men ever."

"We lived with them for a while," said Dahlia.

"You mean they live *together*?" asked Matthew.

"Well, duh," said Dahlia.

"Where shall we put it?" asked Camille, hands on her hips as she scanned the apartment.

But Josie had already rushed across the room, her small hands pointing toward the wall beside the dining table. "Here. Where we can always see it."

Camille smiled. "Perfect."

Ben went downstairs and returned a few minutes later with a hammer and a handful of nails. He and Matthew hung it, while Josie and Dahlia supervised. When it was level and secure, the five of them stood together, admiring it.

"It must be worth a great deal," Ben said. "The label says it was insured for quite a bit of money."

"It's a Perez," said Camille. "He's quite famous in New Orleans."

"What's the Quarter?" asked Matthew.

"The French Quarter," said Dahlia.

"The Vieux Carré," Camille said, the words fluttering off her tongue. "It's the oldest part of New Orleans."

Josie smiled. "Isn't it magical?"

Later on, while they cleaned up the packaging, Camille moved close to Ben and said, "I'm sorry."

Ben folded cardboard under his arm. "Sorry for what?"

"I overheard Maryanne Foster in the Laundromat talking about Rowena's pregnancy. I'm sorry to have caused you such embarrassment, Benjamin. I never imagined working a few spells would get so out of hand. I suppose I should have."

Ben glanced to the kitchen, where the sisters and Matthew were digging into a fresh batch of pralines.

"You haven't caused me any embarrassment," he said gently. "I don't give a fig what people say. I never have. I never will."

Camille smiled. "You say that now. . . ."

"I'll say it then too."

A week later, it was discovered that Rowena had lied about her pregnancy, but by then it was too late.

Camille would never again sell her spells on Little Gale Island.

Part Two

The holy trinity:
peppers,
onions, and celery

Thirteen

Little Gale Island
Saturday, June 15, 2002
7:40 a.m.

Main Street was just waking up when Dahlia pulled her truck against the curb and darted under the café's purple awning, jiggling her key in the front door until the old lock gave way.

"Joze? You here?"

Coming inside, she found the jukebox playing Billie Holiday and the smell of chicory coffee thick and strong. The counter was lined with rows of bouquets, note cards sticking out of each one like tiny flags.

"She's in the back."

Dahlia looked around the counter to place the disembodied

male voice and found Danny Warner sitting at a corner table. She could still picture the policeman as a freshman in his KISS T-shirt, picking his nose and wiping it under the cafeteria bench when he thought no one was looking.

"Little Dan," she said, sauntering over. "What are you doing here?"

"It's Officer Warner now, Dahlia, if you don't mind." The policeman tried to sound firm, even as his full cheeks flushed pink. He wiped his mouth, then his brow, just missing a long thread of perspiration alongside his temple. Dahlia peered over her sunglasses at his plate and grinned to see the remains of the café's famous Spicy Scramble. She should have known from the telltale navy crescents of sweat spreading out from under his arms.

"I usually recommend people undress before they eat the scramble," she said, pouring herself a cup of coffee. "It takes off hair better than a bikini wax."

"Dahl, leave the poor man alone." Josie came out of the kitchen with a plate of corn muffins and set them on the counter. "He's here to keep an eye on things. Jack sent him over in case any reporters start banging on the door. How was the scramble, Dan?"

The officer offered a bright thumbs-up as he mopped his forehead with his napkin.

Dahlia emptied three sugar packets into her coffee, stirring it with a knife. She gestured to the flowers.

Josie smiled wistfully. "I couldn't even get through the front door at first," she said. "Danny had to help me bring them in. There's a bunch more in the kitchen." She looked at Dahlia. "Did you go by the house?"

Dahlia blew on her coffee. "I couldn't."

"Wayne says Jack didn't put up any of that yellow police tape, thank God." Josie offered Dahlia a muffin; she took two. "I couldn't bear to think of the lilacs tangled up in that awful stuff. Any word from Matty?"

"No. You?"

"No. I tried Jack too, but he didn't answer."

The front door chimed. The sisters looked up to see Willard Riley leaning in the doorway, the older man's brown eyes big on them, looking like a kid peering over the railing on Christmas morning for a peek at the tree.

"Morning, Mr. Riley," said Josie.

"Morning, girls. Listen, I know you're closed and I don't mean to bother you, but I promised Luanne I'd bring pralines to the board meeting this morning, and she'll kill me if I show up empty-handed. You know how she is about her sweets."

Josie smiled patiently. "I'll see what I can do," she said, and disappeared into the back, returning a few minutes later with a heavy brown bag that she walked to the door.

Willard took the bag, beaming. "You're a lifesaver. How much do I owe you?"

"The register's locked. Don't worry about it."

Willard nodded, his eyes filling with concern. "We're all pulling for him, you know. The whole town."

"I know," Josie said, waving as Willard slipped back out the door.

Dahlia sighed. "I bet if you listen carefully, you'll hear the popping of a thousand champagne corks all across the island."

Josie frowned. "Don't say things like that."

"Why not?"

"You know why not. It's bad luck to talk about the dead before they're—" Josie stopped, her gaze catching on the view of the street. "Oh, God."

"What?" Dahlia turned to the front window just in time to see Robert Clark's bright green tow truck pulling up beside her parked pickup.

Dahlia slammed down her muffin. "That miserable *troll*!"

"Dahl, please." Josie reached out as Dahlia stormed past her. "Don't make a scene."

"Bobby Clark!" Dahlia burst out the front door just as the hooks were lowered, shouting as she approached, "Bobby Clark, don't you dare put my truck on that tow!"

The short, mustached man held up his grease-stained hands. "Sorry, Dahlia. Nothing I can do. Orders from the top."

Dahlia spun around and glared at Atlantic Antiques' frosted front doors with their matching lavender wreaths. She thought they looked about the right diameter to fit around a certain shopkeeper's fat neck.

Inside the café, Danny Warner squeezed himself out from behind the table. "I'll handle this, ma'am," he said, his voice lowered with sufficient authority.

Josie smiled gratefully as he stepped past her and outside, but it was too late. Dahlia had already climbed through the truck's passenger window, shimmied across the seat, and started up the engine. "She wants me to move my truck?" she yelled out her open window. "Fine! I'll move my goddamned truck!"

Then, only seconds after Danny Warner and Robert Clark were able to scoot out of the way, Dahlia slammed the truck into reverse, driving the rusted back end up over the curb and straight into the side of Margery Dunham's neatly written sandwich board, sending the hinged panels toppling like an unsteady toddler off the edge of the sidewalk and into the street. Dahlia put the car into drive, pulled it down off the curb, then steered her front end over the flattened boards, hearing the crack of the frame, then taking off down the street.

Jack was waiting for Matthew in the Sand Dollar's lobby when Matthew came downstairs at nine fifteen. The old friends reunited with a handshake and heavy hearts, taking cups of complimentary coffee out to the back porch and settling into a pair of painted Adirondacks that were misted with dew.

"Still no news?" Jack asked.

Matthew shook his head, setting his cup on one of the chair's long, flared arms. "They hope Pop'll come out of it within a few days. They're just not sure how he'll be when he does."

Jack nodded, knowing there wasn't much more to say on it.

Matthew let out a heavy sigh. "I can't believe that cocksucker finally did it, Jack. All those years we worried, you know? But, Jesus . . . I never really thought Charles would be crazy enough to actually come back here and try to hurt Pop."

Jack set down his cup. "I know."

"So when did he get out?"

"Monday."

"Monday?" Matthew rubbed his forehead, stunned. "Jesus, Jack—why the hell wasn't anyone told?"

"It all depends on the nature of the offense, Matt. Sometimes the prison will try to inform next of kin in the event of a parole hearing; sometimes they won't. But in most cases, if there are no priors for domestic abuse, the state doesn't have to notify the family unless they request the release information, which apparently no one did."

"Are you telling me Camille never pressed charges against that son of a bitch?"

"It's not uncommon. A lot of times women don't because they worry it will only escalate the violence."

Matthew let go a sad chuckle. "So much for that theory," he whispered, more to himself than to Jack. He picked up his coffee, took a sip.

"Matt, I want you to know I'm doing everything I can to push this investigation through," Jack said, "so everyone can just move on from this. You and Ben. Josie and Dahlia."

At the reference, Matthew looked up, meeting Jack's eyes. Jack's tone had been casual, but Matthew wasn't fooled. He hadn't forgotten how deeply in love Jack and Dahlia had been with each other, how their breakup had confounded and wrecked Jack. For a long time, Matthew thought that Jack was jealous of him for his relationship with Dahlia, as if the proximity of their living quarters and the time they had spent together had automatically forged a deep passion between them, as if it had been that easy. Matthew had only wished.

But there was more, of course. Jack had a right to his grudge.

"I haven't spoken to them since I left Miami," Matthew said. "They said the hospital wouldn't let anyone but immediate family into Pop's room."

"It's true. The waiting's been awful for them. I'm sure they'll want to go over with you as soon as possible." Jack paused, the next question obvious, and prudent. "Did Holly come with you?"

Matthew looked out at the inn's yard, the winding trails of flower gardens, wondering if they were Dahlia's handiwork.

"No," he admitted quietly. "We broke up a few months ago."

"Oh, Christ, I'm sorry. I know how tough it can be."

"Thanks." Matthew remembered hearing about Jack's

divorce. Dahlia had told him in a phone call, sounding relieved.

"The house is still *technically* a crime scene," Jack said, "but if there's something you need or you want, I can get it for you. Just let me know, okay?"

Matthew nodded. There were a thousand things and nothing he wanted from the old house. He couldn't begin to think on it.

The men rose together.

"I'll be in touch soon," Jack said. "In the meantime, let me know if there's anything I can do."

Matthew said he would and they parted at the steps.

Alone again, Matthew squinted up at the sky. The morning cloud cover had finally burned off, leaving behind a choking blanket of humidity. He returned to his room to change into a T-shirt; then he climbed the hill toward Walnut Street.

Dahlia was weeding flower boxes on her back deck when Josie called.

"That was a wonderful performance this morning, Dahlia Rose. What are you planning to run over for tomorrow's show?"

"Very funny." Dahlia pushed hair out of her eyes with the heel of her dirt-caked hand. "I think one of the nails from that goddamned sandwich board got stuck in my front wheel."

"Serves you right," said Josie. "I just talked to Matty and he said he's on his way. Why don't you come over to the café and we'll all have lunch? I told him we wanted to go to the hospital first thing, but would you believe they're running a bunch of tests this afternoon, so we *still* can't see Ben yet after all thi— Dahl? Dahl, are you still there?"

Dahlia lowered the phone, her eyes fixed on the side of the

house, where Matthew had just appeared from the street: head bowed slightly, hands in his pockets as always, hair still curly and a few weeks overdue for a cut, still sandy blond but graying.

A dormant possessiveness awoke within her; selfish as it was, she wanted him to herself for just a while.

"Joze, I have to go," she said quickly. "I have to be at the Harrises' at noon."

She hung up and set the phone back on the railing.

There wasn't time to consider how wretched she must have looked, or how her heart thumped behind her dirt-streaked T-shirt. Just a single thought blasted through the mess of them, filling Dahlia with pride and relief:

He'd picked her.

Matthew told himself it was simple math that he'd come upon Dahlia first, since her house was closer to the inn than Josie's. But he'd taken the less direct route to every one of his destinations since arriving, so that wasn't entirely accurate.

Maybe he'd come to Dahlia first because he knew she'd be alone.

Maybe he had picked her after all.

"Hey, Dee."

"Hey, Matty."

They met in a patch of lavender and looked a while at each other, until Dahlia finally reached for him. Grateful for her lead, Matthew gripped Dahlia's waist and pulled her close, the sharp, coppery scent of crushed soil filling his nose.

He drew back, blinking away tears. Dahlia looked past him.

"Holly didn't come," he said.

"Oh." Dahlia wanted him to say more, to say why, but he

didn't and she didn't press him. "Why don't we go inside? I
have some sweet tea."

"Fuck that." He gave her a tired smile. "How about a beer?"

It was a great house. Small, open, bright. Dahlia had
bought it the year he'd met Holly. Matthew remembered when
Bobby Chapman and his family had lived in it. All pine panel-
ing and wall-to-wall shag.

She was still a hopeless slob, he thought, looking around at
the cluttered room, the coffee table overflowing with stacks of
planting books and old newspapers, empty wineglasses and
oversize mugs. Yet there was still a certain charm to the mess,
an undeniable warmth that he'd always missed when he was
away. He saw the old love seat in the corner, the faded plum
velvet buried under a pile of clean laundry that would probably never find its way into dresser drawers.

Dahlia came into the living room carrying two beers.

She handed him one and nodded to the love seat. "Remember that old thing?"

Matthew smiled. "Do I ever."

"Josie and I couldn't agree who should have it when
Momma died, so we trade off. I keep it from June to December; then she gets it for the other half of the year."

He grinned. Shared custody of a love seat. Only the sisters
could invent such a thing.

"Do you share the Perez too?" he asked, gesturing to the
empty square of wall above the fireplace.

Dahlia glanced reflexively to where he looked. She was
surprised he remembered her mother's beloved painting.

"No, it's all mine," she said. "It's just at the restorers'."

"I remember when it came."

"You thought it was ugly."

"Yeah, well." Matthew shrugged. "I had a lot to learn about art." Their eyes met. "I had a lot to learn about a lot of things."

In the silence, the room seemed too close, filling up quickly with memories once the floodgates had been opened.

Dahlia pointed them to the porch. "Let's go outside."

On the deck, they sat around a plastic table covered in opened bags of potting soil. They drank awhile, saying nothing, waiting for the air to settle around them as the sea breeze fluttered by, making the deck's collection of wind chimes sing.

"It's been awful not being able to see him, Matty. And now Joze said something about tests today?"

"Yeah. Assessment tests. GCS, or GSC, or some fucking thing." He frowned, glanced to her. "I'm sorry they haven't let you guys see him, Dee."

"Jack's been letting us know whenever he talks to the doctor," Dahlia said. "It's helped."

Matthew nodded, feeling a fresh clump of tears rising. He forced them back, sniffing deeply. He scratched at the corner of the beer label with his thumbnail, not sure what to say next. A part of him wanted to rage at Dahlia, to blame her for her father's violence, for all the years Charles had made anyone who cared for the Bergeron women suffer. But the bigger part of him knew that Dahlia had suffered too.

The label surrendered and Matthew peeled it off.

"I got a room at the Sand Dollar," he said.

"Josie told me. We were wondering why you didn't find a hotel in Portland, where you could be closer to Ben."

Matthew shrugged, swigged his beer. The truth was, it

hadn't occurred to him *not* to stay on the island. No matter where the hospital was.

"I guess I just figured I would be over here most of the time anyway," he said. "Seeing Jack. Seeing you and Jo . . ."

Dahlia reached for his hand across the table, pressed her fingers between his.

"You know you could stay here," she said. "There's an extra bedroom upstairs."

Matthew knew that; he remembered the layout well. Maybe he'd visited Dahlia first so that she could offer her room before Josie, and that out of courtesy he'd have to accept Dahlia's offer, the one he'd wanted in the first place.

"You should, Matty. Save yourself the money."

It was a lame excuse and they both knew it. He made a good salary; cost wasn't the issue.

"Or not," Dahlia said. "I know that wouldn't sit well with Holly."

A new stretch of silence arrived, longer this time. Dahlia sipped her beer. Matthew studied her when she looked away, wondering what she would say if she knew that Holly had left him, wondering why he hadn't told her yet. Back on the island, the desire to have Dahlia's attention, her affection, overwhelmed him. He could have been seventeen again.

God, he thought, the burning hunger for revenge racing through him, if only he were.

"When was the last time you talked to your dad?" Dahlia asked.

"Last week." Matthew paused, fighting back tears. "We talked about me coming up for Thanksgiving. He sounded tired. Not like himself somehow. How has he seemed to you?"

Dahlia shrugged, smiling sadly. "Honestly, Matty, ever since Momma died, your dad hasn't seemed like himself."

"What do you expect? She was his constant companion for almost twenty years, Dee. They were each other's whole world." He looked at Dahlia as the memories flooded him. "We all were."

Dahlia stared at her hands in her lap, the black crescents of dirt packed under her nails. "We should get going," she said, dragging her wrist across her wet eyes. "Josie's waiting."

Jack watched the Casco Bay ferry glide into the landing, evicting a snug pack of seagulls with its arriving horn. The birds rose in an angry arc, still squawking as they landed farther down the dock.

Forty-three years on the island and he still felt a shudder of awe watching the great boats arrive against the piers. He took a seat on a sun-parched bench nearby, leaned back, and sipped his coffee while the ship's heavy lines were tossed out and tied down. The crush of the departing passengers followed, the seasonal mix of residents and tourists marching down the gangplank.

Jack spotted Keith Hewitt right away in the crowd of attendants, all dressed in their white polo shirts and khaki shorts, but Keith's bleached crew cut was hard to miss. Keith was a good kid, nearly twenty-three and bright as hell. Jack had helped the young man to get the job as a deckhand for the *Island Explorer* when the paper mill in Westbrook had closed down the spring before. The pay wasn't nearly as good, but it did keep the young man closer to home, where he was sole guardian of his teenage brother, Shawn, which was a full-time job in itself. In the past six months, the seventeen-year-old had been caught twice with dope, the most recent time in the company of a woman nearly twice his age who ran a sex shop in Saco.

Jack drained his coffee while the last passengers disembarked, mostly parents with loose children and unwieldy strollers (Jack remembered Jenny's that folded up like a pocketknife) and islanders toting bags from the shops on the mainland.

When the boat was finally empty, Jack made his way down the ramp.

"Hi, there, Keith."

The young man's face brightened when he looked up. "Oh, hey, Chief Thurlow. You waiting for someone?"

"As a matter of fact, I am." Jack stepped up onto the deck. "Got a second?"

The young man gave him a quizzical look, the sunburned skin of his forehead knotting. "Yeah, sure." He took off his sunglasses, hooking them on his collar, and followed Jack to a quiet stretch of the deck. "This isn't about Shawn, is it?" Keith asked, a flicker of panic shuddering across his face. "He's not in trouble again, is he?"

"No, nothing like that. This is about Ben Haskell. The office said you were on Thursday night when Charles Bergeron came over on the boat."

"I worked that shift, yeah. But I don't know if I saw him or not."

Jack took out the faxed picture of Charles's most recent mug shot and held it out to Keith. "I'm just trying to confirm the time line," Jack said. "Anything you can remember would help."

"Oh, yeah, that guy," Keith said, nodding. "Sure. I saw him. I remember thinking his hair was even crazier than mine."

Jack grinned as he tugged a small notebook out of his back pocket, pulled the pen off its front, and clicked the tip out. "How did he seem to you?"

Keith shrugged. "Fine, I guess. He bought a cup of coffee while me and Kip were working the snack bar. Told me to keep the change."

Jack made the note. "Anything else you can remember?"

"Not really. I didn't see the guy again after that."

"So you didn't see Bergeron get off the boat?"

"Nope."

Jack nodded, making more notes. "And this was the ten-forty, right?"

"No, the seven-forty."

Jack looked up. "The *seven*-forty? Are you sure?"

"Positive."

Jack frowned. It didn't add up. Ben's call to dispatch had come in a few minutes after eleven, and it sure as hell didn't take three hours to walk from the landing to the old house, which meant Charles had stopped somewhere on his way to Ben's.

One logical answer as to where rushed at Jack, forming a knot in his throat. Josie and Wayne had been with him having dinner at his house, but Jack had never gotten around to asking Dahlia where she'd been that night. Now he'd have to. Jack only hoped she could she tell him.

He slipped the notebook into his jacket.

"Thanks for your help, Keith," he said, already walking back down the ramp. "And tell Shawn I said hi."

Fourteen

Little Gale Island

Saturday, June 15, 2002

11:50 a.m.

Matthew smiled to see the same Open sign hanging lop-sided in the café's front door, and when he followed Dahlia inside, the smell nearly toppled him.

It didn't matter that the walls had been redone, or that the rose blossoms they'd once painted so carefully on the wide floorboards were nearly gone, stomped and mopped and scuffed away over the years. Or even if a pair of overstuffed chairs sat in the corner that used to be reserved for boxes of paper goods and dried beans. The jukebox was still there, playing Ella Fitzgerald, and if Matthew had dared to close his eyes, he could have been sixteen again, squeezing past Camille to rinse garlic peel off his hands.

"Matty!"

Josie appeared behind the counter in a sleeveless blouse and a knee-length denim skirt, her delicate hands lost in a pair of oven mitts. She wove through the tables and collapsed against him, rocking back and forth. Matthew smoothed the soft red bowl of her hair, seeing the rows of flowers on the counter. He smiled.

"They're for Ben," she said. "They keep coming."

Matthew glanced around, seeing customers he'd never seen before. A group of young people crowded in the window booth, probably children of classmates, kids not much older than he and the girls had been when they'd opened the café. A new generation of gumbo converts. Camille would have been pleased.

"Hi, Matt."

Wayne emerged from the kitchen. Josie stepped aside and an awkward silence fell over the café while the two men walked carefully toward each other. Close enough, they exchanged a strained embrace, then drew back quickly. Wayne moved to Josie, taking her hand.

"We're all really sorry, Matt," he said.

Josie pulled her hand gently out of Wayne's grip and gestured to the kitchen. "Hungry, Matty?"

Matthew wasn't the least bit. He hadn't had an appetite for the last two days. He had barely been able to force down a sandwich at the airport.

But when Josie brought him the first bowl of gumbo, and he saw the fat wedges of sausage in their satiny broth, he inhaled it and asked for another.

They closed the café early and returned to Josie and Wayne's, letting the hours of the afternoon slip away over pots of coffee and a thawed pecan pie. When it was time for dinner, Josie implored Matthew to stay, as if there was any question he wouldn't, and they ate oyster bisque and crab cakes in the dining room, reminiscing between second helpings and pours of red wine. When bowls and plates were empty, Wayne complained of a headache and excused himself to the den to watch the Red Sox. He'd been subdued at dinner, saying little the entire meal, and Josie was grateful to see him depart.

"The house looks great, JoJo," Matthew said, glancing around the candlelit room. So many memories in the smallest details, strings of Mardi Gras beads swinging from doorknobs and cabinet pulls.

"The best part is outside," Josie said, rising with a pile of dirty plates and heading into the kitchen. "Dahlia did some beautiful new plantings around the deck this spring. You'll have to go take a look."

Matthew met Dahlia's eyes across the table. "You always were talented, Dee." They looked at each other for a moment, looking away when Josie returned for more dishes.

Dahlia rose to help clear the table. Matthew joined her.

In the kitchen, he said, "It's late. I should really be getting back to the hotel."

Josie nodded, smiled. "So, eight o'clock at the café tomorrow, right?"

"Right," Matthew said, moving toward the door.

"Wait." Dahlia grabbed her keys off the counter. "I'll drive you."

"Don't be ridiculous," said Josie. "You're drunk!"

Dahlia grinned. "So I am."

She tossed her keys to Matthew. He caught them easily.

"Then I guess Matty will drive *me*."

It was a clear, cold night. Jack leaned back in his wicker porch swing and studied the ceiling of stars as he sipped a beer. A rush of guilt coursed through him; he had to admit it had been nice seeing Dahlia again, having the opportunity, the excuse, to be close to her again. And he couldn't deny the relief that had settled over him at thinking that they were all finally free of Charles. Especially Dahlia.

But his conversation with Keith Hewitt gnawed at him. He wanted to believe there was some explanation for the gap in the time line; that maybe Charles had lingered over dinner at one of the island's restaurants before climbing the hill to Ben's. But after an afternoon spent canvassing the island's shops and eateries, Jack couldn't find a single person who could remember serving an old man with wild orange-and-white hair.

Still, there were other possibilities. Maybe Charles had found himself lost; maybe he'd stopped to rest in Watson's Park and fallen asleep, like old men did sometimes, even old men with scores to settle. A man could go unnoticed in Watson's Park late at night, could sit there for a long time without being seen from the street.

Or maybe Charles had just stopped to buy himself some time. Maybe in the eleventh hour he'd wrestled with his violent plan, had second thoughts, only to find his conviction return to him.

Jack scanned the horizon, feeling the soft, salty air flutter across his porch, grazing his temples, his jaw. Three lost hours. Three hours in a lifetime of hours. Even now he could barely believe it was more than twenty years ago that he and Dahlia had ended things, that last night on Ben's porch when he'd waited for her until dark, only to realize she was already long gone. But then, she'd warned him from the start the one thing she didn't have was patience.

Jack drained his beer and rose.

Patience or not, he just hoped the one thing Dahlia *did* have was an alibi.

Matthew pulled the pickup against the curb and put it into park, leaving the engine running. He and Dahlia looked up at the Sand Dollar's front porch, the stained-glass insert in the door, shades of amber and violet, lit from inside, warm and inviting.

Matthew studied Dahlia as she watched the street. Her cheeks were still hot from the wine, her dark eyes heavy. Dahlia felt his gaze on her. The question was on the edge of her tongue; she wanted so badly to ask: *Why didn't Holly come, Matty?*

She glanced over to her keys dangling in the ignition. He hadn't turned off the motor. He didn't mean for her to come up, and an alcohol-induced hurt bloomed within her.

But in the close quiet, Matthew wasn't as certain. He could feel the possibility floating between them. It wasn't so different from that night on the beach, or any of the other nights when he'd let her have her way. All she ever had to do was say the word.

Dahlia saw his brightening expression. "What?"

"Nothing." Matthew shrugged, blushing slightly. "I was just remembering something."

Something. Dahlia grinned. "It's nice to see you smile," she said.

"It's nice *to* smile." He studied the streetlight, the balloon of moths at the edge of its glow fluttering madly. He let go a deep breath. "Pop had a good life here, Dee. A really good life. No matter what happens."

"We all did, Matty. The best."

She covered his hand where it lay on the steering wheel. The truth poured out of him like sap from a pierced maple. "She's fucking an architect. An architect she met in her yoga class."

"Oh, shit." Dahlia squeezed his knuckles. "We wondered why she didn't come."

Matthew turned to her, feeling the alcohol stirring, warm and smooth. "I'm worried about you driving home. Maybe you should leave the truck here. I could walk you back."

"It's only a few blocks."

"If it's only a few blocks, then we can walk it." *Or you could just stay here*, he thought reflexively. *Help me forget things. We were always good at that, weren't we, Dee?*

Dahlia leaned over and kissed his cheek, lingering awhile against his jaw. He smelled good. Familiar. Warm. Safe.

"Get some sleep, Matty."

He nodded, climbing out. While she moved across the seat, Matthew rested his hands on the driver's window, waiting for her. Dahlia shoved the car into gear.

"Seat belt," he ordered, tugging the strap toward her.

Dahlia pulled it across her breasts, snapping it into place. Dear Matty, she thought. Still trying to take care of her.

"See you at eight," she said.

"I'll be there." Matthew pushed off from the door, patting the window rim, and watched Dahlia pull away, flats of mums sliding across the bed, the rusted pink tailgate spotted with peeling bumper stickers.

Josie dipped the last of the dishes into the sink of soapy water, watching her husband at the deck door. The smell of crab lingered in the kitchen, rising with each sunken plate. She took off her dish gloves, laid them on the edge of the sink.

"We're meeting at eight to go to the hospital tomorrow morning," she said.

Wayne scratched at the thick hairs of his beard, his gaze fixed on the view.

"I think it's best if you all have some time alone with Ben first. Four people's a lot to cram into a tiny hospital room."

Josie frowned at him, confused. "Baby, that's crazy. We've been waiting to see him."

"I know," Wayne said, his voice as far away as his gaze. "But I thought I might take the boat out tomorrow morning. Maybe try to clear my head on the water."

Too shocked to argue, Josie just turned off the counter light and walked to the stairs. She stopped at the first step, her hand on the newel post. "You coming up?"

"In a little while," he said without turning.

She nodded, then resumed her climb. Putting her hand in her pocket, she gripped the gris-gris bag she'd recently filled and dressed, feeling the long-lost relief of its bulk, the safety of its warm red felt.

A swell of longing filled her. But she wasn't sure, even as she climbed into bed a few minutes later, what—or whom—it was for.

Dahlia answered the phone shortly after eleven. It was the sisters' routine to call each other before bed, but tonight

Dahlia couldn't help wondering whether Josie had called to make sure she hadn't stayed with Matthew at the hotel. Dahlia had heard the relief in her younger sister's voice when she picked up.

"Holly left him," Dahlia said, cradling the phone against her shoulder while she smoothed lotion on her peeling heels. "For some architect in her yoga class. He just told me."

"Oh, God. How could she?"

"Maybe she really liked his downward-facing dog."

"Don't joke," Josie scolded. "When?"

"He didn't say."

"Poor Matty. On top of all this. Why didn't he tell us?"

"He just did."

"No, I mean before. When it happened."

"We're not exactly meeting at the cove anymore, Joze."

"Well, obviously," Josie said, hurt that Matthew had kept this from them, from her. "Do you think it was because they couldn't get pregnant?"

"I don't know. Maybe."

"So what did he say?"

"I just told you."

"Well, what else?"

"That was it."

Dahlia could hear Josie nibbling on her thumbnail, the nervous tapping of teeth.

"I bet that's exactly why she left him," Josie said. "God, I wish he'd told me. He knows I know what that feels like. I know how hard it is on a marriage to want to have a baby and not be able to."

"They weren't married, Joze."

"So? Neither were Momma and Ben, and they loved each

other more than most married people do." Josie paused, sighed. "God, it must have been because of Holly all along. Then again, Matty doesn't know that, does he? Oh, God, what if he thinks he was the reason they couldn't conceive?"

"What does it matter now?" Dahlia asked, wishing she'd never brought it up.

"Of course it matters, Dahl. You know Matty. He's probably been beating himself up over this."

"I think he has other things on his mind."

"I know that. I'm just saying maybe we should tell him now."

"We can't. You know we can't."

"We could," Josie said. "We *won't*. There's a difference."

The line went silent. Dahlia pumped out another dollop of lotion, rubbing it over her dry hands.

"What if Ben doesn't wake up, Dahl?"

"He will," Dahlia said firmly. "The doctors are almost sure he will."

"But they don't know how he'll be if he does. You heard what Matty said. Just because Ben comes to doesn't mean he'll recover. He could be a vegetable, Dahl. What kind of life can he have like that? It's too cruel."

"You can't think that way."

"I know. That's why I'm going to do one of Momma's cleansing rituals tomorrow. Just to be sure." Josie paused. "Wayne isn't coming with us to the hospital."

"Why not?"

"He says he thinks it's too many people at once. Does that make any sense? He's still downstairs. It's weird, Dahl. I can't help thinking it's because Matty's here and Wayne's just, I don't know, *sulking* or something. I can't believe he'd be that selfish."

Dahlia set her lotion on the nightstand, the memory of Wayne's visit the night before flashing back to her. "He's just upset, Joze. Don't read so much into it."

"Maybe."

"Try to get some sleep, okay? I'll see you in the morning."

"Okay. Love you."

"Love you too."

When Dahlia hung up, she stared awhile at her hand on the phone, wondering whether the rest of her looked as old and unfamiliar as her fingers did, and why she never noticed before now.

Fifteen

Little Gale Island

February 1978

Camille and the girls had three glorious months of freedom before Charles found them. The dreaded reunion came on a bitterly cold afternoon. It was Josie who saw him first, on her way back from the village with Camille and Dahlia. He was pressed against the railing on Ben's porch, his hands shoved under his armpits, the collar of his thin coat flipped up, the flaming points of his hair poking out from under his cap like sparks from a dry-wood fire, a short cigarette dangling from his chapped lips, two cases at his feet.

Josie heard her mother suck in a sharp breath behind her, but it was Dahlia who said, "Oh, fuck."

"Dahlia Rose," Camille said softly. "Let's keep our wits now."

She took their mittened hands, squeezing them reassuringly.

"Look at y'all," Charles said, grinning as they approached. "All y'all look like Eskimos!"

Panicked, Josie looked to her sister, but Dahlia's eyes were hard on Charles, as level as their mother's. Josie looked down, hoping he wouldn't call on her first, but he did.

"You in there, Julep?" Charles reached out to pry apart the thick shell of her puffy hood.

She smiled reflexively, ashamed at once at herself.

"Man, I've missed my girls," he said weakly, his eyes fixed on Camille. "I've missed y'all real bad." He turned to Dahlia, tilting his head. "I know what you're thinkin', darlin'. That I'm mad at ya for cuttin' your daddy like that, but I ain't. Promise."

Dahlia met his eyes, her own without remorse.

"Girls, your daddy got carried away that day, and I'm real sorry about that. I understand why y'all took off like you did. Had a hell of a time findin' y'all, though. Cost me too. That new girl they hired at the beauty parlor wouldn't hunt up your forwardin' address for me for less than fifty. Can you believe that?" Charles took one last drag off his cigarette, then flicked it over the railing. "But that's all water under the bridge—look who made the trip with me!" He reached down and picked up the trumpet case at his feet, his grin huge now as he swung the case through the air. "Donna and me thought we might teach these Yankees what real music sounds like. Whatcha think about that?"

Josie swallowed, sure she would throw up all over her salt-lapped boots.

Less than ten minutes later, Charles was in his stocking feet and lounging on the couch, railing at the indignities of his two-day bus ride and smoking enough cigarettes to fill a chipped tea saucer.

"I can't believe these people up here, Camille," he called out to their mother, who was already in the kitchen, warming up leftover biscuits for him. "You know I couldn't get a decent bowl of grits outside of Virginia? I mean, how hard is it to make a bowl of grits?"

Josie glanced quickly to Dahlia, but her older sister wouldn't lift her eyes from her soda. A Miles Davis record blared on the player. Josie could only imagine what Ben and Matthew must have been thinking on the other side of the house.

"I still can't understand why y'all came all the way up here," Charles said, looking around at the unfamiliar furnishings. "Where'd y'all get this stuff, anyway?"

"The apartment came furnished," Camille said.

"Oh, yeah. So who runs this place?"

Camille gave the girls a silencing look through the kitchen doorway.

"It's owner occupied, Charles. We don't know much about our landlord."

"Well, shit, baby. I ain't askin' for blood type. Man or woman?"

"Man," she admitted carefully.

"Man, huh? He come on to you yet?"

Their mother didn't respond. Charles grinned at Josephine

as he pulled out a new cigarette from the crumpled pack and lit it. "Oh, I'm just kiddin' with your momma, ain't I, Julep?"

Josie shrugged lamely. Charles laughed.

"Now, listen up, 'cause I got news." He sat forward. "Your daddy's got himself a steady gig. Gonna be makin' some *real* money now. Gonna be a salesman."

"Selling what exactly?" said Dahlia, arms folded.

Josie gave her a quick look. Charles frowned. "What difference does it make?" he said. "Shit, I could sell a snowball to the devil if I had to."

But Dahlia knew he wouldn't be selling snowballs, and from the tight smile on Camille's face, Dahlia could tell her mother knew it too. Only Josie seemed oblivious to their father's intended product.

"That's wonderful, Charles," Camille said, handing him his biscuits.

"You bet your ass it's wonderful," said Charles, beaming again. He slapped the cushion beside him, ordering her company. Camille obliged him, an unwelcome sense of familiarity coursing through her at the feel of his arm over her shoulder, his callused fingers tapping against her skin. "I was waitin' for y'all to celebrate, so tonight, we're gonna go get ourselves a proper meal," he announced, snuffing out his cigarette and tearing into a biscuit.

Dahlia cleared her throat loudly. Camille nodded, understanding her signal. "Charles, tonight isn't a good night," she said carefully. "The girls have a Valentine's Day dance to go to. The town puts it on for all the young people. They've been looking forward to it for weeks."

"A dance?" Charles cackled, spraying biscuit crumbs all over Camille's folded hands. "No shit. Well, I guess you'd have to dance to keep warm in a place like this!" Charles reached down, stroking Camille's thigh. "Maybe you and me go with 'em? Show these uptight Yankees how to really dance."

Camille saw the look of panic cross both girls' faces. She patted Charles's hand, returned it to his own thigh. "The girls deserve their night. Besides, they'll have their friend Matthew with them."

"Who's that?"

"He's our landlord's son," Camille said. "He and the girls have grown close."

"Shit, not *too* close, I hope." Charles looked right at Josie. "Boys your age are filthy, nasty little pricks, Julep." He grinned. "I should know."

"Charles."

"What?" He sat back. "It's true."

"You girls go get changed now," Camille instructed brightly. "Go on."

Dahlia and Josie rose quickly, disappearing into their room.

Dahlia closed the door behind them. Josie collapsed on her bed, her head in her hands.

"Don't you dare cry," Dahlia said, already pulling off her shirt and yanking her dress from the closet. "Ignore him and he'll go away. That's what I'm going to do."

"Ignore him?" Josie said, looking up, bewildered behind her tears. "How are we supposed to do that? He's going to ruin everything."

"Only if you let him." Dahlia shrugged into her dress, tugging down the ruched shoulders. She crossed to the mirror and fixed her hair with a pair of combs. "Momma will be nice to him tonight; then tomorrow she'll tell him what's what. We just have to get through tonight, that's all."

"How can you know that?" Josie whispered, wiping at her eyes. "She can't make him leave. He's her husband. He can stay here as long as he wants. Oh, God . . ." Her face crumpled at the thought. "What if he wants to *move* here?"

"Oh, please." Dahlia threw Josie a flat look in the mirror as she tied a black velvet choker around her neck, centering the plastic cameo. "He wouldn't survive this place for ten minutes. I wouldn't be surprised if he hightails it out of here in the middle of the night."

Josie sucked in a sob and nodded, hopeful.

"Now get dressed," Dahlia said, reaching for her lip gloss. "Before he gets any more brilliant ideas."

Charles hadn't moved from his station when they emerged from their bedroom; only the pile of bent butts in the chipped tea saucer had grown. Their mother remained seated beside him, looking at turns captive and compliant. Josie wondered how much longer their father would be content with just cigarettes and sweet tea. Soon he'd need something stronger, and she knew the only liquor Camille kept in the house was brandy for cooking.

"Well, look at you, Julep." Charles sat up, shaking his head. "I hardly recognize you, you so beautiful."

Camille gestured to the closet. "Wear your boots, girls. Ben said there could be snow later."

"Ben?" Camille realized her error at once. Charles dragged his gaze around to her. "Barely know him, huh?" He considered Camille a moment, then stood up, tugging her to her feet with him. "Come on. I think I need to meet this landlord of yours."

Camille felt a spark of panic. "Now?"

"Why not now?"

"Charles," she pleaded, "you just can't show up at someone's door. This isn't New Orleans. People here like a little warning. . . ."

Charles reached down, tugged out his trumpet, and blasted out a short tune.

"How's that for warnin'?" he declared, laughing.

The sisters looked at their mother, mortified. Camille smiled patiently.

Ben was loading the washing machine when Matthew found him. "Pop, Mr. Bergeron's here. He wants to meet you."

"Who?" Ben stopped, realizing at once. "Oh." He dropped the top on the washer and wiped his hands on his seat. "Is he waiting in the living room?"

"Nope. He refused to come in. Said he just wanted to get a look at you."

Ben frowned. "He said that?"

Matthew nodded nervously.

"All right then."

They met Charles in the foyer, his arm draped over Camille's shoulder. Ben gave her a brief smile, seeing the flash of concern in her eyes.

"I'm Camille's husband," Charles said, thrusting out his hand as if he were delivering a sucker punch instead of a handshake. "Charles Bergeron."

Ben accepted warily. "Ben," he said. "Ben Haskell."

The men shook hands, considering each other.

"This is my son, Matthew."

Charles extended his hand to Matthew, shaking it roughly. "Boy's got a firm grip," Charles said. "That's real good. Tough guy, ain't ya?"

Matthew withdrew his hand, looking over at his father.

"I take it that was your work on the trumpet just now, Charles?"

"You take it right." Charles lifted his chin. "I'm real well-known in New Orleans. I'm sure Camille's told y'all that."

Ben glanced at Camille, but she kept her eyes fixed on Charles.

"Yes, she has," Ben lied. "I was quite impressed."

Camille delivered him a grateful smile.

"The girls are nearly ready, Matthew," she said eagerly. "I'll go tell them you're ready too, all right?"

Matthew nodded. "Sounds good, Mrs. Bergeron."

"Nice meeting you, Charles," Ben said. "Maybe we'll see you again before you leave."

Charles gave Ben a cool look. "Oh, you will," he said. "Y'all gonna see a lot of me."

The edge of challenge was clear and thick, but Ben chose to ignore it, even as a fierce worry gripped him the second they'd walked up the stairs and disappeared through the apartment door.

Heavy, wet snowflakes fell as Matthew and the sisters walked toward the elementary school, pressing into thick crescents around the toes of their galoshes.

"Your father's pretty loud," Matthew said, walking between them.

"Don't call him our father," Dahlia said, pulling stuck hair off her glossed lips. "His name is Charles. Or Asshole."

"I don't want to talk about him," Josie said, pulling her scarf tighter around her throat. "I just want to forget he's here."

Matthew nodded, sliding his hand under Josie's elbow

when she stumbled on a slick patch of sidewalk. She looked up at him, a grateful smile blooming on her pink cheeks. "You'll dance with me, won't you, Matty?" she asked.

"Of course I will. I'll dance with both of you."

Dahlia exhaled, watching her breath plume. "I don't plan to do much dancing," she said, searching the lines of fellow teens who filed up the front steps of the yellow clapboard building.

Josie smiled, slipping her arm through Matthew's. *Good*, she thought.

Streamers and balloons dangled from one side of the auditorium to the other, Christmas lights blinking shades of green and red and blue across the scuffed wood floor.

They hung their coats along the wall, peeled off their galoshes to reveal their shoes, and tossed them into the pile. It was a good turnout, Dahlia decided, looking around hopefully at the darkened clumps of students who wreathed the dance floor and crowded the two tables of refreshments.

"You look handsome," Josie said, seeing Matthew without his coat and hat for the first time that night.

"Thanks." He smiled distractedly, watching Dahlia make her way toward the punch table. "Do you want something to drink?"

"Sure."

Polly Patrick, the town librarian, and Miles Barker, the town manager, stood together, surveying the students, whispering back and forth. Josie walked by them, keeping her eyes down, knowing Polly had been in Camille's kitchen the month before, waiting on a love potion, Miles Barker's wife coming in the week after. Josie didn't understand love at all.

The musicians gathered on the small stage at the end of the

auditorium, band students in matching yellow sweatshirts. A Billy Joel song rang out, slow at first, then gaining in speed and meshing eventually. Couples took to the dance floor slowly, nervous pairings and a few brave singles shuffling to the erratic beat. Josie watched with envy, looking over the rim of her plastic punch glass. They'd managed to find Dahlia in the crush of students, and Matthew insisted on staying close, even as she made her way around the dance floor, eyes peeled.

"He's not here," she murmured. "Shit."

"Who?" asked Matthew.

"Nobody." Dahlia tossed her empty cup into the trash. "I need to pee."

"Let's dance, Matty," Josie pleaded. "I love this song."

Matthew let Josie lead him out onto the dance floor, settling them between Lawrence White and Olivia Peaco. Matthew moved stiffly, tugging at his tie knot to loosen it, feeling suddenly choked.

Ben heard the knock shortly after eight. Camille stood in the foyer looking distraught. "I'm sorry to bother you."

"It's never a bother." Ben glanced up the stairs. "Where's Charles?"

"That's why I'm here." She sighed. "He went through my brandy—which wasn't much—and then he went into town for more. I insisted on going with him, but he wouldn't hear of it, and that was almost an hour ago. I'm worried."

Ben nodded, knowing that it wasn't Charles's well-being that worried her. In their brief meeting, Ben had gleaned that Charles was not the sort of man who could be trusted unsupervised. Especially not out of his element.

"I'll go look for him," he offered without waiting for her to ask.

"Thank you," Camille said, relieved. "He can get a little . . . carried away."

"I'm sure it will be fine," Ben said, reaching for his coat. But he wasn't sure. Not one bit.

Dahlia was walking toward the water fountain when a pair of hot hands swept over her eyes; then a deep voice said in her ear: "I've been watching you."

Dahlia swatted at the hands, spinning around to see Billy Forester's white smile gleaming at her. He tugged her around the corner and into the supply closet, kicking the door closed behind them. "I've been waiting for you to get here," he mumbled.

"Yeah, I noticed." Dahlia turned her head when he tried to kiss her. "You looked really impatient making out with Tracy just a few minutes ago in the hall."

"What am I supposed to do? She's my girlfriend." He dipped his head to kiss her, spreading lip gloss across her chin, kneading her breasts roughly.

"Easy," Dahlia ordered, slowing his hands. "I'm not a lump of dough."

"No kidding." Billy kissed her again, deeper this time, tasting of chewing tobacco. The pointed collar of his polyester shirt scraped her neck. "I can only stay a sec," he whispered. "Tracy's waiting by the punch. She thinks I'm taking a piss."

Dahlia pulled away, turning to fix her loosened comb, adjust her dress. "Then go."

"I can meet you later, you know. Tracy gets talking to her friends and she barely even notices when I'm gone."

"Don't bother. I'm not staying much longer."

She squeezed past him and pushed out the door, only to

collide with someone waiting on the other side. Looking up, she paled.

"Oh, hey, Jack." Billy arrived behind her, one hand shifting his crotch, the other nudging her out of the way. "Bummer about the game last night, man."

Dahlia stepped to the side, wanting to run but frozen there, wishing she could melt into the wainscoting. She gazed off to the side, as if she were looking for someone, Billy's cocky voice dropping beside her. She heard the word *nothing* and then, "Thanks, man." The short, sweet sealing of a male pact to keep the other's secret, no doubt. She stiffened, pulling out her tube of lip gloss and reapplying it calmly. To hell with both of them, she thought.

"Nice to see you again."

Dahlia looked over. Billy had gone and now only Jack Thurlow stood there, in chinos and a navy sweater over a white collared shirt. She leaned her head back against the wall and gave him a disinterested look to mask her embarrassment, digging her fingernails into the soft wood behind her.

"Run into any difficult ketchup bottles lately?" he asked.

She grinned in spite of herself, biting gently at her lip. "Nope. I think I finally got the hang of it."

"Good for you." Jack looked down the hall, looked back at her. "You don't have to do that, you know."

"Do what?"

He nodded to the closet. "That."

She folded her arms, looking away.

"I'm just saying there are plenty of guys on this island who'd be thrilled to be seen in public with a girl as interesting as you. That's all."

Thrilled. Interesting. Dahlia felt heat flood her skin. "Name one," she said.

Jack smiled knowingly. "I'm just saying I think you deserve better than that. Better than *him*." He turned toward the hall. "Enjoy the dance."

Dahlia watched him walk away, warmth spreading through her, feeling at turns elated and heartbroken. She forced herself back into the auditorium, nearly crashing into Josie on her way.

"Dahl!" Her younger sister was wild-eyed and breathless as she waved her forward. "Dahl, you've gotta come—you won't believe it. Daddy's here!"

"What?"

"He's here and he's on the stage!" Josie cried over her shoulder as they hurried back into the auditorium. "He took the trumpet right out of Corey Rice's hands and now he's demanding the bandleader let him do a solo!"

"Oh, Jesus." Dahlia reached the edge of the room, finding herself behind a small crowd that had gathered to watch the ensuing drama onstage. Josie tried to press through them, but Dahlia tugged her back. "What the hell are you doing?"

"What do you think?" Josie shook off her sister's grip. "We have to stop him. He'll humiliate us!"

"He already has," Dahlia whispered harshly, pulling Josie out of the crowd and toward the door. "Let's just go before he sees us."

"Josephine!"

The name seemed to last a whole minute as it sailed across the room. Josie cringed, frozen in place as if Charles's hand had landed on her shoulder.

"Julep, is that you over there, sugar? Don't be shy, now!"

The auditorium fell quiet as Charles stumbled toward the edge of the stage, squinting into the crowd.

"Josephine, baby, come on up here and help me show these folks how to play some *real* music."

"I have to go," Josie said weakly, already turning back.

Dahlia gripped her arm. "Don't you dare. We're leaving."

"But he'll be furious," Josie said, fighting Dahlia's lead.

"So let him be. Let the cops come and throw his crazy ass in jail and get him the hell away from us."

"Aw, come on now, girls," Charles yelled out again. "Dahlia, I know *you* ain't shy, girl!"

Dahlia felt her cheeks flush, disgraced. Josie began to cry. The other students turned toward them, figuring out their location now. Dahlia swept her gaze across the line of them, determined not to let them see her embarrassment. Then she glimpsed Jack Thurlow standing near the end and her heart sank.

"Where's Matty?" Josie looked around, desperate. "I want to wait for Matty."

"Then wait for him," Dahlia snapped, feeling her own tears threatening to betray her. "I'm not sticking around for this." She marched to the entrance, past the parted rows of wide-eyed students and chaperones, and fumbled through the coats until she found hers, forsaking her galoshes, knowing there wasn't time to rifle through the pile.

As she reached the steps, she saw the Jeep pull up to the curb. Ben climbed out, calling to her. "Get in," he said gently. "I'll be right back."

Dahlia nodded, knowing somehow she didn't need to explain. Barely five minutes later, after she'd taken a seat in the back, she heard the crash of the front doors hitting the side of the school, then a familiar cry booming out into the flurrying night. "Get your fuckin' hands off me!"

Charles appeared at the top of the stairs, Ben beside him, the shadowed figures of Josie and Matthew following. Halfway down the steps, Charles slipped on the snow and Ben reached out to steady him, only to have Charles shake off his help.

Dahlia kept her eyes forward as they reached the Jeep, looking out the window when Charles labored into the front seat, muttering incoherently and slamming the door behind him. Matthew and Josie crawled in beside her. Finally Ben climbed in, turning on the engine and looking up to give the children a reassuring smile in the rearview mirror.

Charles shoved a cigarette into his mouth and struggled to find the lighter on the dashboard. Ben calmly reached over and helped him.

"Thanks," Charles grumbled, the last word that would be uttered in the car as they made the short trip back to the house, driving through a galaxy of snowflakes.

When they arrived, Charles stumbled again on the porch, but this time Ben didn't offer his help. He was already walking ahead with Matthew and the sisters, making sure they got safely inside.

Camille was waiting in the foyer when they came in. She searched her daughters' drawn faces, her heart sinking. She touched them each on the cheek as they marched by, walking up the stairs with weary steps. Ben steered Matthew into the parlor.

"Hi, baby." Charles fell against Camille, nearly toppling her. She winced at the stench of spilled liquor on his coat. "Bottle fell and broke on the goddamned ice," he muttered against her temple. "They wouldn't let me play, baby. Assholes.

Don't know shit about music and they tell me to go home. Fuck 'em all. I say let 'em play their Lawrence Welk shit."

Camille glanced at Ben over Charles's shoulder, her eyes bright with apology. She mouthed, *Thank you*. Ben nodded, but a swell of panic rushed over him as Camille turned to lead Charles toward the stairs.

"Charles," Ben called out. "I keep some Scotch. Maybe you'd like to join me for a glass?"

Charles turned, his arm hanging off Camille's shoulder. He shrugged. "Why not?" He peeled himself off Camille and staggered toward Ben, grinning. "I should warn ya, Haskell. I can drink most men under the table."

"I don't doubt it." Ben looked to Camille. "I'll see him back."

She nodded, but her expression remained fixed with doubt when she turned to go.

Inside the parlor, Ben settled Charles on the couch, barely hearing the drunk man's rantings as he walked into the kitchen for the bottle of Scotch. Matthew waited in the doorway, eyes wide, and watched his father draw down a pair of juice glasses, then an amber bottle.

"Aren't you gonna pour any?" Matthew asked, seeing his father's hands stalled on the counter.

"No need." Ben nodded toward the parlor.

Sure enough, the rantings had stopped, replaced with thick, dragging snores. Ben met his son in the kitchen doorway and both men looked out into the parlor together, seeing Charles's sleeping body twisted along the length of the couch.

Matthew took in a deep breath. "He scares me, Pop."

Ben put a hand on Matthew's shoulder, his eyes fixed on Charles. "Me too, son," he said quietly. "Me too."

———

Josie felt the wet spot from her tears on her pillow when she rolled over.

"What if they want us to leave now?" she whispered into the darkness.

"Who?" Dahlia answered from the other side of the room.

"Ben and Matthew. What if they think we're too much trouble? What if they kick us out? What if that's what Ben's saying to Daddy this very minute?"

"They can't do that."

"Of course they can!"

"Hush," Dahlia ordered sharply, not sure if her impatience was from weariness or her own fear of the same thing. "Just go to sleep."

But neither sister could. And in the living room on the pull-out, Camille tossed and turned in the same awful quiet. She was almost relieved when she heard the door creak open two hours later and Charles's uneven steps cross to the pullout, stumbling as he kicked off his pants. When he climbed in behind her and pulled her to him, she didn't dare make a sound. She just reached out to brace herself against the wall, hoping she might slow the couch from its proclaiming beat.

Sixteen

Little Gale Island
February 1978

By eight o'clock the next day, news of Charles Bergeron's episode at the dance was covering the island like freezing rain, filling the crowded counter of the hardware store and causing shopping carts to stop in the aisles at Larson's Grocery. If Ben sensed the tension, he didn't say a word when he greeted Matthew and the sisters in the foyer on their way to school, but the children had their suspicions.

"Don't worry," Dahlia said firmly as they marched down Ocean Avenue for the ferry landing. "Everything will be fine once we get to school. Nobody cares about what happens on this stupid island over on the mainland."

But it wasn't so. As soon as they stepped into the halls of the high school, it was clear that the span of the bay had done little to keep their secret.

"Everybody's staring," Josie whispered frantically as they walked down the length of the lockers.

"You're imagining it," Matthew said, even as he too could hear the whispers, feel the prying glances. "Just ignore them."

Josh Moody scurried up beside them, his glasses still speckled with sleet. "Hey, is it true?" he asked. "I heard you guys' dad busted up the dance last night!"

"I'm going to the bathroom," Dahlia said, steering them around the corner.

Josie nodded. "Me too."

Matthew followed.

"I'll wait for you two," he said firmly, settling against the tile wall when they arrived at the double doors.

Dahlia frowned at him. "What for?"

But Josie was delighted. "Thanks, Matty."

Stepping into the bathroom, Josie's heart sank to see the notorious trio of Marsha Daley, Peggy Posner, and Tracy Jenkins standing in front of the soap-splattered mirror, brushing their feathered hair and putting on lipstick.

"Just keep walking," Dahlia said low as they moved toward the open stalls. Dahlia's stream came effortlessly, but Josie couldn't manage even a trickle and gave up when she heard Dahlia's flush. They crossed back toward the door, avoiding the sinks.

They were almost out, almost safe, when Marsha's lilting voice called, "I hear your dad was a big hit at the dance last night, Dahlia."

Dahlia stopped. Josie glanced up at her, panicked. "Don't, Dahl."

It was Tracy's turn next. "It's really disgusting not to wash your hands," she said, tracing her lips with cotton-candy pink.

"And their mother doesn't even shave under her arms," announced Peggy. "Lucy Warren's mom saw her in the Laundromat and said so."

Marsha's nose wrinkled as she feathered back her wings. "That's so gross. No wonder that apartment smelled so weird. Here I always thought it was from all that Voodoo stuff, and turns out it was just BO."

Josie tugged Dahlia forward. "Let's just go, Dahl. *Please*."

But Dahlia had waited too long for this confrontation. She left Josie at the door and walked back to the sinks with a level stare.

"Don't let her touch you," Peggy warned, grinning. "She'll put a curse on you."

Tracy Jenkins giggled, but it was a nervous sound. Dahlia snatched the hairbrush from Marsha's hand and calmly yanked out a handful of hair from the bristles.

Marsha gasped. "What are you doing?"

Dahlia held up a fistful of the girl's blond hair with a proud smile. "You can do almost anything with someone's hair," she said, her eyes narrowing. "I'd start buying more zit cream if I were you. *Lots* more."

Tracy and Peggy looked at each other nervously. Marsha cried, "You *bitch*!"

Dahlia just tossed the hairbrush into the sink, then turned and walked out, pulling Josie with her.

Charles managed to bear the cold for nearly three days before he announced he had to return to New Orleans for a while, that he had "business commitments" he had to see to, but that he would return as soon as he could and they should plan to be ready to move back with him when he did.

It was the declaration the sisters had been dreading, but their mother listened with great patience, letting him drain the last of his coffee before she said calmly, "This is our home now, Charles. You're welcome to come back, but I can't uproot the girls again. Not now that they've just settled into a new school."

Dahlia and Josie stood at their bedroom door, waiting for the outburst, but it never came. Perhaps their father saw the change in their mother, the new determination, and perhaps out of New Orleans he felt less powerful, his control over her diminished. Dahlia suspected that in future visits Charles could maintain some degree of ownership of them. That he was smart enough to know that it was the best he was going to get.

"I ain't happy with this—I'll be honest with ya," Charles said when Camille walked him to the door with his suitcase and trumpet. "This ain't your home, Camille. It ain't never gonna be home. These folks here don't understand our kind."

"There are some good people here, Charles," she defended carefully. "You hardly gave them a chance." He snickered, prompting her to add quickly, "And you said yourself, you have *commitments*."

Charles pushed his tongue against his cheek, considering

his options. After a moment, he sighed wearily but his eyes flashed with indignation.

"It's not right, y'all not comin' to see me off," he said sulkily, tugging on his coat.

"We would if we could, Charles. But the girls have to get ready for school, and it's so cold."

"Yeah, yeah." He frowned, still pouting. "Just makin' sure it ain't 'cause y'all embarrassed to be seen with me."

Camille glanced briefly at the girls. "Don't be ridiculous."

There was the rage, Dahlia thought, watching her father narrow his eyes, unconvinced of their loyalty. The anger, raw and cold. She'd known it would come out again eventually.

"Y'all come here, then," Charles demanded, arms spread. "Come give your daddy a hug for the road. We gonna make peace. Come on, now."

The girls walked reluctantly across the room. Dahlia allowed him a brief but stiff embrace, though his arms were tighter around Josie, his hold longer, so long in fact that Camille eased his hands off her younger daughter and handed him a bag packed with biscuits and slices of baked ham for the bus.

Charles reached around and flattened his palm over her buttock, gripping her flesh possessively through her robe. He tipped her face up to his. "You're still my wife, Camille, and you belong to me. That ain't never gonna change. You know that, don't ya?" She nodded, motioning for the girls to depart, which they did at once, disappearing into their room. They remained there, hearts racing, until they heard the closing of the door and the thumping of feet on the stairs; then they rushed to the turret window to make sure that Charles had disappeared down the street.

When they came out, Camille was moving around the living room, neatening the piles Charles had left behind.

Josie walked to the window, carefully parting the curtains to look out. Dahlia stormed across the room and fell onto the sofa, fuming. "This is horseshit. We came all this way to get away from him and you tell him he can come back anytime?"

"Don't you raise your voice at me, young lady," Camille said firmly, her eyes shifting between them. "That isn't at all what I meant."

"Does he know that? What if he gets the idea to move here?" Dahlia said, the mere suggestion draining the color from Josie's face. "What if he comes back for good next time?"

"He won't." Camille picked up an overflowing ashtray and carried it into the kitchen. "He couldn't bear living here. The snow alone would kill him."

But Dahlia wasn't convinced. Glancing at Josie, still at the window, she could see her younger sister wasn't convinced either. Josie began to weep softly. Camille dumped the cigarette butts into the trash and returned to the living room, clapping ash off her hands. She pointed to the table. "Sit down. Both of you."

When they'd taken their seats, Camille joined them, making a chain of their hands around the table.

"Now you listen to me," she said. "No matter how many times he comes here, no matter what trouble he starts, this is our home. Not his. *Ours.* You both understand me?"

The sisters nodded. Camille looked at Josie, her brow arching suggestively. "Josephine."

Josie rose at once, knowing what her mother wanted. She

walked to the kitchen and returned with Camille's box of gris-gris and a pair of white candles.

As soon as she set them down on the table, Dahlia stood up. "Count me out," she said.

Camille snapped her fingers. "You'll keep your seat, Dahlia Rose."

Dahlia sighed, sitting back down.

Camille opened the box, releasing the smoky scent of patchouli into the air. "This is one spell you won't want to miss."

That night Camille carried a dish of bread pudding downstairs, filling the foyer with the sweet steam of warm vanilla and orange zest. She walked into the parlor and found Ben just returned from his woodshop, brushing sawdust off his sleeves.

"For you," she said simply. "For being so understanding."

"You didn't have to do that." He gestured to the kitchen. "Join me for some? I can make coffee."

"I can't. I've got something on the stove." She turned to go, then stopped, her eyes still lowered as she said, "I was so young when I met Charles. I was so afraid of the world, and he wasn't afraid of anything. That abandon was irresistible."

Ben nodded, understanding. Camille smiled.

"I owe him so much, Benjamin. So much of who I am is because of him. My love of music, my beautiful daughters, my passion . . ."

She paused, tears glistening when she looked up at him at last.

"It's a strange thing," she whispered. "To be so grateful to someone, and wish they'd never been born."

Part Three

Add stock

and

bring to a boil.

Seventeen

Little Gale Island

Sunday, June 16, 2002

9:10 a.m.

They took Dahlia's truck to the mainland, the three of them squeezed together in the pickup's front like a trio of teenagers cutting school for a day at the beach, though they couldn't have felt older. The short ride across the bay brought with it many memories for Matthew: sea-sprayed benches that had been blocks of ice in their winter commutes; heavy doors that led to the cabin, where they'd finished homework on their laps; even the coffee, as weak and tasteless as ever. Driving up Commercial Street, they pointed and chuckled, even laughed, to see landmarks of their shared youth. The city had changed and yet Matthew still recognized plenty.

It was only when they reached the hospital and stepped out of the elevator into the ICU that the pleasant flooding of memories finally stopped, the torrent ceasing as abruptly as a faucet turned off.

"Wait here." Matthew moved to the reception desk.

Dahlia glanced down the hall, seeing a police officer reading a magazine. "What's a cop doing here?"

Josie shrugged. "I'm sure it's just routine. Probably to keep out any reporters."

Dahlia clamped a hand over her forehead, suddenly sure she was running a fever, but her skin was cool. She swallowed. "I can't do this, Joze."

"Do what?"

"This." Dahlia swept her arm around the lobby, her expression strained. "Be here. See him in there like that."

"Don't be ridiculous," Josie said firmly. "What's the matter with you?"

"Nothing. I just don't like hospitals, that's all."

"I'll bet Ben doesn't like hospitals much either, you know. God, first Wayne and now you."

"I think I'm going to throw up—"

"Shh. He's coming back."

Josie reached for Dahlia's hand and tugged her forward. They followed Matthew down the corridor and all joined hands in the doorway before stepping into the room.

"Oh, God," Dahlia whispered, seeing Ben at last.

Josie sucked in a pained breath.

"It's okay," Matthew said. "Come on."

He draped his arms around the sisters and steered them gently to the bed. He reached down and touched his father's hand, the skin around the IV almost translucent.

"Pop, it's me. Dahlia and Josie are here too. We're all here, Pop."

"Can he hear us?" Josie whispered.

"He looks so cold," Dahlia said, reaching out to tug Ben's blankets closer to his shoulders.

"He's okay," Matthew said, easing her hands back. "You don't want to move the tubes."

Josie dug through her purse and pulled out a lump of waxed paper.

Dahlia frowned. "What is that?"

"What does it look like?" Josie asked, sniffling as she unpeeled the paper to reveal a glossy praline. She set it on the nightstand. "I read that it's a good idea to stimulate patients with things that are familiar to them. The book said music and reading, but I don't see why the smell of a fresh praline isn't just as good."

Matthew smiled at Josie. "I don't see why not either, JoJo. Thanks."

"We're so sorry we couldn't get here before now, Ben," Josie said, leaning closer. "We wanted to but they wouldn't let us." Josie looked up between Matthew and Dahlia. "I don't want him thinking we just didn't come," she whispered. "Unconscious patients can still hear what you're saying, you know. I read that too."

"He knows, JoJo. Don't worry."

A cell phone chimed. Matthew fumbled in his pocket, his face brightening for a moment when he saw the ID screen. "It's Holly," he said, glancing to the door. "I should really take this."

Dahlia and Josie exchanged a wary look. "Of course," Josie said, forcing an understanding smile. "We'll be here."

Matthew pushed through the waiting room door and walked to the window. "There isn't much to tell. I haven't talked to the doctor yet."

Holly's voice was tight, nervous, on the other end. "I couldn't sleep last night. I had the worst dreams of my life," she said. "I was in this huge house and I was supposed to meet your dad in one of the rooms but I couldn't find my way back to the stairs and . . . God, it's so awful."

"I know."

"How are they holding up?"

Matthew knew she meant the sisters. "As well as can be expected."

"What about you?"

"I'm getting through, I guess. Whatever that means." He glanced up at a TV on the wall, a news channel with the sound turned off. He turned back to the window and watched a man walking his dog across the street. "How's Hoop?"

"He's fine."

"Has he crapped in any of Peter's shoes yet? I've been training him with overpriced Italian loafers. His aim is remarkable."

Holly gave in to a weary laugh. "You don't quit, do you?"

"I never used to." An old woman shuffled into the waiting room, a young woman carrying a baby behind her. "Lately, I don't seem to have a choice."

A heavy silence landed on the line.

"This isn't why I called, Matt. I just wanted to make sure you were okay."

Matthew leaned against the window, the glass cold on his cheek.

"And if I'm not?"

"Matt, I've been thinking about things," she said. "I want us to talk."

It was a brief but palpable promise; he seized it helplessly.

"We're talking right now," he said.

"No, I mean face-to-face. When you get back. When do you think you'll leave?"

"It's hard to say. It'll depend on whether . . ."

"Of course." Holly rescued him. "I'm sorry. I didn't mean it like that."

"I can call Maggie if you can't keep Hooper that long."

"Of course I can. He's our dog, Matt."

Our dog. She might have said her dog too, but she'd hadn't, and the simple word filled him with relief, with stupid hope.

"I miss you, Holl," he said, almost as if she weren't still on the line.

She sighed. "I have to go, Matt. I'm really sorry; it's just that I have this meeting and . . ."

Matthew closed his eyes, confusion swirling through him. The plea sat on his tongue, thick and useless: *Don't hang up, Holly. Please.*

But she did. And after a moment, so did he.

"Hey, Chief!" Danny Chandler set down a pair of pint glasses and leaned his meaty hands on the long slab of varnished oak as Jack approached the bar. "Pour you somethin'?"

Jack smiled, sliding onto a stool. "Much as I'd love to, Dan, I can't."

Shell's Pub was quiet on a Sunday afternoon. Jack glanced around, waved to a few familiar islanders at the end of the bar, watching baseball on a mounted TV.

Danny sighed as he wiped his hand on a bar towel, slung it over one broad shoulder. "What a friggin' mess. Christ, I couldn't believe it when I heard about what happened."

"Is Kip here?" Jack asked.

"Yeah, he's in the back breakin' down boxes. I'll go get him."

The pub owner ambled down to the end of the bar, cupped his hands around his mouth, and shouted toward the back, "Hey, Kip!"

When no answer came, Danny motioned for one of the customers to try. Larry Betts leaned over on his stool and bellowed in the same direction.

Danny returned, shaking his head. "He wears those goddamned things in his ears all the time. It's like livin' with a mime, I swear to Christ."

A few moments later, Kip Chandler came out of the back, wiping sweat from his red cheeks. "Hey, Chief Thurlow."

"Son, tell the chief what you told me," Danny said. "Tell him what Bergeron said to ya."

The young man came around the bar and pulled a Coke from the cooler. "He didn't say much. Mostly asked me about Ben Haskell, wanted to know if he was still around and stuff. I told him I thought so but I wasn't sure."

"Tell him the other thing," Danny said. "The thing about directions."

Jack looked to Kip. "Charles Bergeron asked you for directions?"

"Yeah."

Dread crawled up Jack's back. "Directions to where?"

Kip thought on it a moment, his nose wrinkling; then he said, "Walnut. He wanted to know the quickest way to Walnut."

"You're sure?"

"Yeah. I'm sure."

Jack released an aching breath.

Walnut. Dahlia's street.

The sisters left Matthew at the hospital just before noon with the promise that he would join them for dinner. When they passed the café on their way home, the curtains were still drawn in the tall windows.

"Wayne wants to close the café for a few days," Josie said. "Just until this all blows over."

"What do you think?" said Dahlia.

Josie shrugged. "I don't know. A part of me likes having it to ourselves again. Reminds me of how it was when we first opened. How we all used to go in there, getting it ready, getting excited."

"You were so nervous," said Dahlia.

"I was a wreck," Josie concurred cheerfully. "And I was right to be."

"At first. But it all worked out."

Josie considered her sister's phrasing as Dahlia steered them out of town along the island's southern coastline, where boats dotted the olive green swells just beyond the jagged rise of rocks still slick with the tide's retreat. Had it all worked out? Josie wondered. She wasn't so sure.

"Wayne must still be out on the water," Josie said when Dahlia pulled them into the empty driveway. She turned to her sister, her expression suddenly serious. "Dahl, you didn't mention anything to Matty about us working with the adoption agency, did you?"

"No. Why?"

"Good," Josie said, relieved. "Then let's not bring it up, okay? I just think it would be really insensitive right now, what with Holly leaving him and everything." Josie looked down at her hands in her lap and shrugged. "I'm not even sure it's such a good time for us, anyway. I mean, there's no way our application would be approved when they realize who we are, who *I* am. And besides, if Ben . . . *when* Ben wakes up, Matty's going to need my help taking care of him, and I need to be there."

"Joze, I'm sure Matty'll have to hire a nurse or someone—"

"A nurse?" Josie stared at her sister. "Dahl, how could we let some total stranger take care of Ben as long as we're here?" She looked back to the house, her lips set in a determined line. "No, ma'am," she said firmly. "I wouldn't feel right about that. I'd do it for Momma as much as for Ben."

Dahlia studied Josie's profile, surprised at her sister's insistence, her burst of reasons for preventing the child she'd wanted her whole life.

"Have you talked to Wayne about any of this?"

"I don't see any point in bringing it up just yet," Josie said. "It would only upset him, and I'm sure our application is the farthest thing from his mind right now."

Dahlia wasn't nearly as certain as her sister, but still she said, "Sure, Joze. Whatever you think."

"Thanks." Josie sighed, as if something deeply burdensome had been resolved.

The sisters hugged and Josie climbed out.

"Oh, hey," Josie said, "whatever happened with the Hobart job this weekend?"

Dahlia shrugged. "Nothing. They canceled the party."

"Maybe that's for the best." Josie grinned. "See you back here for dinner? I'm making étouffée."

"Show-off," Dahlia yelled as she shifted into reverse and pulled back out onto the street. She was all the way down the block before she saw the reflection of the cruiser's lights in her rearview mirror and her breath caught in her throat.

Jack.

Eighteen

Little Gale Island

August 1978

$It\ was\ Ben's$ idea to open the café.

The inspiration came to him one afternoon in late summer when he watched Camille deliver a tub of pralines to the AMVETS hall for their end-of-season bake sale. He made his suggestion official at dinner that night and the whole table darted forward enthusiastically.

Everyone except for Camille.

"Oh, no," she said. "I've already tried selling my wares on this island, and you remember what a complete failure that was."

"Now, that was different," insisted Ben.

"How was it different?" Camille asked.

"You know how," Ben said gently. "People here don't understand Voodoo. But food is different. There's no scandal in eating a bowl of gumbo. Besides, you already sell giant tubs of it."

"At school fairs," she argued. "That's hardly a business."

"But it could be."

"He's right, Momma," said Josie. "You know he is."

Camille waved her napkin, flustered. "Oh, come on, now. I
don't know the first thing about running a restaurant, Benjamin."

"So what?" Ben said. "I'll help you."

Camille laughed loudly. "You don't know the first thing
either!"

"No," he admitted sheepishly. "So we'll learn together."

"How? You already have a job."

It was kind of her, but they both knew his work as an island
handyman was hardly steady employment.

"Come on, Camille," he said. "We'd make great partners;
you know we would."

"Oh, yes!" said Josie. "Can we, Momma, please?"

Camille had to admit her heart raced at the idea. And she
was so tired of the Laundromat, waking up with sore bones
and aching feet. Not that running a restaurant was any easier.
But at least she'd be doing something she loved.

But . . . *partners*. Camille studied Ben's face, letting the
strange word wash over her. She had no idea what it meant to
have a partner. Someone to help, to support, to cheer. She
realized, almost blushing when she did, that Ben *had* been her
partner, nearly from the day she'd stepped into his house.
Surely more of a partner than she had ever known in Charles,
and she and Ben didn't even share a bed, though the thought
had crossed her mind more times than she dared to admit.

Still, to hear the word *partner* sent a curious shiver curling down her back. It had been almost eight months since Charles's disastrous visit, and in his continued absence she'd grown fond of her independence. Even in business, Camille suspected a man could be as controlling as he might be in the bedroom. Maybe even a kind man like Benjamin Haskell could reveal ugly tendencies in the unpredictable moments of stress. . . .

Camille studied him while he served Josie another spoonful of rice. No, she decided. Benjamin wasn't like most men. She could search for days to see a glimmer of reckless anger in his soft brown eyes, but she'd never find it.

Still, one thing was certain: If Ben was serious about this café business, he'd have to learn to make a proper gumbo.

Their first class was conducted in Camille's kitchen on a damp September afternoon.

"The hardest part is the roux," she said, standing beside Ben at the stove.

"The what?" Matthew asked, leaning over his father's shoulder.

"The roux," Camille said again, whisking the mixture of butter and flour in a cast-iron pot. "The base of the gumbo. What helps give the gumbo its rich flavor. We Creoles like our roux lighter than the Cajuns do, but it really depends on the dish. Roux can be really light—*blond*, they call it—or as dark as bittersweet chocolate. The darkest are the hardest to make, but every roux requires the cook's undivided attention. They cook quickly and are easily ruined."

"Like love," Josie chimed in from her post on the other side of her mother. "That's what Momma's friend Miss Willa used to say. That a roux was a lot like love. Isn't that right, Momma?"

Camille glanced to Ben, blushing slightly. "Never mind all that, Josephine," she said, biting back a smile. "All I know is that chatty cooks make for a burned roux."

Josephine nodded dutifully. "Yes, ma'am." She leaned toward Matthew and whispered, "I got my roux perfect the first time. Momma said even *she* didn't get it right her first time."

"What about you, Dahlia?" asked Matthew, suspecting he already knew what her answer would be.

Dahlia sat behind them at the table, doodling on her notebook, her stack of schoolbooks beside her untouched. "What about me?"

"Dahlia hates to cook," said Josie, as if Matthew were asking to find a suitable wife. "She hasn't the patience for cooking, or the imagination. Momma said so."

"She did not," said Dahlia.

"No, I certainly did not, Josephine," Camille agreed. "I said Dahlia's talents lay elsewhere. It's not anyone who can grow roses with blossoms that big," Camille said, nodding to the pair of overflowing pots on the windowsill. Camille winked at Dahlia; Dahlia smiled. "Now pay attention, gentlemen."

When the roux was the color of peanut butter, Camille pointed to the counter and said, "Hand me that blue bowl, please, Josephine."

Josie did, and Camille poured the contents into her pot, a mix of finely chopped vegetables.

"We call this the holy trinity in New Orleans cooking," she explained, blending the diced pieces into the roux. "Equal parts onion, celery, and bell pepper. Next we add the stock. This is where the real flavor comes in."

She gestured to the pot on the rear burner, the source of the heady scent that had been filling the house while it had simmered all morning, a blend of shrimp shells, lemon slices, parsley, thyme, and bay leaves.

"Strain that, will you please, Benjamin?"

Ben's turn to play sous-chef; he returned to her side a few moments later with the strained liquid and poured it slowly into the pot while she stirred, letting the mixture grow hot.

"So who taught you to make this?" asked Matthew.

"My momma," Camille said. "But everybody's got their own gumbo recipe. You ask a dozen New Orleanians how to make gumbo and you'll get a dozen different recipes." She pointed back to the pot. "Now we add the garlic, chopped tomatoes, and seasonings. Matthew."

At Camille's direction, Matthew selected a variety of herbs, which she sprinkled over the mixture: thyme, basil, oregano, and bay leaves.

She pointed to the counter with her free hand. "The chopped okra, please, Benjamin."

Ben delivered her the bowl and watched as she folded the green coins into the stew.

"Smells good, doesn't it?" asked Josie, watching Matthew closing in.

Camille turned down the flame. "Now we let this simmer for a while, so the okra has a chance to break down and thicken the gumbo."

"So when do we add the shrimp?" asked Matthew.

"At the very end," said Camille. "You don't want to overcook them."

Ben leaned in for a whiff. Camille smiled at him, their shoulders touching.

"And there you have it," she said, setting the lid on her pot. "Gumbo." She wiped her hands on the skirt of her apron.

"Tomorrow we'll work on étouffée and pralines. You can't call yourself a partner in a Creole café and not know how to make a praline, Benjamin Haskell."

Ben nodded, smiled. "No, I suppose I can't."

While Dahlia scrawled on the edge of her notebook and Josie scooped handfuls of onion skins and celery ends into the trash, Matthew watched his father and Camille at the stove, transfixed by the unspoken affection that passed between them in the sweet-smelling room. Most of all he watched his father's spreading smile, Ben's eyes glossy with a determined devotion that Matthew made up his mind in that instant to inherit, whether he realized it or not.

A week later, Ben leased the empty storefront three blocks down from the police station where Harry Martin's diner had lived for almost twenty years, getting nearly all of the fixtures and appliances and even the old man's jukebox in the deal. He and Matthew and Camille and the girls spent a blissfully mild weekend in early October coloring the exposed brick walls violet and mustard and painting fat-blossomed flowers on the floor. Camille took it upon herself to fill the jukebox with only jazz and blues, even as the girls pleaded for their favorite Fleetwood Mac and Carly Simon songs.

A few hours before opening on a crisp and bright Saturday morning, Ben hauled the ladder out onto the sidewalk and hung the sign he'd made in his woodshop above the door.

The Little Gale Gumbo Café was officially open for business.

No one came.

The five of them wandered through the café all morning,

busying themselves with small chores, glancing up every time someone passed by the tall front window only to slow, peer in, and keep walking. When ten o'clock arrived and still no one had come in, Ben assured them that the lunch rush was imminent, but as the minutes ticked away on the clock above the counter, it seemed their great plan might be a miserable failure.

"This place sucks," declared Dahlia, falling into a chair. "These people wouldn't know good food if it came up and bit them on the ass."

"Dahlia," Camille said gently, neatening a plate of pralines for the tenth time that hour.

"I can't believe it," Josie wailed. "After we've worked so hard!"

"Oh, come on, everybody," said Ben, patting Matthew on the back. "Cheer up. It's early."

But it wasn't. The clock read three ten. They'd be closing in less than an hour. Then, just when they began to ferry plates of pralines and pots of gumbo back to the kitchen, the front door opened and in spilled half a dozen high school boys in sweatpants and sweatshirts, red cheeked and sweaty. Dahlia, Josie, and Matthew recognized them all, but it was the dark-haired one in front with the basketball wedged under his arm who captured Dahlia's attention.

Ben came around the counter, smiling. "Hi, Jack."

"Hi, Mr. Haskell," Jack Thurlow said to Ben, even as his eyes searched the restaurant. "We just finished a pickup game and we're starved." When Jack found Dahlia behind the counter, his gaze settled. He waved. She waved back, her stomach dropping. She'd heard that he and Janet Miller had broken up that summer, and the news had thrilled her.

At the other end of the counter, Josie made kissing faces behind her tented hands. Dahlia flicked ice water at her.

"You boys are just in time." Ben steered the posse toward the largest table and handed out menus. "We're having an opening-day special—buy one entrée, get five free."

The team chuckled, taking their seats. "I'll be there in a sec, guys," Jack said, turning to Dahlia. When she saw he meant to approach her, her hand rushed to her hair, a desperate attempt to tame the curls she had given up on hours earlier. She tugged on her apron, hoping the sweat stains under her armpits hadn't spread too badly.

Jack arrived at the counter.

"Hi."

"Hi."

He gestured to the clock on the wall. "Looks like we just made it."

"Looks like y'all did," she said, checking too, even though she knew exactly what time it was. "Good thing, too. Otherwise my sister and I would've had to eat three pots of gumbo each. Not to mention four pies."

Jack chuckled. "Four, huh?"

"Four." Dahlia grinned. "And don't even get me started on the tubs of shrimp Creole."

Matthew came out of the kitchen, his eyes fixing on the new arrivals. Seeing Jack, he moved at once to the counter.

"Hey, Matt," Jack said.

Matthew nodded, glancing pointedly at Dahlia. "Hey, Jack."

"It looks great in here," Jack said, glancing around. "I've been watching you guys get the place ready." His eyes wandered back to Dahlia and stayed there. "I've been looking forward to coming in."

Matthew looked between them. "Your mom needs help in the kitchen," he said.

Dahlia gave him a dubious stare.

"I'll go," offered Josie, slipping behind Dahlia and disappearing into the kitchen.

"Matthew," Ben called from the table, "let's get these boys some food, son."

Matthew marched out to the floor. Dahlia and Jack shared a nervous smile.

"Here." He withdrew a small package from his pocket and held it out to her. "It's for your mother. Sort of a congratulations gift. Handmade soap from my mom. She said your mother was always really helpful to her at the Laundromat."

"Thanks." Dahlia took the package. "Does your mom like pralines?"

"I'm not sure. What did you call them—praw-what?"

"Pralines."

"Pralines," he repeated, smiling. "Got it."

"Stay here," she ordered. "I'll be right back."

Dahlia could feel Jack's eyes on her as she walked down the counter and fumbled to slide a half dozen pralines into a paper bag, cursing helplessly when she dropped two, catching them in her apron. When she came back with the folded brown bag, Jack pulled out his wallet, but Dahlia wouldn't hear of it.

"Then I guess I'll just have to come back," he said.

She smiled. "I guess you will."

For the next hour, the six young men inhaled bowls of gumbo and emptied baskets of crusty bread, ending their meals with fat slices of pecan pie topped with whipped cream before they tried to pay their bill, which Ben refused to give them.

They left at four fifteen, full and tired, promising to be back with their parents, their sisters, their brothers, and everyone else they knew.

Nineteen

Little Gale Island
Fall 1978

The basketball team made more than good on their vow. As quickly as gossip had spread about Camille's arrival, so did the news of her luscious food. Suddenly islanders who had once crossed the street to avoid her were now lining up at the café's counter for a steaming bowl of her signature stew.

Camille herself could hardly believe how quickly her business grew. Within weeks, she was serving nearly seventy bowls of gumbo a day, and selling pralines faster than she and Josie could make them.

It didn't hurt, of course, that it was Ben who greeted the

customers and Ben who served them their meals. But sometimes, for fun, Camille would slip out from the kitchen just to
watch customers take those first spoonfuls, their eyes closing,
their cheeks and necks flushing, their fingers tensing around
their spoon handles, and then the sounds, the rhythmic groans
of rapture that came from their throats, so similar to another
primal release that a person passing by might have looked
twice at the sign above the door.

Just as he'd promised, Jack Thurlow returned to the café
on a windy Saturday morning in November, when Louis
Armstrong played on the jukebox and the restaurant was so
full that the only free seat he could find was at Alma Cooley's
corner table. The town manager's secretary looked up from
her gumbo, her spoon suspended in disbelief.

"Good morning, Mrs. Cooley," Jack said cheerfully, sitting
down. "Don't mind me. This'll only take a second."

"Hi."

Jack looked up to find Dahlia had arrived. She looked
quizzically between him and the older woman. "Mrs. Cooley,"
Dahlia teased. "You didn't tell me you were waiting for your
date. He's very handsome."

"Oh, for goodness' sake," Alma Cooley huffed. "Just get on
with it, Jack Thurlow. My soup's getting cold."

"Yes, ma'am." Jack grinned and Dahlia's face bloomed into
a wide smile, her heart racing. "I was wondering if you'd like
to go out with me next Friday night?"

"Yes," she said, without hesitation.

"Great." Jack rose, driving his hands into his pockets.
"Then I'll pick you up at six."

"Wait." Dahlia fumbled for a pen. "Let me write down my address—"

"That's okay. I know where you live."

Dahlia stilled, smiled. Jack smiled back.

Behind them, Donald Wylie held out his empty coffee cup, clearing his throat to get Dahlia's attention for a refill. In her elation, Dahlia turned and walked right by him. Jack smiled politely at the older man, then turned to Alma. "Have a great day, Mrs. Cooley," he said, then wove back through the café and out into the brisk morning, smiling proudly. He knew the nearby customers had been watching, listening in expectantly.

Jack was counting on it. He'd wanted to take Dahlia Bergeron out on a date for a very long time, and he wanted the good news of her acceptance to travel as fast and as far as possible.

That evening, spread out in the window booth, as had become their routine every Saturday night after the last of the customers had gone home, the two families made dinner out of the day's remainders, but Dahlia barely touched her food. Matthew had noticed her dreamy expression all afternoon, but only when Dahlia passed him the salt when he'd asked for the rice did he finally demand, "What's with you?"

"Oh," Dahlia said, correcting her error. "Nothing."

But Josie was bursting with the news. "Jack Thurlow's what's with her. He asked her out."

"Jack Thurlow?" Matthew repeated.

"You know Jack," Ben said to Camille, buttering a cold biscuit. "Irene's son. The basketball player who brought in his friends our first day. He's in Matthew's class."

"He's so handsome," added Josie breathlessly. "And he's really nice. Tell them, Matty. Isn't Jack Thurlow a supernice guy?"

Matthew reached for the hot sauce, stalling. But he couldn't deny it was the truth. And maybe that was the problem. He hadn't ever had to worry about the jerks who showed interest in Dahlia. They never stuck around, but Jack Thurlow . . . A girl could really fall for a guy like that, a decent guy . . .

Dahlia may not have watched the expression change on Matthew's face as they continued with their meal, but Josie did, and her heart ached to see how his brow twisted, his jaw fixing with a hurt he hadn't expected, and truly disliked.

Friday night came too quickly for Matthew and not soon enough for Dahlia. All week she had planned what she would wear (her off-the-shoulder peasant dress), how she'd fix her hair (swept up with a comb on one side), where she'd spray the tiny sample of Shalimar she'd sneaked from Porteous last spring (behind her ears and along her wrists), but when the evening finally came, a thunderstorm came with it, bringing sheets of rain and winds so strong that branches that usually hung far from the Queen Anne's tall windows were brushing against the glass, screeching like a flock of angry gulls.

"Fuck you!" Dahlia shouted at her bedroom window, her pinned hair sagging over one cheek, her peasant dress crooked around her shoulders. Josie watched her sister rage around their room, hurling shoes and bracelets in her disappointment, but it was hard to tell which sister was more crushed. When the limb snapped off the great maple in the front of the house, it dangled helplessly for a few seconds before it crashed onto the porch roof like a cat too fat to turn itself over in time. The aging shingles tore like newspaper under the weight, sending a shriek and a shudder through the whole house. When it had subsided, the sisters looked at each other, then charged out of the apartment and down the stairs, yelling as they ran.

Camille was already in the foyer. The front door was open, a cold spray blowing in as Ben and Matthew studied the damage. The branch had rolled off but not before leaving a noticeable gash in the roof. A ribbon of rainwater came down on the porch floor as if poured from a pitcher. Josie shivered. Camille pulled her close. Dahlia dropped onto the stairs, burying her face in her hands. When she looked up, Matthew was standing over her, looking so calm and relieved she could have kicked him in the shins. When he offered to help her up, Dahlia glared at him as if he were to blame for this, when she knew it wasn't possible.

But Josie knew it was. She knew for a fact that storms this vicious didn't come around without reason, and a heavy sorrow sank in her stomach. It was Matthew's doing. There was no other explanation. Matthew's love for Dahlia was so strong that the sky had dumped out its very worst to keep Jack Thurlow from coming between them.

Camille must have thought so too, because she looked especially worried, Josie thought, her mother's hazel eyes fluttering nervously.

When Dahlia ran back upstairs and slammed the apartment door, Josie said softly, "I knew I should have dressed another love candle, Momma."

Camille pulled her daughter tighter. "There's no need for it."

"But the storm . . ."

"Hush." Camille smiled, gently brushing her daughter's

long red hair behind her ears. "Don't you worry about your sister and this young man. I'm not."

Josie glanced over and saw Matthew at the window, his eyes fixed on the street. She swore she saw him flinch, as if he had heard Camille's decree and the very thought had briefly stopped his heart.

When Josie heard Jack's voice a few seconds later, sailing in on a gust of rough, chilled air, she exhaled as if it had been hours since her last breath.

While the women fixed food in the kitchen, Ben, Matthew, and Jack worked together to secure a tarp across the hole in the roof. They returned nearly thirty minutes later, drenched. Jack had come over in a tie and his nicest chinos. Now his shirt was soaked through, his tie loosened. Camille looked at Josie and nodded toward the stairs. "Go get the men some towels, Josephine." Josie leaped to her feet, dashing up the stairs two at a time. "And take one of Matthew's clean shirts from the pile on the dresser!"

The suggestion implied an intimacy that Jack chose to ignore. He'd heard the rumors of their communal living, but he didn't care what people said. Standing in that kitchen, Jack knew he was in the presence of a true family.

He smiled apologetically at Dahlia. "I looked better an hour ago," he admitted, running a hand through his wet hair.

Dahlia couldn't imagine how that was possible.

"Best-dressed handyman I've ever seen," said Ben, patting both young men on the shoulder. "You're a lifesaver, Jack. We couldn't have done it without you."

Matthew smiled in agreement; he had to. He hadn't been glad to see Jack arrive, even less so to have his broad-shouldered, smiling face on the roof with him, but as the chore had lingered and the rain had slowed, he'd had to admit that Jack wasn't playing at being nice. He wasn't up on the roof, sopping and filthy, just to impress Dahlia. Jack Thurlow genuinely wanted to help. It was going to be hard to hate him if he kept this up.

"We should be fine if another front comes through," Ben said. "Tomorrow morning, first light, I'll get up there and see what's what."

"Please sit, gentlemen," Camille implored, drawing two chairs out from the table. "I've made coffee with brandy to warm you up."

"Camille!" Ben scolded gently.

"What?" Camille bit back a mischievous smile. "It's only a pinch."

Josie returned with a stack of towels and a new shirt. "You can change in the bathroom, Jack," Camille said, pointing to the hall. "It's down at the end. Dahlia can show you."

Dahlia rose quickly and Jack followed her out of the kitchen. They took the corridor slowly, savoring their first chance to be alone, trying to walk side by side even though the hall was much too narrow. They bumped against each other, apologizing foolishly. Jack smelled of cool, soft dirt. Dahlia wanted to comb his wet hair with her fingers, pull at the places where his shirt stuck to his body.

At the bathroom door, Dahlia pressed herself against the wall, her heart racing. Jack glanced down the corridor, just to be sure they were still alone. "I wanted to take you to dinner. Someone waiting on you for a change."

Dahlia reached out and touched the wet edge of his cuff.

"Momma says I'm the worst waitress she's ever seen. Josie said she heard a few customers complaining just the other day."

Jack watched her thumb trace his button, feeling his groin ache when her fingertips grazed the inside of his wrist. "Tell me their names. I'll straighten them out right now."

Dahlia smiled, flushed. When he wouldn't move into the bathroom, she gave him a gentle push. "You should change before you start to mold."

After a lively meal around Camille's table, Jack and Dahlia sneaked out to the porch and sat close on a bleached wicker couch. They sat without talking, listening to the soft spattering of rain overhead, their bodies settling against each other in the cool damp. All around them, blown leaves lay pasted to the floorboards, glistening under the porch light.

"Looks like it's finally letting up," Jack said.

Dahlia toyed with the hem of her dress. "Bet you wish you'd stayed home, huh?"

He smiled. "Not at all. I loved hearing those stories about New Orleans. All the different places you lived, those people you knew. It must have been a pretty exciting place to grow up." He peeled a stray leaf off the side of the bench, turned it over in his palm. "Maine must seem like a graveyard after that."

Dahlia watched the absent way he rubbed his thumb over the wet leaf, her skin warming. "Sometimes," she said.

Behind them, Camille closed the parlor curtains.

"Momma likes you," Dahlia said. "But then, I have a feeling everybody likes you, Jack Thurlow."

"I'm not interested in everybody," he said, glancing at her.

Dahlia looked out at the night. "You don't have to do that."

"Do what?"

"Pretend you want something serious with me."

"Is that what you think I'm doing? Pretending?"

"I think it doesn't work this way."

"What way?"

"You know," she said. "Team captains are supposed to go out with cheerleaders and prom queens."

"Says who?"

Dahlia shrugged. "It's a law of the universe."

"Ah." Jack nodded authoritatively. "One of those. Just like you're not supposed to go swimming after you eat, right?"

She grinned helplessly. "I didn't know about that one."

"You didn't?" He grinned too. "Oh, yeah, that's a big one."

She reached over to take the leaf from his fingers. He caught her pinkie with his thumb, trapping her briefly. The leaf curled over his knuckle.

They sat awhile without talking, hearing the faint sounds from inside the house: dishes clearing, voices and footsteps nearing and disappearing. It all seemed gloriously distant.

Dahlia laid her head back on the rounded edge of the seat. "Why do they do that?" she asked.

"Do what?"

"Paint the underneath of porches blue."

"I think it's supposed to look like the sky," Jack said, watching her. "So it'll seem like the days last longer." His expression turned wistful. "That's what my dad used to say, anyway."

Dahlia looked over at him. "Ben told me about him," she said. "I'm sorry."

"Yeah, me too." He turned to Dahlia. "You would have liked my dad. He was like you. He could grow anything. I swear he could pick up an old peach pit off the ground and we'd have big, fat peaches growing in our yard the next summer."

"God, I'm not *that* good," she said.

"You must be," he said, nodding toward the house. "Your mom showed me your roses in the kitchen. She said you practically brought them back from the dead. They're beautiful."

She shrugged. "It's not that hard."

"Says you. I'm sure that took a heck of a lot of patience." Dahlia chuckled.

"What's so funny?" he said.

"Just that if you knew me, you'd know the one thing I don't have is patience."

"I'd like to know you," he said firmly, reaching for her hand. "I'd like to see you again."

Dahlia let him capture her fingers in his. "If you want to."

She felt her skin flush hot, her moment of steely indifference as fleeting as a hiccup.

"Yes," she said, then one more time, suddenly afraid he might not understand how much she wanted it, "Yes."

Upstairs, Matthew rolled around on his mattress, wishing the wind would stir again so that he couldn't hear Dahlia's and Jack's voices floating through his window. When he heard the door creak open, he assumed it was Ben coming in to say good night, but when he squinted into the sliver of light and saw Josie's silhouette there, the hall light ballooning out the skirt of her nightgown, he sat up, confused. She came toward him without a word, and when she stepped into the light of his window, there was just enough reflection to reveal her cautious expression.

"Don't say I have to go back to my room," she whispered, sliding in behind him before he could refuse. "We don't have to talk if you're tired. We can just sleep. I don't mind."

Matthew lay down on his back, slowly, not sure whether he should even look at her. They'd lain side by side a hundred times in the grass, on the beach, their toes and elbows touching without their thinking anything about it, but this . . . this was different.

Or maybe Josie didn't think so.

When she slipped her arm over his stomach and lifted it carefully up to his chest, Matthew froze. "JoJo . . ."

"Just for a little while," she said, her voice quavering as if she might cry at any second. "In case there's another storm. I can't bear the thunder. And Dahlia's still not back."

He lay there, unmoving, saying nothing, and eventually he felt her body soften against his, her breathing quieting to the easy rhythm of sleep. When her hair brushed his cheek and he took a whiff of her apple shampoo, he clasped his hand over hers, and even though he wasn't sure he would be able to fall asleep with her there, he did.

He slept deeply, waking a short time later. It was a long moment before he realized that Josie had already returned to her own bed, the thick scent of licorice left on his pillow.

"*Jack Thurlow likes you.*"

Dahlia turned at the sound of her sister's small voice in the darkness. She'd been sure everyone was asleep when she'd crept back into the apartment.

"Shh," Dahlia whispered. "It's almost midnight."

Josie sat up. "He kept looking at you all through dinner. I mean really looking at you. Didn't you about die when he pulled your chair out for you? Matty's never done that. I can't believe they're the same age. Can you? Jack seems so much older."

"Go to sleep, will you?"

"Momma's worried you're gonna mess it up with him."

"When did she say that?"

"She didn't," Josie admitted. "But I saw her dressing a love candle for you just before I came to bed."

"Oh, Jesus." Dahlia unsnapped her necklace and dropped it on the dresser. "It was one date, y'all."

"Did he ask you out again?"

When Dahlia didn't answer, Josie frowned.

"Well, did he?"

Dahlia smiled helplessly, glad for the darkness to hide her delight. "Yeah. He did."

Josie said nothing, just lay down and sighed, relief and joy traveling all the way to her toes.

When Camille was certain that the house slept deeply, she slipped out from under her blanket, pulled on her scarlet kimono, and stepped carefully out of the apartment. For several weeks now she had been learning the home's bones, discovering which floorboards squeaked, and which stair treads groaned. But all of her careful study was for naught: The moment she reached the door to Ben's room and pressed it open, it let go a yawning creak that nearly propelled her under his bed.

"They'll know now," she whispered, feeling Ben's hand close around hers in the near darkness.

"No, they won't," he assured her, pulling her into his room and carefully closing the door behind them, knowing the perfect speed to keep the hinges quiet. He switched on the light atop his dresser, casting the sparse room in a soft glow. Camille looked around at the tidy bed, the bare floors, the tall dresser with a curious collection of pencils, drill bits, and change. She had an urge to slide out one of those drawers, to see inside.

When Ben reached up to spread apart the neck of her silk robe, he had to stop, his fingers were shaking so badly. He blew out a ragged breath, lowering his hands. "I can't believe how nervous I am," he said.

Camille smiled, lifting his hands once again and settling them above her breasts.

"Are *you*?" he asked.

"Of course," she said, her own skin prickling with anticipation.

"Silly, isn't it?" he said, his mouth dry as her bare flesh began to be revealed, the cappuccino-colored skin so smooth, the faint smell of rosewater rising as the fabric fell away. When he closed his wide palms over her bare breasts, they both exhaled.

"Everything was firmer once," Camille confessed when Ben carried her to the bed and laid her down.

"Me too," he said, lowering himself beside her. They took their time—after all, they had waited a year; what was another few minutes when there was so much to explore, to touch, to taste? When Ben finally eased himself down on top of her, Camille shifted beneath him, settling him inside of her, watching the familiar lines of his face deepen, the rough skin of his jaw flush with each thrust. She could feel her own skin reddening too, the forgotten splotches of heat that always appeared below her neck when she made love.

After several minutes, Ben slowed. "I have trouble," he admitted quietly. "Sometimes I just can't—"

"Shh . . ." Camille pressed her fingers against his lips. When he tried to withdraw, she wrapped her legs around him, keeping him inside of her.

"I never could have imagined," Ben whispered. "I thought this part of my life was over. And then you came here. . . ."

Camille didn't know how it was possible. Her falling so deeply in love, and she'd never even dressed a candle for him.

Twenty

Little Gale Island
Spring 1979

When the fly appeared in the café kitchen on a soft May morning, Camille was too busy stirring praline syrup and chopping piles of okra and onion to see it. If she had noticed the insect, she would have been warned that Charles was on his way back to the island; a lingering fly always signaled the arrival of an unwanted guest.

So when Charles stepped off the ferry that same afternoon, swinging his precious trumpet case and greeting strangers with a confident grin as he climbed Ocean Avenue to Main Street, Camille was far from prepared.

When the knock came on the apartment door, Camille was

folding laundry in the living room. She was sure it was Ben, couldn't conceive of anyone else being on the other side of the door, so when she found Charles standing there, she had to grip the knob to keep from falling over.

He spread his arms. "The new me, darlin'. What do ya think?"

Camille hardly recognized him. He wore an ivory suit under a long wool coat, leather gloves, and polished shoes. His hair was combed flat, his jaw clean-shaven.

"Charles," was all she could manage, though he wouldn't have waited for more.

"Told ya I'd be back."

He tossed his belongings into the apartment and swept her up, spinning her around as he steered her toward the couch, his linen shirt sticky with sweat under her splayed hands.

"You should have called," Camille said, breathless as he dragged them both down to the couch, nuzzling her neck as she tried to gather her wits. A prickling fear flooded her. She searched the room over his shoulder, seeking evidence of her new lover, pieces of her guilt. Just that morning, Ben had slipped from the pullout at five, making sure to be back in his own bed when Matthew rose at five thirty. Camille felt sure the flush of their dawn lovemaking was still evident on her skin, the cushions still hot beneath Charles's seat.

"Where the girls at?" he demanded, pulling off his coat and gloves, tossing them easily onto the love seat.

"School."

"School, huh?" Charles tugged at his collar, plucking buttons from their holes.

"You must be thirsty," she said, seeing her chance to flee. "I don't have much in the house."

"You're lookin' at a new man, Camille," he announced

proudly, lifting his chin. "Don't touch the hard stuff anymore. Haven't had a drop for almost a month now."

"A month?" It was unimaginable to her.

He rubbed her thigh through her caftan. "I'd love me a tall glass of sweet tea, though." Camille nodded dully, rising and making her way into the kitchen. "And some beans and rice, or jambalaya or somethin'," he said, tugging out his cigarettes and snapping open his lighter. "I'm starved. Jesus, I forgot how god-awful the food is up here."

Camille's hands shook as she drew the pitcher from the fridge, then set the pot of red beans on the stovetop. From the kitchen, she watched him, dumbfounded, sure there had been some mistake, that the real Charles Bergeron would appear at any moment, bursting out of his clothes like a dancing girl from a cake.

"You look pale, baby," he observed coolly, squinting through the smoke of his cigarette when Camille came out with his food and tea, setting them down carefully in front of him. "You feelin' okay?"

"I'm fine," she managed. "It's just . . . we hadn't heard from you in a while."

He rested his smoke on the edge of the tray, scooped up a wedge of bread, and chewed it. "I know," he said, "and I'm sorry for that. But I had to get some business squared away. Certain things straightened out."

Business. Her stomach lurched at the word. She knew there was only one kind of *business* that would allow a man like Charles to afford expensive clothes.

She glanced nervously at the clock on the table. Four ten. The girls would be home soon. And Ben was to come by to fix the light in the bathroom.

She swallowed, clearing his plate the instant he'd scooped up the last spoonful of beans.

"How long are you here for this time?" she asked, fleeing to the kitchen again.

"Well, now, that's just it." Charles reached back and draped both arms across the back of the couch, stretching out his legs. "I decided if y'all won't come home, then I was gonna bring home to y'all."

"Wha . . . what do you mean?"

Charles reached into his coat pocket and produced his wallet, parting the billfold so that she could see the thick fan of bills. "It's just for starters." He tossed it onto the coffee table. "Business been so good lately I was thinkin' I might take a little break. I think I'm gonna buy me a lobster boat and start pullin' up some of them ugly sons a bitches myself."

"Charles . . ." Camille came back into the living room and gave him an even look, trying to keep the panic from her voice. "Charles, you can't be serious. You don't just *become* a lobsterman. There are licenses, and the weather here can freeze, and you don't know the first thing about trapping lobsters or owning a boat."

"Well, shit, Camille." He snorted, lighting a new cigarette. "Bergerons been shrimpin' the gulf for generations. Pullin' shit out the water is in my blood."

"That may be," she said, the panic now creeping into her tight voice, "but catching shrimp and trapping lobster are very different things."

"Oh, come on now, darlin'." Charles grinned at her, his expression utterly carefree. "I told ya. You're lookin' at a new man. I been livin' wrong for too long now, but I got things straight in my head. We gonna be a family again. I swear to you, Camille."

She managed a weak smile, even as her heart sank, as deep and heavy as a lobster trap into the bay.

"A lobsterman? Is he out of his goddamned mind?"

Dahlia paced in front of the window while Camille explained Charles's plan to them that night. Josie sat on the love seat, bent at the waist, as if she were warding off nausea.

"What about Ben?" Dahlia said. "Have you told him about you and Ben?"

"Of course not," Camille said. "And I don't want either of you saying a word; do you understand?"

Josie nodded obediently. Dahlia flopped beside her on the love seat. "He'll drown. He'll fall overboard within a day."

Josie gnawed on her thumbnail, wincing when she drew blood.

"Where is he, anyway?" Dahlia asked, looking around.

"At the grocery," Camille said. "He insisted on buying steaks for dinner."

Dahlia stood up. "Well, I can't stay," she announced. "I have plans."

Josie looked up, panicked. "You're leaving us?"

"I am if I want to catch Jack on his way over here." Dahlia crossed to the bedroom. Josie followed.

"At least wait until Daddy comes back," Josie pleaded, closing the bedroom door behind them. "At least say hi."

"If I say anything, it won't be hi." Dahlia walked to their dresser and snapped on the radio to drown out their conversation. Rod Stewart came on. She turned it up. She shook off her flared jeans and walked to the closet, finding a denim miniskirt in a pile on the floor and tugging it over her hips.

"Where's Jack taking you?" Josie asked.

"Portland," said Dahlia. "Joel Hardy's parents are away and he's getting a keg." She returned to the dresser for a tube of pink gloss and dragged it over her lips, smacking them loudly.

"Sounds like fun," said Josie.

"Not really. All those basketball players' girlfriends still look at me like I'm about to burst into flames."

"They're just jealous because you're Jack's girlfriend. All the girls in school are."

Girlfriend. Dahlia still didn't know how she felt about that word. The truth was, she'd been dating Jack almost six months now, longer than she'd ever stayed interested in any one guy, and that equation wasn't sitting well with her either. Worse than that, every time she thought about breaking up with him, she felt undone. Like leaving the house and being sure you'd forgotten to turn off the stove. She couldn't stand the thought of not being near him.

"Are you going to tell Jack that Daddy's here?"

"Jesus, no," said Dahlia.

"You have told him about Daddy, haven't you?"

Dahlia shrugged. "What's to tell?"

"I don't know," said Josie. "It just seems like something you'd tell someone who loves you."

Dahlia turned on her sister. "Who said anything about him loving me?"

"Well, of course he loves you," said Josie, suddenly confused. "Why else is he still with you if he doesn't love you?"

Dahlia dropped onto the bed and pulled on a pair of cowboy boots. "You don't know anything, Joze."

Josie frowned, dejected. She watched Dahlia move back to the dresser and snap the top off a bottle of perfume.

"I knew you'd do this," she said.

Dahlia glanced back at her sister in the vanity mirror. "Do what?"

"Ruin it. Pretend Jack's just like all those other creeps when you know he's not."

"That's crap. I'm not ruining anything."

"Not yet. But you will," said Josie. "I know you will. And you're obviously in love with him."

"I'm not in love with him," Dahlia said firmly.

"You are too. I see how you look at him. How weird you get if he's late or if he's not on the boat in the morning. You never cared this much before."

Dahlia sprayed her wrist, rubbed it across her neck. "You should go downstairs and find Matty," she said, eager to change the subject. "Ask him to take you to the movies or something. Get yourself the hell away from here tonight."

"I can't." Josie sighed. "I can't leave Momma here with Daddy all alone. Not when he just got here."

"Fine. Do what you want."

"It isn't what I want," Josie said, annoyed. "I'm not the one doing what I want here."

"Don't start, Joze. Stay if you want to stay, but don't guilt-trip me."

Josie followed her sister back into the living room, defeated, but it was already too late. To Dahlia's horror, she walked toward the door only to meet Charles blowing in with an arm-load of groceries, and Jack right behind him.

"Hey, darlin'!" Charles shoved the groceries into Dahlia's motionless arms, pushing past her to find Josie. "Where's my Julep at?"

Josie waved meekly from the love seat. Charles bounded to her, scooping her up into a suffocating embrace. "Found this fella tryin' to break into y'all's house," he roared, gesturing to Jack. "Says he's your boyfriend, Dahlia." Charles reached over and stroked Josie's cheek. "Don't you break your daddy's heart and tell me you got one of them nasty boyfriends too, Josephine?"

Josie shifted toward the front edge of the love seat, her fingers gripping the worn velvet seams like toes over the edge of a diving board. "I should help Momma," she said, rising.

Camille emerged from the kitchen, wearing a strained smile. She moved to Dahlia, relieving her of Charles's bags and offering her an understanding smile.

"Hello, Jack."

"Hi, Mrs. Bergeron. My mom wanted me to thank you for the étouffée you sent over on Monday. She said it was delicious."

"Good. I hope she's feeling better."

Charles pried off his shoes and stacked his stocking feet on the coffee table. "You know, Camille," he said, "I thought you was kiddin' with this restaurant business, but I walked right by the goddamned place just now and almost pissed myself."

"I told you when you called the last time, Charles. It's become very popular."

"No shit?" He shoved a cigarette into his mouth, fumbled in his shirt pocket for his lighter. "Well, don't get used to it, darlin'. I'm makin' enough money for y'all now, so you can quit this foolishness with the restaurant. Let Haskell make his own goddamned gumbo."

Jack gave Dahlia a curious look. She took his hand, steering them toward the door, thinking there was still time to escape unscathed.

"Where y'all going so fast?" Charles pointed to the kitchen with his cigarette. "Dahlia, girl, go help your sister and your momma and leave me and your boyfriend alone awhile to get to know each other."

Dahlia looked up at Jack, panic filling her eyes. He gave her a reassuring smile and squeezed her hand. Jack had heard the stories about their father, even seen Charles's takeover of the band at the island's dance with his own eyes the year before, a painful scene that had only made his affections for Dahlia grow stronger.

Jack took a seat across from Charles, his gaze steady but cautious.

Charles offered him a cigarette. Jack refused. "My lungs would kill me," Jack said. "I'd never be able to get up and down the basketball court."

"Horseshit." Charles sucked in a long drag. "I been playin' the trumpet near my whole life. Need lungs the size of Texas for that. Ain't hurt me none."

Jack shrugged agreeably, glancing toward the kitchen, sure Dahlia was straining to overhear.

Charles saw where Jack's eyes roamed and he grinned. "You like Dahlia, do ya?"

Jack turned back to Charles. "I like her very much."

"Yeah, well . . ." Charles snickered. "Me and Dahlia don't always see eye-to-eye so good. She tell you she tried to kill me once?"

"No," Jack answered carefully. "I don't think she mentioned that."

"Sure did. Went at me with a goddamned carving knife." Charles flicked ashes off his cigarette. "She's a hellion, that one," he said, nodding to the kitchen. "You gotta watch her real good."

Jack studied Charles as he stubbed out his cigarette, wondering just what sort of attack Dahlia had endured before managing to defend herself. Just let the bastard try to pull something like that here, Jack thought, protectiveness rising in him primal and hot.

He stood, offering his hand. "It was nice meeting you, Mr. Bergeron, but we really have to go if we want to make the ferry."

Dahlia appeared in the doorway, relief spreading across her face.

"Ready?" Jack asked.

Dahlia sighed. "God, yes."

Jack waited until they were in the car before he asked, "So when did he get here?"

Dahlia watched the house slide out of view in the side mirror, her heart still racing. "A few hours ago," she said.

Jack reached across the seat and touched her cheek. Her skin was hot. "We don't have to go to this party, you know," he said. "We could just get some fried clams and go down to the cove. I've still got that blanket in the trunk."

Dahlia bit at her lip, torn. She didn't want to go to Joel Hardy's, but she didn't want to stay on the island, either. Tonight it wouldn't have been enough to disappear into the cove. She wanted a moat between her and Charles larger than just a slip of sidewalk or a hundred yards of pavement. Give her the widest part of the bay. With luck, maybe she and Jack would miss the last ferry and be stuck on the mainland till morning.

"No, I want to go to the party," she said, forcing an easy smile.

Jack searched her face, unconvinced.

They parked in the lot and walked down to the landing. Spring had arrived, but only barely. Even though the streets had been empty of snow for over a month and the daffodils had started to poke through the softening soil, it seemed winter still held claim to the island's evenings, resurfacing at sunset with a bristling wind.

On the ferry, they found Jack's teammate Eddie Boone and his girlfriend, Mandy Kinney, sitting on the upper deck.

"Hey, man!" Eddie stood, waving them over. Mandy stayed seated and watched them approach, pulling the collar of her peacoat under her chin.

"You guys going to Joel's?" Eddie asked.

Jack took Dahlia's hand. "That's the plan. Hi, Mandy."

Eddie's girlfriend smiled, brushed back her straight blond hair. "Hi, Jack."

"You know my girlfriend, Dahlia Bergeron, right?"

Dahlia swore Mandy's nostrils flared. "Sure," she said, meeting Dahlia's gaze. "Hello."

Dahlia lifted her hand. "Hey."

The air fell silent between the two couples. Jack pointed inside. "I was going to grab us a couple of Cokes," he said. "You guys want something?"

Mandy rose, pushing past Eddie. "I'll go," she said tightly. "I'm freezing out here."

The four of them walked indoors, choosing a booth near the windows. Dahlia and Mandy took seats while Jack and Eddie crossed to the snack bar.

"The guys are getting together for a pickup game tomorrow at TJ's," Eddie said. "Want to come?"

"I can't." Jack fished a pair of singles out of his wallet. "I'm helping Dahlia start some seeds for her beds."

"Very funny." Eddie grinned. "That's a joke, right? Seeds and beds?"

Jack turned to him. "No joke. She wants to get started on some plants before summer. I said I'd help."

They took their place in line behind an elderly couple, who grumbled loudly as they recited the price list behind the short counter.

"Gardening?" Eddie stared at Jack. "You're serious?"

"Why wouldn't I be?" he said. "Dahlia's incredible at it. Talk about a green thumb. Man, you should see what she did with Haskell's yard. I keep telling her she should open up her own business. She'd make a fortune over on the Foreside."

"Yeah, well, I didn't think you were dating her for her thumbs, Thurlow."

Jack frowned. "Is that supposed to be funny?"

"Oh, come on, man. Don't get pissed off. I'm just surprised that you're still seeing her, that's all. I mean, shit . . ." Eddie lowered his voice, turned toward Jack. "She's not exactly the kind of girl you get serious about."

"How would you know, Ed? You've never even said five words to her."

"Look, don't get me wrong," said Eddie. "I get it, you know. I get what you see in her."

"No," Jack said firmly, handing over his cash and scooping up two bottles of Coke. "You don't."

Back at the booth, Jack found Dahlia and Mandy sitting

across from each other, their gazes fixed on different points out the window. He handed Dahlia her soda, delivering it with a sympathetic smile. Dahlia gave him a wary look and climbed out from the booth, walking away without a word, then pushing through the door to the deck.

"What's with her?" Eddie asked.

Mandy shrugged. "As if I would know."

Jack offered no explanation; he just followed Dahlia outside. She'd chosen the bench farthest out on the stern. Jack looked around the deck, seeing they were alone. He took a seat beside her.

"I don't want to sit in there," she said when he arrived.

"Then we won't."

"Mandy Kinney couldn't say two words to me, Jack. You should have seen her face while you were gone. I swear she looked ready to pop. I'm not even sure she took a goddamned breath the whole time we sat there together."

He chuckled. "She probably took one."

"Maybe," Dahlia relented.

Jack watched her study the water with narrowed eyes, biting at her cuticles.

"Want to talk about him?" he asked.

"Eddie?"

Jack gave her a weary look. "Your dad."

"Oh." Dahlia shrugged. "There's nothing to talk about. He's an asshole and I couldn't care less if he's here."

She closed her eyes then and raised her face to the darkening sky, the wind off the water loosening the hair from her combs. Jack reached out and smoothed the stray strands behind her ear, watching the familiar transformation. Her face relaxed first, then her body. Her legs, crossed before so snugly they were nearly knotted, now came undone. She threw one leg over his, her skirt riding up her thigh. He could see the gooseflesh above her knee, the tops of her wool socks peeking out from her cowboy boots.

He put his hand on her leg as if trying to still a spinning top. She exhaled.

"Why didn't you ever tell me?" he asked.

She rubbed her thigh against the smooth cotton of his chinos. "Tell you what?"

"About the fight with your father."

"It was just a fight, Jack."

"You had to defend yourself with a *knife*."

"It wasn't a big deal."

"Not a big deal?" He frowned. "Jesus, Dolly, he could have really hurt you. Did you call the police?"

"No."

"Well, why the hell not?"

"Because we got the fuck out of there instead." Dahlia swung her leg off him and sat up, impatient. "You don't have any right to judge us. You weren't there."

"I'm not judging you," he said. "I just want to know what happened."

"Well, maybe I don't want to talk about it, okay?" she said. "It has nothing to do with you."

"Nothing to do with me?" Jack looked at her, incredulous. "Jesus Christ, Dahlia. You're my girlfriend. It has everything to do with me."

"Says who?" she demanded, turning on him. "You don't own me, Jack. You don't get to own things that belong to me just because you think you do."

"What does this have to do with owning anything? I care about you."

"Well, maybe you shouldn't care so much."

Dahlia rose from the bench, suddenly dizzy. She thought of what Josie had said earlier in the night, the suggestion that she'd grown soft and weak with love, and a fierce panic gripped her.

When she moved to leave, Jack reached for her hand, stopping her. "So I should care about you like Billy Forester?" he said. "Only care about going all the way in the janitor's closet? Care about you like that jerk?"

She stared at his sleeve. "You make it too hard."

"Because I give a shit?"

"I never asked you to."

He stared at her. "That's the idea, Dolly. Jesus, that's the point."

She swallowed, feeling the burn of tears in her throat. "Maybe for you."

Jack considered Dahlia a long moment before he let go of her hand and stood up. "The hell with this," he said. "Do what you want. I'm going in."

He turned and walked toward the door. Dahlia watched him go, feeling at once a sharp stab of fear, irrational yet bottomless.

She called out in a voice she didn't recognize as her own, "Jack!"

He stopped and turned to her, his eyes full, his expression worn, strained.

She walked to meet him.

"Now what?" he said.

Dahlia reached out and hugged him fiercely. "Now you hold me," she whispered against his cold neck. "Just hold me."

Ben knew Charles had returned. He had only to see Camille's face when she appeared in the foyer later that evening, the drawn expression he'd blissfully forgotten in full view on her usually radiant face. That same night, he turned restlessly under his blankets, trying to fight off the jealousy that surged within him, knowing that Charles was sharing Camille's bed.

The next morning, he left for the café by himself, making coffee and thawing gumbo, stacking pralines and stirring grits in the soft quiet before dawn. When Camille hadn't arrived by noon, Ben put in a call to the house but no one answered. Finally, at four, when the daily coffee-break crowd had finally begun to trickle back out onto the sidewalk and Ben could safely flip the Closed sign over and lock the door, he heard a knock. A heavy dread crawled along his skin as he crossed to the front and let Charles inside.

"Hey, there, Haskell." Charles stepped in, looking around. "Bet you thought you'd never see me again." Ben closed the door, surveying the man's gait, surprised at how steady his steps were as he walked toward the counter. "Not a bad-lookin' place y'all got here." Charles lifted up the glass cover and tugged out a praline, taking a large bite. "Pretty good," he said, leaving the rest of the disk on the counter and wiping off crumbs on his thigh. "My momma's were better, though."

"Camille never made it in today," Ben said. "No one answers at the house. Any idea where she is?"

Charles ambled over to a table, slid in, and stretched out. "She's takin' care of some business for me at the town hall. Gettin' me forms for my fishin' license."

Ben frowned warily, in no mood for details. "Fix you something to eat, Charles?"

"Oh, no, I ain't stayin'. I just wanted to have a word with ya. Make sure we all on the same page."

"All right." Ben took a seat on the other side of the table. "What's on your mind?"

"It's like this." Charles laced his hands across his stomach. "I don't know what kind of shit you been pullin' this last year since I been gone—and I don't want to know—but I'm here to stay now, and I don't care to see much of you near my wife."

Ben sat back calmly, crossed his arms. "That's going to be difficult, Charles, seeing that Camille and I work together."

"Not for much longer, you don't. I told her straight out: I make the money now. I want her cuttin' loose from this here contract y'all got goin'."

Contract. Ben might have laughed out loud at the suggestion if he didn't worry that Charles would have reached across the table and strangled him. The truth was, legally speaking, Ben was the sole owner of the café, and though others might have recommended some kind of official document to clarify their respective roles as business partners, Ben had declined such an article for his union with Camille. As he saw it, there was no question they were in it together.

"Lobstering is hard work, Charles. You may find you need a bit longer than a few weeks to start seeing some return on your investment."

Charles's cool eyes narrowed. "Says you."

Ben shrugged. "Says the lobstermen I know. Smart men who've been doing this for a long, long time."

Charles considered this amendment, working at a piece of

pecan in his molar; then he slapped his palm down on the table, signaling his departure. Ben rose with him, followed him to the door.

At the threshold, Charles paused, turned.

"I know what you think of me, but I'm done with all that," he said. "The other women, the booze. Camille's gonna see that, and we're gonna be a family again. I'm gonna start lookin' for a new place for us to live, too. Somethin' bigger. You might wanna start lookin' for a new tenant soon as possible."

Ben closed the door behind Charles, a sinking ache filling him, the longing and despair swift and so staggering that he fell into the first chair he came to.

After supper, Ben managed to find Camille alone in the backyard, taking clothes off the line. He glanced around for signs of Charles, and seeing none he moved beside her, slipping behind a flapping sheet. She wore one of his old wool cardigans over her violet caftan, the shimmering fabric billowing out like waves in the wake of a boat. He wanted to reach out and take her hand as it danced down a row of clothespins, wanted to bury his nose in the nape of her neck. But he did neither.

"Missed you today," he said low.

She turned slightly, her eyes still fixed on the laundry. "I know."

"You don't have to go through this," he said. "If you don't want him here, the police can—"

"No." Camille's eyes flashed quickly to his, then dropped. "It would only make it worse," she whispered. "He isn't drinking anymore."

"So he says."

Camille shrugged. "So he says."

Ben helped her take down the last sheet, folding it into halves until they came together like dance partners. A flood of wants and fears piled up at the bottom of his throat, clumped, and stuck. When she took the sheet and scooped up the basket, he remained silent, saying nothing as she climbed the lawn, leaving him in the flat shadows of dusk.

Two days later, Charles led Camille and the girls down to the town landing, beaming.

"There she is, y'all. The SS *Bergeron*. Ain't she a beauty?"

The women looked down the pier at the small silver skiff that bobbed lazily above the chop, the dory dwarfed even more by the large lobster boats that surrounded it.

"That's not a real boat," Dahlia said. "It's what you use to *row out* to a real boat."

Charles's proud smile waned. "Well, sure, it ain't one of those giant things," he huffed, "but it'll get me out on the water good enough. After a while, I'll get me a bigger one. I figured I'd get my feet wet first on this one. Get my sea legs, as they say."

"And everyone knows you name a boat after a woman," Dahlia added.

"Bergeron is your momma's last name too, ain't it, smart-ass?"

Dahlia just stared at him, knowing damn well he hadn't named the boat for his wife, but she imagined their mother was more than relieved not to see her first name scrawled on the side of that pitiful-looking shell.

"It's nice-looking, Charles," Camille said. "I'm happy for you."

"Happy for *us*," he corrected, swinging his arms out, laying one over Camille, another over Josie, and tugging them into his embrace. "I'm gonna catch so many lobsters, there ain't gonna be room for me in that thing. And Dahlia ain't gonna get a single one."

But it wasn't nearly that simple. Too stubborn and smug to listen to the wisdom of the other lobstermen who watched him toil unnecessarily for almost a week, painting buoys and collecting used traps, Charles waved off their inquiries as to where he planned to hang his gaff to haul the traps in, or where he intended to store his catch. By the following Friday morning, Charles decided he was ready to drop his traps, arriving at the dock much later than the other fishermen, some of whom were already back with their bounty and who shook their heads at the sight of the red-haired man in linen pants and a fussy-looking slicker steering a dented boat crowded with lobster pots into the open water, especially with the wind picking up, and a storm headed their way.

Donald Burton, coming back in with his son Arnold on their family trawler and passing the overloaded dory, called out to warn Charles of the incoming clouds, but got only a dismissing wave for his trouble and a roar to mind his own business.

A crowd had already gathered at the wharf when Charles and his boat were hauled in just before dark. Charles regarded them all with hateful eyes, daring each and every person to speak their whispered comments aloud as he climbed down to the weathered boards of the dock, still soaked from his unintentional swim. Ben had offered him his coat for the ride, but Charles had refused, just as he had refused any conversation, including Gary Masterson's patient and generous assurances that it had been a rough day on the water and that the capsizing of Charles's boat had been an easy error under such conditions.

"Don't you say a word to Camille about this, Haskell," Charles warned through chattering teeth as he climbed into the Jeep.

Ben assured him he wouldn't, but it didn't take long for the news of Charles's performance to reach her. Try as Charles did that next morning to convince Camille and the girls that he was a natural on the water, their eyes revealed their lack of faith, but it was Dahlia who gave her disgust a voice.

"Serves you right," she said from the kitchen doorway. "Everybody told you you were doing it all wrong, but you wouldn't listen."

Charles shot up from the table and charged across the room, grabbing Dahlia's upper arm and yanking her against him. "Don't you tell me my business, girl."

Camille rushed behind him. "Charles, don't!"

Dahlia met her father's cold eyes, steadying herself for a blow, but it didn't come. Charles gave her arm one last sharp squeeze, then released her roughly and stormed back to his breakfast.

When he finally managed to haul his small stash of traps out of the water a few days later, he had caught only two lobsters, one of which pinched his fingers when he reached in, and the crustacean found itself hurled back into the waves, leaving only a single, scrawny lobster in his sloshing bucket.

Arriving home, Charles presented his embarrassing yield to a silent table. Camille gave the sisters a quick glance, encouraging their admiration, but only Josie could manage a small congratulation, and Charles already seemed attached to his misfortune.

"The jerks on the dock tell me it's too small to keep, but I don't give a shit," he muttered. "It's still bigger than a crawfish." Then he swaggered down to Shell's, ending his short stint of sobriety over a single-malt.

That night, when the house was finally still, Dahlia rose and dressed. It took her nearly a half hour to carry the heavy bucket down to the landing, where a small circle of fishermen stood smoking. If they saw her raise the lobster out of its salty bath and lower it down to the water, they didn't say so. But Dahlia would swear she heard those shiny green claws clap happily as the lobster went over the side, like the high five of a teammate landing the winning basket in a championship game.

A week later, Charles announced he'd had enough.

"This time I ain't takin' no for an answer," he told Camille while she folded laundry at the table. "I gave it a real try, but I was right about these people. You don't belong here, and I hope you see that now."

Camille said nothing, just continued to fold her clean dish towels into neat squares.

"Two months, Camille. If you and the girls ain't back home by then, I'm comin' back for ya."

She raised her eyes briefly, flashing with challenge, but she didn't argue.

Late that night, Camille knocked on Ben's bedroom door and stood before him in her silk robe, letting him undo the slippery knot while she wove her fingers through his hair. The next morning, as fog crawled over the island like white moss, she stood at her kitchen sink with a piece of paper on which she had written Charles's name in bright red ink, the color of protection and power, and she cast it under the faucet, letting the water run until the basin turned pink.

Within a month of his return to New Orleans, Charles Bergeron was caught selling heroin and sentenced to eight years in prison.

Twenty-one

Little Gale Island
Sunday, June 16, 2002
1:15 p.m.

Dahlia's hands shook as she pulled the truck over to the side of the road. The cruiser slid in behind her, Jack climbing out soon after.

She watched him approach in her side mirror, her heart racing. "What, no sirens, Chief?"

Jack slid off his sunglasses, his expression strained. "Not today, Dahlia."

"Okay, look," she began wearily, "I know I shouldn't have run over the stupid thing, but she had no right to get my truck towed, Jack. I'll buy her another one, but if it's an apology that old witch wants, then she can kiss my a—"

"Dahlia." Jack came closer, his eyes serious. "This isn't about Margery's sandwich board."

"What then?"

He nodded toward the water. "What do you say I buy us a couple orders of fried clams at Joe's?"

Dread flickered up Dahlia's limbs. "I already ate."

"Okay." Jack stepped back. "Then I'll buy one for myself and you can keep me company." He put his sunglasses back on and tapped the door to signal his departure. "See you down there."

Joe's Sea Shack stood at the entrance to the pier, a bleached, shingled shed just big enough to hold Joe Greeley, his tiny wife, Ellen, and an impressive amount of fried seafood that passed over the counter and into the mouths of both tourist and local alike every summer without pause from ten to five thirty, seven days a week. Today, like most bright island days, the weathered picnic benches outside the shack were crowded with diners. Dahlia found an empty table and sat down to wait while Jack walked to the counter and ordered, greeting Joe, who waved through a curtain of steam.

"Here you are, Jack." Ellen Greeley handed him a soda and a basket of crusted clams. A mischievous smile bloomed on the proprietor's pink cheeks when she glimpsed Dahlia in the distance.

"About time you two found your way back to each other," Ellen said, winking as she handed Jack his change. "We all wondered how long it would take."

Jack considered telling Ellen the truth, but a foolish delight sprang up in him at her suggestion, and he didn't want to correct her. He crossed through the picnic tables, waving at familiar faces. Glancing around when he took his seat across from Dahlia, he could see that Ellen wasn't the only one to make assumptions about their meeting. He couldn't help being reminded of how eager he'd once been to have the whole island, the whole world, see him with Dahlia Bergeron.

He dragged a fried clam through a puddle of tartar sauce, crunching on it as he pushed the basket toward Dahlia. "Sure you don't want one?"

She shook her head. "So what's this about, Jack?" she asked, doing a quick survey of her own. "Or did you just bring me down here to start a little gossip?"

"Not exactly." Jack wiped his hands on a napkin, rested his elbows on the table. He looked at her for a long moment before he said, "I need you to tell me where you were Thursday night between the hours of eight and eleven."

She frowned at him. "Why?"

"Josie said you were meeting someone on the mainland about a landscaping job."

"I was. They canceled."

"So where were you?"

"I was at home."

"Doing what?"

"I don't know, Jack. Doing what most people do at night. Sleeping."

"Was anyone there with you?"

Jack knew how the question had sounded, and, looking up, he saw a smug smile tugging at her lips.

"If you want to know if I'm seeing someone, Jack, all you have to do is ask."

"Okay." He sat up, accepting her challenge. "Are you?"

Dahlia drew back, surprised at his candor, the intent in his warm brown eyes. For a moment, she considered lying, telling him she was dating a sexy, much younger man from away, just to see the look on his face. But she couldn't.

She looked off at the water. "No," she admitted quietly. "I'm not."

"That still doesn't answer my question."

Dahlia turned back to him, stung by his insinuation.

"No, I'm not seeing anyone, and no, I'm not *sleeping* with anyone, either. What are you, chief of the morality police now too?"

Jack dug out another clam. "What you do is your business," he said, trying to keep the hard edge of hurt out of his voice and failing miserably. "It always has been, right?"

Dahlia watched him as he took a long swig of soda, crunching down on a mouthful of ice. "I thought you said this wasn't personal, Jack."

He looked at her, remorse flashing in his eyes. "I'm sorry. I didn't mean that."

"The hell you didn't. Are you this sweet to all your suspects?"

"I never said you were a suspect."

"Then why are you asking me where I was Thursday night?"

Jack rubbed his forehead, frustrated. Hell, this wasn't how he'd wanted this conversation to go, and yet how could he have expected anything else? He'd come here as the chief of police, not as a lover, yet sitting across from Dahlia, watching her, he felt such longing again, as if their lives had never veered off course from each other. It was just like it always was: him trying so hard to get her to confide in him, to let him in, and her pushing him away whenever he'd start to get too close.

So much had changed between them, and yet so little.

He sighed wearily, lacing his hands against his mouth. "The problem is that if no one can confirm you were at your house on Thursday night, it makes for a weak alibi."

"Alibi?" Dahlia said, her voice rising. "Why the hell do I need an alibi? I thought you said this case was as good as closed. Now you're talking about my *alibi*?"

Jack glanced around, seeing customers shift their gazes toward them again.

"We shouldn't do this here," he said.

"Do what?" Dahlia's heart was racing now. "Defend myself?"

"Look, it's okay if you did see Charles. I just need to know."

"Why are you doing this?"

Jack leaned forward, looking Dahlia square in the face. "I'm doing this because your son-of-a-bitch father walked off that ferry at seven forty Thursday night and he didn't get to Ben's until eleven, which means he was somewhere else on this island for three hours."

"And so you just assume he was with me?"

"I'm not assuming anything, Dahlia. One of the deckhands said Charles asked for directions to your street."

He saw the flash of panic in her eyes, and it was all he could do not to reach for her.

He dropped his voice even more. "Dahlia, if he came to you first, I understand if you're feeling guilty; maybe you think you could have stopped him from going after Ben; maybe you even tried, but you have to know that you couldn't have possibly—"

"Oh, my God, Jack." Dahlia was breathless now. "Don't you think I would have called the police if I'd known what that asshole was going to do? You think I would have sat on my hands and watched him just jaunt off to Ben's if I thought he might try and hurt him, if I thought Ben was in danger?"

"Of course I don't."

"Then what?"

Jack sighed. "I don't know," he said wearily. "But I can't make this go away without answers." He met Dahlia's eyes and held them. "And I can't protect you if you don't tell me the truth."

"Protect me?" Dahlia drew back, pulling her hand off the table as if it were a hot stovetop. "I don't need to be protected, Jack."

"No, of course not," he said tightly, the years of frustration rising up in him, too fast to hold back what he'd wanted to say for so long. "Except by Matthew, right?"

Dahlia shot to her feet, feeling the tears sting in her throat. "Go to hell, Jack." She climbed out from the table and marched across the wharf toward her truck. He caught up to her just as she reached her pickup, stepping beside her when she tried to open the door. Dahlia kept her eyes fixed on the handle, afraid of what she might reveal if she looked at him.

"I know what it was like for you with Charles. But he can't hurt you anymore." Jack reached out and touched her hand where it rested on the door, making a final, tender plea. "If you're not telling me something because you're afraid, I promise I won't let anything happen to you. Just tell me the truth, okay? Jesus, Dolly, just talk to me."

Dahlia would never have expected his old nickname to

break her, but it did. The tears she'd managed to swallow surged, filling her eyes so fast she couldn't talk over them.

"I'm late," she lied, struggling to climb inside the truck and slam the door with trembling fingers.

Jack stepped back and let her go. He watched her peel out of the parking lot and lurch up Ocean Avenue, an all-too-familiar regret knotting in his stomach.

Josie stood in her kitchen and stared at the loose puddles of praline syrup she'd just spooned onto the cookie sheet.

She couldn't remember the last time she'd ruined a batch of pralines. Not even when she was learning to make them as a girl, standing on a step stool in the kitchen of their St. Claude shotgun. She wanted to cry; she wanted to break something. So she did a little of both, sniffling as she gathered the still-warm sheet of waxed paper into a big ball and threw the whole runny mess into the trash hard enough to shake the can, but even then she didn't feel better.

She knew why she'd ruined the pralines. It was the same reason she'd started a pot of coffee without any grinds in the filter ten minutes earlier. She would tell Wayne that she wanted to withdraw their application from the agency. He'd understand, she told herself as she took off her apron and laid it on the counter. He'd have to see it wasn't the right time. They had to think about what was best for Ben now. What was best for Matthew. That was what family did for family.

But even as she drew out a pen, scribbled a short note on a Post-it, and pressed it to the top of the stove, Josie knew there was more to her decision, and the guilt swept over her like a chill. She took her purse and stepped out onto the porch.

She glanced quickly to the sky, seeing a soft bruise of gray spreading across the horizon.

Rain was coming. She didn't have much time.

Dahlia was sitting on the front steps of the Sand Dollar when Matthew returned from the hospital, his head lowered until he saw her; then a relieved smile spread helplessly across his face.

She held up a bottle of Maker's Mark. "Join me for a before-dinner drink?"

He glanced around nervously. "Out here?"

"Why not?" she said, already chipping away at the wax seal.

He chuckled, wondering suddenly why she wore sunglasses when clouds covered the sky. "This isn't New Orleans, you know, Dee."

"Oh, really? I hadn't noticed."

"You could get arrested."

Dahlia snorted, yanking off the cork. "I doubt it," she said, taking a quick swig. "Jack's already taken his pound of flesh from me today. And not in the way I would have liked." She climbed to her feet, gesturing to the sidewalk. "Come on. Let's walk."

They started down Birch Street and took the right at Dover, as if they had no idea where it might spill them out, so that when the entrance to the cove appeared before them, they each pretended to be surprised. Dahlia kicked off her clogs at the first sight of sand and tossed them into a stretch of rugosa roses, the sprawling bushes fragrant with white and pink blossoms. Matthew did the same, fumbling with the laces of his running shoes, feeling every bit as clumsy as he had the last time they'd ventured to their favorite beach.

When they'd walked the short stretch of shore, back and forth, taking turns swigging from the bottle and watching the fingers of the foamy surf grasp at the pebbled sand, Matthew said, "So what's this about Jack taking a pound of flesh?"

Dahlia put out one bare foot and made an arc in the water with her toes. "You know Jack," she said with a shrug. "He's always been jealous of us."

With good reason, Matthew thought, guilt fluttering through him, shameful pride trailing not too far behind.

"He made some crack about how I always let you protect me," Dahlia said. "It was stupid. He was just being mean and I told him to go to hell."

Matthew studied her profile, a strange and sudden discontent rising in him. "What's so stupid about it?"

Dahlia's foot stopped its sweep. She turned and looked at him. "Only everything," she said. "The idea that you, or anyone else for that matter, ever had to protect me is ludicrous. Let alone insulting."

"Insulting?" Matthew turned from her, resuming their pace. "Jesus, you have some fucking nerve, Dee."

"Me?" Dahlia rushed to catch up to him. "Why are you mad at *me*? I was only defending you!"

"Defending me?" Matthew stopped and spun around to face her. "What the hell do you think I was doing all those years? Of course I was protecting you—*all* of you! Jesus Christ, Dahlia, my father's on fucking life support because of all the years we protected you."

"Don't you dare put that on me. We never asked you to protect us. Not once."

"Bullshit! You pulled me all over the place. You never had to ask—you never went anywhere without me!"

"That's how *you* remember it," she said. "I remember you wouldn't let us out of your sight. I remember you hovering over us all the time like a goddamned streetlamp!"

"A streetlamp? Jesus, you ungrateful bitch."

They glared at each other, the speed and ferocity of their rage shocking them into silence. Matthew knew his earlier accusation had been unspeakably cruel, and yet he couldn't take it back. He wanted to watch Dahlia suffer its power, wanted to punish her awhile longer.

But Dahlia wouldn't let him. When she marched past him toward the top of the beach and ordered him not to follow her, Matthew didn't. He couldn't. Hurt and ashamed, he stood in the path of the tide, watching her storm up the crest of the dune and out of sight, ropes of seaweed threading between his toes, rubbery tethers that could have easily kept him bound there for hours.

Jack might never have noticed the blur of movement on Ben's wraparound porch if Joel Cunningham hadn't stalled his Cavalier coming out of the four-way stop, but when Jack turned his head in impatience, he saw something flash just behind the railing and pulled into the Queen Anne's driveway. When he reached the top of the ribbed gravel, he leaned across the seat, squinting to make out the front door, and was startled to find the police seal torn down the middle, one side blowing in the breeze. He yanked the cruiser into park, turned off the engine, and climbed out.

Reporters. That was his first thought as he mounted the

four crooked steps to the porch, tabloid hounds not content with a straightforward self-defense case.

He tapped the cracked door open with his foot. The thick smell of burning leaves greeted him, earthy and sweet. Stepping inside, he found his intruder in the parlor, fanning the air with a small bundle of smoking sticks, her back to him.

He would have known that shiny bowl of red hair anywhere. "Jo?"

Josie spun around, drawing the trail of smoke around her like a hula hoop.

"Jack!" She pressed her free hand flat against her chest as if she were making sure her heart was still beating. "Oh, my God, you gave me a fright."

He saw the assortment on the floor behind her, the tall bottle, the dish of incense, a single white candle.

"Jo, sweetheart, this is a crime scene. You can't be here."

"Oh, I know," she said with absolute conviction, "and I swear to you, Jack, I didn't touch anything except with the very tips of my fingers—except for that tape thingie on the door." She winced. "Sorry about that."

Jack wanted to laugh. After the gravity of his talk with Dahlia, this moment was practically comical. He knew he should have been annoyed, even concerned, but instead he felt a curious relief.

"It's just that I wanted to do a cleansing ritual," Josie explained. She looked down at the bundle in her hand, the smoke thinning. "See, Jack, this is all my fault."

Amusement and relief slipped from his face, her admission returning him to earlier suspicions; it had never occurred to him that Josie might have known of Charles's arrival.

"What do you mean, it's your fault?" he asked carefully.

"It's my fault Daddy came back," she said, so plainly that Jack thought for sure she must have been kidding. But he knew her well enough to know she didn't kid. That was Dahlia's forte. For Josie Bergeron, life was a desperately serious matter.

She looked up at him, her eyes swimming with tears. "I was just so busy with the café and the adoption application, I didn't—" She stopped to dab at her eyes with her fingertips. "I didn't make time for my spells. I didn't protect us. I didn't protect *Ben*."

"Jo . . ." Jack reached out and touched her cheek. She closed her eyes, sending down a fresh stream of tears. "You don't really believe that, do you?" he asked tenderly.

"I don't know." She looked around the room. "It's so hard being here. I didn't think it would be so hard." She glanced up to find Jack staring toward the foyer, wondering if he were lost in his own memories. She moved to him. "She still misses you, Jack. We all do." Jack smiled appreciatively. Josie, still trying to play matchmaker, the hope in her eyes no dimmer than it was that night on Ben's porch, when Jack had come to take Dahlia out for their anniversary dinner.

"It's complicated, Jo."

"I know." Josie sighed. "Dahl's pushed guys away her whole life, Jack. When we were kids she made this stupid vow that she'd never fall in love, that she'd never be like Momma, under the thumb of her own heart." She shrugged. "That's the only reason she let Matthew get so close to her."

Jack frowned, confused. "What reason is that?"

Josie smiled. "She was never in love with him."

Jack turned back to the altar she'd made on the floor. Josie looked too.

"I'm almost finished," she said. "I just have to sprinkle the room with Florida water." She touched his sleeve. "Maybe you could help me?"

He put his hand over hers. "I'd like that."

Wayne came inside the house to find Dahlia poised at the stove, her hair balanced on top of her head in a beehive knot, wearing a pair of men's reading glasses and peering into a cookbook.

"Tell anyone I use a recipe to make étouffée and I'll smother you in your sleep," she warned, squinting. "God, does Joze know you're this blind?"

"Where is she?" Wayne asked, pulling a soda from the fridge.

"Don't ask me; I'm just the cook." Dahlia gestured to the Post-it note on the counter. Wayne picked it up. *D, Make dinner, will you? I could be a while. Étouffée and bread pudding. Stock's in the fridge. xoxo, J.*

Wayne frowned. "Maybe I should go look for her."

"I wouldn't," Dahlia said. "It must have been something pretty serious for her to leave me to make dinner."

Wayne gave Dahlia a dubious look but he didn't push. He knew better. He had already stepped over the trail of redbrick dust on his way inside.

He moved to the deck door. "I have to finish the lawn before it rains."

"She wants to tell Matty about the baby."

Wayne stopped halfway through the slider. He came back inside, turning slowly to Dahlia.

She took off the reading glasses. "She thinks that's why he and Holly broke up. Because they couldn't have children. She thinks it would help him to know."

"Oh, God." Wayne blew out a long breath, leaning into the jamb. "What did you say?"

"That it was a terrible idea. But you know how she gets."

"Well, even if she does tell him, it doesn't mean she has to know about the . . ."

"No," Dahlia said quickly. "No, it doesn't."

They looked at each other for a moment; then Wayne made his way outside.

Josie saw the dented silver belly of the boat as Jack turned the cruiser into their driveway, Charles's failed attempt at a lobster fortune propped up on the bulkhead, a web of ropes still dangling off the top of the Buick where Wayne had hauled it to the water that morning.

Jack parked behind Dahlia's pickup.

"Stay for dinner?" Josie asked.

"I can't," he said. "I still have a few phone calls to make."

"Then how about a beer?"

Jack glanced at the truck. "Sure, maybe a quick one."

They climbed out. Josie gestured to the backyard, where they could hear the whir of the lawn mower.

"Go on in and help yourself," she said. "I'll just let Wayne know we're here."

"Shit!"

Jack heard Dahlia's exclamation from the door even before he'd arrived in the kitchen. When he did, he found Dahlia lunging for the stove, her knot of hair flopping over one eye as she reached for the bubbling pot on the front burner.

Jack darted for the dish towel hanging from the refrigerator door and swooped in, wrapping it around the handle and carrying the hissing pot of rice to the sink, where it toppled a mountain of dishes, sending a cascade of dirty dishwater over the side.

The pot sizzled and smoked.

"Now I see why they never actually let you *cook* at the café," Jack said, tossing the towel onto the counter.

"That wasn't it," Dahlia said. "They just didn't want to waste me in the kitchen when I had such a way with the customers."

He grinned, thinking of a certain bowl of gumbo that had ended up in a rival's open pocketbook the summer after graduation. "Yeah, I remember."

Dahlia pulled the lid off a shallow pan, the sweet scent of simmering shrimp floating toward him. "You know, Jack, if you've come by for round two . . ."

"No, that's not why," he said. "I was just giving Josie a ride home."

"Oh." Dahlia looked at him, his dark eyes steady on her, warm again, open. Too open. She looked away. "I meant what I said on the pier." She made wide strokes with her spoon through the étouffée. "I wish to hell I could have had the chance to stop Charles before he got to Ben, but I didn't. And if you don't believe me, there's nothing I can do about that."

She drew out her spoon and laid it on the porcelain rest.

"It isn't just about what I believe, Dahlia. I have the department to think about. I just know how loose ends can unravel. Sometimes taking the whole sweater with them."

"So let it unravel." Dahlia leaned back against the counter, folding her arms. "It won't be the first time on this island a Bergeron woman has been blamed for something she didn't do."

The reference to Rowena Parker's false pregnancy hung

there a long while. Jack watched Dahlia resume her cooking, seeing the flush of an old wound spread across her face.

The apology poured out of him. "I'm sorry for what I said about Matt. I had no right."

"Yes, you did," Dahlia said gently, meeting his eyes. "You had every right." She gestured to the open bottle of wine on the counter. "Want a glass?"

"Actually, Josie promised me a beer."

"A beer it is."

Jack wandered to the deck door while Dahlia pulled a bottle from the fridge. He looked out at the flower gardens beyond the steps. Dahlia's work, for sure. He suddenly wondered whether she modeled her landscaping after herself; it seemed her gardens were always lush and tall, slightly hectic, yet intoxicatingly colorful. He wondered why he'd never made the connection before now.

"Here you go."

She held out the bottle and he crossed back to take it, their fingers touching briefly in the exchange. They each chose a side of the kitchen, forcing a stretch of linoleum between them.

"How's Jenny?" Dahlia asked.

"She's good. She's great, actually. She's heading to Brown this fall."

"Brown's a good school."

"Yeah, it is." Jack smiled proudly. "She wants to be an astronomy major. How about that, huh?"

"Astronomy. Wow." Dahlia took a sip of wine, studying him over the rim of her glass. "I heard you were seeing someone in Cumberland. A Realtor, was she?"

"She was. Still is, probably. I stopped seeing her a few months ago."

"Oh." Dahlia feigned nonchalance even as relief settled over her. "That's too bad."

Jack shrugged. "It wasn't serious."

Not like us, Dahlia wanted him to say, but he didn't, just swigged his beer, lowering the bottle to his thigh and resting it there, his fingers curved around the neck. She'd always liked his hands.

She turned to the window, the sky a deep gray now. "Matty thinks Ben isn't going to pull through this."

Jack looked at her, watching her profile. "Is that what he told you?"

"Not in so many words," Dahlia said. "But I could see it in his face at the hospital." She bit at her lip, pulling gingerly at a flap of chapped skin.

"We used to think everything was so complicated, didn't we?" she whispered.

"It seemed it then."

She smiled sadly. "Yeah, it did, didn't it?"

Jack returned the measured smile, feeling the familiar tug of nostalgia creeping in around him, the easy exchange of memories, too tempting.

He set down his bottle. "I should get going."

"Already?" Dahlia turned back to him, panic flashing in her eyes, startling and raw. "What about dinner? I'll make new rice—and I promise the étouffée hasn't spent any time in the sink."

He chuckled. "Josie already offered, but I can't stay."

Disappointment swept over her, stronger than Dahlia would have expected, but it had been a long time since things had been so easy between them, like they used to be, and the craving for more was instinctive.

When Jack came beside her to leave his beer on the edge of the sink, she reached for his hand, grazing his knuckles, just enough to stall him. "I'm sorry too, Jack," she whispered, her fingers still outstretched.

It didn't matter that she hadn't quantified her apology. They both knew what she was talking about. Jack looked at her fingers, reaching out into the air, and he told himself there was no harm in taking them for just a moment, like he'd done a hundred times before. Their fingers laced naturally, squeezing several times like a pumping heart.

When he finally released her hand and moved toward the hall, she followed him to the front door, feeling the swell of urgency with every step, as if time were running out and there were things still to say, years and years of things.

But at the door, opening it to let the world back in, time returned.

"Take care of yourself, Dahlia."

She nodded. "You too, Jack."

She stood in the doorway and watched him jog down the steps to the driveway, watched him climb into his patrol car. Walking back inside, she had to chuckle to see the faint trail of red footprints he'd unknowingly left behind.

It figured. The one man she'd never wanted to keep out.

Josie had been watching Wayne fight with the mower for almost fifteen minutes, driving it over stubborn swells of ragweed and around Dahlia's beds, before she stepped into his field of view. Glimpsing her, Wayne reached down to turn off the motor. He crossed to her, wiping his hands on his baggy shorts, long threads of sweat snaking down his temple, disappearing into his beard.

Little Gale Gumbo 249

He swallowed, trying to catch his breath. "How long have you been back?"

"Not very long. Jack dropped me off."

"Jack?" Wayne craned his neck to glimpse the side of the house, looking for the cruiser but not seeing it. "What was Jack doing here?"

"I was taking a walk and he gave me a ride home."

"Oh." Wayne dragged a hand across his forehead. His sneakers were covered in shredded grass, the hair on his calves tinted green. "Look, I'm sorry I wasn't here when you got back. I wanted to be; I just lost track of time and . . ." He stopped, his eyes misting. "How is he, Jo?"

"It's hard," she said. "It's like he's just sleeping but he's not. And no one knows anything, and if they do, they aren't saying it. You should go see him, Wayne. Soon."

"I know. I will."

Josie glanced up at the house. "Matty's coming for dinner."

Wayne brushed grass off his arms, reminded of Dahlia's warning in the kitchen. He wanted to ask Josie not to tell Matthew about the pregnancy, to plead with her to keep their secret, but the words seemed to stick in his throat.

He just nodded lamely and she moved back toward the house, touching his arm on her way.

The Queen Anne looked bleached and flat in the shapeless light of dusk.

Jack stared up at it from the front seat of his cruiser, not entirely sure why he'd come back to Ben's massive house on his way home. He wanted to believe Dahlia when she told him she hadn't seen Charles Thursday night, but still the missing hours of the time line gnawed at him. His gut told him the answer was here, in the last place Charles had been before he died, and so Jack had found himself pulling up the gravel drive for the second time that afternoon.

He walked through the first floor, then the second, scanning the rooms with a care he hadn't taken the first time he'd gone through the house, but still he saw nothing new. He even climbed the stairs to the apartment door but found the dead bolt locked and didn't feel like making a trip back to the station to retrieve the keys.

Now he came slowly around to the front of the house, letting his eyes drift over the porch as he walked past, wondering if there was something outside he hadn't seen, some tiny clue. At the steps, he turned and walked backward, lifting his eyes, his gaze moving slowly across the weathered facade.

After a moment, he realized what he'd missed, and his stomach seized.

The apartment window was open.

Maybe Ben had been mistaken, Jack thought. Maybe Charles had broken in through the upstairs and not the front door, but—

No. Jack studied the roofline. It was a treacherous climb. There was no way a man of Charles's age could manage it without a ladder. Of course, it was also possible that Ben was just letting air into the apartment during the stuffier months.

Then Jack noticed the gravel path at his feet. Maybe it was just the way the evening light fell, but he could swear there were indents in the rocks. He crouched and studied the area closer, seeing at once that it wasn't a trick of shadows. There were unmistakable grooves where the gravel gave way to the dirt below, sharp crescents that spread out into even lines.

Jack looked back to the porch, a new theory beginning to

grow in his tired brain. What if Charles had come to the house looking for more than revenge? What if he'd come hunting for something else? A document, maybe. An old will, or Camille's life insurance policy? And what if Charles had found the front door locked? He would have remembered that he could access the house through the apartment, Jack realized. Or maybe the front door *wasn't* locked, but Charles had wanted to make a less conspicuous entrance so he would have had more time to look around?

Jack's eyes darted to the shingled outbuilding behind the house. Ben's treasured woodshop. What if Ben was holed up in there Thursday night? he wondered. Jack knew how Ben was when he was in the middle of a woodworking project. Ben could go hours without coming up for air. And with earplugs in to protect him from the whir of his router, Ben would never have heard Charles's invasion.

Jack looked down at the disturbed gravel, then back up to the dormer. Taking a few more steps, he peered around the side of the house and saw exactly what he'd expected. An extension ladder rested against the house on its side. He looked again to the path. A ladder would explain the gouges in the dirt, the drag lines. A ladder would have been tall enough to get Charles to the roof, and from there he could have managed the short climb over to the dormer window. Then, once inside, Charles would have found the apartment dead bolt locked, just as Jack had, and would have had to climb back out the window. Back on the ground, Charles might have realized for the first time that Ben wasn't even in the house, but in the woodshop, at which point Charles might have simply used the front door after all.

Coming back to the island for some urgent treasure would

certainly explain why Charles had violated his parole. But even more, it could explain the missing hours in the time line. If Ben was deep in his project, Charles could have been free to rummage through the house for as long as he pleased, as long as he needed. Then, hearing Ben return, Charles might have found himself caught inside and waited for Ben, then surprised him at the top of the stairs, only to lose his footing and drag Ben down with him, the stress and trauma causing Ben to suffer a stroke. Suddenly Jack remembered the broken teacup in the parlor. He'd always assumed it was proof of the location of the attack but what if Charles had simply knocked it over during his search instead?

Jack scanned the roofline again, feeling unsettled. He'd been so quick to judge the scene, so sure he'd understood everything in an instant.

Now the sour taste of doubt burned in the back of his throat.

Across the bay, rain began to fall. Matthew watched the drops as they brushed against the tall hospital windows, making no sound at first, then gaining strength like fingernails drummed across a tabletop. He knew the sisters would be wondering where he was, why he hadn't yet arrived for dinner. He'd expected Josie to call, knowing Dahlia never would. He doubted she'd even told Josie about their fight. Even now, he felt prickles of shame for what he'd said, conflicted by the unavoidable surge of rage that quickly followed; he had meant every word—he hadn't meant to say them, was all.

The afternoon had passed slowly in his father's room. Between visits from nurses, Matthew had babbled and rambled, whispered and cried. He had told his father things he knew Ben already knew, and even told him things he never thought he would, confessions of fears and regrets, all the while searching his father's still face for a hint of recognition, of understanding. Once or twice, Matthew had thought he saw a finger twitch, an eyelid quiver. The nurses had just smiled politely.

He hadn't dared to think about the what-ifs of his father's recovery. It still seemed to require an unmanageable amount of effort just to comprehend that the frozen man beside him was the same man who had built him a tree house in a single afternoon, or taught him to drive a stick in a blizzard. The same man who had struggled to learn to make blueberry pancakes without burning them, or macaroni and cheese from scratch; who'd washed his son's clothes, packed his lunch, and filled his humidifier. The man who'd crept out onto the roof to leave reindeer prints on the snow-covered gable so that Matthew would be sure to know Santa had come through the minute he woke on Christmas morning.

Matthew dragged his sleeve across his wet eyes.

With the memories came the longing, stronger than the anger, so heavy and cloaking he could almost forget the rage had ever been there.

He'd kept the sisters waiting long enough.

He kissed his father good night and left for the ferry.

Twenty-two

Little Gale Island

Summer 1979

"We need to hire someone," Ben said.

It was the end of June, and in less than a year the café had grown so popular that Ben and Camille could barely keep the praline trays and gumbo pots filled. In a few months, Matthew would be leaving for college. Signs for bed-and-breakfasts had recently appeared in house windows around the village with cozy names like Seabreeze Inn and Oceanview. The ferry line had added another boat to its fleet. Island beaches that could go whole days without seeing a single pair of bare feet were now crowded with umbrellas and coolers by noon.

Barely two hours after Ben posted the Help Wanted sign in

the window, a young man with curly brown hair and a round, ruddy face came into the store and asked to speak to the owner. Camille and Josie were in the kitchen picking out meat from a towering pile of crabs when Ben walked in with his guest.

"Ladies, this is Wayne Henderson. Wayne, this is Mrs. Bergeron. The talent behind this place."

"Camille," she said sweetly, wiping her fingers on her apron. "And I'm hardly a one-woman show here," she said, flashing Ben a small grin as she extended her cleaned hand. "This is my daughter Josephine."

"Nice to meet you, ma'am," Wayne said, though his attention was already elsewhere. He was so eager for his introduction to Josie that he knocked several crab bodies to the floor reaching across the pile to offer her his hand. "Oh, man . . ." He shook his head, embarrassed, and immediately dropped to the floor to retrieve them.

Josie jumped down from her stool. "Oh, don't worry about it," she said. "They're all empty. Here. Let me help you."

They smiled at each other, then rose together, each with a handful of crab shells.

"It's really nice to finally meet you, Josephine," he said, suddenly breathless.

Her smile broadened. "You can call me Josie."

"Wayne's in Matthew's class," said Ben. "He's going to be helping us out this summer. Why don't you show him where things are, Jo."

Josie led Wayne out into the café, where Dahlia was behind the counter, fighting to loosen her fingers from a jammed napkin dispenser. "Motherfucker."

Josie flushed with embarrassment. "I'm sure you already know my sister."

Dahlia turned to them, sucking on her pinched thumb. "I still don't see why we can't just put out napkins in stacks on the table, for Christ's sake."

Wayne smiled politely. "Probably because they'd spill and make a real mess."

Dahlia frowned at him.

"Wayne's going to be helping out at the café," Josie said cheerfully.

"Since when?"

"Since Ben just hired him."

"Hey, Wayne." Matthew arrived with a stack of cardboard boxes stamped with the words DRIED KIDNEY BEANS and set them on the counter.

"Hi, Matt. Jeezum crow, that's a lot of beans."

"Jeezum crow?" Dahlia chuckled. "What are you, ten?"

Wayne gave her an even look. "We don't use swearwords in my house."

"I think that's nice," Josie said, glaring at Dahlia. "Momma says you get only so many words on this earth, and I don't want to waste mine on cusswords."

"What can we get you, Wayne?" Matthew asked.

"I'm working here now," Wayne said. "Your dad just hired me."

"No kidding? Just till school starts, huh?"

"I'm not going to college, actually."

"Really? I thought I heard you were going to Orono?"

"I was. But then my dad had a . . ." Wayne cleared his throat. "Maybe you heard."

Matthew had, and he felt bad for remembering too late. When Josie looked at them all blankly, Wayne explained, "My dad had a heart attack last spring and the bills have been crazy. He had to stop working, so it's not really a good time to leave."

Josie nodded quickly, her eyes rounding with sympathy.

"You'll like working here," she said.

Wayne smiled gratefully at her. "I'm sure I will."

Wayne Henderson proved a hard worker and a fast learner. By the end of his first month, he was opening the café four days a week, and manning the counter by himself three. A native islander, he knew all the customers by name and quickly learned their favorite dishes. Even Camille had to admit his first attempt at making a roux wasn't half-bad, and his enthusiasm for the business seemed genuine.

But it was his enthusiasm for Josie that was most apparent. Especially to Matthew. If Matthew hadn't known better, he might have thought Wayne had applied for the job only to get to know Josie better.

But Wayne imagined he knew a few things about Matthew too. He knew that Matthew was the sisters' bodyguard, and that it had been a rare day to see them around school without him.

Wayne knew too that Josie was terribly fond of her escort. He'd seen her face light up when Matthew came near, her cheeks flush, her fingers wind nervously around her red ponytail. But more than that, Wayne had seen the clear lack of nerves in Matthew when Josie crossed his path. The attraction wasn't mutual, and Wayne was relieved for that simple fact.

"You can go home early if you want, Wayne," Matthew said one afternoon at the beginning of August. "It's quiet. Josie and I can close up."

They could hear Josie's faint singing in the kitchen. "Someone to Watch Over Me."

"Jesus, you'd think she only knows one song," Matthew said, wiping down the display cases.

"I think she has a great voice," said Wayne. "I like her. Very much."

Matthew frowned, confused at first. "Well, no kidding, so do I. I was talking about a stupid song. . . ." But even as he said it, Matthew knew that Wayne hadn't misunderstood, and yet Matthew added for good measure, "I like Josie very much too, actually."

"Not the way I do." Wayne shifted nervously against the counter. "I just . . . I just want to be clear on that, all right?"

Matthew might have pressed his classmate if Doris White hadn't come in just then for two pecan pies.

And so Wayne's bold statement fell away with the old woman's order, and Matthew didn't care enough to bring it up again for the rest of the summer.

For Jack Thurlow, summer pleasures were fleeting. In another month, he'd be going to the University of Southern Maine, commuting to the mainland for classes and keeping his part-time job packing seafood on the wharf. He knew with his new demands it would be hard to find time for Dahlia, but he had no intention of breaking up with her. Quite the opposite: His affection for her was stronger than it had ever been, his commitment to her unwavering.

Not that loving her had been easy. Oftentimes he'd felt like a naturalist observing an exotic animal in the wild, fearful of scaring it off before he'd had the chance to win its trust. For every week that had brought them lighthearted chases on the beach or excursions north to explore garden spots and greasy spoons at her urging, there had been episodes of frustration, her continued accusations that he was too demanding, his that she was too detached, both arguments that would drive them apart for days at a time until Dahlia would plead for his return, clinging to him as soon as he did, her affection so naked in those moments it shocked him.

But it was all worth it. Tonight they would celebrate their eight-month anniversary. Jack had been hard at work on the plan all week, arranging to use the roof patio of the fish market after hours. The owner's wife, Marcy, had even offered to set aside a pile of scallops for him, and promised to leave an extra quart of blackberry custard in the freezer. He'd decided it would be the perfect night to announce his devotion, though he still didn't understand how Dahlia could have doubted his love after all this time.

Boarding the ferry for home that afternoon, Jack saw Matthew on the upper deck and shared his plan.

"Does Dahlia know?" Matthew asked.

"She knows we're going out," Jack said. "Nothing specific. You know Dahlia. She likes surprises."

"Yeah, I know." Matthew frowned into the wind. "So you guys are going to stay together through school then?"

Jack glanced over at him. "Of course. Why wouldn't we?"

"I don't know." Matthew watched an old man wipe sea spray off a bench with his sleeve before sitting down. "I guess I just figured with all those college girls, you'd want to be free and clear."

"You'd think, wouldn't you?" Jack grinned. "Maybe if I wasn't so damn crazy about her. But I am."

Matthew turned back to the view, squinting out at the

nearing island, the familiar tufts of trees like the scalloped edges of a collar. "Good for you," he said, then again, as if he might mean it this time: "Good for you."

Dahlia watched the clouds from the porch steps, her heart so heavy she could hardly breathe. Her fingers stung where she'd been pulling at the skin around her nails. A pair of zits had appeared on her chin, and another one was starting on her forehead. She touched it compulsively, sure it was getting as big as a walnut.

It wasn't any wonder. Ever since Jack had told her two weeks earlier that he was going to USM, she'd been a nervous wreck, distracted with useless jealousies and swirling fears. She'd tried to tell herself she wouldn't care if he fell in love with some high-and-mighty college twit, but she did care, desperately, and the thought of his being attracted to another girl left her feeling so hot and feverish she couldn't sleep.

She knew there was only one thing to do: She'd leave Jack Thurlow before he left her. Then things could go back to the way they'd always been. The easy way, the safe way. She could be free again, free of all the complications of a relationship, free to breeze in and out of a person's line of vision, to flirt and fool around and move on. She'd go back to being the girl who announced she'd never get married, never get serious about one man. There was too much trouble and heartache in it otherwise. If this was what love did to a person, she'd been right to say she didn't want any part of it.

Looking up, she saw Matthew climbing the path to the porch, carrying a soda.

"Anyone else home?" he asked, dropping down beside her.

"Nope." Dahlia took the bottle from his hand. Matthew

watched her sip and hand it back, seeing the flash of abandon in her dark eyes. Something was wrong, he thought. Something had happened.

"Jude Parker is having a bonfire at the cove," she said without looking at him. "Want to go?"

"I thought you and Jack had a big date."

Dahlia turned back to the view, knowing she couldn't lie if she had to look Matthew in the face. "Jack and I are breaking up," she said, the words coming out slow and thick, as if her throat were sore.

Matthew didn't believe it. And when silence fell between them, he knew this was his chance to correct her, to discourage her from this course she'd set for herself in a fit of panic and foolish fear. It would have been easy—painless, really—to tell her just how much work Jack had gone to for their evening, how determined he was to take their relationship as far as it could go. How much he loved her. The silence lingered, taunting him. But he let it go, letting the chance go with it, and when the weight of guilt took residence in his throat, Matthew forced it down.

"You want to go or not?" she said.

"Yeah," he said. "Yeah, sure."

He told himself Dahlia already knew what she claimed was a lie, and that made it okay to be her accomplice. He told himself that Jack should have known she'd do this, and he wouldn't be surprised when he came to the house in an hour and found her gone.

But even as he followed Dahlia inside, even as he waited in the kitchen while she ran upstairs to change, Matthew knew this made him a terrible person. And yet, even as he walked beside her down to the beach, the sky streaked violet and the dusky sand cold between their toes, he knew too that he couldn't help himself. He'd wanted her too long.

When they reached the edge of the bonfire and each took a beer, Dahlia could see the night spreading out before her, the way it would go now that she had set things in motion. She couldn't stop it now. She only hoped it wouldn't hurt as much if she did it like this.

Looking at Matthew, seeing the growing buzz in his narrowed eyes as he stared at her through the popping flames, Dahlia knew for certain. Jack would break her heart if she let him, and Matthew couldn't if he tried.

"*Wayne is working out* well, don't you think?" Ben said, turning the sign to CLOSED and snapping off the light above the front door.

"Josie certainly thinks so," said Camille, putting away the last of the day's leftovers. "He asked her to a movie tonight. It's just nice to see her interested in someone other than Matthew for once."

"Now if Matthew could just do the same." Ben crossed back to where Camille stood and laid his hand on hers where it rested on the counter. They watched their fingers awhile, opening and closing together.

Camille sighed. "Dahlia's broken his heart, hasn't she?"

"He'll move on," Ben said. "Everyone does eventually."

"You can't be sure. He loves her terribly."

Ben took Camille's face in his palms, caressing her velvety cheeks, her temple, her mouth. "I loved Leslie like that," he said. "Then I met you."

Camille turned her face to kiss his thumb, her eyes heavy with want.

"Come to the pantry," she said. "There's something I've been meaning to show you."

Ben smiled.

Matthew found them a place under the rock ledge where the tide couldn't reach and the sand was smooth enough to lie on. They made love without undressing, their union so fast that he couldn't help but be surprised when Dahlia stood up right after to tug her skirt back down over her hips. He watched her brush the sand from her rear, her thighs, her arms; watched her shift her breasts around in her bra, breasts he'd barely touched, breasts he hadn't even seen. He'd imagined the hundred ways he'd make love to her body, the hundred places he'd touch and taste, and he'd barely had time to kiss her before he'd come inside her and she'd rolled off him.

He stared at her now, confused.

"What's your hurry?" he asked.

"I'm cold," she said, when he'd never known her to be cold, not even in the dead of winter, "and you know they always run out of beer."

"I don't care about the beer," he said. "Come on, stay."

Her hair fell across her face but she didn't seem to want to tie it back. She was hiding something, Matthew thought at once, and when she sniffed, he knew. She wiped her eyes in quick strokes.

"What is it?" he asked, wanting to believe it had something to do with him.

She gave him a tight smile, then leaned down to kiss him quickly on the jaw. "It's nothing," she said. "I just got sand in my eye, that's all."

Out of instinct, Matthew grabbed her arm to pull her back down to his lips but Dahlia gently wriggled free.

"Don't go yet," he asked one last time.

"I'll save you a cup," she promised.

Then she dashed over the rocks before he could zip up his shorts and catch up to her.

Jack waited on Ben's front porch until nine. When he heard the click of a woman's shoes on the sidewalk, he felt a last swell of hope, a brief spark of relief. Then Josie appeared around the curtain of forsythias and his broad smile fell.

"My goodness!" she exclaimed, beaming with excitement. "Back already?"

"Never left, I'm afraid." Jack forced a good-natured grin that any other night would have suited him.

"I—I don't understand," Josie said, her voice suddenly small. Jack saw her eyes fill up. "Maybe she got caught in town. Maybe the ferry was late."

Jack smiled, grateful for her effort, but they both knew there was no emergency, no good excuse for Dahlia's absence. He rose and wished Josie good night.

"What should I tell Dahlia?" she asked, her voice desperate as Jack made his way down the front steps.

He shrugged. "Tell her I was here. Tell her I was here the whole time."

Josie nodded dully as she watched him walk down the sidewalk and climb into his car.

On her way inside she stopped, smelling the smoke rise over the dunes, sharp and thick, and she burst into tears.

Twenty-three

Little Gale Island

Sunday, June 16, 2002

8:30 p.m.

Wayne had gone upstairs for the night, leaving Josie and Dahlia to linger in the kitchen, stalling over dirty dishes that could easily have waited until morning, but neither sister wanted to surrender the night, hoping there was still a chance Matthew might arrive. Josie had spent the last few hours coming up with reasons for his delay, while Dahlia had offered up agreeable nods, denying her sister the truth of their friend's absence. When the knock finally sounded at nine, they moved to the front door together, their languid movements suddenly urgent with purpose. Josie proved the swifter in the race, claiming the doorknob for her own.

Matthew stood on the porch, his Windbreaker shiny with rain.

"I hope I'm not too late for dessert."

He held up Dahlia's forgotten bottle of bourbon. She reached out to take it, their eyes meeting.

"You were supposed to finish it," she said.

He pushed back his hood. "I tried passing around shots to the hospital staff, but they weren't interested. More the white-wine types, I guess."

Josie drew him inside, taking his coat. "We wanted to call," she said softly as they walked into the kitchen. "But we didn't want to disturb you."

"Where's Wayne?"

"Upstairs."

Matthew looked between the sisters. "It's late," he said, as if the hour had only just then occurred to him. "I should have called first."

Josie reached up and kissed his damp cheek. "I'll get us some glasses."

Matthew made a fire in the living room while Dahlia picked out music and Josie reheated bowls of bread pudding. Ready, they gathered barefoot around the coffee table to the familiar strains of Louis Armstrong. Matthew poured them generous shots, one round, then another. The logs burned, crackling and spitting.

When their bowls were nearly empty, Josie gasped. "All this drinking and we haven't made a toast yet."

Matthew cleared his throat, lifting his glass. "To the three of us. Like old times."

"Like old times," Dahlia echoed.

They clinked their glasses in the center of the table and threw back their shots. Matthew poured again, sloppy now, and he splashed a pillow covered in a familiar scarlet silk.

"Jesus," he whispered. "Is that . . . ?"

"Momma's kimono robe," Josie said. "Do you remember it?"

"Of course I do. Jesus, do I ever."

"When it tore too badly to repair, she saved a few squares to make into gris-gris bags, then turned the rest into pillows," Josie said proudly.

Dahlia chuckled into her glass. "Now Momma can't say she never drank."

The sisters fell against each other, laughing.

Watching them, lost in their amusement, Matthew felt the lightness of the alcohol, the welcome warmth and ease of it. The bourbon was loosening his thoughts, like thread unspooled.

"I miss this." He reached for them. "I miss us."

The sisters gave him their hands and the chain was complete.

"I performed a cleansing ritual for Ben today," Josie said. "It wasn't as perfect as one of Momma's, but I think it will help rid the house of whatever negative energy Daddy might have left behind. I really do."

Matthew squeezed Josie's hand, her thin fingers warm. "Thanks, JoJo. That would mean a lot to Pop."

Josie rose to her feet, steadying herself on the side of the couch. "Bathroom break," she said. "And one of y'all'd better get to making some coffee while I'm gone or no one's going home."

Matthew grinned. "Yes, ma'am."

As Josie disappeared down the hall, Dahlia slid around the coffee table and scooted in beside him.

"Sorry I missed dinner," Matthew said.

"You should be. I made it."

"Oh, then in that case . . ."

She gave him a playful push. He pushed back. They smiled at each other, their expressions cautious at first, then yielding quickly.

"I'm sorry for what I said, Dee. I was just so damn angry. . . ."

"Don't." Dahlia reached out, pressing her fingers against his lips. When he had quieted, she lifted her hand and smoothed back a chunk of his hair. "It's forgotten."

Matthew looked into her eyes. "It's about the only thing that is."

Dahlia let her fingers drift down to his ear, his jaw, the hint of beard there so much coarser than when she'd touched him as a lover. She noticed the wrinkles where his ear met his cheek, the slight pleating of skin, that subtle but undeniable cue of middle age.

"I'm sorry too," she said. "I was mad at Jack today and I took it out on you."

It wasn't the first time, Matthew thought. Then again, it wasn't the first time he and Dahlia had found themselves together in the wake of some crisis of the heart either. What a difference a few hours made. He'd left the hospital thinking of Holly's phone call, the spark of promise still fresh and bright in his mind, yet here with Dahlia, it seemed that everything else dimmed. The bourbon and the fire, the warmth and the jazz—he was reminded of how much he'd wanted her, how deeply, how long. Safely lost in their old world, Holly seemed another lifetime, another life. It was always so easy on the island, knowing their places, their wounds, how little it took to mend them.

Matthew's eyes blinked open, languid and heavy. "God, I've missed this."

"Me too," Dahlia said, knowing even as she said it that she didn't mean it like he did. But there wasn't any point in making the distinction. They were too drunk now. It was the guilt talking, and she knew it. The unbearable ache in her chest, knowing what she'd done, what she'd kept from him, and would have to now, knowing Matthew might never forgive her. He reached for her face and Dahlia let him catch her cheek, let him ease her closer. When he slipped his tongue between her parted lips, Dahlia regretted it immediately, but then Josie appeared, saving Dahlia from having to push him away.

Her sister stood before them, her face crumpling.

"Sorry to interrupt." Josie lowered her eyes so they couldn't see the pained flush that had spread across her skin. She gestured to the stairs. "You know, I didn't realize it had gotten so late. I think I'm just going to leave y'all alone and get to bed."

"Don't go," pleaded Matthew, catching her wrist, trying to tug her back down to the floor even as she grew as rigid as a fence post. "Come on, JoJo. Stay. Just a little while longer. We haven't had coffee yet."

Josie looked to Dahlia, but Dahlia couldn't meet her sister's wounded eyes.

"I can't, Matty. I'm sorry." Josie leaned down and kissed him on the mouth. "Tomorrow, okay?"

He nodded, wondering how it was that bourbon from Josie's lips tasted more like vanilla lip gloss as he watched her climb the stairs, her head hanging, the opposite of okay.

"Late night, huh?"

Wayne's voice startled Josie when she crept into the bedroom. "You can turn on the light if you want," he said.

"That's okay." Josie undressed quickly, slipping her nightgown over her head. Wayne lifted the sheet for her and she climbed in beside him.

Dahlia's bursting laugh sailed up the stairs, filling their quiet room.

"Sounds like old times down there, doesn't it?" Wayne whispered.

Josie rolled against her pillow, wishing he hadn't said so.

He reached for her, his hands still smelling of cut grass.

"Sometimes it's better to let things go, Jo," he said. "Better for everybody."

Josie felt the tears seep through her closed eyes, the shameful envy that she'd worked so hard to abandon, filling her up again as if it had never left.

She steered Wayne's hands down from her hip. "We should get some sleep, baby."

But as she lay there, her heart raced at every laugh, every cheery, teasing sound that came from downstairs, and even though she wished desperately that Matthew and Dahlia might just leave and end her suspense, when she finally heard the clap of the door and the growl of the truck's engine, the silence that followed was so much worse. She'd almost forgotten just how much worse.

Twenty-four

Little Gale Island

Summer 1984

Wayne's proposal came on a crisp June day, when the lilacs had finally bloomed across the island, fat sprays of lavender and white. He'd been nervous at the café all week, spilling orders and forgetting change, but only Ben and Camille had known why. If Josie suspected, she didn't let on. Wayne didn't imagine she would say no. For as long as they'd been together, Josie had made it clear how badly she wanted children, how she couldn't wait to start a family.

For the most part, it had been a quiet start to summer at the Haskell house. Newly graduated from college, Matthew had decided to spend the summer on Martha's Vineyard, living with five roommates in a rustic stable apartment and painting Victorian cottages in Oak Bluffs; an irony that hadn't been lost on Ben, who had been pleading with his son to paint their peeling Queen Anne for years. Dahlia spent little time at the café, having started her landscaping business in earnest, securing contracts with several wealthy summer people and buying a pickup truck that she painted hot pink. Matthew had invited her down several times for a visit, though she had yet to commit to a date.

"I can't imagine Matty has time to entertain," Josie said, counting the register drawer shortly before closing. "Ben says he's working seven days a week out there."

Dahlia made herself an iced coffee with the last of the pot. "He'd make time for me."

Josie didn't argue. They both knew it was true.

"Want to catch a movie later?" Dahlia asked.

"Can't," Josie said. "Wayne's taking me to Florentine's for dinner."

"Ooh. So fancy."

"I think he wants us to move in together."

"In where? His mom's garage?"

"Very funny." Josie pushed the drawer closed. "For your information, we've been looking at rentals. Claire Watson is renting out her carriage house. It's more than we can afford, but she said she'd cut us a deal."

"You mean she'd cut *Wayne* a deal. If it was just you looking, she'd charge double."

"That's not true. Lord, Dahl, we've been here almost seven years now. You can stop thinking everyone is still looking to chase us out of town."

"Well, if they aren't, it's only because you-know-who hasn't been out of jail long enough lately to visit."

"Shh, don't say that." Josie groaned, walking to the door and flipping the sign in the window. "Now I'll have to dust the stupid steps again."

Dahlia followed her sister to the front, dropping into the window booth. "Sounds like ol' Wayne's getting serious."

"Maybe." Josie shrugged, joining Dahlia on the opposite bench. "I do love him, you know."

Dahlia leaned across the table. "Well, it doesn't mean you have to marry him, Joze. You're twenty-one, for Christ's sake."

"So? Momma got married at eighteen."

"And look what a fucking disaster that turned out to be."

Josie sighed. "I'm not like you, Dahl," she said softly. "I don't want to be alone."

"I never said I wanted to be alone." Dahlia turned to the window. "I thought I saw Jack leaving here while I was parking."

"You did," Josie said, watching her sister's wistful expression. She'd worried Dahlia might have seen Jack. The island seemed to get smaller every day.

"He was getting pralines for Irene. You remember how much she loves them."

Dahlia nodded, smiling sadly. If only she could forget.

A heavy silence landed between them. Dahlia rose, needing air. Lots of it, she decided.

She climbed out from the booth, kissing her sister on the cheek. "See you in a few days, sweetie."

"A few days?" Josie turned, strangely panicked. "Where are you going?"

But Josie knew, of course, even as Dahlia grabbed a stack of pralines on her way by the counter.

"You give Matty my love, you hear me?" Josie yelled as the kitchen door swung closed, as if she were offering for the first time, instead of the hundredth.

"You sure you won't have some of this, Jo?"

Wayne pushed his plate of linguine with mussels across the stiff white tablecloth. Josie shook her head. She'd barely managed to eat half of the filet mignon he'd insisted on ordering for her. Dahlia's spur-of-the-minute road trip had left her annoyed and undone, and she felt guilty for it. Josie knew how much Wayne had planned for this evening, how much he loved her.

"Save room for dessert," he said when she set down her fork.

"Dessert? Wayne, I can't even finish dinner. . . ."

"Oh, come on," he urged gently. "I already special-ordered it. I had to. It takes a while to make."

The hope in his soft eyes, made brighter by the table's candle, seemed almost stubborn. Josie knew he was determined to see this night through. And somewhere between the parking garage and the waiter handing them their menus, she'd known why he had gone to so much trouble. Just as she knew what was in the ramekin even before it arrived in front of her, a small ring box, set in a nest of rose petals, and a thousand feelings charged through her.

"Let me," Wayne said, his hands shaking as he slid the ring on her finger.

Josie could sense the tables around them growing quiet, hear the telltale shifting of chairs, diners turning to watch. After years of being watched so closely, she wished Wayne had chosen a more private space to propose, but it didn't matter now. What mattered, Josie told herself, lifting her eyes to find Wayne's crinkling with excitement and watery with tears, was that he loved her and he always had. With luck, he always would.

When she returned home, Camille and Ben were asleep, and Josie told herself it wasn't fair to wake them, that the news of her engagement could wait until morning. Passing through the parlor, she saw one of Camille's red love candles on the sideboard, and her heart sank to think her mother had as little faith as Josie did herself in her answer.

She walked back to the kitchen and found the sheet of paper on the fridge with Matthew's summer address and a phone number where he could be reached in an emergency, which, Josie realized as she dialed, was exactly what this was.

By ten that night, the apartment above the stables had finally quieted after a rowdy dinner of lobsters that one of Matthew's roommates had acquired from an enamored waitress in Edgartown. The cramped kitchen had emptied out quickly, no one wanting to clean up the soaking newspapers that still lay stuck to the table like papier-mâché, covered in piles of red-orange shells, drained butter dishes, and empty beer bottles.

Matthew had been down on the beach when Josie's call came in, and the message he received when he returned, sandy and still drunk, seemed almost expected to him. But not so an hour later, when he was deep asleep and a knock came on his bedroom door, his roommate Doug leaning in to announce, "Yo, Matt. There's someone here to see you. Someone hot."

Dahlia.

Matthew tore down the hall, down the stairs, caring too late that he'd be winded when he arrived, that she'd see again how glad he was to see her, when he should be angry that she'd not bothered to call first, that she'd just presumed to find him available. Which he was. And he would have been no matter what.

"You look skinny," she told him as he carried her bag up the stairs. He introduced her to the two roommates who were still awake, sprawled out and drinking beer in one of the front bedrooms. They offered her a bottle and she accepted it.

"My room's back here," Matthew said, leading her down a narrow hallway and into a low-ceilinged room with faded travel posters on the wall to hide chunks of missing plaster.

Dahlia fell onto his bed. "I'm starved," she said. "Let's get dinner."

"Shit, I just gorged myself on lobster. And it's almost midnight."

She grabbed his shirt off the end of the bed and tossed it at him. "Then we'd better hurry."

Nell's was the only place still open when they finally made it into Vineyard Haven. They carried paper trays of fried clams and onion rings down to the docks and watched the floating lights of the yachts in the harbor, the dark sea crowded with them.

"I think Wayne's going to ask Josie to marry him," Dahlia said.

"He did. She just called."

"Of course she called. She wanted you to tell her not to."

"Why would she want me to do that?"

Dahlia gave him a flat look. "Oh, please."

"What?"

"Why do you think?"

He shrugged lamely. "How should I know?"

She dragged an onion ring through a pile of ketchup, smiling. "Did you know that when we were kids, she used to keep a strand of your hair in her shoe to make you fall in love with her?"

"You're so full of shit. . . ."

"I swear to God. She used to sleep with one of your unwashed socks under her pillow too."

"What the hell for?"

"So you'd never leave her."

"Jesus."

Matthew frowned at his pile of clams. He knew there was no point in playing dumb anymore. He'd always had his suspicions, grinding tremors in his stomach, but hearing Dahlia say it out loud sealed it.

"Funny, isn't it?" he said.

"What?"

"Her wanting it to be me, and me wanting it to be you."

"Matty . . ." Dahlia turned her gaze to the water. "I didn't come here to start this. . . ."

"Then why did you come?" he demanded.

"I don't know. I just thought you might like to see a friendly face." She sighed. "Why does everything always have to mean something?"

"Fuck, because it does, Dee. You'd think so too if I was Jack."

Matthew knew it had been the wrong thing to say. Dahlia's eyes darted to him, looking wounded. "I don't want to talk about Jack."

"Fine," Matthew said, rising. "That makes two of us."

But even as they walked back to the car and drove the

green VW Bug down the island's dark and twisting roads, Matthew knew there would be no salvaging the night. Back at the stable, he gave Dahlia sheets for the pullout, but by three a.m., she had padded into his room and slid into bed behind him. His skin smelled of salt; his fingers, draped over his shoulder, still reeked of lobster.

"He's marrying Mandy Kinney," Dahlia whispered. "She's pregnant."

Matthew rolled around to face Dahlia and pulled her against him. He felt her tears wet his neck, even as her hands slipped inside his boxers.

When Ben opened the café the next morning, Wayne and Josie had still not arrived for work. Camille was in the kitchen, flattening garlic cloves with the heel of her hand. Ben could see she was anxious.

"I didn't even hear her come in last night. Did you?" she asked.

"It's obviously a good sign," Ben said. "Maybe they just went ahead and eloped."

Camille gasped. "Don't you dare say it. A mother deserves at least one wedding, doesn't she?"

"I agree." Reaching over to take the pan of corn bread Camille had just pulled from the oven, Ben kissed her cheek and whispered, "Why do you think I've been offering for years?"

Camille blushed, smiling down at her crowded cutting board. It had become a joke between them, his asking and her declining. After nearly seven years as best friends, six as business partners and almost as many as lovers, they had both come to the conclusion that marriage would have been redundant. Even if she were to ask Charles for a divorce, which Ben knew would have been far more trouble for both of them than it was worth. As it was, they were as good as married. Maybe even better.

"Sorry we're late."

Josie appeared, hurrying to tie on her apron. Wayne followed, looking flushed. After a few moments of silence while they unloaded muffins and pralines from the pantry, Camille slammed down her knife and exclaimed, "Now you both just stop this right now and 'fess up before I expire!"

They all burst out laughing and the news was shared quickly with handshakes and hugs before the day's first customers forced Wayne and Ben out to the front.

When they were alone, Camille drew Josie to her and kept her close.

"Are you happy, baby?"

Josie nodded, tears rising. "I want to be, Momma. I know I can be now."

Camille smoothed her daughter's long red hair. "It's all going to work out. You'll see."

"Is that why you dressed the love candle?" Josie pulled back, the hurt so clear on her face. "I saw it on my way upstairs last night."

"Oh, baby girl . . ." Camille cradled Josie's cheeks in her hands as her own eyes began to water. "That candle wasn't for you. It was for your sister. Because she doesn't know that she can be loved. And I'm starting to worry that she never will."

Twenty-five

Little Gale Island

July 1987

It was going to be another rainy week, Wayne thought as he turned the café's Closed sign around at four o'clock. The forecast had predicted storms by the next morning, and sure enough, the afternoon sky was already blooming with heavy clouds. He hoped Josie didn't get caught in any showers on her way back from the store. He'd pressed her to take the car, but she'd insisted on walking, claiming she needed the fresh air, a request she'd been making more and more often. He knew she missed her sister. Dahlia had been living on the Cape for most of the summer, tending to the gardens of a lawyer from Boston. Probably tending to the lawyer too, Wayne had suspected but never said outright. Matthew had also left the island for the season, working at a summer camp up north. Wayne wasn't sure whose absence upset his wife more. Two years into their marriage and he hadn't yet figured out how to be Josie's whole world.

He gave the sky one last look, then moved into the back to clean up. He had filled the sink when he heard the bells of the front door jingling and he cursed under his breath, realizing he'd turned the sign but not the lock. When he came out from the kitchen, he found a red-haired man wandering the length of the counter, peering into the empty cases.

"Sorry, sir. We're closed."

When the man stood up and Wayne could see the trumpet case in his hand, he felt as if he'd swallowed ice cream too fast.

Charles Bergeron looked just as Wayne had imagined him, rangy and slick. Everything about the older man seemed to wear a slippery shine: his pumpkin orange hair, his green polyester shirt, his pointed shoes. Only his eyes, the same blue as Josie's, didn't shine. They were as dull as a pair of unwashed headlights.

"Camille here?"

"No," Wayne said. "She had to run an errand. . . . You're Charles, aren't you?"

Charles's pale eyes narrowed on Wayne, as if he weren't sure whether to be flattered or nervous at being identified.

Charles answered slowly, his long nostrils flaring out. "Do I know you?"

"No, sir, but you should. I'm Wayne Henderson. I married your daughter Josie."

Well, I'll be goddamned. My little Julep's a married lady."

Josie smiled tightly at her father across the booth. Shell's

Pub was quiet at the early hour of five, the bar empty except for Rick Harris at the far end and Danny Chandler behind it.

"Get us some drinks, will ya, Wade?" Charles said when they'd settled against the cracked red leather.

"It's Wayne, Daddy," said Josie.

"I like bourbon," Charles said. "Josephine knows how I like it."

"Charles," said Wayne, "why don't you just tell me—"

"Neat," Josie said dully, her eyes meeting Wayne's. "In a highball glass."

"All right." Wayne leaned down, kissing her cheek. "I won't be long."

When he'd gone, Charles reached across the table and took Josie's hand.

"The pearls look real nice," he said, fingering the loose bracelet around her wrist. "You do like 'em, don't ya?"

Josie nodded dutifully, resisting the urge to lower her hand into her lap and out of reach. "Of course, Daddy. They're beautiful." She kept her eyes fixed on the bar, waiting for Wayne to appear out of the darkness.

"How long you been married then?"

"Two years."

"You pregnant yet?"

She looked up at him, embarrassed. "No," she answered, then said again, "No."

Charles raised his hands. "Hey, I'm just askin', is all. It ain't like I don't know from experience how that all goes."

He chuckled. Josie forced a small smile, knowing he expected one.

"You know, Julep . . ." He leaned in then, his voice dropping, "I was hopin' you might do one little favor for your daddy. Just a little thing."

Dread prickled the skin of her neck. For her father, nothing was little. And if he introduced it as such, it was all the more reason to be suspicious.

"What kind of favor?" she asked.

"Well, it's like this. . . ." He paused to smooth down his hair, one side, then the other. "I've been makin' money again, good money, and you know how I don't trust banks. But see, I can't keep all my money with me in New Orleans. It ain't smart. A man with my connections can't risk that. People steal, take shit that ain't theirs. So I was thinkin' I could leave some money here with you. Just for now. Just till things cool off a little bit for your daddy."

"How much money?" she asked warily.

He sniffed. "Twelve thousand dollars."

"Twelve thousand dollars?"

"Shhh," he said gently, glancing around. He smiled. "Now, I could ask Vivian's family and all them, but you know I don't trust 'em like I trust you." He patted her hand. "God's truth is there ain't nobody I trust more than you, Julep. Nobody. Not your momma, not Dahlia, not nobody."

Josie could feel his eyes on her, waiting.

"So what do you say, baby? Do this little thing for your daddy, will ya?"

Josie looked up to see Wayne slipping through the haze of smoke. "Okay," she said, the desire to appease her father still involuntary, still urgent, the need to keep calm whenever he was around. Her loyalty was always the price for peace.

Besides, she told herself, it wasn't as if she had to tell her sister or mother.

"Here you are, Charles." Wayne set down the highball glass and two Cokes.

Charles raised his bourbon. "To your weddin', Julep." They indulged the toast. Charles waited until he'd taken several sips before he looked at Wayne and said, "You know, it's usually courtesy to ask the father for his daughter's hand. Guess all y'all Yankees do things different, huh?"

Wayne glanced to Josie. "We couldn't get in touch with you, Charles."

"Horseshit." Charles tugged a pack of cigarettes out of his jacket and shook one out. He snapped open his lighter, sucking hard until the flame caught and the paper began to burn. "We get letters in prison, you know. Some of us get phone calls, too. You coulda told him, Julep."

As they left, Wayne reached for Josie's hand but she kept it close to her side.

Driving home in a light rain, Wayne felt a useless regret bloom in him. He wondered what Matthew might have done in his place.

"*See y'all still got* that little café thing goin', Camille."

Camille glanced briefly through the kitchen doorway to where Charles sat at the dining room table, nursing a cup of coffee. She lifted the kettle and poured herself a cup of tea. "That's right."

"Y'all usin' my mother's recipes too, no doubt?"

"My own mother's, actually." She added sugar. "I never cared for Lorraine's gumbo."

She could feel Charles's eyes on her as she calmly stirred her tea and set the spoon in the sink. The past half hour had been shocking for him, she suspected. Arriving to find her in the bath, in no hurry to come out and greet him, let alone prepare him food. When she'd finally emerged from the bathroom, the warm smell of lavender powder trailing behind her, he'd watched her intently as she'd moved around the apartment, no doubt waiting for some sign of pleasure at seeing him, some hint of allegiance, and she'd given him nothing.

Times had changed. Camille wondered if he'd expected that. He should have.

"So where's Dahlia at?"

Camille took the seat across from him, setting down her cup and saucer. "She's away this month."

"A little vacation, huh? Shit, does that girl ever work?"

"She works incredibly hard, Charles. She runs her own business, as a matter of fact."

"Well, I know about work, Camille. Been workin' since I was old enough to reach a doorknob, for Chrissake, and waterin' some rich man's flowers ain't my idea of hard work."

She blew on her tea. "How long do you plan to stay this time?"

"I ain't sure. I wasn't even gonna come, but I was in Atlantic City and I figured what the hell. Vivian ain't doin' so good. Cancer. It's real touch-and-go."

"I'm sorry to hear that."

"Yeah, well. We all pullin' for her." He paused, sipped his coffee. "Y'all probably wonderin' about that business over in the Quarter, ain't ya? I tell you what—they got all bent out of shape over nothin'. I barely laid a hand on that son of a bitch. Let alone his goddamned car. What the hell do I want with an 'eighty-two Chrysler? You tell me that."

Charles tugged out his cigarettes. Camille's eyes snapped to him.

"I'd rather you not smoke in here."

He frowned. "Since when?"

"Since I decided I can't bear the smell."

Charles returned the pack and looked around the room, the harsh reality of his cool reception sinking in at last.

His hands fisted in his lap. "You know you can't marry him if you're still married to me. You do know that, don't ya?"

Camille looked at him evenly over the top of her cup. "That's quite a bracelet you gave Josephine."

"What? Can't a daddy give his baby girl a present?"

"Not when it's paid for with drug money."

His lips thinned. She hadn't expected him to deny it.

"You never minded my money when you was young, Camille."

"I didn't know better."

"Well, it ain't your business. Josephine's all grown-up now. She don't have to play by your rules no more."

"She won't keep it, Charles."

"Don't be so sure. Money does things to people who don't got much of it."

"You would know."

Camille watched the corner of his mouth twitch, wondering if she'd finally pushed him too far. She'd grown so bold in his absence, maybe too bold. But she held his gaze, determined now.

"From what I see, you ain't exactly living like a queen here, Camille."

It was true. The previous summer had been bleak, plagued by long bouts of rain that had kept the tourists off the island for much of July and August, the café's most profitable months. Then there was the matter of the freezer and the oven that had needed replacing within a month of each other. She'd had no idea kitchen equipment could cost so much.

"Restaurants are a hard business, Charles. Some months are better than others."

"Yeah, well. I'm just sayin'. You might want to be careful you don't need somethin' yourself soon. Be a real shame to have to come back grovelin' after talkin' to me this way."

Her eyes rose to his, her voice tight. "I would never take money from you. Never."

He snickered. "I'll remember you said that, darlin'."

"Hello, Charles."

Ben appeared in the doorway. Camille turned and gave him a reassuring smile.

Charles didn't get up, just offered a stiff wave and muttered, "Haskell."

"I thought I recognized that trumpet case in the hall." Ben crossed behind them, touching Camille briefly on her shoulder as he walked by.

Charles saw and his eyes narrowed. "I'll just go bring my things in."

"Don't bother," Camille said. "We haven't room just now."

Charles looked at Camille, the shock bald on his face, but she wouldn't meet his eyes.

In the strained silence, Ben stepped forward.

"There are several inns on the island, Charles. You're welcome to use the phone to call for a room. I'm sure you'll find them all quite comfortable."

Charles looked coldly between them. "I'll use your phone, all right. But I ain't sleepin' in no motel. Not tonight. Not ever."

Camille sipped her tea. Ben's calm smile never faltered.

Josie moved to the other side of the pullout and snapped the fitted sheet over the corner.

"It's just one night," she whispered across the mattress to Wayne. "We'll find him a room tomorrow."

"Why can't we find him a room tonight?" said Wayne.

"It's too late now."

"No, it's not. God, Jo, you didn't even try."

"Wayne, please. Just let it be for tonight, okay? I promise tomorrow he'll go."

Wayne sighed, handing her a folded blanket. "You know he won't."

Josie fluffed it open, settling it neatly over the mattress. As she did, an envelope spilled out of her pocket and landed on the bed. Wayne picked it up, frowning as he felt the bulk between his fingers. "What the heck is this?"

Josie moved to him, her cheeks flushing, and took the envelope. She stuffed it back in her jumper pocket and returned to the pullout. "It's nothing."

Wayne followed her. "I know what cash feels like, Jo."

"It's not mine."

"Then why did you just slip it into your pocket?"

The toilet flushed at the other end of the hall. Josie looked up at Wayne, her bright eyes pleading. "He'll be coming in."

"Is it his money?"

"Yes." She hurried to tuck under the edges of the blanket, her heart racing. "He just asked me to keep it for him, that's all."

"Why?"

"Because he says he's nervous having it in New Orleans."

"Then put it in the bank, for God's sake."

"Daddy doesn't trust banks."

"Doesn't trust banks?" Wayne leaned closer. "Jo, did it ever occur to you the reason he won't put it in a bank is because it's drug money and he *can't* put it in a bank?"

She felt the hot tears of regret and failure rise in her throat. Why did Wayne have to make this so hard? Her whole life she'd done it this way. It was too late to stop now.

"You don't understand," she said wearily. "It's just easier to say yes to Daddy. It always is."

"Easier on who?"

"On *everyone*."

Wayne sighed. "Does Dahlia know?"

"No," said Josie, panicked, "and she can't know. Not Momma either. Please, Wayne."

The bathroom door creaked open; then Charles's heavy footsteps clicked along the bare floorboards.

"I'll send it back to him as soon as he's home," Josie whispered.

Wayne looked at her. "Promise me."

She touched his hand. "I promise."

𝐵𝑢𝑡 𝑡𝘩𝑒𝑟𝑒 𝑤𝑜𝑢𝑙𝑑 𝑏𝑒 no need for a hotel. During the night, Vivian took a turn for the worse and Charles decided to leave the next morning on the seven-fifteen ferry. No matter the chilly reception upon his arrival, he was sure Josie would be hard at work in the kitchen with a proper send-off for his departure, but when Charles came downstairs, he found the first floor of the cape quiet, and only Ben present, standing in the living room.

"Ready, Charles?"

"What are *you* doin' here?" Charles looked around. "Where's Josephine at?"

"She and Camille went in early to the café. Busy day. Have a big order of jambalaya for the Historical Society this afternoon. I said I'd be glad to give you a ride down to the ferry."

"I'm sure you would," Charles said, snatching up his cases as Ben reached for them. "Like to make certain I get on the boat, wouldn't ya?"

"There's a bad storm coming, Charles." Ben pointed to the window, his smile pleasant but firm. "Wouldn't want you to get caught in the rain."

"Horseshit." Charles gave the downstairs a final searching, as if refusing to accept the lonely state of his departure. "Horseshit," he said again.

Ben opened the front door and let Charles exit first.

The Jeep was silent as Ben steered them through town. Charles's eyes stayed fixed out the window, one weathered hand tapping anxiously on his left knee, the other hand fondling the bulk of his cigarettes through his shirt pocket.

Ben flexed his fingers over the wheel. "I think it would be a good idea if you didn't come back to the island again, Charles."

Charles squinted. "What did you say?"

"You heard me."

"You arrogant son of a bitch. You got no right!"

"I've got every right." Ben pulled them against the curb, throwing the car into park. He turned to Charles, his eyes fierce behind his glasses. "And I'm saying it again: I don't want to see you on this island anymore."

There was a long pause; then Charles spoke tightly, his teeth clenched so hard Ben could see his jaw pop. "You gonna be sorry—you know that, Haskell? Up until now I been real patient and tolerant of you, but no more. You gonna be real sorry you said that to me."

"I don't want a war with you, Charles."

"Yeah, well," said Charles, his eyes hard on Ben's, "you

shoulda thought of that before you poisoned my wife and baby girls against me."

"No, Charles." Ben's gaze remained leveled behind his glasses, his voice even. "I'm fairly certain you did that all on your own."

For several agonizing seconds, Ben believed Charles would finally strike him, and he readied himself for the blow, his hands fisting on top of the wheel. But the punch never came. Charles just reached for his bags, threw open the car door, and climbed out.

He lowered himself to glare through the passenger window. His eyes were slitted, tiny blue specks rimmed in pink.

"It don't matter what you say, Haskell, or what you do. I ain't got much in my life, but what's mine, I keep. And I ain't never gonna let them go. You got me?"

Ben turned forward, his heart racing. "Have a safe trip, Charles."

Charles stepped back from the window, his eyes still fixed on Ben.

"I'll see you soon, Haskell," he said. "*Real* soon."

Ben watched Charles amble down the road, seeing the ferry in the distance, and he stayed parked at the curb until Charles appeared on the upper deck and the ferry belched out its departing horn.

Only when the boat was too far from shore to be called back did Ben finally loosen the knot of his fists, his fingers unfurling like an exhaled breath.

Twenty-six

Little Gale Island
Fall 1988

On the first day of November, the island woke to a dusting of wet snow and shiny streets. Matthew had to walk to the café, his car refusing to start, but he didn't mind the brisk exercise, not this morning. When he came into the restaurant, Josie was at the counter. Ronnie Powell and his grandson occupied the window booth, three-year-old Troy Powell using his gumbo as finger paint. Matthew grinned as he passed them, waving to the old man.

"Congratulate me, JoJo." Matthew slid in behind Josie and gave her a quick peck on the cheek.

She spun around. "For what?"

"I got the job."

"You're kidding! The one in Portsmouth?"

"No, the one in Florida."

"Oh." Josie smiled but her eyes gave her disappointment away. Matthew couldn't believe she still cared so much, when she and Wayne had been married almost three years already.

"Come on, kiddo," he said. "It only sounds far."

She nodded firmly, turning as the tears came.

"Hey, there, Matthew," Ronnie Powell called out. "Did I hear you say you got a job?"

"Sure did, Mr. Powell."

"So where you goin', young man?"

"Florida. Miami."

"Oh, Christ, don't do that."

Matthew laughed. "Have to, Mr. Powell. My pop says he's tired of me messing up his paper every morning."

"Maybe *he* is," Josie said, knocking used coffee grinds into the trash.

"Hey . . ." Matthew rubbed her shoulders, dropping a kiss on the top of her head. "It's not like this place will go under without me."

"Don't even joke," Josie said, her expression suddenly strained.

Matthew's grin faded. He knew Josie was right to be nervous. He'd seen his father's features grow heavy in recent months, pulled down by fear for the future of the café. For the first time since the Little Gale Gumbo Café had opened, they'd reduced their hours to save on heating costs.

"I'm really worried about this place, Matty. Momma won't come right out and say it, but I know it's bad when Ben's calling the bank and asking for an extension."

"He did that?"

"Last week, in the kitchen. He didn't know I could hear."

Matthew shrugged. "They'll figure it out, JoJo. They always do. Besides, they can always let you go when you're up to your neck in diapers and mashed peas."

Little Troy had climbed out of the booth and toddled over to the jukebox, his tiny fingers stretching to reach the buttons. Josie watched him, smiling sadly. "Not likely."

"Trust me," Matthew said, "my father won't let you stand on your feet all day."

"That's not what I meant."

Matthew turned Josie gently around to him, trying to read her lowered face, the fragile set of her mouth, the lips ready to crumple at any second. She didn't have to explain. He knew that she and Wayne had been trying to get pregnant for two years now and that it wasn't working. He'd overheard Josie telling Dahlia that they were going to see a fertility specialist in Boston. That had been a month ago. Matthew had wondered about the visit, but he hadn't wanted to pry. They weren't teenagers anymore, huddled around a bonfire on the beach, spilling out their guts about every tiny thing that had irked or crushed them that day. Failed math tests and embarrassing slipups in gym class. Defeats that had seemed so life-ending. Now in their mid-twenties, there were some things they simply couldn't tell one another.

Josie smiled up at him, her eyes full. "That's great news, Matty. Really it is."

In the next moment, Wayne appeared from the kitchen and saw them standing there, Matthew's hands on his wife's slight shoulders, fingers kneading.

"I can't believe he's really leaving," Josie said later that day while she and Dahlia shared a beer on Ben's porch, watching Wayne change the oil on the Wagoneer.

"He's been gone before," Dahlia said.

"Yeah, for college. But he always came back."

"He'll come back this time too."

"But it won't be the same. You know it won't."

Dahlia shrugged. "People leave, Joze."

"Not everyone," she said. "Jack didn't."

The sisters fell quiet, each gazing out at a different point on the horizon. Wayne glanced up from under the hood and waved.

"You could always just tell him, you know," Josie said, waving back, then pulling her jacket sleeves down over her chilled fingers.

"Tell who?"

"Jack. Tell him you still love him."

"Who says I still love him?"

Josie gave her sister a flat look. "Don't be dim, Dahl. And don't make me out to be dim either, thank you very much."

Dahlia sighed. "He made his choice, Joze."

"Baloney." Josie grabbed the beer and took a sip. "You made it for him."

"They have a little girl. A sweet little girl who doesn't need her heart broken. It's too late, and I've made my peace with that."

"Right," said Josie. "And that would be why you haven't had a steady boyfriend in over three years now."

Dahlia took the beer back, swigged it.

Josie reached out and rubbed her sister's arm. "People change their minds, Dahl. That's all I'm saying."

Dahlia looked across the lawn at Wayne, hunched over a pan of old oil. "Did you?"

Josie smiled weakly. "Yes," she said. "A little bit more every day."

Matthew stepped into the café the next afternoon to see Thomas Dunham walking out of the kitchen, looking as guilty as a cheating spouse as he wiped his mouth with a napkin.

"Delicious as always, Camille," Margery's stern husband said on his way past the counter. "Matthew," he added with a stiff nod, setting his hat on his head and heading for the front door.

Matthew watched the older man hurry out. "Why was Thomas Dunham coming out of the kitchen?"

"Because that's where he eats his bowl of gumbo," Camille said simply.

"Since when?"

Camille grinned. "Since Margery caught him eating it in a booth and threatened to leave him. We decided after that he'd be more comfortable taking his lunch in the kitchen."

Matthew smiled. "*We?*"

Camille took him by the hand. "Come on back. I have some things for you."

Matthew stood in the café's kitchen and watched while Camille packed him enough gumbo to feed the entire island.

"How far do you think I'm going?" he teased, sliding up beside her. "The moon?"

"It might as well be. Florida's awfully far from here."

An urge to defend himself rose up unexpectedly. "It's not like I was *trying* to find the farthest place, you know."

Camille smiled gently, reaching out to smooth down a wild curl at his temple. "Or maybe you were."

Matthew watched her return to the sink to wash her hands. "Josie said the café's in trouble."

He saw her eyes flutter nervously, but she masked her discomfort with a smile as she shook water off her fingers.

"We'll get through it, baby," she said evenly. "It's nothing for you to worry about."

But Matthew wouldn't be discouraged. "How bad is it?"

Camille shrugged, smiled, but Matthew could see the faint sheen of tears sparkling in her eyes.

He sighed, his own heart sinking. "That bad, huh?"

She returned to him, her hands still damp, and cupped his face in her palms, reaching up to kiss each cheek. "I have something else for you too," she said, releasing him and crossing back to the sink.

"No more! I'll weigh three hundred pounds before I get to Edison. They'll have to use the Jaws of Life to get me out of my car."

Camille winked at him. "It's not for eating."

She reached up to the shelf above the sink and came back with a red pouch tied with a black ribbon. Matthew eyed it curiously.

"It's a gris-gris bag," she explained. "Each one is made differently, for different reasons. This one is for good luck in life transitions." She pressed it against his heart. "Made with love."

Matthew pulled Camille to him, holding her tightly. When they broke apart and she had returned to her dishes, he looked around the kitchen, unprepared for how quickly the tears rose. He gripped the bag in his fingers, thinking about Camille's words, and an unexpected hope bloomed within him.

After dinner, Matthew told his father and Camille that he was going out. It was his last night on the island. He had to make the rounds, he explained. Say good-bye to old friends. The ones who wouldn't be stopping by the house to see him off in the morning.

He forced himself to take the long way to Dahlia's house, steering through town first, as if there was another reason he'd climbed into his car at nine o'clock at night. But the island roads were too quiet, any tourist traffic gone for months now, and hope as he did for some delay, he had none. When her rented cottage came into view, he released the gas pedal without hesitation.

He had nothing to lose, he told himself as he mounted the steps to her front porch. Maybe she'd be thinking what he was thinking: that there could be only one right way for the two of them to say good-bye. Sweeping open the storm door and stepping inside, he promised himself he hadn't arrived with expectations, only desire. Pure and clear.

The music was loud. Marvin Gaye. He had to shout.

"In the kitchen," Dahlia called, and he walked quickly down the hall to the back of the house.

She was at the sink, wearing an oversize sweater and a pair of jeans. "Hi, stranger."

"Shit, don't call me that yet," he said, glancing around the cluttered kitchen.

If he'd come at a bad time, she didn't let on. She sipped

from a glass of red wine and pointed him to a bottle on the other end of the counter. He poured himself some.

"What are we having?" he asked, coming beside her.

"Pizza." She nodded to an empty box dangling off the top of an overstuffed trash can in the corner. "I thought you were eating at the house?"

"I did," he admitted. "Your mom made blackened trout and ginger cake. But you know I always have room for your cardboard store-bought pizza."

"Ha-ha," Dahlia said, licking sauce off her finger. "We should call Joze."

"Sure," he said. "Later."

Dahlia nodded agreeably and bent down to check on the pizza. She'd been expecting him somehow, she realized—how could she not have been?—and he knew it. She poured herself more wine and watched him move leisurely around the kitchen, swaying and tapping the air in time to the music. His leaving struck her suddenly, though she'd been aware of her refusal to confront it for weeks now. She'd miss him deeply. She didn't dare consider how much. Seeing the flush of his cheeks, his dizzy smile, she knew he had tallied *his* feelings. He'd come here with the balance.

They sipped their wine. Matthew rested against the fridge.

"I'm thinking of getting a dog when I get down there."

"You should," Dahlia said. "A really big one that eats everything and sheds all over the house."

"You mean to replace you?"

She chucked a dish towel at him. He caught it, laughing.

The smell of the cooking pizza, fatty sausage and salty olives, filled him with a fierce giddiness. The wine was warm and smooth. He began to feel its effect. The familiar, always pleasant beginnings of the buzz, a weightless ease, slow and carefree.

The kitchen looked cozy to him, the pile of dirty dishes in the sink somehow charming.

"Gonna miss me, Dee?" he asked finally when she wouldn't confess on her own.

"Jesus, how can you even ask me that?" Dahlia pulled the pizza from the oven, set it on the stovetop. "It was hard enough with all of us moving out of the house. Adjusting to that distance. Knowing you weren't just down the hall anymore. Somebody to sneak a beer with."

"And do your algebra homework for you."

"One time!"

"Bullshit," he said. "Try a dozen."

Dahlia shrugged, chuckled. "A lot of good it did me. I still got a C-plus."

"Serves you right."

They carried the pizza into the living room and ate on the couch, draining the bottle of wine.

"Let's open another," Matthew said, starting to rise.

Dahlia touched his arm to slow him. "Let's wait for Joze."

"Why bother?" he said. "She won't come. It's too late."

"Not for us."

He reached for Dahlia's cheek, ran his thumb down her throat. "I'll see her tomorrow, Dee."

Dahlia saw the familiar yearning in his eyes. He hadn't come here for a reunion with both of them, and she knew that too.

She let her head fall against his hand. "We shouldn't, Matty."

"Why not?" He smiled, even as her expression remained serious. "Not even for old times' sake?"

"Matty . . ."

"Come on, Dee. Think of it as my going-away present."

She looked at him sharply. "What a shitty thing to say."

"I'm sorry. I didn't mean that."

"Didn't you?"

He wanted to repair the moment quickly, knew he had to. He cupped her face in his palm, emboldened by the wine, by the knowledge that he was leaving.

"I just thought it might be nice," he said. "Does it have to mean more than that?"

Dahlia smiled, reaching out to push his bangs back. "You once told me everything means something, remember?"

Matthew remembered it clearly, but still he shrugged.

"It won't make it any easier, you know," she said.

"I'm not expecting it to."

"Liar. You always do," Dahlia whispered as his mouth came down over her face. First he kissed each cheek, then her lips, one at a time, lingering until he felt her kiss him back.

Looking into her eyes, in an unmistakable flash, he saw what might have been obligation—or worse, pity. But he chose to see it as something warm and familiar. What he'd always imagined he saw in Dahlia's face when she looked upon him. Something binding. Something real.

They lay down on the couch. He turned off the light before she could.

"The house is so quiet."

Camille stood at the parlor window the next evening, smiling at the faded folds in the curtains she'd hung for Ben so many years ago. Ben stood behind her, his hands resting gently on her shoulders. She turned her face just slightly, enough to brush the hard peaks of his knuckles with her lips. It didn't matter that the children had moved out years earlier. Somehow, their daily activities had always brought them back to the house, even allowing for the occasional extended stay in their old bedrooms between rentals, breakups, or new jobs.

But tonight was different, and both Camille and Ben knew it. Matthew had left the island that morning, and Dahlia and Josie had finally made their own lives, their own homes. Even the café seemed to be slipping away from them.

Camille almost didn't dare ask. "Did you hear from the bank?"

Ben kissed her neck, rested his chin against her soft, graying curls. "They want to be patient, but . . ."

"But they're not a charity, right?" Camille finished softly. She frowned, feeling useless tears rising in her throat. "We just need a few more months. Winters are always tough. They have to understand that. Every business on the island has lost money in the past few summers. We can't be the only ones."

Ben wrapped his arms around her shoulders. "I know."

They spoke little as they made their way up the stairs to his room. For years, Ben had asked Camille to move out of the apartment and into his side of the house, but she had refused, and he had finally come to accept her simple terms. It didn't matter that she no longer needed the space, that there were only two of them in the rambling house now. Camille loved her home, though they had shared it as one almost from the start.

They made love on top of the sheets, then lay side by side under them. When the phone rang, neither wanted to leave the soft nest they'd built, but Camille implored Ben, suggesting it might be Matthew from the road. She snuggled deeper, stretching leisurely, warm and content, her worries abandoned for a moment. When Ben returned a few minutes later, his face was drawn. Camille sat up, panicked.

"What is it?" she asked. "What's happened?"

"That was Charles's brother Louis," Ben said, his voice oddly flat. "Charles told him to call. He said Charles was sentenced today in New Orleans. Eighteen years."

Ben climbed back into bed and Camille rolled into his embrace. They lay there, wide-eyed and silent, their hearts swelling with a relief they had never imagined.

At last, it was possible.

Charles Bergeron might never darken the shores of Little Gale Island again.

Wayne watched Josie in the moonlight, her knees drawn up to her chest on the window seat.

"You were supposed to send it back, Jo. You promised."

"I meant to. A hundred times."

"So why didn't you?"

She shrugged uselessly. "What does it matter? We need it now."

Wayne sighed. "What happens if he gets out and he wants the money back?"

"He won't," Josie said firmly, her eyes fixed on the night sky.

"He won't what? Want it back?"

"Get out." Josie turned to her husband and smiled calmly. "Eighteen years is a long time. Daddy's not a healthy man. He won't see the end of it."

"You don't know that," Wayne said gently. "He'd survive it just for spite."

"Then we'll cross that bridge when we come to it," she said. "We can always save it back."

Wayne considered that, frowning down at his hands where they lay in his lap. "What do we tell Camille and Ben? You know your mother. She won't take it if she knows where the money came from. She'd sooner see the café go under."

"I've already thought of that," Josie said. "We'll tell her it's your money. That you've been saving it in an account since you were a teenager."

"What if they *still* won't take the money?"

"They'll take it," she said. "They have to take it."

And they did have to; Wayne knew that. The café would close if they didn't. The threat of that unthinkable event had been on their minds for months now. Ben had cleared out his savings and taken out a second mortgage on the house and still they'd come up short. The summer season was still months away. They'd never get through the stretch otherwise.

Josie came back to bed, pressing herself against Wayne as they lay back down together.

"We can't tell Dahlia either," she whispered. "She'd never forgive me."

"We won't tell her."

But even as Josie nodded in the darkness, even as the thin, warm layer of relief began to settle over her thumping heart, she felt the crushing weight of regret land with it.

It was a law of the universe: Sisters weren't supposed to keep secrets from each other.

Part Four

Simmer for one hour.
Add shrimp
at the very end.

Twenty-seven

Little Gale Island
Monday, June 17, 2002
7:00 a.m.

Morning came quickly to the island, like something in the grip of a current, a stream rushing after heavy rain, the early sky brushed with soft gray clouds that barely moved no matter how long and hard Dahlia glared at them from her bedroom window. She lay back down, yanked the sheets above her head, and tried to find sleep again, but thoughts flickered, some almost blinding in their clarity, others so dim she could barely grasp them before they fled again. She'd never been so drunk that she'd blacked out—native New Orleanians knew how to hold their liquor, thank you very much—but today she wished for such amnesia, a few portions of the previous evening plucked from her brain: Matthew's caressing of her face, his gentle but firm pressure on her hand, the look of hurt when she'd pulled away. She thought he'd wished her good night on the steps of the inn, but she might have merely hoped for the words.

Surrendering at last, she dragged herself out of bed and down the stairs, facing the flat light of dawn that fell in fuzzy streaks across her wood floors, the dishes in the drainer, the dusty collection of sea glass above the sink. The stretch of wall where Lionel and Roman's painting had hung until recently looked somehow brighter to her, or maybe it was only her imagination.

She pushed through the back door and stepped out onto the deck to find the mist still clinging to her porch railing and the rows of seedlings lined along it. It was all right, she decided. Rising in the company of the fog might be a good thing: cloaking her, hiding her from her lies as she tried to begin this impossible day.

"Morning, Chief."

The short, broad-faced officer climbed to his feet when he saw Jack coming toward him down the hospital corridor.

Jack patted the officer on the shoulder. "Take a break, Brian."

"Thank you, sir."

Jack pushed through the door. The smells that had accosted him in the lobby seemed stronger in Ben's small room, the cloying odors of chemicals and the thick scent of synthetic sweetness meant to mask them but somehow managing to enhance them instead. But it was the stillness of the room that chilled him the most, the distinct lack of air and life, even though Ben lay inside a web of tubes just a few feet away.

Jack drew in a resolved breath and pulled a padded folding chair to the head of the bed. He sat down, letting a few moments pass before he said in an easy voice, as if he and Ben had run into each other at one of Clem's pumps on a Friday night, "Hi, Ben. It's supposed to be a hot one today. They're saying upper eighties."

He drew closer, his elbows on his knees, his hands fisted.

He sighed deeply. "Wish you could help me out here, Ben. I'm pretty sure Charles was at your house that night, long before you knew it. I'm thinking he came looking for something, but I don't know what that would have been, and I'm betting you might."

Jack paused, studying Ben's profile, his drawn flesh almost as pale as the pillowcase that cushioned his motionless head.

A memory overwhelmed Jack; he smiled broadly.

"I keep thinking about that time we got up on your roof in that crazy storm, and you told me how you used to look at that branch every day, and that you knew it was only a matter of time before it snapped off, but that you couldn't bear to take it down." Jack's smile lessened, the irony too painful. "I can't help wondering if you felt that way about Charles too. Christ, if maybe we all did."

The door opened. Jack straightened reflexively, smiled at the nurse who came in.

"Don't let me disturb you," she said. "Are you his . . . ?" The nurse stopped, seeing the badge hanging from Jack's neck. "Oh." She smiled. "Guess not."

Jack rose to let her by, moving to the window. He watched as she toured the various machines, changing the IV bags, neatening tubes. "Is it still raining?" she asked, moving to the other side of the bed.

"Just a drizzle. It's supposed to clear." Jack folded his arms, leaned back against the glass. "You have much experience with stroke victims like this?"

"Some. But every patient's different, you know."

"I'm sure. Is it true that people in this condition can hear things, conversations?"

"Some doctors think so."

"Do you?"

The nurse shrugged. "I think it's hard to sit in a room with someone and not talk to 'em, don't you?"

Jack smiled, nodded.

"I do know one thing, though." The nurse glanced over at Jack, her small brown eyes creasing with conviction. "People can surprise you."

Josie was brewing a fresh pot of coffee when Dahlia sailed into the café at ten thirty. Rhonda Simon and her sister Stella were gossiping over a plate of beignets in the window booth, while Horace Anderson sat over a bowl of cheese grits at a table against the wall. Behind him, the Finnegan brothers chuckled over scrambled eggs and sausages.

"Morning, all," Dahlia said, giving the room a broad wave. Wayne looked up from the register, hoping to warn Dahlia of Josie's mood before she reached the counter, but she refused to meet his gaze. Wayne knew it wouldn't have done any good. He'd learned long ago that when the sisters wanted a fight, there was no stopping them.

"In case you're wondering, bourbon and I are no longer on speaking terms," Dahlia said, coming behind the counter to stand beside Josie. She reached into the case for a blueberry muffin. "I mean it. Bourbon is dead to me. If he calls, I'm not here." Dahlia tore her muffin in half and sprayed crumbs across the counter, which Josie scooped up and clapped noisily into the sink.

"There's this crazy new invention called a plate, you know." Josie snatched up a wet towel and marched around the counter to clean a vacated table, clearing a pair of coffee cups and plates.

Dahlia sighed. "You're mad."

"Gee, you think?" Josie glared at her sister on her way back to the counter, dropping the dishes into the bin with a crash. The Finnegan brothers glanced at one another over their mugs and rolled their eyes. Over the years, café customers had come to accept the complimentary side of sisterly bickering with every meal.

"This is because Matty and I kissed last night, isn't it?" said Dahlia.

Josie said nothing, just stormed back behind the counter and pushed through the swinging kitchen door.

Dahlia followed her. "Oh, come on, Joze. He's in a lot of pain. What did you want me to do?"

"Don't you dare," Josie said, whirling around. "Don't you dare play the great saint like you did the last time you and he were together, like you were doing him some great big favor. This has nothing to do with Matty—this is all about *you*. You wanting one more chance to prove that you still have him wrapped around your finger!"

"Me?" said Dahlia. "What about *you*? Walking around here lit up like a goddamn Christmas tree, hanging on his every word? And that was hardly a peck on the cheek you delivered last night, you know. How do I know you didn't slip him a little tongue yourself?"

"God, you're disgusting!" Josie shoved her sister out of the way of the sink, snapping on the faucet and splashing her hands under the stream. "You can't ever let me have one special moment with him, can you? One moment that's just mine. You never could."

"What is that supposed to mean?"

"Don't be dim," Josie said, wiping her hands on her apron. "You know exactly what it means. You never think about anybody but yourself. And speaking of which, why didn't you tell me the truth about sending the Perez to be cleaned?"

Dahlia groaned, wishing she'd never said anything to Matthew. Josie could bleed information from people like a goddamn mosquito.

"Because I knew you'd freak out," Dahlia said. "And it needed it. It was filthy."

"Filthy? This coming from a woman who never cleans her bathroom."

"I clean my bathroom every month, thank you very much."

"You spilled wine on it, didn't you?" Josie said. "God, I knew I never should have let you keep it."

"For your information, Momma gave it to me."

"So who'd you take it to?"

"Some guy in Portland."

"Some guy? You gave Momma's favorite painting to *some guy*?"

"He's legit, Joze."

"Like you'd know the difference," Josie snapped, moving to the pantry.

"Well, I do know one thing, baby sister." Dahlia followed Josie across the kitchen. "I know why you're putting the brakes on this whole adoption plan, and I know it has nothing to do with taking care of Ben."

Josie pulled out a bag of pecans and slammed the pantry door shut. "Is that right?"

"You think there's still a chance with him, don't you?"

"Who?"

"Who do you think?" said Dahlia. "You never stopped carrying a torch for Matty. Admit it! And now that he's back, you're falling for him all over again."

Josie dropped the bag onto the counter. "You're a crazy woman, you know that? You are one hundred percent certifiable."

Dahlia crossed her arms, decided now. "Then why did you never mention taking care of Ben until after you found out that Holly and Matty had broken up?"

"Why should I have to mention it? It's obvious!"

"And you think that's what Ben or Momma would want? To have you put your life on hold to empty bedpans and drool cups?"

Josie's eyes filled instantly. "That's an awful thing to say."

"It's the truth."

Josie yanked off her apron and threw it on the counter, pushing past Dahlia to pull her purse down from the shelf. "I don't expect you to understand," she said, storming out the back door to the delivery dock. "It would never occur to you to put someone else's needs before yours. Not in a million years."

"Horseshit!" Dahlia said, right behind her. "If you want to live out some teenage fantasy, you go right ahead, baby sister, but don't you dare play the righteous nursemaid."

Josie rushed to the parked Buick and climbed into the driver's seat. Dahlia reached the car, gripping the open window as Josie revved the engine.

"Nothing happened last night, okay?" Dahlia said wearily. "Matty wanted me to come up but I didn't. I couldn't."

"How big of you," Josie said, shifting the car into reverse. "Remind me to order your medal the next time I'm in Portland."

Dahlia stepped back and watched the Buick lurch out into the street.

Wayne appeared in the doorway, hands on his hips. "Where's she going?"

"Where else?" Dahlia shrugged. "Away from me."

Jack left Ben's room and took the stairs to the morgue. He'd been dreading the autopsy all weekend. Despite his recent theory of Charles's whereabouts in the hours before the crime—a theory Jack had grown very comfortable with—his police report remained unfinished, and now he'd have to explain why to Frank Collins.

Reaching the heavy door at last, Jack steeled himself for Collins's usual jabs, but when he stepped inside the cool, tiled room, he was surprised to find the medical examiner's assistant sitting alone at a stainless-steel desk, papers spread out around him.

"Hey, Jason."

"Chief." The pathology student spun around in his chair and smiled broadly. "You're early. Frank won't be in until one. He had to go to Topsham for that murder-suicide they had over the weekend."

"Yeah, I heard about that," Jack said, looking around. "Awful. Christ."

"Husband and wife," the young man said. "Makes me glad I never got married."

"Not everybody wants to kill their spouse, Jason."

"Yeah, right. Try telling that to my folks." He reached for a tin of Pringles, shaking them at Jack. "Want one?"

"No, thanks," Jack said, turning to go. "Hey, don't let Collins see you eating those in here. He'll have *you* under one of these sheets."

The young man laughed. "I'm not too worried. Your vic's already a mess. I found pieces of gravel in his hair, his clothes. He even had gravel in his shoes. Weird, huh?"

Jack frowned at the wall of drawers. Maybe a little weird, he thought. But then, Charles might have struggled getting up the ladder that night, might have stumbled a few times in the growing dark.

"Want me to tell Frank you'll be back at one, Chief?"

Jack shook his head as he opened the door. "Just tell him I'll call him later."

Much later, Jack thought as he took the stairs to the parking lot two at a time.

Matthew squinted at the silver travel clock on his nightstand and groaned. He should have been relieved to find it so late, grateful to finally have just cause to stop flopping around on his mattress chasing sleep. The memory of the night before returned to him, clearer now in the prickly light of morning. He wanted to blame the bourbon for his clumsy pass at Dahlia, but he couldn't. Any more than he could blame her rejection of him on the same. After twenty-five years of friendship, they'd grown too old to salve their wounds against each other. He understood that now.

He dressed and went downstairs, fixing himself a cup of coffee in the lobby. Thoughts of Holly flooded him, warming him as he took a seat on the porch and considered what lay ahead.

He'd call her; that's what he'd do. He'd tell her once and for all that she'd been right to blame him for keeping her at arm's length for so many years. He understood why she'd run to Peter, but now she could run back.

Pulling out his cell phone, Matthew imagined how the conversation would go. Holly would tell him that they'd have to take it slow, that what was broken between them couldn't be repaired in a weekend, and Matthew would agree. Of course he would. If she still wanted a baby, then they would keep trying. Lots of couples weren't a perfect match that way. The doctors didn't know everything. Getting pregnant was as much in the head as the . . . well, head. Matthew chuckled at that as he settled the phone against his ear. He'd remember that joke, and Holly would chuckle too.

After several rings, she picked up, sounding so groggy Matthew thought he had dialed the wrong number.

"Holl?"

"Matt?" She paused, her voice weak when she began again. "Is it Ben? Has something happened?"

"No, he's the same. That's not why I'm calling." Matthew frowned at the horizon, thinking she should have been at the office by now. "Did I wake you?"

"No. I'm staying home today, that's all."

"Are you sick?"

"No . . . no, I just . . ." She stopped. He heard her take a hard swallow. "I think I just ate something bad, that's all. You know how those places on the beach are."

Matthew's gut told him to end the call, to let the promise of their earlier conversation lie, pleasant and hopeful, but he couldn't help himself.

"Holl . . ." He stood, building strength as he paced the long boards of the porch floor. "I know we said we'd wait until I got back to talk, but if there's something you want to say, I don't want to wait. I've been doing a lot of thinking here. You were right about everything. About me not wanting to let go of the island and my life here, but I'm ready to do that now, and I think tha—"

"Matt." Holly's weary voice found a burst of force, startling him. She drew in a shaky breath. "Oh, God, I didn't want to have to do this over the phone."

The next pause felt endless. Matthew fixed his gaze on the porch railing, feeling his heart race.

"I'm pregnant."

He reached for the railing.

"Matt? Are you still there?"

He gripped the rounded edge, his knuckles whitening.

"Matt, please. Say something."

He stared out at the harbor, thinking how cold the water looked. "Congratulations."

Then he clapped the phone shut.

The attendant on duty at the Merry Manor smiled as Jack approached the reception desk carrying a small brown bag in his hand.

"Hi, Bonnie. Is she in her room?"

"I think she's scrapbooking, Jack. The craft room. Down the hall to your left."

"Thanks." He walked to the end of the building, finding the

small room where several old women were crowded around a card table, singing along to Tony Bennett.

"Good afternoon, ladies."

Irene Thurlow looked up, her round face flooding with delight. "Jack!" The rest of the table greeted him while his mother wheeled herself away from the table. "Ooh!" she squealed, seeing the bag. "You're wonderful!"

He held open the door and pushed her through.

"Thank God you came when you did, Jack. If I had to listen to another story about Joyce's son-in-law the brilliant doctor, I was going to put my head through a three-hole punch."

Jack chuckled, steering them around a maid's cart. "I thought scrapbooking was on Thursdays."

"It was," Irene said, waving to an old man coming out of his room. "But we changed it to Mondays when Althea started PT again."

"Ah. Of course."

At the cafeteria, they settled into a sunlit corner with navy sectionals and an arching ficus. Irene dug a praline out of the bag, moaned as she bit into it. "Still as good as ever," she said. "I'll never forget when you brought me home that first bag, Jack. I'd never had anything so wonderful in all my life."

"I remember."

Irene sighed. "It's just so awful what happened. I feel terrible for Matthew, and for Ben, too, of course. And those girls, Jack. After everything they've been through. You know how much I always liked Dahlia. So did you, if memory serves."

Jack smiled, seeing the searching look in his mother's eyes. "Yes, I did," he said. "Very much."

"I'm sure you've been seeing her during all of this."

"Some."

"Strange she never married, isn't it?"

"Not everyone gets married, Mom." Jack glanced at the clock on the wall. "I should get going."

"Oh, stay," Irene pleaded. "I thought we could have some coffee cake. Look, Bernard's putting out some fresh now."

"I can't," Jack said, rising. "I'll come by tomorrow, okay?"

"Jack?"

"What?"

Irene smiled up at him. "Everyone deserves a second chance, you know."

Jack leaned down and kissed her cheek. He knew.

Josie couldn't remember the last time she'd come to the cove. Certainly not like this, crying like a heartsick schoolgirl. She rested at the top of the dunes and took stock of the scene. It used to be that the cove was deserted most of the day, that it was effortless to slip into anonymity beneath the slick rocks. Now families and couples crowded the short strip of pebbled sand, their delighted children crouching over the tidal pools to pluck out crabs and periwinkles. Another reminder of how much time had gone by.

She took off her sandals and carried them down to the water, slipping between a pair of girls who trolled the sand, bent at the waist. Josie sat close to the water, uncaring of the nearing surf, and stared out at the horizon.

"Do you want that one?" a little voice asked.

It took Josie a moment to understand that the question was directed at her. She turned to face the taller of the two girls, her long curls pushed away from her eyes by a pair of swimming goggles, making a high wall of tangled blond hair that flopped like a rooster comb.

"That piece," the girl said, pointing to Josie's hip, where a chunk of green sea glass was visible. "Do you want that one?"

Josie plucked the smoothed shard free, wiped it clean, and held it out. "Finders keepers," she said. "It's a nice one. Green was always my favorite."

"Blue's the best," the girl said firmly, dropping the new treasure into her swinging pail. "I have two pieces at home. But I got those on another beach. This beach doesn't have very much. Look." The girl held out her plastic bucket. Josie peered in, seeing only a few pieces skidding around the bottom.

"There used to be lots of sea glass here," Josie said.

"Really? Where did it all go?"

"People found it. My sister and I found quite a bit, actually."

"I have a sister too." The girl pointed up the beach to a toddler wobbling around in an orange two-piece. "She eats sand."

Josie smiled, her eyes filling with tears. "You're very lucky. Sisters are special."

"That's what my mom says."

"Your momma's right."

"Molly!"

Josie saw the girl's mother waving from the top of the beach. The girl swung around, shrugged. "I gotta go. Mom says we can't stay all day today."

Josie watched the girl race back up the sand, her friend following, their excited cries folding over one another, buckets sailing behind them, and the ache returned within her, deeper and heavier and more coiling than ever.

She looked back at the rocks, a memory returning to her. The five of them on a blustery spring day. Momma insisting on a group picture. They'd debated for several minutes where to pose, settling finally on a stretch of rocks flat enough that

Matthew could set up the timer on the camera, but not so flat that the portrait hadn't turned out tilted. Still Momma had adored it, hanging it above the café's stove in a Woolworth frame and moving it only to clean the grease off its edges every few months.

Josie wiped her eyes, the waves of longing and remorse sweeping over her. She'd been so sure, so adamant she'd given up her feelings for Matthew, when all she'd really done was fold them away and store them like blankets, keeping secrets like currency, as if she might use them to buy back the past.

She rose and started up the beach, headed back for the car, her steps slow at first, then hastening as sudden panic charged through her.

Oh, God, she thought. Silly fool. What had she done?

Twenty-eight

Little Gale Island

December 1988

Dahlia knew it didn't take more than one test. If there were two lines, there were two lines. There was no such thing as a false positive. And still she had peed on a total of eleven plastic sticks and now sat on the rounded edge of her tub and stared at the pile of them in her sink, wondering what the hell she was going to do.

Josie was struggling to carry a tray of gumbo bowls around four full tables when Dahlia burst into the café an hour later and blocked her passage. "I need to talk to you."

"Can't it wait?" asked Josie, wide-eyed. "Momma's at the

store and Wayne and Ben had to run out a delivery and I'm up to my ears!"

Without another word, Dahlia took the tray from Josie and set the three overflowing bowls down in front of the closest customer. Martin Glover sat back, withered hands up. "I didn't order these!"

"They're on the house," said Dahlia over her shoulder as she dragged her sister past the counter and into the kitchen.

"What in the world is the matter with you?" Josie demanded, pulling free of Dahlia's grip when the door had swung closed. "Those were going to the Templetons!"

"I'm pregnant," Dahlia announced flatly.

Josie looked as if she'd been punched. "What?"

"Yup." Dahlia walked to the shelf above the stove and began riffling through the lineup until she found a bottle of cooking sherry and yanked off the top. When she put it to her mouth, Josie rushed across the room and grabbed it from her hand.

"You can't drink that!"

"I'm not keeping it," Dahlia said.

"You can't know that yet." Josie corked the bottle and returned it to the shelf. "You just found out."

"Yes, I can."

"No, you can't. You have to at least talk to the fa—" Josie stopped herself, seeing Dahlia's eyes drop. Josie paled. "Oh, no."

Dahlia sighed. "Oh, yes."

Josie reached behind her to make sure a stool was there and she fell onto it. She couldn't bring herself to look at Dahlia.

"When?"

"The night before he left for Florida. He wanted to and I didn't want to hurt him. I know it sounds awful, Joze, but I felt like I owed it to him."

"Owed it to him?" Josie's rage was immediate and scalding, piercing right through the shock. *"Owed it to him?"* she said again, her voice straining. "God, you have no shame!"

"Joze, don't start," Dahlia said. "It's done. I have bigger problems right now."

Josie looked away, her heart racing with anger and despair. "You have to tell him. "

"No." Dahlia shook her head repeatedly. "I can't." She moved to Josie, her eyes pleading, panicked. "He can't know, Joze. And you can't tell him. You can't tell anyone. Promise me!"

Josie studied her sister, feeling numb. This couldn't be happening. It was simply too cruel. Josie, who'd always wanted a child and still couldn't get pregnant after years of trying. And Dahlia, who'd never cared to have kids, now carried Matthew's baby after one night. *Matthew's baby . . .*

Josie struggled to her feet, dizzy. "I can't deal with this right now. I have to get back out there. I'm sorry. I can't just—"

"Jeezum, Jo!" Wayne burst into the kitchen, shrugging out of his jacket. "The customers are going nuts—what are you doing back here?"

Dahlia retreated to the sink. Josie turned to her husband and forced an easy smile. "Hi, baby." She took his coat, even as he glared suspiciously at Dahlia. "How are the Keatings?"

"They're fine," he said slowly, still watching Dahlia. "What's going on?"

"Nothing," Josie said, trying to keep her voice light, even as stubborn tears crept up her throat. "Dahl just had a fashion crisis, that's all. You know, a date tonight. She wanted to borrow a skirt. No big thing. I'll be right out, okay?"

Wayne looked at Dahlia, unconvinced. Camille came in

with two bags of groceries. "I swear it could snow any minute!" Wayne took the bags from her and she plucked off her gloves. "I hope you finally got a chance to wrap those rosebushes in the front, Dahlia Rose," she said, moving to the pantry door for her apron. "Those poor things were shivering like newborn babies when I left the house this morning."

"I was on my way over right now, Momma," Dahlia said, glad her mother hadn't glimpsed her guilty face. Dahlia hugged Josie on her way out. "Come by later?" she whispered against her sister's cheek.

Josie nodded, still smiling at her husband. She knew Wayne didn't believe a word of her story. Their faces must have been ghastly when he'd first stepped in, she thought, like two caught burglars. Never mind the fact that Josie's dress size was four sizes smaller than Dahlia's. Or that their taste in clothes was night and day.

But still Wayne waited until Dahlia had left the café and he and Josie were filling orders behind the counter before he leaned over and whispered, "Are you going to tell me what that was about?"

"Later, baby," Josie assured him, snapping the top on a tub of étouffée with shaking hands. "Later."

A soft snow had been falling for almost an hour when Josie came to Dahlia's house that night, flakes so light that they blew across the stone path like feathers. Josie rubbed her arms as she walked through the downstairs looking for her sister. The choking smell of burned food was thick in the house.

She found Dahlia on the back porch, sitting on the swing, knees to chest and staring straight ahead.

"Dahl? Sweetie?"

"I charred a chicken," Dahlia reported dully. "I think I actually cremated it."

Josie smiled. She sat down and slid up against her sister, the nylon of their down jackets whistling against each other.

"Did you tell Wayne?"

Josie shrugged. "I didn't really have to. He knew it was something big."

Dahlia smiled sadly. "Not yet, it isn't."

"Dahlia . . ."

Dahlia rose and moved to a porch post, wrapping herself around it, sighing wearily.

"Then you haven't changed your mind?" Josie asked carefully.

Dahlia shook her head, her gaze fixed forward.

Josie looked down at her hands in her lap. "What if I raised the baby?"

Dahlia released the post and turned around. She blinked at her sister, sure she had misheard.

"Don't look at me like that," Josie said, pulling the edges of her jacket tighter around herself. "Why is it such a crazy idea?"

"Why?" Dahlia fell back against the post, wide-eyed. "Jesus, Joze!"

"Just hear me out, okay?" Josie leaped to her feet, crossing to Dahlia's side. "I've been thinking about it all afternoon," she said breathlessly. "Wayne and I have been talking about adoption—how would this be any different?"

"Joze!"

"Tell me—how is it any different?"

"I can't believe you're even asking me."

"I know how it sounds, but put yourself in my shoes. Please."

Dahlia fell back into the swing and buried her face in her hands. Josie dropped beside her, hot tears sliding down her cheeks.

"Please just say you'll think about it."

Dahlia lowered her hands, dragging a sleeve across her eyes. "What did Wayne say?" Josie bit at her lip. Dahlia sighed. "You haven't discussed this with him, have you?"

"I know he'd be okay with it."

"Okay raising Matthew's baby?" Dahlia stared at her sister, unconvinced. *"Matthew's?"*

Josie shrugged lamely. "I don't see what difference it makes whose baby it is—"

"Oh, Joze, don't be stupid."

Josie frowned at the silver-pink horizon. "He could learn to live with it, Dahl," she said after a moment, her voice soft and faraway. "I know he could."

"Well, maybe I couldn't."

Josie turned to her sister, her eyes pleading and desperate. She'd never asked Dahlia for anything. All the years, all the times she'd put everyone else's needs first, and she'd never once asked her older sister for anything.

"What about Momma and Ben?" Dahlia asked. "What are we supposed to tell them?"

"You could say it was some guy you were dating, some jerky guy, and that he wouldn't want anything to do with a baby, so you won't be telling him."

Dahlia shook her head. "This is crazy. You're twenty-six! You can't possibly know at twenty-six if you can't have children."

Josie's eyes filled. "But the doctors can."

"I don't believe them." Dahlia took both of Josie's chilled hands and pulled them to her. "And don't you either, damn it."

"It's not about believing or not."

"Since when?" said Dahlia. "Sprinkle oil, dust the steps, light a candle, for fuck's sake. You and Momma pull out that crap when you burn a roux—don't you dare tell me you give up now."

Josie laughed, but it was a sad, tired sound. "I already did all those things, Dahl. Over and over. Nothing can change this."

Dahlia drew her sister's hands to her cold, wet cheeks and held them there a long while.

"Please, Dahl," Josie asked again. "Just say you'll think about it."

Dahlia drew in a shaky breath, her eyes closed.

"Okay," she whispered finally. "I'll think about it."

When Josie arrived home, Wayne was waiting in the kitchen, sitting stiffly at their small table.

"She's not keeping it, is she?"

Josie took off her coat and sat down, her hands shaking so badly that she had to make them into fists and drive them deep into her lap. "She's not sure yet."

"Dahlia doesn't want kids, Jo. She never did."

"No, but . . ." Josie lifted her eyes to his. "We do."

Wayne stared at her a long moment before he pushed back from the table and charged to the sink.

"Baby, just hear me out," Josie pleaded. "Matthew would never have to know it was his. Dahlia could say it was somebody else's, somebody she barely knew. . . ."

"God, Jo." Wayne gripped the edge of the sink, his eyes

fixed on the window, his own strained reflection in the glass. "Just listen to yourself."

"I know how it sounds—"

"Do you?" He turned to her, the wash of hurt on his face so plain Josie had to look away. "Do you have any idea what you're asking?"

"Dahlia said she'd think about it."

"I'm not just talking about Dahlia, Jo. I'm talking about me. About *us*."

Josie nodded. She knew. Of course she knew.

Wayne sighed, turning back to the sink. "I need time. You can't just expect . . ."

"I know."

He moved from the sink and crossed to the stairs, stopping at the first tread.

He spoke without turning. "I just wonder."

Josie studied the back of him, her heart racing. "Wonder what, baby?"

"I wonder if you'd have ever suggested this if it weren't his baby."

Josie drew in a quick breath, as if he'd reached across the room and struck her. He lingered on the stairs an extra moment to give her a chance to respond, but she couldn't manage any defense.

It wasn't until the following morning, after Josie had spent the night wandering the downstairs, that Wayne came to her at the counter and gave her his answer.

"Okay," he said, tearing as he drew her into his arms. "Okay."

Four days later, Dahlia and Josie sat side by side in the women's clinic's pink-and-cream waiting room.

"Whoever named it morning sickness was an asshole," Dahlia muttered. "They should really call it every-waking-fucking-second sickness."

Across from them an older woman with her pregnant daughter glanced up from her magazine, giving Dahlia a disapproving look.

Josie patted her sister's hand. "Can I get you something?"

Dahlia closed her eyes and swallowed. "A daiquiri."

"I've got saltines."

"Lucky me." Dahlia stuck out her hand; Josie set a small stack in her palm. Dahlia began crunching them roughly. Josie returned to the clipboard on her lap, tapping the end of her pen against her lower lip and frowning at the dizzying list of health history questions.

"I always hate this part," she whispered. "I have no idea what our family has."

"Just check the box for *nuts*," Dahlia said. "That about covers it."

"What are you going to tell the doctor if she asks about the baby's father?"

"She won't. I know she won't."

A young couple shuffled past them, the woman's large belly straining against her poncho, her feet pinched into a pair of white flats. Dahlia watched her lower herself into a chair, her husband hovering, looking nervous.

"Momma wanted to know why you didn't come in yesterday," Josie said. "I told her you have food poisoning."

"For three months?"

"I'm sorry. It was the first thing that came out of my mouth."

"Jesus, I just wish I could throw up," Dahlia moaned

through a mouthful of saltines. "I would sell my soul for one long, beautiful hurl."

The older woman snapped her magazine closed. Josie smiled apologetically.

"Dahlia Bergeron?"

The nurse in the doorway looked pleasant, young. Dahlia rose, throwing her bag over her shoulder.

"I'll be right here," Josie said, handing her sister the clipboard.

They squeezed hands briefly.

"I know you will, sweetie." Dahlia managed a weary grin. "You and ten pounds of saltines."

In the weeks that followed, Dahlia would swear the sky wore a new shade of gray every morning. Some days it was hard as metal, others soft as ash, but always, undeniably, gray. It seemed the only sun that shone on the island was in the form of Josie, sparkling through each day with an increasing glow, arriving every morning to rouse Dahlia from sleep with a new book on pregnancy, fat and thick, and bags of vitamins and supplements that soon began to overrun the kitchen counter. Not yet ready to tell Camille and Ben, Dahlia had kept her off-season routine intact to avoid suspicion, helping out at the café four days a week and spending the rest of the time ordering bulbs and plants for the spring.

"Did you know that pregnant women have an increased sense of smell?" Dahlia asked during one of Josie's routine visits, sipping coffee at the kitchen table.

Josie gave her sister a pointed look. "That's not caffeinated, is it?"

"Don't start, Joze," Dahlia warned. "And no more books. If I read one more chapter about how I should be looking forward to uncontrollable flatulence and excessive urination, I'm going to kill somebody."

Josie smiled, undaunted. "I brought you more of that ginger tea, and I found a great class at the hospital on what to expect during delivery that I already signed us up for."

"A class?"

"And there're plenty of openings in the Lamaze classes at the Y. I checked."

"Jesus, Joze. Since when is having a kid a graduate program?"

"Maybe you should lie down," Josie said suddenly, studying Dahlia as if she might sprout horns. "You look really tired."

"That would be because I *am* really tired."

"Do you think Momma and Ben have any idea yet?"

Dahlia shrugged. "It's too early to tell anything. But once I start working outside, it won't be so easy to hide it."

"Working outside?" Josie blinked at Dahlia. "You're not actually planning on landscaping this spring?"

"No, sweetie, I thought I'd just live off of our fabulous inheritance and take up soap carving. Of course I'm planning on it."

"But you lift stuff."

"I know," teased Dahlia. "Whole pots of seedlings."

"You know you lift things heavier than that, Dahlia Rose. I'm talking about twenty-pound bags of mulch and topsoil. I'm talking about digging holes for trees!"

"Of course I won't do that," Dahlia said, growing restless and more than a little annoyed. She rose, adding more coffee to her lukewarm cup. At the counter, she spied a jar of liquid and turned to give her sister a wary look. She held it up. "What is this?"

"Oh, it's nothing." Josie waved her hand. "Just a little Florida water."

"Joze . . ."

"Look, I'm not saying you have to splash it on yourself *every* day, just once in a while for a quick cleansing. Just think of it as perfume. Like Momma does."

Dahlia set the jar back down on the counter, surrendering for the moment. She glanced out the window, watching a female cardinal dance along the edge of a frosted bough. "I haven't seen much of Wayne at the café lately."

Josie stopped her unpacking a moment, looked up. "He's been helping Roger out on the new garage. He says we need the extra money if we're going to be raising a child."

Dahlia knew it wasn't the whole truth, but she didn't press her sister.

Finished, Josie folded the empty paper bags neatly and tucked them under the sink.

She hugged Dahlia on her way out. "See you at the café," she said. "And don't forget to keep taking your folic acid."

Dahlia forced an agreeable nod, but her strained smile fell as soon as Josie was out the door, her cheeks aching almost as much as her heart.

It was a thawing Sunday morning a week later when Dahlia found Wayne in the backyard, painting Charles's boat.

"You're not honestly going to keep that thing?" she asked, taking a seat at the old picnic table.

Wayne shrugged, dragging his brush across the hull. "If you're only looking to catch bluefish, it's not a half-bad boat."

Dahlia squinted up at the house. "Joze here?"

"Nope. She went into Portland for supplies."

Dahlia turned to look out at the horizon, her eyes watering. "We need to talk."

Wayne just nodded gravely, setting his brush into the can at his feet.

He made them a pot of coffee. Dahlia sat in the window seat, watching Kitty and Douglas Chase navigate their way down the sidewalk, back from church. They had four children, she recalled. Grandchildren too. Great-grandchildren, probably.

When Wayne came out with their mugs, she tried taking a sip but couldn't. She set down her coffee. "I can't do this."

Wayne looked at her. It had finally come. The confession he'd yearned for, the ugly, guilt-soaked admission he'd wished for in the loneliest hours of so many sleepless nights in the past month.

The relief came so quickly it made him sick to his stomach.

"I know," he said quietly. "I can't either. I wish to God I could, but . . ."

Dahlia licked tears from the top of her lip. "I love my sister. I would do anything for her."

Wayne sniffed, dragging a sleeve across his wet eyes. "So would I."

"I'll need you to drive me," Dahlia said.

He nodded, still staring down at his coffee. "What will we say?"

"We'll say I lost the baby. The doctor said a lot of women miscarry their first pregnancy. Especially in the first trimester."

The room fell silent, the guilt spinning between them like a bicycle chain around two gears.

Wayne walked her back to her truck.

"She can't know," Dahlia said, climbing into the cab. "Not ever."

Wayne gripped the edge of the door, a fresh wave of nausea roiling through him.

"She won't."

They each told Josie a different reason for their absence on the following Tuesday, taking the ferry across the choppy bay at noon, then climbing the hill to Congress Street in Wayne's sedan, saying little as they drew near the clinic, the windshield wipers brushing away a light snow.

Headed home afterward, they sat in the dark of the ferry's garage, watching Dusty Cuttle retie his roof straps almost four times, saying nothing until a young mother walked past with her newborn.

It was hard to know who cried first. Only that when Wayne reached for Dahlia she let him pull her into his arms, let him bury his face in her hair as their sobs collided, clinging to each other as if they might otherwise drown.

An hour later, Josie met Wayne at the door, her eyes bright, streaks of paint covering her arms and thighs.

"Come see," she said, pulling him up the stairs even as he tried to shrug out of his coat, leading him down the hall to the tiny spare room at the end. Stepping inside, she was winded with excitement as she said, "What do you think?"

Wayne stared at the fence of stripes that lined the far wall, shades of peach and blue, purple and green.

"I went a little overboard, I know," Josie said, gesturing to the sample pints stacked in the corner. And she hadn't even confessed to the week's other purchases, the embroidered linens and crib bumper she'd been unable to resist at a new boutique on Exchange Street, the changing table with the musical mobile she'd put on order at the mall.

She pressed herself against him, waiting for him to wrap his arms around her.

Wayne swallowed thickly. "It's . . . They're all great," he said, turning away before she could see the strain on his face. "I've gotta go empty the car, 'kay?"

"Sure."

When he'd gone, Josie looked at the wall again, a fresh burst of hope swelling in her. Life was so funny, she thought. The way things worked out, even when she'd been so sure the spirits had chosen other paths for her. Now she would be a mother. A mother! And to Matthew's baby. Was it so wrong of her to take joy in that sweet and simple fact? No, she decided brightly. Not a bit. Maybe this was how it was meant to be all along. Maybe Dahlia was right to have her doubts about the spirits' powers. Maybe there was some faith to be had in the universe on its own.

Even still, after Wayne had gone to bed, Josie lit a protection candle at the kitchen table for their continued good fortune, for the continued health of her sister, and the baby she had already imagined born and grown, his or her whole life spread out before Josie like a perfect, never-ending bloom.

Twenty-nine

Little Gale Island

Monday, June 17, 2002

2:30 p.m.

It had to be Josie, Dahlia thought when she stepped up to the café's front door and heard the soulful singing through the glass. No one else blasted Billie in the middle of the day like her younger sister.

Coming inside, Dahlia was startled to find Matthew behind the counter instead, head thrown back in mock singing.

"Matty?"

He spun around, arms wide. "Hey, perfect timing!"

Dahlia came behind the counter and lowered the music. "Where is everyone?"

"Don't know. Closed early, I guess. God, I love this song. Do you remember this one?"

"Of course I do, Matty. I still hear them all ten times a day." She eyed him warily. "What are you doing here?"

"What does it look like?" Matthew gestured to an opened case of beer cans on a nearby table.

Dahlia counted four empties and sighed. "Crap."

"Oh, come on." He laughed, taking her by the hand and tugging her toward the table. "It's not great beer, but it's far from crap."

"You're turning everything into a stupid joke," she said flatly, taking the chair across from him. "Something happened."

"Ahh, Dahlia, the great psychologist."

"Look, Matty, if this is about last night . . ."

"Hush." He grabbed a beer out of the case and pushed it at her. "Drink."

She snapped open the can and took a sip, watching Matthew over the rim. He was edgy, she thought. Too edgy.

"How did you get in here?" she asked.

"How do you think? The key's been in the same place for twenty years."

Dahlia set down her beer, licked her lips. "So do we have to go through this whole case before you tell me what's wrong?"

Matthew drained his can and slammed it down. "She's pregnant."

"Who?"

He gave Dahlia an even look. She sat back, stunned. "Oh, fuck."

"Yeah. Exactly." He pulled out another beer, snapped it

open. "Fucking architect sperm. And I always thought they built huge buildings to compensate for their small dicks."

Dahlia leaned across the table and took his free hand. "We'll talk to Joze. She can do things to him. She can make him wake up with moss all over his balls. The really thick, prickly stuff, where slugs hang out."

Matthew laughed helplessly. "Suddenly you're a believer, huh?"

"I make exceptions."

"Yeah. Don't we all." He looked down at her hand in his, turning it over and running his thumb across her palm. "I don't know, Dee. It's funny."

"What is?"

He shrugged. "I've been sitting here thinking maybe there's a reason Holly and I couldn't get pregnant."

Dahlia felt his hand tighten around hers.

"I'm sure the doctors had their theories, Matty."

"I'm not talking about what the doctors said."

"What then?" she asked.

"Maybe the reason it never worked was because I never really wanted to have a baby with her."

Dahlia tried to ease her fingers out of his grip but he wouldn't release her.

"That's crap and you know it," she said. "You were with Holly for ten years."

"So? You've known me almost my whole life, Dee. Did you ever think I'd have kids?"

"I don't know. I never thought about it."

"Well, neither did I. Out of all of us, Josie was always the one who wanted kids. But what about you and me?"

"What does that have to do with anything?"

Matthew lifted his eyes to her and smiled sadly. "Because in my whole life, I think the only person I ever thought about having a baby with was *you*."

Dahlia pulled her hand free. "Very funny."

"You think I'm lying?"

"I think you're drunk."

"Right." Matthew swigged his beer, swallowed hard. "I figured you'd say that."

The front door opened. They turned to see Josie come in, wide-eyed and winded. "Why's the Closed sign turned around?" she said, looking between them. "Where's Wayne?"

"JoJo!" Matthew stumbled out from behind the table, lurching to meet Josie. He grabbed her around the waist, hugged her tightly. "My little JoJo . . ."

Josie managed to raise her chin above his shoulder, locking eyes with Dahlia. The sisters shared a nervous look. Dahlia gestured to the beers and shook her head.

"Dance with me," Matthew insisted, spinning Josie around a pair of tables before she could protest. "You always wanted me to ask; you know you did. Here's your big chance."

"Matty, stop," Josie said gently, trying to loosen his hands from her waist. "I think you should sit down."

"Oh, fuck all that," he said. "I'll sit when I'm dead. Isn't that what they say?" He tugged Josie closer to the jukebox. Dahlia rose to help, stepping between them.

"Joze, why don't you go make us something to eat."

"Good idea." Josie finally slipped free and moved out of Matthew's reach, grabbing Dahlia's hand on her way to the kitchen and bringing her along.

The sisters hurried through the swinging door. When they were safe inside, Josie exclaimed, "What's going on?"

"Holly's pregnant."

"Oh!" Josie's face brightened.

Dahlia frowned. "It's not his."

"*Oh*," Josie said again, quieter this time. "No wonder he's drunk." She moved to the refrigerator, opened it, then stopped. She looked at Dahlia over the top of the door, her expression determined. "I'm going to tell him."

"What?" Dahlia moved to the fridge, frantic. "Don't you dare. You promised."

Josie shut the door. "That was before this."

"Joze, it won't help. You'll only hurt him more."

"I don't believe that," Josie said.

"Well, it's not up to you!"

"Why not? It's as much my secret as it is anybody's. Maybe I'm tired of feeling guilty about it all the time. Aren't you?"

"Shhh!" Dahlia glanced to the door, sure she heard Matthew approaching. "Of course I feel guilty," she whispered. "How can you even ask me that?"

"Then let's tell him," Josie said. "Let's tell him so he can get on with his life."

"How is telling him going to help him get on with his life?"

"Because he can try again with someone else. He has time—he just doesn't know it!"

"Jesus, listen to you two!" Matthew burst through the swinging door. "I can't even hear the music. What the hell are you yelling about in here?"

"Nothing." Dahlia glared pleadingly at Josie across the kitchen, but Josie wouldn't meet her gaze.

"We have something to tell you, Matty."

"No, we don't," Dahlia said, moving to Matthew and urging him back out into the café. "I want another beer."

"So go get one," Matthew said, turning to Josie. "What do you want to tell me?"

"Joze," Dahlia warned evenly, "so fucking help me . . ."

"Dahlia just told me about Holly, Matty."

Matthew shrugged. "Yeah, what are you gonna do, right? Life's an asshole." He strolled between them, looking around the kitchen. "I thought you guys were getting us some food."

Josie moved toward him, her hands clasped under her chin. "I know you're upset," she said calmly, "and you think you can't have a family, but you need to know that there's still time for you to try with someone else."

"Jo, come on. . . ." Matthew turned back to her, his head rolling to one side. "I don't want to talk about this, okay?"

"Hear that, Joze?" Dahlia stared at her sister. "He doesn't want to talk about it."

But Josie was too determined now. "You *can* have babies," she said. "As many as you want."

"Jesus, what is this?" Matthew said. "Some kind of fucking intervention? I told you I don't want to talk about it anymore."

"It's the truth," Josie said. "We wanted to tell you a long time ago. It just never seemed like the right time."

Matthew looked at Dahlia. "The right time for what?"

Dahlia couldn't meet his eyes. The room seemed to grow hot, the air thick. Her heart thundered in her chest. She looked at Josie instead, determined to let her sister gasp for breath alone. This confession was, after all, Josie's grand plan. Dahlia would be damned if she'd rescue her sister halfway across the high wire she'd walked herself out onto.

"Go on, Joze," she said coldly. "Tell him already."

If her sister regretted her decision, she didn't reveal it. Josie's expression remained tender, her smile small but insistent, even as her eyes filled with tears.

"Matty," she said, "Dahlia was pregnant with your baby."

For a few seconds, the admission seemed to hang in the air like incense smoke, heavy and unmoving. Matthew just looked between the sisters, his eyes slitted with confusion. "What did you say?"

He'd heard, of course he had, but he wanted to hear them say it again. To hear Dahlia say it.

So it was Dahlia he looked at when he ordered, "Say that again."

Dahlia lifted her eyes to his. "I was pregnant, Matty. When you left for Florida."

Reflexively Matthew counted the years, the sum of such a lengthy betrayal making the news even more unbearable. He charged at Dahlia, his rage blinding. "So, what, you decided not to have it? Without even telling me?"

"No!" Josie rushed to Dahlia's side. "We *lost* the baby, Matty."

"We?" Matthew blinked at them, his features twisting with disgust. "*We?*"

"I was going to raise it," Josie said. "Wayne and I."

Dahlia stepped toward him, even as he backed away. "Matty, you were starting a whole new life. It wasn't the right thing for us to have a baby, and Josie and Wayne wanted to—"

"Jesus Christ!" He looked between them. "Listen to you

two. My best fucking friends, planning to raise my own child without telling me. Standing there and acting like you were doing me some great fucking favor. You're sick, you know that? You're both out of your fucking minds!"

Josie reached for him, tears spilling down her cheeks. "We never meant to hurt you, Matty."

"Don't touch me," he said, stumbling backward. He pointed at each of them, his hand shaking. "Don't you come near me." Then he punched open the kitchen door and marched through the café, bursting out the front with such force that the jukebox record skipped.

Josie fell against the sink, weeping.

"Feel better now?" Dahlia said.

Josie looked up, her eyes swimming. "That's a hateful thing to say."

Dahlia turned away, knowing it had been the worst thing to say, but it was the shame of what hadn't been said that tore at her in the silence Matthew had left in his wake. Even after his suggestion that she'd terminated the pregnancy, Josie had never considered the possibility that Dahlia had lied about losing the baby. The relief was almost as overwhelming as the shame.

They remained in their corners for a long time, staring at each other's feet, blanketed in their anger and frustration. They might not have moved or spoken for even longer if the phone hadn't rung.

It was Josie who moved to answer it, her face expressionless at first, but soon her puffy eyes widened, alert again.

She hung up.

"That was Jack." She took a quick breath. "The hospital called the station. Blessed be—they're bringing Ben out of the coma."

Thirty

Miami, Florida
1992

Matthew came into the headmaster's office to find Adam Dennis seated at his desk wearing a heavy expression.

"They're threatening to sue," Adam announced, handing Matthew a letter from Chace Burrough's parents.

"What?" Matthew took the letter and dropped into the empty seat across from Adam's desk. He scanned it quickly. "Can they do that?"

"What do you think?"

Matthew blew out a long breath. He had always had a good relationship with the headmaster, from the first day he had come in as the guidance counselor at the Windsor School four years earlier.

"You gave the kid condoms, Matt. He's fourteen, for Christ's sake."

"He's fourteen and having unprotected sex in the dugout, Adam."

"I know, I know. But this isn't Planned Parenthood. He can buy a box at the drugstore like everyone else." Adam leaned back in his chair and smoothed his thinning brown hair. "You crossed a line on this one, Matt. I don't know how else to say it."

The headmaster tugged open his pencil drawer and rummaged around, finally pulling out a business card and handing it across the desk to Matthew.

"Her name's Holly Newcomb. She's an attorney. Claudia and I used her for that bike accident mess last year. She's sharp," Adam said, then grinned as he added, "And single, last I heard."

Matthew studied the card, flicking the edge with his thumb.

"Call her," Adam said. "Call her before the board gets wind of this. Make sure you have a leg to stand on."

Holly Newcomb sailed into the wine bar at four-thirty in a crisp white suit, with long blond hair pinned back in a neat bun, her hand already outstretched even before she'd reached the table Matthew had saved for them. Her speed and beauty flustered him. When he rose and took her hand, the smell of her perfume distracted him. He managed a clumsy shake and sat down, glad there were no glasses or plates in front of him to knock over. Even at thirty-two, confident women still made him nervous.

"Can I get you something?" Matthew asked, handing Holly a wine list. "They have some really nice reds. I usually order a glass of the Pennington merlot—"

"Scotch," Holly said firmly, snapping open her leather bag and pulling out a pen and notepad. "Chivas. No ice."

Matthew raised his hand to alert the waitress. The young woman dressed all in black sauntered over, rolling her bright red lips together as she took their order. When she'd gone, Matthew pulled at his polo collar, wishing he'd worn a nicer shirt, maybe even a tie.

"Not used to it yet, are you?"

He looked at Holly. "Excuse me?"

She smiled. "The humidity."

Jesus, he thought. Was he sweating that badly?

"I should be," he said. "I've been here four years now."

"I've been here my whole life," she said. "Trust me. Give yourself at least ten." Holly snapped the top off her pen, set it to the blank page in front of her. "Now, you said the parents sent a letter informing you of their intent to sue, but so far there hasn't been any action taken toward you?"

"That's right," Matthew said. "It's not like I hand out condoms with homework assignments, you know."

Holly regarded him a moment, grinning slowly. "You have a sense of humor," she said, taking notes. "Good. You might need it. I've heard of several cases like this where the parents throw a fit and threaten to see the teacher fired, but it rarely goes any farther than a suspension. A slap on the wrist."

Suspension was more than a slap on the wrist. Matthew had worked too hard to suffer that stain on his record. He leaned forward, his voice low. "I'm good at my job, Ms. Newcomb."

Holly looked up from her notes. "I'm sure you are, *Mr.* Haskell." Her blue eyes were bright and warm. "So formal. You sure you're not from the South?"

"Far from it," he said. "Maine."

"Maine? I've always wanted to get to Maine. It's supposed to be beautiful."

"It is."

"You must miss it."

He shrugged. "Some days."

The waitress arrived with their drinks, setting the glasses down on black napkins.

Holly took a sip of her Scotch. Matthew sipped his wine, wishing he'd ordered a beer instead. Her pen lay on the notebook, signaling a break in their business.

"So you're from here, then?" he asked.

"Fort Lauderdale."

"What brought you to Miami?"

She took another sip. "*Who*, actually."

"Ahh," Matthew said, nodding.

She smiled. "You too?"

"Sort of. In my case I came here to escape the who, not follow her."

Holly studied him, her eyes flashing with interest. "Did it work?"

"I think so." Matthew felt his hands grow warm. "What about you?"

"It worked out great," she said. "He dumped me three months after I got here to move in with a cocktail waitress. I got an apartment on the beach all to myself and started law school a month later."

"And your ex?"

"The waitress kicked him out a few weeks after he left me. He moved back to Lauderdale and got a job at his father's appliance store." Holly grinned. "Karma's a bitch, isn't she?"

Matthew chuckled. "You sound like a friend of mine."

"An old friend?"

"You could say that."

They looked at each other a moment.

Holly took up her glass, chuckling. "I can't believe I just told you all that. We're supposed to be talking about your case. You must think I'm a real quack."

"I think you're human."

"God, that's even worse." She rolled her watch around, wincing at the time. "I'm sorry to run out on you, but I have to make a five-thirty in Coral Gables." She slipped her notebook back into her bag, and closed it. She rose, holding out her hand. Matthew took it, rising too. "You have my card," she said. "Call me if there are any developments, okay?"

"What about for this?" Matthew said, gesturing to their table. "How much do I owe you for this?"

Holly waved her hand, slipping on sunglasses. "There's no charge for a consultation. But thank you for the Scotch. And the conversation."

"It was my pleasure."

Matthew stayed on his feet, watching Holly push through the door and disappear into the daylight.

That night he called Ben.

"You did the right thing," Ben said. Camille was cutting his father's hair; Matthew could hear the snip of the shears in the background. "Camille thinks they should be giving you a promotion."

"I sure do, baby!"

Matthew chuckled. "Tell her thanks." He reached into the fridge for a beer and confessed, "I met someone, Pop."

"That's great. Who is she?"

"Well . . . I sort of met someone. It's this lawyer I got put in touch with. In case the parents sue me. We had a meeting today. I won't see her again unless they press charges."

Ben laughed. "Well, then you'd better hope they sue, hadn't you?"

Just as Holly had predicted, Chace Burrough's parents never made good on their threat to sue, and Matthew was elated to hear the news when Adam Dennis came to report it in Matthew's office two weeks later.

"But just in case," said Adam, turning to go, "I wouldn't keep a condom collection in your drawer for future offerings."

Matthew made a mock salute. "Thanks, Adam. Really."

Halfway out the door, the headmaster stopped, turned back. "You ever meet with that lawyer?"

Matthew nodded, and his relief gave way briefly to disappointment. Now he didn't have an excuse to see Holly Newcomb again.

Unless, of course, he wanted to share his good news. Matthew told himself it would be the courteous thing to do. Maybe along with some flowers. He knew just the shop to deliver.

When Holly called several days later, Matthew had just come in from a run on the beach.

"They're lovely," she said. "Irises are my favorite, actually."

"You don't have to say that." Matthew peeled off his T-shirt and tossed it on the couch

"I'm not just saying it. I'm a lawyer. I can't lie. I'd be disbarred."

Matthew laughed. "I'll have to remember that."

The line went quiet for a moment.

"Would you like to come over for dinner sometime?" she asked.

Matthew felt a fresh stream of perspiration travel down his spine.

"Sure," he said. "When?"

"How about tonight?"

They never got around to dinner. Instead they spent an hour on Holly's deck with a bottle of red wine and a round of smoked Gouda. When the bottle was finished, they found a box of Girl Scout cookies. When the cookies were gone, they put their shoes back on and walked the thirty blocks to Matthew's apartment, where they raided his kitchen, managing to find a pair of frozen pork chops and a bag of yellow rice. They ate on paper plates on his fire escape, catching the upbeat strains of a reggae record out of Matthew's next-door neighbor's open window.

It was Matthew's idea to suggest Holly stay the night, his idea that she take his bed and he take the couch. But it was Holly's idea to make love, which they did, nervously and with several fits of bloated laughter, until they fell asleep, half-dressed, on top of his sheets.

When the phone rang at one, Matthew thought he was dreaming. Until Dahlia's voice drifted out of the machine in the hallway, so strangely somber it took him a moment to place it.

Momma and Ben didn't want to worry him, but Dahlia thought he should know.

Camille had been to the doctor and they'd found something.

Thirty-one

Miami, Florida
1996

Holly sat on the edge of their bed while Matthew packed, her arms crossed, her expression tight. Hooper lay curled up in the doorway, the golden retriever's furry brow flexing nervously.

"How could you think I wouldn't want to come, Matt? Camille was practically your mother. Of course I'd want to be there for you."

Matthew shrugged lamely, stuffing rolled socks into the side of his bag. "I just assumed after the last time that you wouldn't want to go back."

Holly glared at him. The last time. What he should have said was the first and *only* time she had joined him on a trip to his precious Little Gale Island and he'd done nothing to help her feel at ease, barely acknowledging her as soon as he was back in the company of the sisters, who had their own hand in making her feel like an interloper in their private universe.

"This is Camille's funeral, for God's sake," Holly said. "How could you think I would make this about me?"

Matthew laid down a stack of shirts. "Maybe I wanted to spare you. But fuck me for protecting you, right?"

"You jerk," she said. "This isn't about protecting me. This is about you wanting to keep me out of your treasured island club. Like you always do."

When Matthew didn't respond, Holly rose.

"Tell them I'm sorry," she said, quietly but firmly. "And don't you dare make something up to your father about why I'm not there. You tell him the truth, Matt. I couldn't bear them all thinking I don't care. They already resent me."

"That's not true. . . ."

"Yes, it is, and you know it. So you tell them the truth, damn it. I deserve at least that."

Matthew nodded, but he knew he wouldn't need to explain. Ben would know at once why Holly had stayed behind. They all would.

On the drive to the airport, Holly said little to him. When she pulled up to the curb and he climbed out, Matthew leaned in to kiss her, tasting the tears she'd been hiding behind her sunglasses.

"I'm sorry for your loss," she said. "I know how much she meant to you."

"Forgive me, Holl. I can be such an asshole."

But as soon as he had closed the door, she pulled back out into the travel lane, denying him an answer.

Dahlia met him at the landing, wearing sunglasses in the growing dark. They held hands as they walked the narrow sidewalks to the old house, where Ben was waiting for them on the porch, nursing a cup of tea, his eyes red-rimmed but alert.

Matthew looked around for Josie.

"She wanted to come," Dahlia said. "She just can't seem to leave the house yet."

Matthew smiled, his tears arriving at last. "I know."

Dahlia sat with Matthew while he made up his old bed, her eyes fixed numbly on the tidy corners he tucked under the ends, the way he flattened his palms over the old quilt, trying to smooth down creases that wouldn't be softened. Afterward, they climbed out the dormer window and shared a glass of bourbon on the roof. The sky seemed smaller to them than it ever had as teenagers, the whole island spread out before them; once it seemed endless, but now all they could see was the boundaries of its shore.

"You won't believe the flowers," Dahlia said. "The bouquets were three deep in the entryway. You couldn't even get to the front door. We finally had to move them inside the café."

Matthew took a sip and passed the glass to her. "I'm sorry I couldn't get back this last year. I know it's been hard."

"Your dad was amazing, Matty. He wouldn't let anyone else care for her."

"Camille was the love of his life. There's nothing he wouldn't have done for her."

Dahlia swirled the liquid in the glass, watching it settle. "The doctors wanted her to go into hospice on the mainland, but your dad wouldn't let them. He even tried to find a real Voodoo priest to come and perform the burial, but she said she didn't want that. She said . . . " Dahlia swallowed, her eyes filling. "She said she didn't need rituals to make sure her spirit found its way back to him."

Dahlia looked to Matthew, her tears coming too fast to catch on her sleeve.

He reached across the asphalt tiles for her hand, their fingers linking in the dark.

Ben and Wayne opened the café at eleven the next day, and by noon, the dining room was full. Familiar faces, those down the street, and those who'd long since moved away, came to pay their respects to the Creole woman who had arrived on Little Gale Island nineteen years earlier, intending to stay only a single season. To everyone who entered, the smell of chicory coffee and simmering gumbo seemed somehow stronger, the crumbling pralines even creamier traveling around their mouths. Josie stayed behind the counter, as if it were a boundary keeping her from the truth of the event on the other side. The jukebox blared Camille's favorites, Billie Holiday and Dinah Washington, Ella and Louis. Josie had set up an altar in the window booth. Wayne had found a photo of Camille and the girls from their first spring on the island, and he'd had it made into a poster so Camille's bright smile would be visible from every corner of the crowded room. Beside the picture stood a kerosene lamp that would stay lit all night and into the morning, and a sampling of Camille's favorite foods. Even though their mother had chosen not to abide by the customs of a Voodoo burial, Josie had insisted on some, and no one had questioned her.

"I just wanted to say how sorry I am, Dahlia."

Dahlia looked up to see Mandy Thurlow in front of her in a dark blue cardigan and black slacks, her blond hair grazing her shoulders. Jack's wife looked drawn, nervous. "How sorry *we* are."

"Thanks, Mandy. I really appreciate that."

Dahlia glanced around the room for Jack.

"He's parking the car," Mandy said, her blue eyes flashing knowingly. "We can't stay long, I'm afraid. We tried to find a sitter at the last minute but we couldn't. Jenny's with my mom."

"You could have brought her," Dahlia said, gesturing to the clumps of small children scattered throughout the crowd. Mandy nodded politely, but Dahlia knew an invitation wasn't the issue. An awkward silence landed between them; Mandy turned to the door. "I guess I should go look for Jack."

"Sure."

"Take care, Dahlia."

"You too, Mandy."

By four, the crowd had thinned. Wayne had taken Josie home and left Matthew and Ben to see to the final visitors. Dahlia stood behind the counter, making a last pot of coffee, when she heard her name. She turned to see Jack in a tweed sports jacket, corduroy pants.

A rush of relief coursed through her.

"I thought Mandy said you had to go pick up Jenny."

"We did," he said. "She did. She's there now, actually. I just came back because I didn't get a chance to see you myself and . . ."

Jack reached for her hand across the counter. Dahlia gave

it, his palm so warm she wanted to slide her whole body inside his grip. She looked up at him, the tears rising uncontrollably. She wiped her eyes with her free hand, laughing at herself.

"I had my sunglasses here for a while, but I put them down somewhere and now look at me."

He *was* looking at her. Dahlia could feel his eyes, warm as his hand.

"I loved her too," Jack admitted softly, his own throat closing up. Their eyes moved at the same time to the door, where Ben was accepting a hug from Bitsy Masterson.

"Momma was his whole world," Dahlia whispered.

Jack smiled. "We should all be that lucky."

Dahlia looked at him, her eyes questioning.

"Loving someone that deeply, that long," he said, meeting her gaze. "That's a gift."

Across the café, helping Alma Cooley into her coat, Matthew watched Jack and Dahlia, unprepared for the rush of envy that rose in his throat. Even with so much sorrow in her heart, the clear wash of regret was still evident on Dahlia's face when she finally let go of Jack's hand and watched him walk away.

The next day, when the fog was still so thick that the other side of the street was lost in the mist, the sisters stood beneath the awning with clasped hands, neither one wanting to unlock the café door. Before this early morning, Josie had opened the café a hundred times on her own, been in charge of cooking and baking for whole weeks at a time while Camille had been failing, yet somehow she'd always felt their mother's presence. Today they would enter the café truly without her for the first time.

Dahlia's hands shook as she turned the key. They eased the door open slowly, as if unsure of what they might see on the other side. Somehow, they'd hoped to find the café changed, *needed* to find it different. But except for Camille's altar, the restaurant looked as it had always looked, smelled as it had always smelled, of bay leaves and chicory coffee.

They walked numbly through the room, seeing everything as if for the first time. The painted roses faded into the floorboards. The bottles of hot sauce on each table. The dull whir of the ceiling fans. The jukebox.

Josie made it as far as the counter before she fell against the cases, a deep sob leaving her. She held on to the curved glass, like a passenger to the hull of her capsized boat. "I don't know if I can do this."

"Yes, you can," Dahlia said firmly as she pulled her sister close. "You've been making everything on your own for almost six months now."

"I'm not talking about the stupid food," Josie said.

Dahlia's eyes filled. "I know." She looked around the café, the anguish scooping out a hole in her stomach as it did every few minutes, knocking the wind out of her. "Everything Momma was is in this room, Joze." She smiled, tears spilling over. "Her dreams, her loves."

Josie wiped her eyes with the side of her hand, wiped her nose with her sleeve. Dahlia was right. It was up to them now to preserve their mother's life work. The Little Gale Gumbo Café was their legacy now.

Josie let go a long and quivering breath.

"I'm just so scared, Dahl," she whispered. "I don't know who we are without her."

"Then we'll find out together," Dahlia said.

Just then the front door opened and Sam Milkie peered in,

thick white eyebrows raised warily. "Too soon for a cup of coffee?"

The sisters parted and looked at each other. They squeezed hands.

Josie smiled through her tears at the owner of the island's hardware store. "Just in time, Mr. Milkie."

Thirty-two

Little Gale Island
Monday, June 17, 2002
4:00 p.m.

"*Now, don't expect* too much," the doctor said as he led Matthew down the hospital corridor. "It isn't like in the movies when the patient wakes up and is right back to normal."

"Did he ask for me?" said Matthew. "Does he know where he is?"

"He hasn't tried to speak yet, Mr. Haskell." The doctor steered them around a meal cart. "It's still early. As I've said, sometimes patients make a full recovery; other times extensive rehabilitation is necessary, even to regain the most basic functions. It's best to take things one step at a time."

Matthew nodded firmly, his heart soaring with the clear promise of this news as he trailed the doctor into the room.

His father had come back to them.

When Jack returned from the cafeteria with coffees, he found Josie and Wayne in the waiting room. Josie took her cup and smiled up at him, her eyes red rimmed. "No word yet," she said. "Matty's still in there with the doctor."

Jack nodded, glancing around. "She's in the lobby," Wayne said, taking his own coffee and leaving the fourth cup in the cardboard holder.

Jack found Dahlia by the reception desk, leaned against a tiled wall.

She took the coffee, sipped it deeply. "Thanks."

Her hands were shaking; Jack could see the coffee shiver in its cup.

"So what happens now?" she asked.

"With what?"

"The case."

"Nothing." He shrugged. "As far as I'm concerned, the case is closed."

"Good."

They looked at each other, their bodies forced closer to keep the passage clear for the nurses who rushed by. When he splashed coffee on his wrist, she wiped it off for him with her fingers. "Jack." She swallowed, sighed. "It's just that . . ."

"He's back." Jack pointed to Matthew, where he appeared across the lobby, headed for the waiting room.

Dahlia nodded, and they followed him in.

Josie and Wayne rose to meet him, eyes wide with anticipation.

"He's out again, but the doctor says that's normal," Matthew explained. "What matters is that he's responsive. The doctor's confident he'll be awake for longer the next time he comes to."

"Oh, Matty." Josie moved toward him instinctively, then stilled, not yet sure he was ready to welcome her back, not even in the midst of their joy. She saw quickly that her decision was wise; he offered her only a tight nod, his arms firm at his sides.

"That's great news, Matt," Jack said.

"Really great," echoed Wayne.

Dahlia kept her distance, knowing better than to try for an embrace.

"Can we see him?" she asked.

Matthew directed his answer to the group. "The doctor asked that everyone wait until tomorrow. I'm going to stay with him awhile longer, in case he wakes up again."

"Of course," Josie said, nodding. She looked to Wayne. "We'll stay too."

"You don't have to do that," Matthew said.

"I know we don't. We want to."

Matthew smiled thinly. "Thanks. Well . . ." He gestured to the door. "I'm going to head back in then."

When he'd gone, Josie moved to the window. Dahlia watched her go, her lips set in an angry line.

Jack drew near. "Something wrong?" he asked.

Dahlia shrugged. "Nothing that hasn't been wrong for a while." She turned to him, her eyes soft. Fragile, he thought. The way he remembered them in their youth, those precious moments when she'd let him see how vulnerable she could be, before drawing the curtain down.

He waited for it, the inevitable veil, but it didn't come.

"Take me home," she whispered. "Please."

Matthew carried the chair across the floor, setting it at the head of his father's bed. Evening light slipped through the blinds, soft ladders of pink that fell across the walls, the bedspread, the monitors.

He looked down at his own hands, clenched in his lap, wondering how it could be that only an hour before he'd been standing in the café, crazed with anger, sure he would hate the sisters forever for what they'd done, for what they'd kept from him, and now the rage had dissolved like a stain soaked in cold water. Watching his father's profile, Matthew could think of nothing but how right the universe was again, how much he couldn't wait to bring Ben back to the island, back home where he belonged.

Home. He sighed. Alone in the stark, silent room, pieces of the afternoon returned to him, making him wince. Christ, he thought. What had he expected Dahlia to do? He had known making love that night was never her idea. He'd known it and still he'd convinced himself that there was some natural course to their sleeping together before he'd left, something unavoidable, something fated. He'd been selfish and careless, and Dahlia had done what she'd had to do. To blame her for that was beyond cruel.

And Josie. Matthew closed his eyes. Dear, dear Josie. He'd been so unfair to her. Pretending not to notice her affection all those years, letting her mistake his caring for love. Like Dahlia, she'd been forced to make an impossible choice too.

He rested his face in his hands. What a chain of mismatched hearts they'd been, he thought. And him, the weakest link of all.

"Mr. Haskell?"

He looked up to see a nurse in the doorway, a portable CD player in her hand. She walked to him, holding it out.

"Betty said you were looking for one of these yesterday. They keep a few on the children's floor." She smiled. "If you're lucky there might even be a *Sesame Street* disk in there."

Matthew grinned. "I'll take it over the stuff I hear my students blasting. God, I thought *my* music was bad as a teenager."

"You're a teacher, then?"

"Guidance counselor," he said, noticing her eyes for the first time. They were light brown and warm. The sort of eyes you'd want to see if you had to wake up in a hospital bed. His gaze moved to her name tag: Beth.

"I hear he came to," she said. "That's great."

"It is. It really is."

She smiled again. "I'll leave you guys alone then." She pointed to the music player. "Don't worry about getting that back anytime soon," she said. "I'm here all night. I'll just come by and pick it up on my way out in the morning."

"Okay," he said. "Thanks again."

When she'd gone, he reached over and sifted through the drawer of Ben's night table, pulling out the CD Josie had left for him. He set the disk in the player and lowered the player onto the table, wheeling it as close as he could to the bed. When the smooth, soulful notes began to sail out into the quiet room, faint but so familiar, Matthew took his seat and watched, sure he saw tiny shivers of recognition at the corners of Ben's mouth.

"The doctor said you might have forgotten a few things, Pop. Maybe a lot of things. He said we might even have to go back to the basics." Matthew smiled. "So I thought we'd start with Billie."

Wayne came up behind Josie where she stood at the waiting room window.

"Want me to get you another cup of coffee?" he asked.

She shook her head, still staring out at the view.

"How about something to eat? You must be starved."

"I'm not hungry."

He set his hands on her shoulders. "You and Dahlia still fighting?"

"Not about this morning," Josie said.

"What then?"

Josie sighed. "I told Matty about the baby."

Wayne took his hands off her shoulders. "When?"

"Just before Jack called the café. I thought I should. Holly's pregnant. I just figured it might make him feel better." Josie frowned. "It didn't."

Wayne came around beside her, his heart thundering. It took him a few seconds to realize that Dahlia hadn't revealed their secret. If she had, Josie wouldn't have been speaking to him.

A wave of relief passed over him. He let go a long breath.

Josie bit at the inside of her cheek. "What if he doesn't forgive us, Wayne?"

"He will. He has to."

"You say it like it's some kind of law."

Wayne took her into his arms. "Everybody has secrets, Jo," he said. "Things they regret."

"I just wanted us to have a family, Wayne," she said against his chest. "I don't regret that."

"And we will, sweetheart. The agency will come through for us."

She closed her eyes, her own apology so late.

"I'm so sorry, baby," she whispered.

He swept back her bangs. His eyes filled quickly.

"Me too, Jo," he said. "Me too."

Jack pulled the cruiser up to Dahlia's yellow cape, its screened-in porch dark except for a wreath of chili-pepper lights strung around the front door. A soft evening breeze blew through the car's open windows, tinged with salt and the sweetness of the rugosa roses that lined her driveway.

"I always liked this house," Jack said, smiling wistfully at the shingled cottage.

"Me too," Dahlia agreed with a heavy sigh. "It just needs so much work. I think my problem is that I love the outside of a house more than the inside. Kyle Champion stopped by the other day and told me I need a new roof, but he tells everyone that. What do you think?"

"Well . . ." Jack leaned toward her so she could see where he pointed. "See that far dormer?"

"I see it," she said.

"That dormer's about ten minutes from becoming a lawn ornament."

She frowned. "So does that mean I need a new roof?"

He bit back a grin. "You need a new roof."

"Shit." Dahlia laughed. After a second, Jack laughed too.

When the car grew quiet again, he said, "I could come over and give it a look for you. Maybe do some work on that seam, just enough to get by until you can get the whole roof done."

"You could do that?"

"Sure. It wouldn't be more than a few hours' worth of work."

Dahlia smiled. "I remember you being good on roofs. In the pouring rain, especially."

"Yeah, well . . ." He looked back to the house. "There are other parts of that night I'd sooner repeat first."

"Right," she said, her eyes teasing. "Like Momma's shrimp pie."

Jack grinned, flexing his hands over the steering wheel, blushing noticeably now. "Yeah, like shrimp pie."

Dahlia leaned back in the seat, smiling sadly. "Josie told me I'd ruin it."

"Ruin what?" Jack said.

"Us." Dahlia turned her smile to him. "That night, after our first date, she was still awake when I came upstairs, and she was so sure I'd screw it up with you eventually. And she was right."

Jack sighed. "You didn't screw it up, Dahlia. . . ."

"Of course I did."

"No, you didn't."

"Then who did?"

"Nobody did." He shrugged, leaning back too. "We were who we were."

"We were young," she said.

"That didn't matter. You didn't want me to love you the way I wanted to love you. I had to accept that."

"But I did want you, Jack. You know I did."

"It doesn't matter now."

"Yes, it does, damn it," she said, twisting to face him, suddenly desperate for him to understand. "I pushed you away because I was scared. Not because I wasn't crazy in love with you. I was." She paused, her skin flushing with her confession. "Jesus, I was."

He smiled. "I know."

"Do you?"

He flattened his hands on his thighs. "We would never have worked then. We wanted different things."

"Which things?"

"All of them," he said. "You never wanted to get married or have kids."

"You didn't give me a chance to reconsider."

"What would have been the point? You weren't going to change your mind."

Dahlia looked at the dashboard. He was right, she thought. More than he even knew.

She turned back to the window. "You moved on so quickly, Jack."

He could hear the hurt in her voice. "What choice did I have?" he said gently. "If I hadn't moved on, I would never have had a family, never had the daughter who means the world to me."

Dahlia smiled. "I know she does."

"And what about you?" he said. "You got a business off the ground, doing something you love. Something you're good at. On your own terms. You honestly think you would have been happy straining peas and ironing my shirts?"

"Ironing?" Dahlia grinned. "What's that?"

He laughed. "Exactly."

They looked at each other a long while.

Jack sighed. "You want me to say I've missed you, Dahlia?" he asked, his voice deepening with feeling. "Christ, yes, I've missed you. But I don't regret my life. I don't regret losing you. We make our choices and we live with them."

She nodded, looking down at her hands in her lap, feeling

a strange mix of relief and regret. "Maybe I want another chance," she said. "Maybe I think we deserve one." She lifted her eyes to his. "What do you think?"

He looked out at the house. "I think I don't want to be someone's husband again. And I don't want to have to fix something I didn't break."

Dahlia nodded. Tears rose, blurring her vision. "Then what *do* you want, Jack?"

"What do I want?" He turned to her, his expression strained with longing. "I want to love someone with everything I've got, and I want them to love me back. I want to have a beer after a long day, make love as much as humanly possible, and grill every night from Memorial Day until the first frost. I want simple."

"Simple." Dahlia moved her hand to where his rested on his thigh. She grinned. "You mean, like me."

"Yeah," he said, grinning too as he reached out and slid his hand through her knotted hair, cupping her cheek. "Like you."

They came together in a deep kiss, twisting around to get as close as they could, banging elbows and heads as they tugged seat belts and shirts out of the way. Dahlia settled herself on top of him, her hair coming undone, falling over his face like a curtain.

When Jack felt her reach down to his erection, he pulled back, breathless.

"What's wrong?" she whispered.

He glanced around at the fogged windows, shrugged sheepishly. "Maybe it's just me, but it seems wrong to have waited over twenty years to make love again and have it be in a police car in your driveway."

Dahlia grinned, smoothing back the graying hair at his

temples. "What could be more right? We both knew it was only a matter of time before you got me into this thing."

"Yeah, but I guess I always worried it would be in the back-seat, and you'd be in handcuffs."

She smiled. "I still could be."

In the end, they made love in several places, outside and in, under twilight, then moonlight, while across the bay Matthew found sleep in a folding chair at his father's side, and Josie and Wayne took the last ferry home, huddled under a cold, clear roof of stars.

At nine, Jack and Dahlia raided her fridge and returned upstairs with leftover cold sesame noodles, feeding each other with chopsticks in her claw-foot tub, then sending soapy water sloshing over the sides. By ten thirty, they had straightened the twisted sheets and surrendered to exhaustion on a mattress plumped and flattened, warmed and smoothed, legs linked, fingers laced.

And it was in those soft, languid moments before sleep that Jack heard the faraway hum of his cell on Dahlia's dresser. Easing Dahlia onto her back, he rose and walked to the other side of the room to pick up his phone, knowing he'd put off his duties long enough.

"So you *are* alive," Frank Collins said on the other end. "I was beginning to worry I was going to have another autopsy on my schedule, Chief."

Jack moved to the window, drawing the curtain back to look out onto the quiet street. "Nice to hear from you too, Frank."

The medical examiner cleared his throat. "Listen, Jack, I'll get right to it. It's pretty much what I expected. That fall killed Bergeron. Must have been one steep flight of stairs; I'll say that much. I've signed off on the certificate. You can pick it all up in the morning."

"Thanks for your trouble, Frank."

"There is one thing, though," the medical examiner said. "Nothing to do with the body."

"What's that?"

"You said no one in the family had been informed of Bergeron's parole; is that right?"

"That's right."

"Well, I read the transcript of the nine-one-one call, and Haskell said something about Bergeron violating his parole when he called in to dispatch."

"So?"

"So how do you suppose he knew that? If Bergeron burst in unannounced, drunk as a skunk and on the attack, it seems kind of unlikely he'd take the time to explain to Haskell how he'd gotten out of prison, don't you think?"

"Maybe Ben just assumed."

Collins sighed. "You're probably right."

But even as he said it, Jack knew he wasn't right. And as he let the curtain drop back over the window, he realized that he'd actually been quite wrong. About almost all of it. In the next instant, he knew why the window was open and the apartment door was locked. He knew why Charles had gravel in his hair and in his shoes, and he knew it wasn't the feet of a ladder that had made those divots in the dirt beneath the apartment window, but the feet of a man.

Ben's nurse was right; people could surprise you.

"Anyway." Collins sighed. "It doesn't matter now. Let's put the seal on this one, Jack. The wife and I are due up to camp tomorrow for a week with the grandkids, and I've got some new flies I'm itching to try out."

Jack nodded numbly. "Night, Frank."

"Good night, Jack."

Jack hung up and turned back to the bed, finding it empty. He walked downstairs, through the parlor and the den, until he found Dahlia in the kitchen doorway, the sink light riding along her naked body.

He came to her, seeing her eyes misting with tears. "You okay?"

She reached out for his hand. "I have to tell you something, Jack."

He took her hand and drew her to him, their foreheads touching. "I know."

Thirty-three

Little Gale Island

June 2002

One week earlier

Josie stood behind the café counter, purse in hand. "You sure you don't mind, Dahl?"

"Go," Dahlia said firmly, already fixing herself an iced coffee in a tall glass. "I think I can hold down the fort for an hour."

"You're the best." Josie gave her sister a quick hug. "If you get in over your head, just kick Harvey and Chip out and lock up." She nodded to the two lobstermen where they sat at a table nursing coffees and slices of pecan pie.

"Oh, please. I used to work the counter by myself all the time."

"Yeah, I remember," Josie said, smiling. "Why do you think Momma fired you?"

"Very funny."

"Hey!" Harvey Waterman turned in his chair, shaking his empty mug. "If it ain't too much trouble, when you girls are done gossipin', we'd like some more coffee over here."

"Oh, just hold your damn horses!" Dahlia winked at Josie. "See? Told you I haven't lost my touch."

Josie rummaged through her purse for her keys. "Now listen. If Wendy McMullen comes in for her gumbo, remind her to check for shells if she plans to give some to little Bo, and to keep the bag upright on the way home because there's a little container of hot sauce in there for Chester 'cause I know he likes his extra hot."

Josie turned for the door and turned back again. "Oh, and Frannie Potts is supposed to come over at four to set up for their knitting group. Those covered plates of pralines in the back are for her. Don't let Patty Sawyer tell you they're for the town meeting. She did that last week and Ben let her walk out of here with the lot of them. I could have killed the woman!" Josie stopped to find Dahlia smiling at her. "What?"

"Nothing," Dahlia said. "Just that Momma would be proud of you."

Josie reached for her sister's hand across the counter, squeezing it as her eyes teared. "She'd be proud of *us*."

When Josie had disappeared through the swinging kitchen door, Harvey waved his napkin. "What's a fella gotta do to get a refill, for cryin' out loud?"

"Tip," said Dahlia, drawing up the pot and sweeping around the counter. She filled both men's mugs to the top, patted them each fondly on the shoulder, and returned to her post. She was about to brew a fresh pot when the cordless rang at the register.

She picked it up. "Little Gale Gumbo Café."

"Julep? That you?"

Dahlia froze. "This is Dahlia."

"Dahlia? It's your daddy, girl."

As if Dahlia hadn't known. A hundred years could pass and she'd recognize that gritty voice in an instant.

"Since when do they let prisoners make toll calls?" she whispered.

"They don't." Charles snickered, a crackling sound like ribbons of birch bark in a swollen fire. "I ain't *in* prison."

Dahlia reached for the counter, her fingers gripping the rounded edge, her legs shaking. "What did you say?"

"You heard me, girl. I'm out. Paroled. Four years early for good behavior. Go figure. I was gonna tell your sister the good news. Where she at?"

Dahlia looked numbly around the room, seeing Harvey and Chip scraping the bottom of their pie plates, licking the sides of their forks; the front door opening, Marion Chase stepping in.

Out. No, it wasn't possible.

Dahlia swallowed. "Josie left."

"So when she gonna be back?"

"Not for a while."

"Well, shit. I gotta speak with her. She's holdin' money of mine and I need to come get it."

Chip raised his hand, nodding to Dahlia for the check. She looked away.

"Horseshit," she whispered tightly into the phone. "Josie would never have kept money for you."

"What the hell do you know? It just so happens family

means somethin' to your sister. Loyalty and respect. You never did have a lick of that. Now, twelve thousand dollars may not seem much to you, but I tell you what—it's more than enough to get me back on my feet."

Twelve thousand dollars. Dahlia's throat tightened. The exact amount Josie had given Camille for the café all those years before. The money she'd claimed was from Wayne's savings.

"Dahlia? You still there, girl?"

Dahlia took in a deep breath, trying to keep the panic from her voice. "She'll send you a check."

"A check? Christ, girl, I can't wait on no check. I'm out with nothin'. I need that money yesterday. No, ma'am, I'm comin' to get it in person."

Dahlia's heart raced. She should have known it wouldn't be that easy. It didn't matter that it had been more than twenty years since she'd last seen him, twenty-five since she and Josie and Camille had left him in New Orleans. Time had stood still for Charles Bergeron. While Dahlia and Josie had watched their mother grow into a bold and independent woman, their father had only become more fixed in his bitterness and greed.

She might have pitied him if she hadn't hated him so deeply.

"I'm comin' up on the bus tomorrow first thing. Already got my ticket."

Tomorrow. Dahlia reached for the wall, dizzy. Harvey and Chip twisted in their chairs, looking pointedly at her. Marion Chase came toward the counter, knotted finger already pointed to the case.

Dahlia turned and pushed through the kitchen door, falling against the sink.

Jesus, she was going to be sick.

"You hear me, girl?" Charles said. "I'm tellin' ya I got my ticket."

She drew in a shaky breath, finding a glimmer of strength and seizing it. "I don't want Josie to know you're coming."

"What'd you say?"

"You heard me."

"Don't you tell me what's what. You think I'm gonna come all the way up there and not see my baby girl?"

"You mean that same baby girl you guilted into taking your blood money?"

"You don't know shit. Tell me somethin'. Just how you figure you gonna get the money without tellin' her?"

"I'll think of a way."

"You got no right."

"Your parole officer approve this trip?"

"Christ, girl, I only been out a day. What do you think?"

"If you tell Josie," Dahlia said though clenched teeth, "if you so much as dial her fucking number and hang up, I'll call your parole officer and tell him you're leaving the state. Then you'll never see your money. How's that for what's what?"

The line went quiet. Then Charles chuckled low. "Shit . . . Same ol' Dahlia. Still can't give up the fight, can ya? Maybe you are my daughter after all."

Dahlia heard the front door open, heard Wayne greeting Harvey and Chip. Her heart galloped.

"Not on the island," she said. "I'll meet you on the mainland. Somewhere near the bus station."

"You just get me that money, girl. I'm gonna be up there Thursday night. Fella at the ticket window said the bus pulls into Portland at eleven fifteen."

Dahlia closed her eyes. "There's a diner next to the bus

station," she said. "I'll wait there for you. And don't you dare try and come over here earlier. I'll call the cops if you do; I swear to God."

She hung up just as the kitchen door swung open and Wayne stepped through.

"Who was that?"

Dahlia handed Wayne the phone and pushed past him. "Nobody."

An hour later, Dahlia stood in her living room, looking up.

Selling the Perez was the only way to be rid of Charles this time, and she knew it. Sure, she could call Jack, have him follow her to the mainland and see to it that Charles was escorted back to Louisiana in handcuffs, but then what? Word would get back to Josie that he was released, and Charles would just try again when he cleared himself, which he would. But with money, he'd leave them alone. At least long enough to find himself in another mess.

But God, it was a beautiful painting. Camille had said it was Lionel and Roman's way of watching over them from far away. Their mother had cried sometimes when she looked up at it. Now Dahlia did the same. But as she lowered it carefully to the floor and began to wrap it in layers of padding, she told herself Lionel and Roman would have understood.

Martin Abrahams from the gallery on Exchange Street would give her a fair price for it. She remembered when Camille had asked him to appraise it a few years back. His eyes had grown huge, but Camille had sworn she'd never sell it, no matter how desperate things got, which, of course, they had.

When Dahlia arrived at the gallery shortly before six, Martin's face lit up all over again.

"What made you finally decide to sell, hon?"

"Lots of things," Dahlia said.

Martin sighed. "The best I can do today is ten. But I'm not going to lie to you. It's worth twice that."

"I know," she said, just as she knew he'd price it accordingly when he set it in his shop window as soon as she left. She'd never have the money to buy it back. But she couldn't worry about that now. It would be a small price to spare Josie the pain of their father's return. Dahlia owed her sister that.

Martin looked at her over the top of his reading glasses.

"You're sure about this?" he asked gently.

Dahlia looked one last time at her mother's favorite painting, swallowing back tears.

"I've never been more sure of anything."

Thursday arrived with a cool breeze. Dahlia watched clocks all day long, seeing them everywhere she went. She canceled her appointments, too anxious to do more than pace the house and wander the yard, chewing at her nails, imagining Charles racing up the coast like a storm. She had decided to take an earlier ferry when Josie stopped by at six with a stack of gardening books.

"I found these at Fern and Clyde's yard sale this morning. Most of them are older than dirt, but some of the plates are really beautiful." She set them down on the coffee table. "I thought you were going over to the Pollard place today."

"I changed my mind," Dahlia said. "It looked like rain earlier."

Josie frowned. "When? There hasn't been a cloud in the sky all day."

"Really?" Dahlia glanced out the window, pretending to be

surprised. "I could have sworn it got really dark a few hours ago."

"Liar." Josie grinned. "You just don't want to hear about Madeline's latest diet."

Dahlia forced a smile. "God, am I that transparent?"

"Only to me." Josie paused, her gaze catching on the wall. "Where's the Perez?"

"Oh, it's . . . it's upstairs." Dahlia waved her hand uselessly, wishing she'd thought up a lie earlier. She should have known Josie would ask. "I thought it was getting too much sun on that wall, so I moved it."

"Oh."

Dahlia watched her sister's face, nervous that she'd press it, unconvinced, but Josie seemed contented with the answer.

"Well, anyway," Josie said, "Wayne and I are on our way over to Jack's for dinner. He's grilling fish. You should come."

"I can't. I told Ginny Hobart I'd come over and look at their rose garden."

"All the way over to Cape Elizabeth?"

"The roses are overrun with cuckoo spit and they've got some big to-do on Sunday, so . . ."

Josie smiled gently. "She's not coming, you know."

"Who?"

"The Realtor. Jack said she was out of town. If that's what you're worried about."

Dahlia only wished that being a fifth wheel was what was worrying her.

"No, sweetie," she said. "That's not it."

Josie studied her sister's face, her eyes so searching that Dahlia pulled Josie into her arms and hugged her fiercely, afraid she'd start to cry if she didn't.

It was almost seven, when Dahlia had finally been sure it was safe to make her way down to the ferry, that she saw him mounting the porch stairs, his red hair streaked white, wound around his scalp like cotton candy.

Charles saw her too, his smile spreading, teeth once as white as a row of chalk now yellowed like old piano keys.

"You gonna invite your daddy in, or what?"

We had a deal, Dahlia said, following him inside. "You were supposed to wait for me on the mainland."

"Sure," Charles said over his shoulder. "So you could send the cops to come pick me up for violatin' my parole? Shit, how dumb you think I am, girl?"

"Why would I call the cops? I don't want anyone to know you're here."

"So you say now." Charles glanced around, his fingers kneading the green polyester of his jacket. "So where is it?"

Dahlia glanced reflexively to the kitchen.

He smiled. "Go get it."

"Don't sit down," she said, seeing him eye the love seat. "You're not staying. I'm driving you back to the landing and you're getting on the next boat."

"The hell I am."

Dahlia watched, chilled, as he settled into the worn velvet cushions and stretched his legs out in front of him, kicking off his shoes, just like the first time he'd come to Little Gale, the first time he'd sneaked up on them in their safe new home. She'd been so sure that would be the only time he'd have the upper hand.

"Girl, I been on a goddamned bus for three days. I ain't about to turn around and get back on one." Charles reached his arms out over the back of the love seat, his shirt pulled taut over his belly, the buttons straining the shiny mustard knit. "You and me gonna get a few things straight now, so go get your daddy his money and somethin' strong to drink while ya in there. And don't tell me you ain't got nothin'. I know you too well."

Dahlia walked numbly into the kitchen, fists clenched at her sides. It was no different from any night in his company, she told herself as she took the envelope out of the drawer, then pulled the bourbon down from the cabinet. How many times had she and Josie watched their mother soften the thorns of their father's prickly coat with the smooth amber of alcohol? Dahlia had learned early and well how to temper the beast of Charles Bergeron.

She returned with the bottle and set the glass and the envelope in front of him on the coffee table. He took up the envelope first. She watched him nervously as he fanned out the bills, hoping he wouldn't count it. She'd emptied her own account to make up the difference and was still almost a thousand short.

When he folded the envelope and slid it inside his jacket, she released a relieved breath.

"Sit down," he ordered. "You look like one of them fuckin' prison guards standin' there like that."

Dahlia took a seat across from him, watching as he reached for his glass. He took it and paused.

"Ain't you drinkin'?"

"I'm not in the mood for a toast just now," she said.

His eyes narrowed. "You gonna poison me. That it?"

"And have you stuck dead on my couch? No, thanks."

Charles chuckled, finally bringing the glass to his lips. Dahlia knew that even if he didn't trust her, he couldn't wait to taste it. She watched him take his first sip, slow and careful, then a second one, longer. The pleasure of it was bald on his face. He grinned foolishly. "God, that's good."

He glanced around the room.

"Sure is weird, though, bein' back here without your momma around. Broke my heart not gettin' to give her a proper good-bye. She never stopped bein' my wife, you know. Don't matter what that asshole Haskell believed." Charles took another sip. "Ain't right," he muttered as he studied the glass. "Ain't right."

He sat back on the love seat, swirling the liquid in the glass. "Whew," he said. "Amazin' what a few years without the good stuff will do to ya."

It wouldn't take long, Dahlia thought. Not long at all to get him drunk enough to be agreeable to leaving. He was already tipsy, she realized. Tipsy and road-weary. She knew too how she could speed it along. It might just kill her to do it, but she knew a surefire way to keep him calm, agreeable, sedentary.

"I've been thinking," she said.

"Oh, yeah?" He snorted, drained his glass, and reached for the bottle. "No shit."

She watched him pour himself another, splashing it over the side.

"I'm sorry for what happened," she said. "I was wrong to attack you."

Charles raised his full glass, looked at her over the rim. "*Now* you're sorry, huh? Ain't that convenient." He patted his pocket with his free hand. "You hopin' to borrow some of this money. That it?"

Dahlia kept her eyes even with his as he drained another full pour, watching his lids grow heavy.

"Yeah, you treated me bad, all right," he mumbled, slouching deeper. "Ain't all your fault, though. Got your mother's Voodoo blood in ya. All that dark, crazy shit."

The glass tilted in his hand.

Dahlia gripped the edge of her chair.

She didn't know how much longer she could keep this up.

Thirty minutes later, he was out. Dahlia waited until his fingers loosened around the base of the glass and it slipped into his lap before she knew it was safe to move.

She walked to the phone. Ben answered on the fourth ring.

"Can you come over?" She glanced back at the love seat. "Charles is here."

She waited by the door, swigging what Charles had left of the bottle. When Ben pulled into the driveway, she rushed out to meet him on the porch. He took the stairs two at a time.

"Where is he?"

"In the living room. Passed out."

Ben moved around her and came inside the house. Dahlia followed, watching his expression when Charles came into view. The wrinkles around his eyes pleated instantly, clenching like fists.

"Does Josie know?"

"No," Dahlia said. "Nobody knows. He said he went to see Josie first but nobody was home."

Ben wiped his upper lip. "Thank God for that."

"What are we gonna do?"

"We'll take him back to the house."

"And do what with him?"

"I don't know just yet." Ben looked at the empty glass on the table. "How much did he have?"

"Probably three-quarters of the bottle."

"He'll be out for a while then." He glanced to Dahlia. "You should have called me right away."

She said nothing, feeling sixteen again, as if he'd caught her smoking pot.

She bit her lip to keep from crying. Ben moved to her and cradled her cheek in his moist palm. "Let's get him in the car, all right?"

She nodded. "All right."

Charles was heavier than she'd expected. She'd taken the envelope out of his jacket pocket before Ben had arrived, had stashed the money in her vegetable drawer, because God knew it never had any vegetables in it, and she was glad she did. If she'd left it to hang out of his lining, Ben would have seen it and would have counted it and he would have figured it all out. As it was, Ben suspected nothing. Dahlia watched him furtively as they took the short drive to the house, her eyes darting back and forth from Ben's determined profile to the side mirror, where she could make out Charles's slumped figure in the backseat. She felt as if her heart would charge out of her chest, just burst through her ribs and land in her lap. "We'll put him in the apartment," Ben said, glancing into his rearview. "The dead bolt only opens with a key. That way I can lock him in there and keep an eye on him until he comes to."

"Then what?"

Ben shrugged, his tired eyes fixed on the road ahead. "Then we'll see."

"I don't want Josie to know he's here, Ben. She'll just die."

"She won't," he said firmly.

Ben balanced Charles against his hip while Dahlia opened the apartment door. Getting him up the stairs was slow. Ben grew flushed quickly, his breathing so labored that Dahlia looked over several times, concerned.

"We can take a break," she said.

"No. We're almost there."

Finally inside the apartment, they reached the sisters' old bedroom and unloaded Charles onto one of the bare mattresses.

"Help me turn him on his side," Ben said. "He'll choke himself if he gets sick."

Dahlia did as he asked; then she followed Ben back out into the living room. She paused in the doorway, glancing back to take one last look at Charles, limp on Josie's old bed, his motionless face pinched with age, the freckles faded into the hollows of his cheeks.

Out in the hall, Ben locked the dead bolt on the apartment door. His color had darkened to scarlet. Dahlia could tell he was struggling to slow his breathing.

She moved to him, panicked. "I should stay."

"No." Ben turned to her, his eyes hardening with the order: "Go. Now. You can take the truck if you want. I'll come get it in the morning."

"I can walk," she said. "He's going to wake up eventually."

"And when he does, I'll handle it." Ben's voice was harsh now. He swallowed, wincing when he did. "I'm telling you to *go*."

Dahlia put her hand over his, thinking his skin felt damp

and cold, like her porch railing before the sun had dried the veil of fog from the wood. It took everything in her to move her feet down the stairs and step through the front door. On the street, she hesitated, staring up at the house, dread and fear stirring deep within her, growing as she turned toward the hill and headed home.

It's just the two of us now, Ben thought to himself as he stood in the foyer and looked up the stairs to the apartment door. All these years later, and he'd lost Camille, and still Charles had crawled back to hassle them one more time.

I'm too old for this, Charles. We both are.

Ben walked to the kitchen, wishing he could catch his breath. A cup of tea, he thought. That would calm him down. He didn't want to call Jack in a panic. It wouldn't look good. Better to be relaxed. After all, it could be hours before Charles came to. Jack would want to keep it all quiet, for everyone's sake. All he'd need to know was that Charles had violated parole. Jack would have him on his way back to Louisiana by morning. Josie would never need to know her father had been there.

The water came to a boil, even though Ben watched it furtively.

He poured his cup, pinched a slice of lemon into it, and carried his tea to the armchair where he'd watched six years of nights pass by since Camille had died. The first few sips went down smoothly. He'd take a few more, he decided; then he'd call the police.

But soon the cup was drained and he set it beside him, telling himself he'd just close his eyes for a minute. It had been a grueling night and he was so tired.

He woke to a banging. In the confused first seconds of consciousness he thought it was the pump or something twisted in the washing machine, but then he heard Charles's voice on the other side of the apartment door at the top of the stairs mixed in among the rapping and the jiggling of the knob.

"Let me out, you cocksucker!"

Ben rushed from his seat, catching the corner of the side table and knocking his cup and saucer to the ground, where they shattered across the brick hearth.

"Haskell!"

Ben climbed the stairs slowly, wondering for a moment whether Charles might be delirious enough to think he could force the door open with his own weight. His eyes dropped to the doorknob, watching it twist and jostle madly.

"Goddamn you, Haskell, let me out!"

Ben wiped sweat from his neck. The doorknob stilled. *Jesus*, Ben thought. *He's going to build up speed and ram the door.*

Ben hurried back down the stairs and moved quickly to the phone in the parlor, his hands shaking as he dialed the three numbers.

"Nine-one-one—what is your emergency?"

"This is Ben Haskell, over on Little Gale Island." He swallowed, his throat so dry it hurt. The words came out fast and panicked. This wasn't how he'd wanted this to go, damn it. "Charles Bergeron's in my house and he's drunk and violent."

"You say someone's in your house, sir?"

"That's right. His name is Charles Bergeron. He's violated his parole and I need an officer to come right away. Please."

"Sir, where is the individual at this time?"

Ben carried the cordless phone back into the foyer, staring up at the apartment door, waiting for another pounding attack from the other side, but it never came. Instead, he heard a rush of movement farther in, then the crash of feet landing on the dormer roof.

Jesus Christ, Ben thought. *He's climbed out the window.*

"Sir . . . sir?"

A muffled, anguished sound outside. The cry of terror.

Ben's breath caught. "Dear God." He whispered into the receiver, "Hurry."

Then he hung up and rushed outside.

"*Oh, God, no.*"

Ben found Charles's twisted body in the middle of the gravel path that led around the house and he knelt down, struggling to turn him over. Charles didn't stir.

"Charles?" Ben tapped his cheek. "Charles, stay with me now. Stay with me."

Ben hooked his arms under Charles and dragged him back to the house, feeling as if his whole head were on fire. He stopped only once to run a sleeve across his feverish face and didn't dare stop again. He told himself Charles could still be alive, that there could still be a chance if he could only get him inside. But at the porch, the pain behind his eyes grew blinding.

With one final heave, Ben hoisted Charles and himself through the front door before the numbness overtook his arm, then his leg, and he slipped out of consciousness, feeling like a leaf swept down a raging stream.

Part Five

Pour over rice
and serve
with French bread.

Thirty-four

Little Gale Island
Tuesday, June 18, 2002

Josie opened the café at seven thirty. She loved the quiet moments of early morning, her precious routine of brewing that first pot of chicory coffee, then choosing the first song to play on the jukebox. Today she picked Dinah Washington's "What a Difference a Day Makes." Fitting, she thought.

She'd already brought out two trays of muffins by the time she heard the bell. The Closed sign hung in plain sight, but Josie knew her first customer wouldn't let that stop him.

"Can I get a bowl a chowdah, deeyah?"

She laughed, turning to find Matthew standing on the

other side of the counter, smiling warmly at her. It was all the proof she needed. He'd forgiven her.

"Not half-bad," she teased, leaning over to give him a soft kiss. "But my accent's better."

"Yeah, yeah. You've been here longer than me, that's all."

"I have, haven't I?" Josie said, amazed. "Do you know I never realized that?"

"But you're still not a native, you know," he said sternly. "So don't go getting all high-and-mighty on me, kiddo. Thinking you can dig clams or make whoopie pies or anything."

"I wouldn't dream of it." She smiled, reaching out to touch his cheek. "Talked to Holly yet?"

He nodded. "I called her last night."

"Does she know what you've decided?"

"Not everything. I told her my dad came to. I didn't want to get into the rest of it over the phone."

"Of course not."

"I was thinking, though. . . ." Matthew came around the counter, helping himself to a corn muffin while Josie poured him a cup of coffee. "Seeing as I am going to be living here again and I do know my way around this place," he said, looking out at the café, "I thought maybe you could use an extra pair of hands for a while."

Josie handed him his mug, excitement flooding her face. "You mean it?"

"Why not? Insurance will pay for a nurse for some of the time, so I'll have to find something to do with myself besides hanging out on the wharf with all the skateboarders."

She grinned. "You should know we pool tips now."

"Communists." He winked at her. "Whatever happened to a little friendly competition?"

"You want friendly competition, open your own café."

"So long as I can still get all the free gumbo I can eat."

Josie squeezed his hand. "You never had to work here to get that."

Dahlia's truck pulled in front of the window. They both looked up.

"I told her you were coming by," Josie said.

Matthew smiled. "I figured you would."

Josie gestured to the back. "Y'all understand if I excuse myself. I have a week's worth of gumbo to make."

"Sure." They embraced tightly; he kissed her forehead. "See you in a couple weeks, JoJo."

Josie blew him a kiss as she pushed through the swinging door. "See you then, Matty."

When she'd disappeared into the kitchen, Matthew turned to face the door. Dahlia came in slowly, stilling when she saw him behind the counter.

Matthew gave her a small wave. "Hi."

Dahlia drew down her sunglasses. "Hi."

"Pour you a cup?" he asked.

"Sure." She came toward him with careful strides, walking as far as the counter but not coming around it. Matthew handed her a full mug over the case, and she walked to the end of the counter to fix it. "I hear you're coming back to the island for a while."

"I thought I might," he said, folding his arms. "See how long I can keep Pop comfortable in the house. The doctors think it won't work, but I think it's worth trying. He deserves that."

Dahlia nodded. "How was he this morning?"

Matthew shrugged. "The doctor says there's always a chance for a full recovery, that it's still early, but . . ."

"He could make a lot of progress, Matty. Your dad's a determined man."

"He was, once," Matthew said with a sad smile. "We'll see."

They fell silent, listening to Ella Fitzgerald while they sipped their coffees.

"How long will you be gone?" Dahlia asked.

"A week, maybe two. I have to talk to the school, pack up my things. Most of it's crap; I'm really just going for my dog."

Dahlia grinned. "How is Hooper?"

"Oh, you know. Old and stubborn."

"Like us," she said.

"Yeah. Like us."

They looked at each other, years of regret and love colliding.

Dahlia's eyes filled. "I'm sorry, Matty. I'm so sorry."

"I'm the one who's sorry, Dee."

She blinked at him, sending tears down her cheeks. "For what?"

"For refusing to see things the way they were. For making you feel like shit for not loving me."

"Don't say that," she pleaded. "I *did* love you. I'll always love you."

He smiled, his own tears rising. "I know," he whispered. He reached for her face, wiped her cheek with his thumb.

He turned to the clock above the counter. "I should go."

"Let me give you a ride," Dahlia said, following him to the booth where he'd left his bag. "I can cancel my morning appointment. It's just Ada Monahan, and she still thinks I'm planting magic beans."

Matthew chuckled, slinging his duffel over his shoulder.

"That's okay," he said. "I want to stop by the hospital before I go to the airport. Square things away with the doctors while I'm gone."

Dahlia tugged a napkin from the dispenser, dragged it across her wet eyes. "We'll be there for him, Matty," she said. "Every day."

"I know you will." He reached out his hand and Dahlia took it, letting him pull her into his arms, linking her hands around his waist and burying her face against his chest. After a few moments, they pulled apart and he walked to the door and let himself out. Dahlia watched from the window as he traveled down the sidewalk; then she crossed back through the café, headed for the kitchen door.

She found Josie at the stove, stirring a cast-iron pot.

Dahlia came beside her younger sister, taking the spoon from her hand and continuing to stir the warming roux.

Josie glanced over. "Don't burn it."

Dahlia frowned. "I never burn it."

"You never make it."

"You never let me."

"Because you always burn it."

They each gave in to a slow grin; then they knocked hips. It was their truce.

Within minutes the roux turned the color of peanut butter. Josie looked over and nodded approvingly. Dahlia pushed the pot off the heat and stole a chunk of green pepper from the pile Josie had been building on the cutting block.

"Matty's coming back," Josie said.

"I know." Dahlia grinned. "I told you he would, didn't I?"

"Know-it-all." Josie poured the holy trinity into the pot and blended the chopped vegetables into the roux, moving the pot back over a low flame. She glanced at her sister as she stirred. "So?"

Dahlia smiled coyly. "So, what?"

"So are you and Jack . . . ?"

"Maybe." Dahlia shrugged, smiled again. "Yeah."

Josie sighed. "Oh, blessed be."

"Hey." Dahlia's eyes narrowed. "You didn't work some spell, did you?"

"Of course I did," Josie admitted. "Twenty-four years ago. It's about time it took."

Dahlia laughed, and Josie joined her. Outside in the café, the jukebox changed songs. The smooth, deep voice of Mahalia Jackson sailed out.

Josie set down her spoon, wiped her hands on her sides. "Daddy came back for the money, didn't he?"

Dahlia turned, startled. "How did you know?"

Josie smiled gently. "The Perez. We drove by the gallery on our way back to the ferry last night and there it was in the window, all lit up."

Dahlia sighed. "Fuck." It hadn't even occurred to her that Josie would see it. She'd been so blind to getting the money however she could, as fast as she could.

"We'll buy it back," Josie said firmly, as if it were no more trouble than returning spoiled milk to the store.

"We can't."

"Then we'll buy something else. How about a new truck?"

"Joze." Dahlia gave her sister a worried look. "Why didn't you tell me it was his money?"

"Because I thought you'd hate me for it. And because I knew it would break Momma's heart. She'd sooner let the café go under than take a single penny of his drug money, and I couldn't let that happen. Any more than I could tell him no when he asked me to keep it for him."

"Did Wayne know?"

Josie nodded. "I didn't think there was any harm in it. I always figured we had time to pay it back before Daddy got out. If he ever did." She shrugged, reaching for a tub of thawed stock and snapping off the lid. "Over the years, I forgot about it."

"Charles sure didn't."

"So how did it start?" Josie asked.

Dahlia sighed. "He called the café that day you had to go to Portland last week."

"Why didn't you tell me?"

"Because I didn't want you to worry about it. I didn't want you knowing I knew."

Josie's eyes filled. "You didn't have to do that. You didn't have to protect me."

"Yes, I did."

"Why?"

Dahlia smiled, her own eyes swimming too. "Because we're sisters," she said.

"What about Jack?" Josie asked after a moment. "Did you tell him?"

"Last night."

Josie frowned nervously. "What did he say?"

Dahlia shrugged. "He said he didn't see any reason to report it. He said the case was closed and nothing would be gained by kicking things up again."

"Wow." Josie shook her head. "What do you know, Dahlia Rose? Sounds like he might still love you."

"God, I hope so."

Josie turned to face the kitchen, looking around as she wiped her eyes.

"She should be here."

"She is," Dahlia said, turning too, sliding her hand into Josie's. "She's everywhere. She's in here; she's out there. She's even in that nasty ol' dust you still insist on putting all over the doorstep every time I turn around."

Josie laughed, even as her eyes filled again.

"I still miss her so much, Dahl," she whispered. "Sometimes it's so bad I can hardly breathe. But she knows, doesn't she?"

"Knows what, sweetie?"

"Knows we're finally free."

"Yeah," Dahlia said, dropping her head against her sister's shoulder. "She knows."

It was a strange and wonderful word, *free*. Fleeting and fragile as any word, maybe even more so, but in that moment, standing side by side, humming along to Billie Holiday and drowning in the smell of garlic and thyme, they were sisters again, and the world opened up around them, as winding as a live oak branch, as endless as an island summer sky.

Acknowledgments

To my agent, Rebecca Gradinger, who championed the story of the Bergeron women and never stopped, thank you from the bottom of my heart.

To my editor, Danielle Perez, for giving *Little Gale Gumbo* a home beyond my dreams; it is an honor to be an NAL author; thank you.

To Svetlana Katz, for being so generous with her time and expertise, my warmest thanks.

To Dr. Eugene Cizek and Lloyd Sensat, gifted teachers and treasured friends, thank you for sharing your boundless knowledge and love of New Orleans—the world is a brighter place because of you both.

While it is virtually impossible to live near the French Quarter and not absorb a good deal of information about Voodoo, I must thank Anna Ross Twichell in particular for her part in helping me to understand the fascinating and often misunderstood culture of Voodoo.

To the city of New Orleans, it was my privilege to call you home once upon a time; to the state of Maine, for welcoming me home when I needed you most.

And to my family, my everything. Home will always be where you are.

PHOTO COURTESY OF THE AUTHOR

A native New Englander who was raised in Maine, **Erika Marks** has worked as an illustrator, an art director, a cake decorator, and a carpenter. She currently lives in Charlotte, North Carolina, with her husband, a native New Orleanian, their two daughters, and their dog, Olive. This is her first novel.

A native New Englander who was raised in Maine, Erika Marks has worked as an illustrator, an art director, a cake decorator and a carpenter. She currently lives in Charlotte, North Carolina, with her husband, a native New Orleanian, their two daughters, and their dog, Olive. This is her first novel.

Little
Gale
Gumbo

ERIKA MARKS

This Conversation Guide is intended to enrich the
individual reading experience, as well as encourage us
to explore these topics together—because books,
and life, are meant for sharing.

FLAVORING A NOVEL:
WRITING
Little Gale Gumbo

Cooking has always been a passion of mine. When I was growing up in Maine, the kitchen was where everyone in the house wanted to be. Maybe it had something to do with the fact that eight months out of the year you embraced any excuse to be in close proximity to a hot stove, but I think it had more to do with my mother's love and talent for cooking than climate. In our house, cooking was a social experience, a reason to gather friends around, and no matter the meal, food was something to be savored.

So it was no wonder when I moved to New Orleans that I fell in love with the city at once. From crawfish boils to king cakes, food in New Orleans is meant to be shared and celebrated. Smoky red beans and rice, creamy shrimp pie, sweet and crispy beignets—there's no end to their culinary treasures or their willingness to make them. When I met my husband there and he made me crawfish étouffée on our first date, I doubted I would ever leave.

But when Hurricane Katrina struck in 2005, we were forced to do just that. In the years since the storm, while we've lived in other places, my husband and I have made sure to keep the spirit of New Orleans alive in our home through cooking. Making the traditional dishes of his native city has been a wonderful way for us to share that piece of our children's history with them.

It was this challenge of how to preserve a place after moving away that was a great inspiration for writing *Little Gale Gumbo*. I wanted to explore how it would feel for a woman like Camille Bergeron with strong cultural ties having to leave her home and make a new life in an entirely different place. And certainly, when the Bergeron women arrive on the chilly shores of Little Gale Island, they feel sure they've landed on the moon, for all of its contrasts to New Orleans. So, to make herself and her daughters feel more at home, Camille promptly cooks up a traditional New Orleans meal, a gesture that secures Camille's commitment to keeping her ties to New Orleans strong, even though circumstances have forced her to leave.

It is that same desire to share her heritage through her cooking that eventually inspires Camille to open the Little Gale Gumbo Café. Once she does, the town finally embraces her, their earlier suspicions dissolving in heaping bowls of gumbo, proving that food has the power to bridge divides between even the most oppositional of people.

In writing *Little Gale Gumbo*, I was also eager to show how food can incite romantic love, as it does with Camille and Ben. On the surface, they are very different people. She is a gregarious Creole; he is a reserved islander. And while their physical attraction is clear from the first, it is only when they share a kitchen and cook together that their love truly blossoms.

I had envisioned the gumbo lesson scene in Ben's kitchen long before I wrote it. In fact, the actual scene itself didn't find its way into the novel until I was several drafts in, but it was the sentiment of the scene—the idea of building intimacy through cooking—that I knew would be the core of Ben and Camille's love story, as well as the foundation of what ultimately bonds the two families. Camille and her daughters, Dahlia and Josie, are barely moved in before they invite Ben and his son, Matthew, upstairs for dinner, and the experience of the two families sharing a meal cements a tradition that will carry them through the years. By the time they finally open the café, they are a fully blended family who cook and eat together regularly, and it doesn't take long before the islanders see that bond for themselves and can't help but be swept up in their evident joy.

In so many ways, food ties us to our past and carries us into our futures. It is a means of preservation and celebration, and one we can all practice. I very much hope this novel inspires you to revisit the foods of *your* history and, better yet, share those treasured dishes with someone, a friend, or maybe a friend in the making. I'm always amazed at how much better something tastes when it's flavored with good company.

RECIPES

Being married to a native New Orleanian, I've been fortunate to learn firsthand many trademark dishes, and it's been quite an education. I can't tell you how many batches of pralines I ruined before achieving one of the buttery disks, or how many roux I burned before I finally conquered the recipes that my husband has been cooking for years. I hope you have as much fun making them yours.

Seafood Gumbo

There is no question that the trickiest part of making gumbo is the roux. As Camille says to Ben, roux "cook quickly and are easily ruined," and it's true. Remember to serve your gumbo with some crusty bread, as you'll want to soak up every last drop.

INGREDIENTS
1 cup oil
¾ cup flour
1 medium-size onion, chopped
1 bell pepper, chopped
3 stalks of celery, chopped
4 cups of seafood or chicken stock
1 28-oz. can of stewed tomatoes, undrained
1 tablespoon each of dried basil, oregano, thyme

3 bay leaves

3 cloves of garlic, sliced

1 teaspoon Worcestershire sauce

1 lb. okra, chopped into coins

2 lbs. raw shrimp, peeled and deveined (medium size)

1½ cups crabmeat, fresh or canned

2 tablespoons Creole seasoning

1 teaspoon of hot sauce

cooked rice

DIRECTIONS

1. Heat oil in cast-iron pot on medium-high heat until it smokes. Slowly add flour, stirring as added. Continue stirring in constant motion very carefully, as splashed oil can burn, until mixture thickens and turns to a caramel color (10 to 15 minutes).

2. Add onion, pepper, and celery and continue to stir. Turn heat down to medium-low and keep stirring until onions are translucent (5 to 10 minutes).

3. Add stock to mixture and stir to incorporate.

4. Add stewed tomatoes, oregano, basil, thyme, bay leaves, garlic, and Worcestershire sauce and stir on medium heat, gently breaking up the tomatoes with the side of your spoon.

5. Add okra and stir. Turn heat down to low and let simmer for at least an hour, stirring occasionally. (Okra will break down and thicken the gumbo even further.)

6. Sprinkle peeled and deveined shrimp with Creole seasoning and toss gently.

7. Add shrimp and crabmeat to gumbo, turning heat up to medium and stirring continually until shrimp are cooked; then lower heat and cover.

8. Serve over rice.

Red Beans and Rice

There are few things more quintessentially New Orleans than red beans and rice. Traditionally they were made on Monday, otherwise known as wash day, because the dish could be left to cook on low heat for a long time. It is an easy and economical meal, and the perfect thing to make for your next big gathering. Be sure to use dried beans and not canned ones, because you'll want the starch to help with thickening. If andouille sausage isn't available, any smoked sausage will do; just make sure it's smoked, or else the coins will fall apart on you.

INGREDIENTS

1 lb. dried kidney beans

1 onion, chopped

3 bay leaves

4 cloves garlic, crushed and peeled

2 tablespoons dried thyme

1 lb. andouille (or any available smoked sausage), sliced into ¼-inch coins

salt and pepper to taste

cooked rice

hot sauce

DIRECTIONS

1. Rinse beans. Soak beans in glass bowl; fill with water an inch above beans and let soak covered overnight, adding water if necessary.

2. Pour beans and leftover soaking water into large, heavy stock pot over medium-high heat; add onions, garlic, and bay leaves. Add additional water, if needed, sufficient to cover beans. Bring to boil.

3. Reduce heat to simmer. Cover. Let simmer, stirring occasionally, until beans start to break down and soften (usually 2 hours, longer if necessary).

4. In final half hour, add sausage and thyme, and salt and pepper to taste.

5. Serve over rice with hot sauce.

(NOTE: Another great thing about the dish is that it can be made the day before and will taste even better the next day.)

Bread Pudding

There are many variations on bread pudding; this one is my contribution. I was on a mission to perfect my own recipe after tasting a sumptuous serving on my first trip to New Orleans in my twenties. I wasn't able to replicate a good whiskey sauce, but this one has enough brandy to make up for it.

CONVERSATION GUIDE

INGREDIENTS

1 loaf of challah bread, cubed (approx. 4 cups)

1½ cups half-and-half

1 cup heavy cream

5 egg yolks

½ cup sugar

3 teaspoons vanilla

½ cup brandy

zest of 1 orange

¼ cup of orange juice

1 cup raisins

1 cup jarred butterscotch sauce

DIRECTIONS

1. Cube challah; put in large bowl; set aside.

2. In separate bowl, mix raisins, orange zest, orange juice, and 1 tsp. of the vanilla. Cover and let sit for several hours (overnight, if possible).

3. Simmer creams in saucepan until warm.

4. In another small bowl, whisk together egg yolks, sugar, and remaining 2 tsp. of vanilla.

5. Add to cream mixture, making sure to temper first, and whisk gently until blended.

6. Whisk in brandy.

7. Pour mixture over cubed bread in bowl, stir gently to soak bread cubes, cover, and refrigerate for several hours (again, overnight is ideal).

8. Add raisins and remaining liquid to bread cubes and stir to combine.

9. Pour mixture into greased baking dish. Set baking dish in water bath and bake, uncovered, at 325°F.

10. After twenty-five minutes, drizzle butterscotch sauce over top of pudding and return to oven for another ten to fifteen minutes.

11. Serve warm with a few splashes of half-and-half.

Pralines

Pralines can be tricky to make but are well worth the effort. For those adept in candy making, the syrup may be deemed ready by dropping a bit into cold water and seeing a ball form. For myself, I still need a candy thermometer to guarantee success.

INGREDIENTS
¾ cup each brown and white sugar
½ cup evaporated milk
pinch of salt
¼ teaspoon vanilla
1 tablespoon butter
1 cup pecans, slightly chopped
a cookie sheet lined with waxed paper
a candy thermometer

CONVERSATION GUIDE

DIRECTIONS

1. In saucepan, heat sugars, milk, and salt. Heat on low, stirring continually and carefully, until the mixture turns the color of caramel.

2. Bring to a boil and insert candy thermometer; keep at a boil (still stirring) until temperature reaches 235°F. When it does, take off heat.

3. Add butter, vanilla, and pecans and stir gently to blend.

4. Drop onto waxed paper and let cool. The cooled disks will be slightly shiny.

QUESTIONS FOR DISCUSSION

1. From a young age, Dahlia and Josie see and react to their father, Charles, in very different ways, differences that bring conflict to the sisters' relationship as they mature. Discuss the opposing views the sisters have of their parents' marriage, and what impact those views have on how each sister secures—or rejects—love in her own life.

2. The themes of loyalty and betrayal go hand in hand in this book. As devoted and loyal as they are to each other, Dahlia and Josie both bear the weight of some potentially devastating secrets. At the end of the book, some secrets have been revealed, but some remain. Do you think it's possible to live a life without secrets?

3. Matthew feels a deep love for both sisters, but romantic love only for Dahlia, a feeling that has been allowed to grow due to his and Dahlia's off-and-on affairs over the years. By the end of the book, do you believe that Matthew has come to accept that Dahlia will never love him as deeply as he loves her? Do you believe he will finally move on from her?

Conversely, do you believe by the novel's end that Josie has to come to accept that Matthew isn't in love with her, and that she and Wayne will be able to move forward to strengthen their marriage?

4. The café is as much a character in the book as the men and women who cook and dine there, eventually becoming a fixture on the island. In your own life, have you ever known a place like the Little Gale Gumbo Café that became a staple in your community? What about it made it so appealing to its customers? Was it only the food or something more?

5. Much like Ben and Camille, Dahlia and Jack's attraction is an unlikely—but undeniable—one. Even though Dahlia insists she doesn't want the complications and risks of love, she can't seem to get past her desire for Jack. What is it about Jack that makes him different in Dahlia's eyes from all the other men she's been with? What about him scares her so much that she works so hard to keep from letting him in?

6. In obvious ways (climate, landscape), Maine and New Orleans couldn't be more different—yet there are some similarities, such as a deep sense of history as well as a dependency on the fruits of their coastlines. At what point in the book do you think Camille and the sisters finally feel as if they are settled in their new home?

7. For most of their lives, Josie is considered the fragile sister, while Dahlia is believed to be the strong one. Do you agree with that assessment? If not, why?

8. Both Josie and Dahlia are devoted to their mother, but see their roles as daughters very differently. While Josie feels a responsibility to protect her mother and help keep the peace with Charles, Dahlia is constantly encouraging Camille to stand up to him, much to Josie's dismay. In your experience, have you observed similar situations among siblings?

9. Charles spends most of the book as an arrogant bully who tries repeatedly to disrupt his wife and daughters' new home until he is finally sent to prison for what everyone believes will be the rest of his life. But when he emerges, he is clearly a broken and bitterly subdued man. Did you feel any sympathy for him by the end of the book, and at any point did you believe he might have the capacity for redemption?

10. For much of the novel, Dahlia is at odds with many of the residents of Little Gale Island, from the time she is a rebellious teen up until she has a well-established business. Yet for all of her frequent grumblings about the island's conservative and judgmental views of her, she never leaves. What, or who, do you think keeps her there?

11. For all the anguish that Charles causes Camille, it might be hard to understand why she never divorces him. Why do you think she chooses not to legally end her marriage, even after she falls in love with Ben?

12. The island ultimately provides a safe and nurturing environment for Ben's and Camille's children, but it could be

argued that living remotely as they grew kept the sisters and Matthew from moving on in certain ways. In what ways do you think the island nurtured their emotional development, and in what ways did it inhibit it? In your own life, have you ever felt held back by a place or a person? What did you do to move forward?